The Zeta Grey War:

New Recruits

by

D F Capps

Copyright 2017

All Rights Reserved

ISBN: 978-0-9774198-1-4

Clearwater Valley Press, LLC

Under License

ACKNOWLEDGEMENTS

An author stands in a circle of people, who, with little recognition, help make a book what it is. First in that circle is my wife, Miriam, who brainstorms with me, reviews my writing, suggests better words to use and points out weak spots in the plot and characters. Thank you for your great patience and understanding.

Next in line is my excellent editor, Phil Athans, who reads through the original manuscript and points out what neither my wife, nor I even thought about. This story is much more complete because of him.

Then come a number of readers who helped go through the story and provide valuable insights and feedback. Among them are Carol Asher, Nick Grachanin, Ron Current, Marci Jenkins, Steven Wagner, and Walt Willis.

Finally, with great appreciation, is Natasha Brown for the beautiful cover design. Thank you Tasha!

I hope you enjoy the story.

D F Capps

Prologue

A cold wind swept past Daniel Zadanski and his twin sister, Diane, as they climbed the half dozen steps to the wide porch on their family home at the end of the day. At seventeen, their life was still a mixture of chores and play. They turned to face the chilly air pushing in from the southwest. Lightning flashed, followed quickly by a loud clap of thunder.

"Storm's breaking," Diane said.

Then it dawned on him, "Oh, jeez, I left my varsity sweater out by the pond." There was still enough light high up in the sky for him to see the ground. "I'll be right back."

In two long strides he reached the ground and took off across the grassy field.

"You better run fast, or you're going to get soaked," she yelled, chuckling at his absentmindedness.

He ran into the numbing wind, watched the flashes of lightning, timed the crash of thunder, and tried to estimate how long it would be before the downpour started. Just before he reached the pond, a large, bright white, glowing, disk-shaped object swooped low over the trees and stopped directly in front of him. It was maybe fifty feet across and so bright that it bleached the color out of everything around him.

His heart pounded in his ears, his breath was rapid and panicked as paralyzing fear flooded his body. He tried to turn around and run back to the house, but only his head would move. Diane was running to him. A tingling, electric energy surged through his body and a humming surrounded him. He felt helpless and unable to move as he floated up into the glowing disc.

* * *

"Danny!" Diane screamed as she raced to help him. "Danny!"

She watched in horror as he was sucked up into the glowing object. She slowed to a stop as the bright white craft swept over her, totally silent, yet terrifying in its power and speed. She turned, unable to take her eyes off the glowing disk.

"No, no, no, no!" she shrieked hysterically as it disappeared over the house and into the gathering clouds.

* * *

Daniel's head throbbed as he opened his eyes. Two bright overhead lights obscured the surrounding room. He sensed movement around him and tried to look to the side. His mind cleared enough to realize he was lying naked on a cold metal table, unable to move. Panic gripped his mind, his breath rapid and shallow as his heart raced. His eyes darted from side to side.

Something touched his right arm. He strained to see what it was. A large gray head with huge black eyes loomed over his right side. It had a tiny nose and a small, horizontal mouth above a scrawny neck. Its long fingers traced a line down his arm, over his elbow, and to the middle of his forearm where it stopped.

No, no, no! Don't touch me! Daniel's mind screamed. Get away from me! He wanted to scream and yell, but he couldn't make a sound.

The thing pressed down on Daniel's forearm with its finger. The creature looked at Daniel's face as pain radiated the length of his arm. His reaction was to recoil away from the creature, but his body still wouldn't move. It continued by touching Daniel's chest and moving its rough fingers downward to his waist and beyond.

No! Daniel's mind cried out. Get away! Don't touch me there!

The creature hooked some kind of device to him down there.

No! I don't want this. Stop! his mind shrieked.

Pain shot through him from the device as his sperm was quickly extracted from his body.

Another creature appeared on his left side. It pulled his left leg to the side and stuck a large needle into the inside of his right leg.

Daniel's anxiety level spiked as he felt the needle penetrate his upper leg bone.

Bone marrow! His mind shouted. They're taking my bone marrow!

More of the creatures were collecting around him, touching him, poking him, probing inside of him, and taking multiple samples from his body.

Daniel felt totally out of control: completely helpless.

One of the creatures leaned over his face, six inches away, and stared into his eyes. The effect was powerful and immediate: He couldn't look away. He couldn't resist. He was aware of the creature searching his memories, thoughts, and feelings; examining and cataloging everything in his seventeen years of life. Nothing was private. Everything was there to be seen by this thing.

Thoughts came into his mind: Violent, dangerous thoughts. His heart felt as though it was thrashing around inside of him. Panic took control. His emotions flared as he saw images in his mind of his mother and his sister, Diane, being tortured and burned. They were screaming in pain and agony. Tears flowed from his eyes, but still he couldn't move.

The creature stepped away from him, but his emotions continued to rage out of control.

This has to stop, he thought. It has to end. Focus. This is my mind. I control it. Not you.

He thought about the hours and discipline it took to learn how to sink his free throw shots on the basketball court: the focus, the practice. In his mind he threw the ball in a perfect arc to the hoop. All net, never touching the rim. Over and over he made the perfect shot. His emotions calmed. His mind returned to his control. He blocked the pain in his body with the focus of his mind.

Index finger, right hand, he thought. Move. He concentrated harder. Move!

He felt his index finger slide against his middle finger. It's working, he thought. I can do this. He concentrated even harder on his hand. It moved! Not a lot but he was gaining back control of his body, one small part at a time.

The creatures didn't seem to notice. They were too busy doing things to his body.

That's it, he realized. He had to dissociate what they were doing from what he was doing. Two bodies; two purposes. They could keep what they were doing to his other body. All he needed was control over his mind and his muscles. Nothing else mattered.

He concentrated with all of his might. He turned to his left. He reached out and grabbed the thin arm of the creature. The thing looked straight at his eyes, but it was too late. Daniel yanked the creature closer to him and punched it right between the eyes with his fist.

The thing fell to the floor. Daniel struck the creature on his right and bolted upright on the table. The creatures around him stood still for a moment as he rolled off onto the floor; then they jumped forward and grabbed him. They were surprisingly strong for their size. More of them poured into the room and held him down on the floor. He struggled to get loose, but there were too many of them.

A tall gray creature appeared close to his head and jammed a sharp device into his forehead. Every muscle in his body went into spasm and cramped. His brain felt the massive electrical jolt from the device and everything went black.

* * *

Rosaq, newly appointed commander of the Zeta Grey Earth Acquisition Force, examined the recent human abductee, now lying back on the table. The subject was male, mid to late teens, Caucasian, and healthy. The usual biological samples were obtained and analyzed. Nothing unusual there. The subject had moved, grabbed, and then struck two of the workers during table procedures when he should have been immobilized. That was a critical concern, Rosaq thought. Not because of any potential injury to a worker, but the break in neurological control was unexpected. Rosaq withdrew the paralyzer from the subject's forehead.

The subject's eyes opened. Rosaq leaned over and

stared into his eyes at close range, using neural engagement to follow the optical nerve to the deeper recesses of the subject's brain. Rosaq examined the memories and emotional experiences of the subject. No history of major trauma or substance abuse was present. The primary emotional structure was formed around the loss of the adult male in the family at an early age and reliance on the female adult in his place.

Rosaq forced images of damage, disfigurement, and suffering of the female adult and female sibling into the subject's mind. As fear and panic escalated in the subject, Rosaq increased the intensity of the traumatic images, and concentrated on the ones producing the greatest emotional response. The state of fear in the subject was extended and heightened until the traumatic psychic energy field surrounding the subject filled the room.

Rosaq soaked in the raw emotional energy, relished every second of agony, terror, and anguish produced by the subject. This was the closest Rosaq would ever get to actually feeling an emotion, such things being beyond the capability of all Zeta Greys.

Rosaq stepped back and observed the subject on the table. This was the six hundred and thirty-eighth subject to be evaluated in his initial assessment of humans on this planet. For the most part these humans were controllable, susceptible to neurological engagement, and memory suppression. More than enough could be recruited and trained to assist in the integration of hybrids and hubrids into the human society, leading to the eventual subjugation and direct control of the population. The hybrid program had been in place for sixty earth years and was now refined into hubrids; beings visually indistinguishable from humans, but part of the Zeta Grey community consciousness.

This subject, however, seemed to be recovering from the emotional trauma too quickly, just as one other subject did several days ago. That was a troubling trend, Rosaq thought. Effective rebellion of humans against the Zeta Greys was uncommon. The last rebellion was on a planet in the Tau Ceti star system, where this same rate of resistance to mind control was observed. That rebellion resulted in the eventual loss of the planet and all of its resources by the Zeta Greys, and was quickly followed by the loss of all access to that entire star system.

Rosaq's advanced analytical abilities indicated the need for a new control strategy to ensure Earth's planetary resources remained in control of the Zeta Greys, with resistance and eventual rebellion avoided altogether.

The memory block technique wasn't going to be effective on this subject. This human was too strong-willed to be trusted, and thus posed a security threat to the operation. Rosaq sent the image of this subject being harvested for organs and their nutritional liquid program to the workers in the room and then left. After being inside the saucer, this human was just too dangerous to be released. His knowledge could corrupt and stimulate intolerance in others.

Overseeing the final conversion of the planet was a demanding job with not only serious responsibilities but potentially catastrophic consequences. As many risk factors as possible needed to be eliminated, Rosaq thought. And to insure the success of the operation, strong-willed humans must be at the top of the list.

Chapter 1

President Jason Andrews, and a man he knew only as Charlie, stood in a wide desert valley in the Kawich Range, one hundred miles northwest of Las Vegas, Nevada. Andrews shivered slightly in the still, cool, early June air and checked his watch: 2:01 a.m. The night sky was solid black with billions of stars thrown across the heavens. They looked up, searching for any sign of the craft as the background hum of thousands of insects continued unabated.

"You sure they're coming?"

"I'm sure," Charlie said. "They will check to see that you and I are the only two people within twenty miles and that there are no aircraft within fifty miles. Those were the conditions. As long as we're alone, they'll be here."

The sound of insects ceased.

"They're here," Charlie said quietly.

Andrews felt the stir of air moving past his face with the tingle of static electricity and the slight smell of ozone growing slowly stronger. The desert night was completely silent now. The small scrub and sagebrush began to quiver for a hundred yards in front of them and fifty yards to each side. Out of the darkness an eerie white glow gradually appeared and then the huge saucer became visible. The craft was at least three hundred feet in diameter and eighty feet in height. It hovered silently in the air, ten feet above the ground.

"Your state of mind is important," Charlie said. "Are you intent on entering the craft?"

Andrews glanced at Charlie. "Yes." His stomach was already tied in a knot, which now grew tighter.

"Remember what I told you. They are telepathic."

Andrews took a deep breath and nodded.

Charlie led Andrews under the saucer. At about a third of the way, they found themselves inside the saucer, standing near the center before a raised platform. Andrews took another long, deep breath, trying to force himself to relax. Despite his effort to calm down, Andrews's left hand trembled. He glanced at Charlie, again.

"It's okay," Charlie whispered. "He expects you to be nervous."

A subdued white light filled the interior of the saucer. Charlie stood with his arms extended to the side so his hands were about a foot from his hips, palms facing forward and fingers apart. Andrews followed Charlie's lead. The universal sign of non-aggression, Andrews reminded himself.

Etnar stepped before them, eight and a half feet tall, large head, huge light blue-gray eyes, a boney face, and small, low ears. He had a thin abdomen with long delicate arms and legs. His skin was a very pale gray, almost white, with a hint of blue. He was dressed in a shimmering white garment that left only his head, hands, and feet exposed. Several other beings, very similar to him, moved within the saucer. The inner surfaces of the saucer were a sleek light metallic material without any visible seams, joints, or connections.

Etnar motioned them to come closer.

"I am communicating with him telepathically and will speak for him," Charlie said.

Etnar glanced at both of them. "You understand the true nature of the beings and the treaty your government has entered into?"

"Yes, I do," Andrews said, trying to at least sound calmer than he actually was.

Etnar stared at Andrews. "What is your decision?"

Andrews breathed out, looked Etnar in the eyes, and said, "I must do everything within my power to break the existing treaty and to rid this planet of them and their influence, forever."

Etnar moved his head in what appeared to be a slight nod. "What about the other leaders of your world?"

Andrews's left hand shook more. He looked down at his hand, trying to will it to stay still. Then he looked back at Etnar. "I will convince them to join with me against this common enemy."

Etnar tipped his head slightly to the right. "You are aware of the technology and power that opposes you?"

"I am," Andrews said, closing his eyes momentarily as he tried to calm his racing mind. "I am also painfully aware of our future should I fail."

Another slight nod from Etnar. "Are you fully committed to the task before you?"

Andrews nodded, breathed in and out, and said, "With every fiber of my being. I will succeed or I, and all those who follow me, will die trying."

Etnar studied Andrews for a minute and then handed

him a small device.

"This is the extent of the assistance you will receive. We cannot appear to be involved in your struggle. You must guard all knowledge and evidence of our existence and presence on your planet and in your star system."

Andrews breathed a sigh of relief. He managed to get through this experience in one piece. "Thank you," he said. "I am grateful for your help."

Etnar turned and walked away. Andrews and Charlie found themselves standing on the ground, out from under the saucer. The dull white glow brightened and the saucer disappeared. A strong movement of air came from behind them as sage leaves and small twigs rushed up from the ground into a twisted conical shape in the center of where the saucer had been. The debris sucked up into the air gently drifted back down to the ground.

"You did fine," Charlie said. "Remember, the military industrial complex is heavily invested in the existing treaty. Some of them may join you, but many will not. What you are doing is very dangerous."

Andrews closed his eyes briefly, breathed out slowly, and turned to face Charlie.

"I have no choice. To do nothing will be the end of us all."

Chapter 2

"How's the pain today?" Diane asked.

Navy Lieutenant Diane Zadanski sat quietly next to her mother's hospital bed in the Minneapolis Hospice Center. The stage-four ovarian cancer had spread too quickly for any therapy to be effective, so her mother had gone straight into hospice rather than remaining in the hospital. At forty-six, her mother was way too young to be dying.

"Much better," her mother replied. "Ever since the diagnosis, I've been feeling panicked—that life wasn't fair, that I should have had more time, you know?"

She should have had more time, Diane thought. This wasn't fair. It wasn't right.

"And now?" Diane asked.

"Now it makes so much more sense. I saw your father

last night, did I tell you that?"

It must be the drugs, Diane thought. Her father died in a car wreck twenty-four years ago. It was just the two of them since her twin brother disappeared nine years ago. Diane never knew her grandparents. They all died early in their lives, just as her mother was doing now.

"Don't worry," her mother said. "It's all going to be fine."

Diane shook her head. "Mom, I just . . ."

Her mother reached out and took her hand.

"I'm at peace, Di, and I want you to be at peace, too."

Diane had never seen her mother this calm, and so serious at the same time. Diane looked down at the floor and thought, How can I be at peace when my last family member is dying?

"I know you must be worried," her mother said. "But don't be. Your father said you have important work to do in this world. He said you have to fight for all of us. There is an evil in the world that you have to confront, battle, and overcome."

What's gotten into her? Diane wondered. She's never been religious, she never believed in a devil. Why was she now talking about an evil in the world that I have to confront, battle, and overcome? Could this, too, be from the pain meds?

Her mother looked up at the ceiling and started breathing harder.

"What is it, Mom? Do you need help?" Worry flooded into Diane's mind as a feeling of helplessness filled her chest.

"Frank," her mother said softly, raising her right arm into the air, her gaze fixed on the ceiling. "The light."

Diane looked around the room. "What light?" Frank was her father's name. "Where's Frank?" Worry quickly escalated into dread.

Her mother pointed at the ceiling. "Frank."

Diane glanced at the ceiling, then back at her mom. The heart monitor went erratic and a male nurse rushed into the room.

"What's going on?" Diane asked, trying to control the urgency in her voice. "Who's Frank?"

"It's her time," he replied nervously.

The line showing her mother's heart beat diminished in strength, slowed, and then flatlined.

"Mom, no . . ."

Tears filled Diane's eyes as her mother's arm fell silently to the bed. A long, slow exhalation issued from her mother's mouth. Overwhelming grief filled Diane's chest as she watched the nurse check her mother for a pulse. He then put a stethoscope to her mother's chest and listened for a minute. Diane felt a rising panic within her heart as the nurse looked at the clock on the wall and entered the time of death on her mother's chart.

"I'm so sorry. You can stay as long as you like," he said as he left the room.

Overwhelmed with panic and loss, Diane grabbed her purse, bolted down the short hall, through the small lobby, and out into the freezing night air. She ran through the drifting snow to her rental car, slid inside, and slammed the door. Here, in the darkness and privacy of the car, she could let loose, wail, and weep for the second major loss in her life.

After thirty minutes she had calmed and regained her composure. She started the engine and waited for the warmth to come from the heater.

Why did she abandon me? How could she leave me alone like this? What am I supposed to do now? Questions and uncertainty swirled in her mind, but no answers were forthcoming. How could she betray me like this? She was supposed to always be here, strong and steady for me whenever I needed her. She wasn't supposed to die!

The warm air blasting from the heater gradually returned her to the present moment. She put the car in gear and drove slowly to the hotel. Once in her room she changed into her pajamas and fell into bed. Emotionally spent and physically exhausted she quickly fell asleep.

Her mother appeared to her, younger, healthy, and confident. A tall, thin man in a light gray suit wearing a fedora hat stood behind her mother.

"It's okay, Di, I'm fine," her mother said. "And you will be just fine, too. You'll see." Her mother was smiling as she turned and glanced back at the man. "Frank was here to greet me. He explained what the evil in the world is. You're going to have to be strong and fearless, Di, just the way I raised you. We know you will be courageous and wise. You will have friends to help you along the way. Be true to yourself and your new friends. Remember, the future depends on you."

Diane woke and sat straight up in bed, breathing hard. She looked, bewildered, at the hotel room around her. It was a dream, she thought. It was just a dream. She got up and wandered into the bathroom, turned on the light, blinked a few times to adjust to the brightness, and looked at herself in the mirror. She kept her brunette hair short and straight. At five-eight and a hundred and forty pounds she was muscular and fit.

"It was just a dream," she affirmed to herself. But it seemed so real—more real than anything she had experienced in her life. If it felt so real, how could it be only a dream? She returned to bed, but sleep would not come to her. She tossed and turned, trying to get comfortable. Nothing was working. She went over the dream repeatedly in her mind: analyzing, dissecting, and evaluating every nuance, each word, and possible implication. Her mind raced at warp speed, as it always did, through endless details and multiple layers of possible hidden meanings. By four in the morning, fatigue finally dragged her back to sleep.

Chapter 3

Diane spent the next few days making arrangements for her mother's funeral, notifying her mother's friends, and talking to the lawyer about the will and her mother's modest estate. From the time Diane was a small child, her mother had instilled a sense of responsibility in her. Now, assuming the duties for her mother's final arrangements actually brought a much needed feeling of peace and control back into her life.

The funeral was held on Tuesday afternoon. The service began at the funeral home, then continued on to the cemetery for the internment. Diane completed the last of the details in Minneapolis and then boarded a Delta Airlines flight to San Diego, California.

Once back at Naval Air Station North Island on Coronado, she rested for the night in her officer's quarters and reported for duty the following morning to Commander Chase, Carrier Air Wing Fourteen, Strike Fighter Squadron 147.

"I expected you to take more time, Lieutenant," Commander Chase said. "You feel ready to return to duty?"

She smiled and stood tall. "Yes, sir. Flying is the best therapy for me, sir."

"I don't doubt that," he said. He looked down at the sheet of paper on his desk. "There's just one thing you need to do first."

This was a new wrinkle, she thought. "What's that, sir?"

"A Dr. Cowen has requested that you have an evaluation as soon as possible. Once that's completed, we can talk."

An evaluation? she wondered. "Medical, sir?"

Commander Chase shook his head. "Psychological, actually. It's a matter of some urgency. You are to report to him without delay." He handed her a card with Dr. Cowen's name and office number printed neatly in the center.

She took the card and examined it. "Yes, sir." Psychological? she wondered. What the hell is going on? Do they think I'm unfit to fly because my mother died?

She walked over to the medical building and looked for Dr. Cowen's name on the building registry. Not listed. He must be new, she thought. She walked up the stairs to the second floor, located the office printed on the card, and entered. The Navy nurse receptionist looked up at her as she entered, apparently wondering what Diane wanted.

"Lieutenant Zadanski, reporting as ordered."

"Yes, of course," the nurse replied. "He's consulting at the moment. I'll call him." The nurse picked up the phone, punched in the number, looked over at Diane, and smiled. "Yes, sir, Lieutenant Zadanski is here." She listened. "Yes, sir." She hung up. "You can wait in his office. He's on his

17

way." The nurse opened the door to the inner office, motioned Diane to enter, and sit in the padded chair in front of the doctor's desk. "He'll be right with you." The nurse left and gently closed the door.

Diane looked around the office. Diplomas and certifications lined the wall behind the desk, but the name wasn't Cowen, it was Gentry. The wall on the left was filled with medical books and journals, all specializing in the various disorders of the mind. She frowned and thought, I was on compassionate leave for a week. Just what do they think happened to me?

The door opened and a man in a white lab coat walked in. He was trim, with a round face, wire-rimmed glasses, and a bald head sporting a shallow ring of gray hair that ran just above his protruding ears. A gold oak-leaf cluster pinned to his shirt lapel identified him as a Navy commander.

"I'm Dr. Cowen," he said, extending his hand. She shook hands, wondering what was coming next. He walked around the desk and sat down. "I understand your mother died recently. How do you feel about that?"

How does he think I feel about that? she wondered. "Disappointed. She was only forty-six. Ovarian cancer."

He grimaced and nodded slightly. "You feel a sense of loss?" Dr. Cowen asked.

She frowned a little. Is this all he wanted to know? she wondered. He could've asked me that on a phone call.

"Yes. She was my only family."

He looked over his glasses at her.

"Do you feel disoriented or overwhelmed?"

He seemed almost as bored as she was with the questions so far.

"Not really. Her death came as quite a shock to me. I was angry at first, but going through the process of tying up all of the loose ends of her life helped me put her death in some kind of perspective. I'm doing better now."

He looked down at the file on his desk. "Do you feel depressed?"

"No." What was he doing? she wondered.

"Are you experiencing a lack of energy or motivation?"

He made eye contact again.

"No." She glanced around the room and wished this whole interview was over.

"Any difficulty sleeping?"

She looked up. "No. I just want to get back in the air. I want to fly my Super Hornet again."

He looked at the folder again. "I noticed in your file that you went through the Naval Strike and Air Warfare Center in Fallon Nevada."

"Top Gun," Diane replied. The change in subject had her curiosity piqued.

"Yes. I see that you graduated at the top of your class."

He watched her closely as she answered.

Diane nodded. "In a fighter jet, it's not about size or strength, it's all about how fast your mind processes information, observes your surroundings, creates situational awareness, and how fast your body reacts."

"You didn't mention intuition," Dr. Cowen said, glancing again at the file on his desk. "The evaluation from Top Gun indicated a high degree of intuitive accuracy in your actions."

"Did it?" she asked. She hadn't seen the actual evaluation, just that she was the best pilot in the eight-week air combat training school. "I just thought I was good at guessing what people would do next."

Dr. Cowen smiled. "How do you feel about being the first woman to fly a combat aircraft for the Navy?"

She frowned a little, wondering where he was going with these questions.

"It's an honor. I believe the Navy struggled as hard with me becoming a combat pilot as I did getting here. I think, in the end, both the Navy and I are satisfied with the results."

He leaned back and tipped his head slightly.

"So tell me, why do you want to fly in combat?"

"It's the greatest challenge I can imagine. It's what gets me up in the morning," she said. She smiled at him, trying to convince him there was nothing else to it. She glanced to the left and then reestablished eye contact with him.

That wasn't her entire reason for flying. Yes, it was challenging, but how could she explain her obsession with flying in combat because her brother was abducted? It was her only real chance of getting close to one of those UFOs again. Only this time, she wouldn't be standing helpless on the ground. This time she'd at least have an arsenal of modern weapons she could use.

I can't mention UFOs, she thought. They wouldn't understand. If they know I've encountered a real flying saucer, I'll lose my certification to fly. They'll think I'm mentally unstable.

Dr. Cowen's face had an odd intensity to it as he studied her. She was left with the feeling that he didn't believe her—that he knew she was withholding something about her motivation to fly in combat. Finally, he nodded slightly.

"How do you feel about shooting down an enemy craft?" he asked.

Good, she thought. He was moving on. Either he decided to believe her or it didn't matter.

"It's what I live for," she said.

He leaned forward and stared at her.

"What about killing the pilots in enemy crafts?"

He seemed genuinely curious about how she would answer.

"If they don't want to die in fighter planes, they

shouldn't be flying them."

No nod, no acknowledgement, just the next question. "No feelings of regret for killing the pilot of an enemy craft?"

What's he doing referring to an enemy plane as a craft? she thought. The only things we fly are airplanes.

"No."

"You fly a Super Hornet," Dr. Cowen said, glancing at the file again. "They fly at over Mach two. How do you feel about that level of speed?"

Now she was definitely curious. "I'm fine with it."

"You're comfortable with speeds like that?" His expression was getting more intense.

"Yes, as I said, it's about the speed at which your mind processes information."

This conversation had come a long way from how she felt about the death of her mother.

"And at fourteen to fifteen hundred miles an hour, your mind has no problem processing things that happen at that speed?"

He was leading up to something, but what? "No problem," she replied.

"Do you ever wish you could fly faster?"

The question took her by surprise. "Yes," she said. Where was he going with this? The SR-91 Aurora flies at Mach six, but that's a high altitude reconnaissance plane, not a combat fighter.

Dr. Cowen shifted in his chair. "How dedicated are you to flying in combat?"

Dedicated? She frowned a little. "What do you mean?"

"In Top Gun, you flew against one other plane, sometimes two opponents. My question is—would you fly into combat against one or more opponents where your chance of survival was minimal?"

She settled back in her chair. "I think that would

depend on what was at stake. Combat isn't something you take on casually."

"What if the survival of your country was at stake? Would you fly into combat even if the odds of your living through it were zero?"

She looked at him feeling stunned and thought, What in hell is going on?

"What would you do? Decide, right now!" he shouted.

She was startled. He appeared intense, but not angry.

"I'd take as many of the bastards with me as I could," she stated firmly.

"You're not afraid to die?"

His intensity held without wavering. This whole interview took a nasty turn in her mind. "It's not my first preference, but if I have to go, flying in combat would be my choice."

Dr. Cowen studied her face intently for several minutes. She stared back at him, confident in her decision.

"Okay. Report back to Commander Chase. You're being reassigned." He closed the file.

What the hell just happened? "Reassigned to where?" she asked.

"Thank you for your openness and honesty. We'll be talking more later." He stood, walked over to the door, opened it, and motioned for her to leave.

"I don't understand." Her mind searched for a reason, but came up empty.

"It's okay. You will. All in good time." He smiled at her as she walked past him into the hallway.

She walked back to the administration building deep in thought. She initially believed the psych evaluation had been about her emotional stability following the death of her mother. Now it was clear there was another, less obvious, purpose behind Dr. Cowen's questions. She felt as if something important had just happened, but she couldn't fathom what it might be. She was still lost in thought when she entered Commander Chase's office.

"You have three weeks of leave accumulated," Commander Chase said. "Do you want to take that leave before you report to your new duty station?"

Her thoughts were still swimming in her head. "No. Where am I being assigned?"

He looked down at the sheet of paper on his desk. "New Mexico."

You've got to be kidding me, she thought. "There's a Naval Air Station in New Mexico?"

He looked at the paper again. A puzzled expression worked its way onto his face.

"I can't imagine there's an aircraft carrier there," she said flatly. What in the world were they doing to her?

"It's classified," he said.

He wouldn't look her in the eye. Not a good sign, she thought. "You can't give me a hint?"

"I would if I could." He finally looked up at her. "There's no destination on your orders, just a travel voucher to Albuquerque, New Mexico. Apparently where you're going, and what you'll be doing, is beyond my level of security clearance." He held out his hand. "It's been an honor having you in my squadron, Lieutenant, and wherever you go, I wish you the very best of luck."

This can't be happening, she thought. It just can't. She reluctantly shook hands and took her new orders from him. She was booked on a commercial flight out of San Diego at four that afternoon.

Chapter 4

Admiral Howard J. Hollis sat quietly on the couch in the Oval Office of the White House reviewing the recent addition to his new team, a talented Navy lieutenant from Strike Fighter Squadron 147, based on the USS *Ronald Reagan* out of San Diego. He stood, as President Andrews entered.

"Howie, how's our project doing?"

Andrews paced nervously in front of his desk.

"We're making good progress, sir. The technology is almost there. The people are the best of the best. Still working on strategy and tactics, I'm afraid, but desperate times demand desperate measures."

Andrews paused and looked at Hollis. "How did the test of the particle beam cannon work out?" Andrews sat on the couch, with the seal of the president woven into the carpeting between them.

"Everything is finally working properly. Effective range is two hundred miles. I have seven specialized ships being fitted with the new cannons. They can be launched in a week to ten days. The ships can stay in international waters and still provide protection for the weapon transmitters in São Luis, Brazil; Lima, Peru; Iceland; India; Indonesia; and Tromso, Norway. The cannons are also being installed to protect transmitters in Wales, West Australia, Alaska, and the Antarctic as we speak."

Andrews glanced out the bullet-proof window behind his desk.

"The aerial spraying?"

Hollis checked his notes. "I'm gradually increasing the coverage. The new nanoparticles of aluminum and barium are staying airborne for eight to ten weeks. The weapon won't work without the metallic ions to conduct the electromagnetic energy through the upper atmosphere."

Andrews nodded, a guilty look on his face. "I hate dousing people with these metals. It's ruining their health, contaminating our food, and our water supply."

Hollis took a deep breath. "I know, but not using the weapon isn't an option. Our new friend told us this was going to be a long and painful process. The situation is already bad and getting worse by the day. I don't see that we actually have any choice."

Andrews closed his eyes momentarily and shook his head. "We don't. Is your security still tight?"

Hollis glanced around the room. "Yes, sir, fully compartmentalized and need to know."

The information was ears only. Andrews didn't have any printed or electronic copies of anything on the project, and he made sure there would be no recordings of any of the meetings that took place.

"Still fully isolated from the military industrial complex?"

"Yes, sir, totally isolated. No cross connections. Our most vulnerable point is the recruitment of top-qualified pilots, but the military system seems to be handling that reasonably well. When asked, we just hint that the pilots are being moved into Special Forces units for classified missions. That appears to be an acceptable reason for losing their best people."

Andrews looked particularly worried.

"What about the rate of alien abductions?"

Hollis stared at the presidential seal in the carpet. "Still increasing," he said. "Worldwide, more than fifty people a day are being abducted by the Zeta Greys. Many show up after a day or two, but some are never seen again. Animal mutilations by the aliens are up, too. More people are noticing. It won't be long before the outcry becomes a public issue. Our official position of denial isn't going to last indefinitely. At some point the people are going to figure out what's happening and that their government has been lying to them all along."

Andrews grimaced. "The timing of this was always a critical issue. Your people have to come up with the necessary strategy and tactics soon, or this whole thing will start to unravel. I'm just afraid that if we fail at this, humanity will be unable to recover. We will lose not only our freedom, but our capacity for self-determination. All of us would be reduced to slaves, at best, and eventually, to little more than farm animals waiting to be harvested for someone else's gain."

Hollis nodded and reflected Andrews's concern for the future. "Believe me, sir—I understand exactly what is at stake. I'll call you as soon as we make the necessary breakthrough on strategy and tactics."

Chapter 5

Diane Zadanski collected her baggage in the Albuquerque Airport and looked around. This was as far as her orders had taken her. A tall, husky man with close-cut blond hair, cowboy boots, faded blue jeans, a muted blue plaid shirt, leather jacket, and Stetson hat approached her.

"Lieutenant?" he asked softly.

Diane glanced around and wondered if this was who was meeting her. He wasn't wearing a uniform, so it felt strange to her.

"Zadanski," she replied. "And you are?"

He checked to see that no one was close to them. He showed her his military ID. "Jed Collier, ma'am. I have a car waiting,"

She followed him out the glass sliding doors into the

cold, dry night air. He opened the trunk of the plain dark blue Chevy sedan and hoisted her luggage into the compartment. Closing the trunk, he opened the back passenger door, motioned for her to get inside, closed the door, walked around to the other side, and got in. He nodded to the driver, who pulled out into the light traffic. She looked him over as the car left the airport.

"Where are we going?" she asked.

He didn't look at her, but just stared straight ahead. "To never–never land."

This whole thing was starting to feel strange. "You're joking, right?"

He turned to face her directly. "Not really. If you're ever asked, you've never heard of such a place, and you never talk about what you're doing there, or where it's located."

Her level of suspicion was rising. "Your military ID was Army," she said. "Why aren't you in uniform?"

He nodded. "Valid question. I used to be a colonel in Army Intelligence."

She frowned. "But you're not now?" She felt alarmed about where this conversation was going.

"Still a colonel, only not in the Army anymore. Just like you're still a lieutenant, but not in the Navy."

He watched her closely to see how she was taking the news.

"What? What do you mean I'm not in the Navy?" She contemplated ordering the car to stop so she could get out.

"You've been promoted into a higher branch of the service. I'll let Admiral Hollis explain it to you when we arrive."

Admiral Hollis? she wondered. She'd never heard his name before, but that wasn't too unusual. There were a lot of admirals in the Navy. The thought that the admiral might not be in the Navy any more crossed her mind, as well.

She felt a little panicked about the sudden change in her life. *I've got to have faith that this is the best thing that I can experience,* she thought. She tried to relax. It wasn't working all that well. "So what do you do now?" she asked.

"I'm head of security at Peregrine Base."

Peregrine Base? she wondered. One more thing she hadn't heard of before. This was getting stranger by the minute. "So you've read my service file?"

He nodded and glanced down. "Honestly, I know more about you than your mother ever dreamed of knowing. I'm sorry about her passing."

Diane closed her eyes and breathed out slowly. Her mind raced to adjust to her new conditions. The fact that he wasn't in uniform was troubling, but he genuinely seemed to be military.

"So do I address you as colonel, or sir?"

He smiled for the first time since they met. "Collier is fine. You'll find military rank isn't much of a deal in the new unit. Most everyone is comfortable using last names, if that works for you."

The mood was definitely lighter now. "It does, Collier," she replied.

He relaxed, too. "I thought it might, Zadanski."

They both chuckled. They filled the long drive into the dark wilderness of southwestern New Mexico with polite conversation.

* * *

"We're here," Collier said as the car came to a stop.

A jolt of panic swept through Diane. They were out in the middle of nowhere: no lights, no buildings, no gate, nothing. For the last half-hour, the car had bumped down what could only marginally be called a gravel road. What had she been sent into?

Collier came around, opened the car door, and illuminated the ground with a flashlight.

"Watch your step; the ground is uneven," he said.

He led her along a narrow path, through scrub brush and sage, in the frozen stillness of the night. A massive outcrop of stone rose above them, barely visible in the dull reflection of his flashlight on the snow. Two men dressed in padded camo fatigues with night vision gear stepped out of a cave. Diane glanced at the M-16 rifles they carried as she passed between the guards, still unsure what was going to happen. Cameras mounted to the ceiling of the cave whirred as she followed Collier deeper into what was clearly an abandoned mine of some sort. She began to feel less uncertain as she entered into the lighted section around a corner in the cave.

Collier led her through a round opening where a twelve-foot diameter blast door, two-feet thick, stood open. The room was generally cubical, fifteen feet on a side, thirty feet deep with rock walls, a security desk, and another blast door off to the left. That door was closed. An older officer stood, waiting for her.

His uniform was a solid dark gray color with a unit patch on the right shoulder. The emblem had a black background with a red border, a yellow nine-pointed star in the lower half of the patch, and USSC in white letters across the top. The collar of the man's shirt was open, no tie, but with four chrome stars on the lapel. He walked forward and held out his hand. She shook hands, glancing at the name tag above his right shirt pocket: Hollis.

"Welcome to Peregrine Base, home of the United States Space Command," he said. "You can keep your personal items. Your new uniform is in your quarters, so you won't need any of your Navy issued clothing."

Space Command? she thought. She didn't know there

was such a thing. That's when Collier's words came back to her: "Never–never land. If you are asked, you've never heard of such a place." She slowly began to relax.

"This is your new home. Your luggage will be in your quarters. Would you like some coffee?"

"Sure," she said. She handed her orders and ID card to the soldier at the desk who processed her paperwork and gave her a new ID card. Two men opened the second blast door.

They trekked through a smooth concrete-lined hall for another two hundred yards, rode an elevator down three hundred feet, and entered the residential section of the underground base. They threaded their way through a moving mass of construction workers carrying supplies and tools in the underground halls.

"Still under construction," Hollis explained. "I'm afraid you'll have to put up with the noise for some time yet. Cafeteria is in here." He turned to the right, walked over to the coffee machine, and poured two cups.

"You'll meet the rest of the squadron tomorrow," Hollis said. "Before you turn in, I'd like you to try something out for me. Do you feel up to that?"

She glanced around at the unfinished dining hall. The construction noise was probably going on twenty-four hours a day.

"What is it?" she asked.

"A flight simulator. You can think of it as a type of video game—on steroids."

She finished her coffee. "Okay, let's go."

Hollis led her down a flight of stairs and into a small room off a long hall, and flipped on the lights. In the center of the room was a pilot's seat with a complex console wrapped around the cockpit, not too different from her Super Hornet's. The cockpit was supported by a number of hydraulic cylinders, which gave the simulator a six-axis range of motion. Three screens were mounted in front of the pilot's seat, simulating forward, right, and left fields of vision. Mounted behind the pilot seat were two displays and another seat.

"It's a two-seater plane?" she asked.

He shook his head and blinked slowly. "Two-seater *craft*. It's much more than a plane."

She frowned slightly. "Okay, but won't I need a RIO?"

He nodded, looked at her, and grinned. "For tonight, I'll be your radar intercept officer. Go ahead and strap in."

She climbed into the pilot seat and strapped the five-point harness around her. Hollis stepped into the second seat and strapped in. He powered up the simulator and the screens in front of her lit up. They depicted a mountainous terrain with blue skies above.

"You're going to encounter a saucer shaped craft sitting on the ground in the middle of your screen. The controls are very similar to your Super Hornet, so you shouldn't have too much trouble adapting. Weapon selection and firing is on the control stick. Your job is to shoot down the scout saucer. We're going to take a few minutes for you to get accustomed to the simulator. Just fly through the air and get used to the controls, okay?"

Her hand trembled slightly and the coffee wasn't helping the nervousness in her stomach, but, she said, "Okay."

"Here we go," Hollis said.

The scenery on the screens started moving. It was a good simulation of flying her Super Hornet at fifteen hundred miles an hour. She banked left then right. The whole simulator tipped and swung in response, just as her fighter jet aircraft moved.

"Okay, you see that valley coming up on your two?"

She checked the screen on the right side. "Yep." The familiarity of flight settled her down into the present moment.

"Fly into that valley and move closer to the ground.

That's where you'll find the scout saucer. As soon as you acquire the target, shoot it down."

She banked into the valley and dived for the ground. As soon as she spotted the glowing silver saucer she froze. It bolted up from the ground and shot a beam of light at her. The screens went dark and the simulator came to rest.

Diane was shaking in her seat, breathing hard, and unable to speak.

"Zadanski?" Hollis said softly.

He waited patiently for her to respond. She finally released her harness and turned to face him.

"It's the same damn saucer!" she shouted. "It took my brother!"

Hollis's expression fell. "I didn't know. I'm so sorry."

"These saucers are real. I saw one." She was furious.

He nodded. "All too real, I'm afraid. When did this happen?"

Tears welled up in her eyes, her hands still trembling.

"Nine years ago," she said. Her voice was shaking as much as *she* was. "My brother had left his sweater out near our pond. It was dusk, but there was still some light in the sky, so he went out to get it. That's when the saucer appeared. I remember him looking back at me just as he was swept up in a bright white light. The saucer flew right over me as it left. It was totally silent—no engine sounds at all. I never saw him again. To this day I don't know if he is dead or alive."

Hollis sighed and looked down, shaking his head. "If he wasn't returned within three days, I'm afraid he's dead."

Diane's trembling increased. She began sobbing. He reached forward and put his hand on her shoulder.

"I'm so sorry."

She felt short of breath and instinctively put her hand on her chest. "Why do you think he's dead?" she asked.

The expression on his face was both grim and sad. For a

few moments he wouldn't make eye contact with her, but then he did.

"Each year approximately ten thousand people are abducted by UFOs and never seen again. Those are just the ones we know about. My guess is that the actual number may be three to four times that high."

This is incredible, she thought. "And nobody notices?"

"Sure, people notice, but without an actual sighting, as in your case, the victims are thought to have left on their own, got lost, had an accident, or some other rational explanation. For most people, UFO abduction isn't even on the list of possibilities."

She shook her head. So her brother wasn't the only one, she thought. The same thing has happened to a lot of people. It's still happening, she realized.

"So what's being done about it?" She turned to face him more and wiped the tears from her eyes.

"You and this new squadron are an integral part of the solution," Hollis said. "I understand, if you don't feel up to continuing tonight."

She turned to look at the screens and the controls in the simulator. Then she swung back to face him.

"We can take them down?"

He shrugged. "We believe we can. The technology is almost there. We need pilots like you to come up with the tactics and skills to make it happen." He looked back at her, hope in his eyes.

She turned forward in her seat. A new determination filled her mind. "So what happened on the first run? The screens went black."

"Hypothetically, you died," Hollis said. "So far everybody dies, every time. Your first problem is slow speed. You ready to try it faster?"

She glanced back at him. "Yes," she said firmly. She

strapped back in.

"Okay, here we go," Hollis said again.

The three screens came back on with an apparent speed of fifteen hundred miles per hour.

"Thruster control is just like your Super Hornet. Push the speed to the edge of where you're comfortable. Same valley, same scout saucer, same action, just faster this time."

She pushed the thruster lever forward. The images on the screen streamed past her at a frightening speed.

"There's your valley."

She banked and dived, spotted the scout saucer, and swung to the side, realigning her aim. The scout saucer shot up quickly. She banked again to the left and pulled back on the control stick, trying to lock her weapon on the scout saucer. The beam of light hit her again and the screens went dark.

"That was better. You ready to try it faster?" His voice was calm, reassuring.

She looked back at him. "How fast will this go?"

"Your last run was at ten percent thrust," he said matter-of-factly.

"Ten percent!" That was a shock. In her Super Hornet, ten percent wasn't even takeoff speed. She'd still be on the flight deck.

"It takes time to adapt to the higher speeds. Our fastest pilot has worked his way up to fifty percent thrust. We think at seventy percent, we can start successfully engaging the scout saucers."

She shook her head. "We think?" Didn't he *know*?

Hollis shrugged. "We'll find out when we get there."

Unbelievable, she thought. "So, faster?"

He nodded. "Faster."

The simulator powered back up. The screens came to life. She pushed the thruster to twenty percent. The images were screaming past her. She located the valley, banked and dived after the scout saucer. It lifted off. She banked and swerved, trying to avoid the beam of light. Just as she was about to line her sights up on the scout saucer she crashed into the side of a mountain. Her spirits fell with the darkened screens and the return of the simulator to its resting position.

"Okay," Hollis said. "Enough for tonight. Welcome to the U.S. Space Command."

"Yeah," she said softly. If she ever wanted a challenge in her life, this was it.

* * *

When Diane returned to her quarters, she unpacked her luggage and put her personal items in the dresser drawers. She held her brother's varsity sweater against her chest, the one treasured item she always carried with her. Tears flowed as she sat on the bed, rocking forward and back, hugging his sweater as tightly as she could. She missed him so much.

The disappearance of her brother, the shock of seeing a real UFO, the breaking storm with the sudden wind, and joltingly close bolts of lightning all swirled in her mind. Her heart pounded as her emotions were swept up in reliving that terrifying event once again. The only difference now was the loss of hope that her brother was still alive, somewhere. The reality of his death was finally sinking in. She wondered once again if he had suffered or had been in pain. How long was it before they killed him? How did he die?

She shook herself out of the downward spiral of morbid thoughts and feelings that flooded through her. He was gone. She looked up at her reflection in the mirror above her dresser. Something in her expression had changed. A steely resolve stared back at her with an inner strength she hadn't recognized, and a determination unknown to her before this moment. After all these years of wondering, now she knew. Fate had brought her into the one place where she could do something to avenge her brother's death. She would not let this opportunity slip away. No. She would find a way to make them pay, and pay dearly, for the loss of her brother.

Chapter 6

"Technology consultant?"

Dr. Theodore Shugart waited while Captain Edwards studied the authorization letter and ID in the beam of his flashlight.

"The army has its own recovery team. Why aren't they here?"

Theo nodded. He had anticipated the MP questioning why the regular team wasn't here. It was an unexpected shift in procedure.

"They may be involved somewhere else," Theo said. "President Andrews personally requested that my team and I take care of the recovery."

Captain Edwards looked skeptical. Furrows in his brow showed his concern over the change taking place. Theo felt he was hiding his nervousness well. What he didn't want was Edwards using his normal chain of command to validate Theo's presence at the crash site.

"How do I know this is actually the president's signature?" Captain Edwards asked.

Theo handed him his cell phone.

"You can call him. It's on the top of the list."

Edwards turned the beam of his flashlight on Shugart's face.

Captain Edwards looked skeptical. "Is this phone secure?"

"Secure and encrypted," Theo answered.

Captain Edwards initiated the call.

"No, this is Captain Edwards, military police. Who am I talking to?"

Edwards sounded nervous, the flashlight beam shifting in the dark.

Lightning flashed in the distant clouds, but no thunder. Too far away, Theo thought. The storm could have contributed to the saucer crash. He'd know more, once they got it back to Ceti Research.

"No, sir. I don't need you to wake the president. I'm just verifying Dr. Shugart's authorization to be here. Can you give me a description of Dr. Shugart?"

Edwards shined the flashlight beam on Theo's face.

"Uh huh."

Edwards returned the light to the ID and letter in his hand.

"Yes, sir, I understand. Thank you, sir."

Edwards handed Theo's phone back to him.

"Sorry for the inconvenience, Dr. Shugart, but we have to verify everyone's authorization before they get access. Corporal Osborn will drive you to the crash site."

Theo took his ID and authorization letter, relieved that

he hadn't been stopped, or worse yet, arrested. At least Andrews wouldn't have to use the cover story they concocted to get Theo released from military custody. He picked up his duffel bag, and climbed into the HUMMVEE. So far, so good, he thought. This would be his first alien saucer recovery.

The crash site was surrounded by multiple floodlights with portable generators running next to them. A ring of a dozen soldiers patrolled the perimeter.

"Anyone been close to or inside the craft yet?" Theo asked.

The craft was definitely Zeta Grey in design: standard scout saucer, fifty-two feet in diameter, and sixteen feet in height. The outer skin was a dull stainless steel gray. The scout saucers were multipurpose craft used for exploration, abductions, and occasionally for combat.

"No, sir. We're strictly perimeter control," Corporal Osborn replied.

The door in the top slope of the scout saucer was sprung open a few inches. Probably from the impact, Theo thought. At least getting into the craft would be easy enough.

"I have a medical team en route. Please see that they're not delayed."

The left circular edge of the craft was buried in the ground with soil plowed up over the upper section.

"Yes, sir. I'll have them brought right in."

The bottom of the door wrapped over the outside edge by several inches, but it was still eight feet above the ground.

"I'll also need two ladders—ten or twelve feet long."

Osborn got on the radio and relayed the request.

"Could be a half-hour, sir, maybe a little longer."

Theo nodded. "We're going to be here all night, Corporal, you got a way to get any coffee out here?"

Osborn shook his head. "Maybe after daybreak, sir. Right now we got nothing."

Which is good, Theo thought. By daybreak they should be back at Ceti Research and out from under the prying eyes of the army.

He pulled his nuclear, biological, and chemical protection suit out of the duffel bag and put it on. He picked up the radiation meter and slowly approached the craft. Radioactivity was elevated, but not dangerous. He nodded and thought, The Element 115 reactor was either shut down prior to impact, or it wasn't damaged in the crash. Element 115 is a super heavy metal used to generate antigravity fields. He'd know more, once he got inside.

He walked slowly around the craft, checking for radiation, and inspecting the exterior surface for any sign of further damage. When he arrived at his starting point, his heart froze. The door was open a foot and slowly rising.

Corporal Osborn had his M-16 to his shoulder, aimed at the scout saucer door. Theo ran to Osborn, waved his arms in the air, and shouted, "Don't shoot. Don't shoot. We need it alive!"

Osborn continued to aim at the scout saucer. "If it poses any kind of a threat, my orders are to shoot it, sir."

"It's injured. It's not a threat. Believe me, if it was in any kind of shape to be a threat, you'd already be dead."

Osborn's radio crackled.

"Medical team has arrived."

Osborn glanced at Theo. "Copy that. I have activity at the site—I need support ASAP."

The door continued to open slowly.

"Roger, support on its way."

Theo turned to face the craft. "What about my medical team?"

Osborn stepped between Theo and the saucer. "Nobody gets close to that thing until it's secure. That includes you, Dr. Shugart; now back away from the saucer, sir."

Theo walked away, shaking his head. The door reached its fully open position without anything appearing in the opening. Three minutes later, a Black Hawk helicopter circled in and took up a position with its machine gun and searchlight aimed at the saucer door.

A rounded gray object slowly appeared in the doorway followed by two small hands with long slender fingers that gripped the bottom edge of the opening. It slowly dragged itself out of the saucer, hung over the threshold, and then fell to the ground below. It lay crumpled in the dirt, its spindly arms and legs twitching.

"Let me get to it while it's still alive," Theo shouted over the thumping of the chopper blades. "You can see it's not a threat. Get my medical team in here now!"

The chopper moved so its bright spotlight illuminated the inside of the scout saucer.

"No movement inside. No immediate threat. Backing off," came over Osborn's radio.

Osborn grabbed his mic. "Site is stable. Send in the medical team."

Theo paced as he waited for his team to arrive. Finally, two more HUMMVEEs pulled up with his three-member team, and four more soldiers. The team put on protective suits and followed Theo to the injured alien, which Dr. Fortner proceeded to examine.

"Is it still alive, Doc?" Theo asked.

Dr. Fortner looked up at him. "As far as I can tell, it's still hanging on. We have a chopper on the way. I'll know more when we get it back to Ceti Research."

Theo walked back to Osborn.

"It's dying. We need to evacuate it while we can."

Osborn checked with Captain Edwards then said, "Okay. Go ahead."

* * *

A half hour later the alien was on a chopper and the ladders arrived. Theo, Dr. Fortner, and his two assistants, Dave Ellis and Sam Laski, climbed into the scout saucer. The doorway led directly into the passenger compartment with three seats in a triangle on a raised center section. One seat was set forward with the other two farther back on each side. The floor-to-ceiling height was only five feet, forcing them to crouch. A six inch diameter tube extended down from the ceiling in the center and flared out in a general tear shaped form mounted to a square section on the floor.

The Element 115 reactor, Theo thought. He checked for radiation leaks and visually examined the tube and flared section for any damage.

Dr. Fortner checked the bodies of the two Zeta Greys crunched against the front wall. "We'll need to get these two back for an autopsy. Get some body bags."

Dave Ellis climbed back down the ladder to retrieve the bags. Theo checked for any other radiation leaks, and slowly descended through a narrow hatch into the lower level of the scout saucer.

Three large coils were attached to the ceiling by a large swivel with control struts allowing the bottom of the coils to swing up to eighty degrees in any direction. Six cables spread out from a spherical central hub, with two cables connected to the top of each coil. The coils produced the antigravity waves that propelled the saucer.

The design was identical to the demonstration saucer provided by the Tau Cetians, with the exception of the control console, which this saucer didn't have. Without the manual controls, Theo couldn't power up the craft, or check any of the control systems.

He supervised Dave and Sam as they put the dead Zeta

Greys into body bags, carried them out of the saucer, and set them on the ground. He called for a Chinook helicopter while Dave and Sam started rigging the nylon strap system that would be used to airlift the craft back to Ceti Research.

Chapter 7

Sean Wells swallowed the last of the Green Spot whiskey in his glass as the two remaining ice cubes gently nudged his upper lip. The fifty-dollar bottle of golden colored Single Pot Still Irish whiskey was a gift from his editor, Ed Schultz, honoring Sean's investigation into insider trading between investment bankers in the derivatives market. After fourteen years as an investigative journalist for the *New York Times*, he had gained a reputation for no-nonsense articles that laid bare the shenanigans of some of the rich and powerful on Wall Street, as well as the political hacks he so vehemently despised.

He pushed the wire-rimmed glasses back up on his nose and read the data one more time. Ed may want his bottle back, he thought. For some time the *New York Times* had been referring to people who opposed the science on global warming as skeptics rather than deniers. That policy was now being changed. Sean's new assignment was to expose the climate change deniers and their fake claims as to the latest global cooling trend.

"The climate isn't cooling," Ed told him, "it just isn't heating as fast as it was. Get the facts and prove the deniers are wrong."

No problem, Sean thought. Digging for the facts was what he did best. How hard could it be? Temperature was temperature, scientifically defined and recorded. He added an ice cube to his glass and poured a second jigger of Green Spot from the half-empty bottle. *If it were only that easy*, he reminded himself. He walked slowly to the glass sliding door leading to the small balcony of his fifth-story apartment on Avenue D in the East Village. Even at ten in the evening the street below was bustling with people and taxis.

The one unerring sense he possessed was his ability to detect BS, and that alarm was ringing loud and clear. The National Oceanic and Atmospheric Administration (NOAA) had set very specific guidelines for the placement of temperature sensors to assure accurate and reliable readings. What amazed him the most was that the temperature sensors weren't read and monitored electronically. The readings were made manually, by volunteers, and sent in to the National Centers for Environmental Information, or NCEI. None of the sensors were accessible over the Internet and data was released only once a month for the previous month's readings.

Critics of global climate change had taken photos of many of the official temperature sensors and posted them on the Internet, complaining that the location of the sensors didn't comply with NOAA standards. Those rules required temperature sensors to be a minimum of one hundred feet from any building, structure, or heat source, such as gravel, pavement, equipment, or exhaust vents. The photos showed temperature sensors located over gravel, on or next to asphalt pavement, mounted on buildings, roofs, and in the direct path of hot exhaust from air conditioning heat exchangers—any of which would push the temperature readings artificially higher.

In response to the photos, the NOAA issued the following statement: "The adjusted United States Historical Climatology Network Conterminous U.S. temperatures are well aligned with recent measurements from NOAA's U.S. Climate Reference Network (designed with the highest climate monitoring standards for siting and instrument exposure), thus providing independent evidence that the USHCN provides an accurate measure of the U.S. temperature."

The problem was, fully 89% of the fifteen hundred temperature sensors were non-compliant with the NOAA rules. What stuck in Sean's craw was the second word in the statement: *adjusted*. A thermometer doesn't lie, but *people*, in his experience, certainly did. What good were the highest climate monitoring standards for siting and instrument exposure if eight out of every nine sensors didn't comply with the standard?

The most disturbing data he read was from the southeast United States. Independent unadjusted temperature records from compliant sensors demonstrated the five-year running average had actually *decreased* by 0.020 degrees over the last decade. The *adjusted* NOAA running average for the same period showed a 0.200 degree *increase*.

Why am I not surprised? Sean thought. Where there are political hacks, there's money flowing. So I follow the money and see who benefits.

* * *

At 7:00 a.m. sharp, Sean knocked on the glass door to

Ed Schultz's office at the *New York Times*. Ed glanced up and waved him in.

"Yeah, I don't care," Ed said into the phone. "If you have documentation that proves our story is wrong, send it to me and we'll print a retraction along with your side of the story. Front page, I promise." Ed looked at Sean and smiled. "Yep, I can't wait to hear from your legal team. Thanks for calling." Ed put down the phone.

"Another satisfied customer?" Sean asked.

Ed grinned. "For some reason they all think the threat of a lawsuit will make us stay away from reporting their crooked dealings. This guy even thought I would care about hurting his bottom line."

Sean shook his head. "I can't imagine."

Ed leaned forward, expectation written all over his face. "So, what have you found so far?"

"Pretty much what I expected—the green supporters and the environmentalists are paying scientists to stack the data in their favor, and the oil cartel is shelling out millions to the global warming deniers on the other side. Some of the data on each side is valid, but a lot of it is bogus. To be honest with you, I don't think there's enough reliable information to determine exactly what the climate is doing, if anything."

"So it's about money?" Ed asked with a hint of disappointment in his voice.

Sean shrugged. "A good portion of it is. On the one hand, none of the dire scenarios and predictions of global warming have come to pass. On the other, we have more severe weather being blamed on a now mostly unseen warming trend, especially if you completely ignore severe weather from the past."

Ed leaned back and shook his head. "And if you include the past?"

Sean sat in the nearer of two seats in front of Ed's desk.

"Depends on how far back you go. Looking at the last fifty years of weather, storms are getting more severe. If we go back six hundred years, we've had worse, and plenty of it. Big storms are cyclical."

"The president says global warming is real," Ed stated dryly.

"He does," Sean replied, nodding. "I need a press pass to the White House and travel expenses to and from Washington to dig out who is getting the money. Maybe then I can figure out why Andrews is pushing the agenda so hard."

Ed looked out the window, his usual frown reforming. "Okay. How long?"

Sean shrugged. "A week, maybe ten days."

Ed looked over at him. "Updates to me every night?"

Sean smiled. "As usual." Time to go hunting for more crooks.

Chapter 8

"How's the Zeta Grey we recovered?" Theo asked as he arrived at Ceti Research. The facility was initially carved out of an extensive system of caves deep in the mountains of the Painted Desert region in Arizona and quickly expanded to four hundred acres underground.

"Still hanging in there, but definitely not conscious. It's in containment chamber eight," nurse Eta Donatello said.

"Where's Charlie?"

She smiled at the mention of Charlie's name.

"He's in the lab, running the DNA sequence on the Zeta Grey."

She likes him, Theo thought as he walked to the design department. Charlie's a friendly enough guy, especially if you don't know he's reading your thoughts all the time. He just comes across as caring, empathetic, and intuitive.

He looked around as he stepped into the design and development room. Forty-two engineers worked at computer-assisted design stations. Sketches and math formulas lined the white boards on the walls.

"The new version of the telepathic blocking helmet ready yet?"

Dr. Kerstov handed him the prototype. "We better get this right soon; we're running out of ideas."

Theo nodded, took the helmet, and headed to the lab to meet Charlie.

Charlie looked at the helmet. He sighed as his shoulders slumped. "You've got to get this right. Your people are dead meat if they go up against the Zetas without effectively blocking the telepathic manipulation."

Theo put the helmet on.

"Okay," Charlie said. "Think of a color."

The two of them used a two-step process: first a color, then a number between zero and ninety-nine. Charlie would use his telepathic ability to plant the color and number in Theo's mind. Charlie scribbled green on a piece of paper and folded it in half.

"I'm having trouble deciding," Theo said. "Either turquoise or green."

"Just pick whatever you think you'd like best," Charlie said.

Theo nodded. "Turquoise."

Charlie handed the folded sheet to Theo.

"Green," Theo said. "First time for a miss, but it was close."

He handed the sheet back to Charlie, who scribbled a number on it.

"Pick a number."

Theo's mind swirled. In previous trials the colors and

numbers came quickly and clearly. This time there was some fuzziness involved. They were getting close.

"Thirty-seven," Theo said.

Charlie handed the note back.

"Forty-seven. Impressive."

Theo took off the helmet.

"Another layer of interactive wave cancellation just might do it," Charlie said.

Theo shook his head. "The helmet is cumbersome now. Another layer and it's going to be like walking around with a large bowling ball wrapped around your head."

Charlie shrugged. "It still beats being dead."

The DNA sequencer beeped and the printer began spitting sheets into the tray.

"So what have you found?" Theo asked.

Charlie pulled the DNA analysis sheet from the printer.

"As I expected, the Zeta Grey DNA is a little different from what it was when we fought them in the Tau Ceti star system. Definite Earth human sequences are present, meaning they have been harvesting human stem cells to overcome the cloning problem for a long time."

Theo nodded. "Not surprised. I've got two dead ones headed into autopsy. Care to join me and Doc? We could use your insight."

Charlie shrugged. "Sure. I don't have to be in Washington until tomorrow morning."

Chapter 9

They put on their bio suits to protect them from unknown alien bacteria and viruses, and followed Dr. Fortner into the autopsy isolation lab.

Each dead Zeta Grey was on its own stainless steel table. The three of them stood around the first table, Doc on one side, Theo and Charlie on the other. Doc turned on the video recorder and the high intensity lights above the table.

"The skin is medium gray in color, slightly rough to the touch, and without hair in any location. Body shape is humanoid in general with a large head, thin neck, moderate trunk, thin arms and legs. No genitalia are present, male or female. The head is very large in comparison to the rest of the body structure. Eyes are also large, almond-shaped, and generally black in color with narrow vertical slits for the pupils. No external ears are observed, just small holes in the skin. A hint of a nose appears above the small and horizontal mouth.

"I'm opening the chest cavity now. Hold on a minute. This skin is really tough. Even with a new scalpel, I almost have to saw through it. The skin seems to have fibers running through it. This can't be natural." Doc took a sample over to the slicing machine, prepared a section, and placed the slide under the microscope. "The fibers in the skin appear to be an artificial web, but there's biological material embedded in the matrix. The cell structure is reminiscent of the lining of the human intestinal tract. This is both artificial and natural skin. Charlie, what do you know about this?"

Charlie leaned over and peered into the chest of the Zeta Grey. "Keep in mind, I haven't seen the insides of one of these either, so I'm going to let the explanation wait for a little while. I think the reason will become more apparent as we go along."

Doc looked annoyed. "Really?" he said. "You're going to make me wait for an answer?"

Charlie shrugged and smiled at him. "You'll figure it out on your own, trust me. From what I've read, it's worth the wait."

"I doubt that," Doc replied, as he returned to the autopsy table.

Theo smiled at the banter that went on between Doc and Charlie. Doc was the practical, materialist scientist, while Charlie was more the cosmic philosopher. They made an entertaining team.

"Blood is dark green in color and thin. No coagulation is present. Ribs appear white and smooth. Taking a sample now . . .

"Huh, that's interesting: it's not bone. Take a look at this. It looks like some kind of synthetic material. It's not biological at all. Charlie, what do you make of this?"

Charlie turned and smiled at Theo before answering, "The Zeta Grey skeletal structure is artificial. It's constructed from a poly-ceramic and fiber material. They aren't born. They don't grow up. They're cloned as full-sized bodies."

Doc looked stunned. He stood there, mouth open, scalpel in hand, staring back at Charlie.

"Doc?" Theo said. "Can we continue?"

"Sure. It never occurred to me that they weren't born," Doc said. "Plus, I've never seen the insides of one of them before, either. This is so strange, you know?"

Charlie just stood there, a self-satisfied smile on his face.

"I know," Theo said. "I've read reports on them, too, but this is my first time actually seeing it for myself. It leaves me with a whole different view of both them and us. You're right, though. It's strange."

Doc continued: "Abdominal organs are similar to human in placement, but different in appearance. Esophagus, stomach, and intestines are all thin, lumpy strings. This is an alien life form. Why would it have organs similar to a human, some of which appear non-functional? It doesn't make any sense."

Theo waited for a moment, but Charlie didn't respond. "Charlie?" Theo asked.

Charlie looked up from the alien body. "Let me start with a hypothetical question."

He just can't help himself, Theo thought. He's got to antagonize Doc.

Charlie looked at him and smiled.

"If you had extensive knowledge of genetics and DNA manipulation, and you needed to create a creature to work in dangerous conditions, where would you start? Would you pick something totally different and unproven, or would you begin where you were most familiar?"

Doc waved his scalpel as he thought. "I'd go with what I knew," he said. "I'd start with my own DNA and make modifications as needed."

"Exactly," Charlie replied. "And you'd end up with a creature that had the same basic physical structure you have."

Doc looked down at the open alien abdomen in front of him.

"But that would mean humans created the Greys."

That was an angle Theo hadn't considered before. What else was going to come out in the autopsy?

"In this case, yes, the Zeta Greys were created by humans," Charlie replied, grinning at Doc.

"Were all Greys made by humans?" Doc asked.

Charlie shook his head. "No. There are many different types of Greys. Some are born and grow up, some are pure clones, and others are a combination of both. Some are benevolent and caring; some aren't."

"But why this?" Doc asked, holding his arms out over the small body on the table. "Why are there Greys?"

"That will become more apparent as we continue," Charlie said. "Shall we?"

Doc obviously didn't like being put off. He scowled at Charlie, shook off the rebuff, and continued.

"The liver is green in color and larger proportionally than a normal human liver would be. Texture is stiffer than a human liver, but still flexible. A spleen is present. It is gray in color, soft and spongy. Pancreas is thin and stringy, similar to the rest of the non-functional digestive system. Cutting through the ribs now."

Doc used an electric saw and then spreaders to open the chest cavity.

"What in the world? I'm cutting the throat open. This can't be."

He sliced into the thin neck, then pulled the skin and muscles back.

"The airway's just another string. The lungs are full sized, but there's no airway, no bronchial tubes. How can they breathe?"

That was a shocking revelation, Theo thought. "Charlie?" Theo asked.

"I'll give you something to think about for a moment," Charlie said. "What happens when a deep sea diver decompresses too fast?"

Doc frowned, stared at Charlie, and paused. Charlie wasn't giving in, so he answered, "They get the bends— nitrogen and other blood gasses come out of solution causing cellular damage, pain, and death."

Charlie nodded. "What happens when people are exposed to the vacuum of outer space?"

Theo could see the frustration building in Doc's expression.

"Essentially the same thing—blood gasses boil out of solution—the body kind of explodes because of it." Doc put his fists on his hips and frowned. "Why?"

"What would happen if there were no dissolved gasses in the blood—if we didn't have lungs—if we didn't need to breathe?"

Doc looked blankly back at Charlie for a moment, studied the chest of the alien and looked back at Charlie. "No," he said, a tone of disbelief in his voice.

"What are you thinking?" Theo asked. It was another cat and mouse series of questions between the two of them, with Charlie as the cat.

"No. You're not suggesting . . . ?" Doc said.

"Theo, what do the Zeta Greys do?" Charlie asked.

"Primarily? They mine natural resources, mostly minerals and metals, and turn them into advanced technology.

They trade that technology for things they want in the interstellar community."

Now he's dragging me into his game with Doc, Theo thought. He knows how I feel about it. Why does he keep doing it?

Charlie smiled and winked at Theo. "Where do they mine?"

Theo sighed. There wasn't any point to resisting. "Well—anywhere—planets, moons, asteroids, comets."

"No," Doc said again, his tone of incredulity getting stronger. He grabbed the Zeta Grey's skin, pulling on it, trying to stretch it. "You can't be serious."

Theo hadn't seen Doc this excited in months. "Doc, what are you thinking?" he asked.

"Take a look at the heart," Charlie suggested.

Doc cut the left lung away.

"It's not a heart. At least not as we understand a heart to be. It has a layer of muscle around it, similar to what the esophagus or bowel would have. It connects to the top of the lung, extends down to the liver, with a branch off to the spleen. If the lungs can't breathe . . ."

Charlie stood there, grinning. "You understand now?"

Doc pointed his face to the ceiling and closed his eyes.

"Oh, my God, they don't need a space suit." He turned to face Charlie. "Their circulation system operates by peristalsis, slow and steady. No beating heart. The tough skin prevents decompression from damaging them. Their body is designed to live and work in outer space. They're not limited to a planet with an atmosphere."

"That's correct," Charlie said, obviously proud of himself. "That's why there are Greys. Their bodies allow them to live and work in space with minimal restriction."

Doc shook his head. "But if they don't breathe, how do they function? How do they stay alive?"

Charlie nodded. "I understand your confusion. Their green blood is magnesium-based, with bismuth and lithium as electrical carriers. For two hours a day, they sit in an electromagnetic field that recharges their bioenergy system. Our bodies work on oxidation—we literally burn food to get energy. Their bioenergy system is electrical-based, while ours is fire-based."

"Huh," Doc said. He shrugged. "Kind of like the difference between a battery and a gasoline engine?"

"Precisely. Only on a biological level," Charlie replied.

Doc frowned. He stared down into the open chest cavity of the cadaver.

Wow, Theo thought. That's efficient. With their advanced technology they can create almost unlimited amounts of electricity. That gives them a tremendous biological advantage over us.

"So the artificial skin must also be an insulator," Doc said.

Charlie nodded. "It prevents heat loss. It also reduces their infrared signature to near zero."

Doc nodded. "That would explain the difficulty I had with the one that's still alive. Our touch thermometers couldn't get a reading on it. I had to insert a regular thermometer into it to get a temperature."

"And?" Charlie asked.

Doc was examining the skin again. He answered without looking up. "High. A hundred and fifteen degrees Fahrenheit."

"Very different metabolism," Charlie said. He looked at Theo.

He's probably tracking Doc's thoughts as he was figuring out the alien skin, Theo realized.

"But that means . . . wait a minute—wait a minute."

Doc cut a section at the corner of a large black eye.

"There it is. The skin is essentially artificial, including the clear section over the eyes. That means the synthetic skeleton and the artificial skin are there first. The muscles, nerves, and circulation system are grown around the skeleton and inside the skin."

"Exactly," Charlie said, a huge grin on his face. "The whole process takes about twelve weeks."

"But how do they eat?" Doc asked.

"You noted the biological component in the skin was like intestinal wall cells. They absorb a nutritional liquid through the skin, once every six weeks."

Doc looked back down at the small body on the table. "And waste materials?"

"Same thing, just the other way around," Charlie said, "through the skin."

Doc nodded slowly. "That would explain the odor they have. What about the brain?"

Even though he didn't like being sucked into this ongoing game between Charlie and Doc, Theo found it at least educational, if not mildly entertaining. That was the primary reason he put up with it.

"Take a look for yourself," Charlie said.

Doc cut the skin away and sawed the skull open in a circle all the way around. He pulled on the top of the skull, but it didn't move. He looked at the cut and found a thin vertical section running from side-to-side inside the skull. He made a saw cut from one side to the other, over the top of the skull, and removed each section.

"It has two brains—one in front, and one in back. They're connected only at the bottom." Doc examined the inside of the skull and the material of the brain. "Uh-huh. Just as I suspected. Cause of death is severe axonal traumatic brain injury. Even if they were wearing seatbelts, the force of the impact would have torn the brain apart. I'm surprised the third one is still alive."

"From the placement of the bodies in the saucer," Theo said, "the one that survived probably sat in the front chair—less distance to the wall—less impact."

Doc nodded. "Reasonable. I see no evidence to suggest otherwise."

Theo turned to Charlie.

"One more nugget for you to find, Doc," Charlie said.

Doc started slicing away thin sections of the alien brain. "It's all consistent material: no lobes, no folds. It looks like it's all cerebellum cell structure." He continued cutting away slices until he reached the bottom core. "And what do we have here?" He dug out a whitish hard piece a half inch wide, a quarter inch high, and thin. He held it up to the bright light above and examined it in detail. "It's been a while since I took geology, but this looks like a slice of quartz crystal to me."

"It is," Charlie said.

Finally, we're getting to the root of the Zeta Greys, Theo thought.

"It's an advanced electronic interface that connects every Zeta Grey to their massive computer system. It also converts their thought patterns into electronic signals that control the saucer. That's why their craft doesn't have a control console. They think, and it flies."

"So let me get this straight," Theo said. "The Zeta Greys aren't born, they don't grow up, and they don't go to school to learn. When their body is fully formed, they what—download everything they need to know from the computer system?"

"Yes, they do," Charlie said. "What you think of as a Zeta Grey brain is actually a neural network computer that runs an artificial intelligence program."

Theo had learned many things about the Zeta Greys from classified documents ranging from technology to speculation on what they were actually doing here on earth. The basic problem was they didn't have all of the classified documents to work with. Those were very closely controlled, so some things they just had to discover for themselves. And this autopsy was connecting dots he hadn't even known existed before.

"So Zeta Greys can't think on their own?" Doc asked.

Charlie shook his head. "That depends strictly on the program downloaded into them. The workers don't think, as we understand it, but the tall Greys do, and certain of those have analytical and thinking skills way beyond the brightest humans."

Theo was stunned by the implications. "So everything we do in the first thirty years of our life, they do in thirty seconds?"

Charlie turned his palms up and shrugged. "Pretty much, yeah."

"Damn, talk about efficiency," Theo said. "Are they smarter than we are? I mean—it's a computer."

"Take a look at the progress that has been made in computer technology in the last fifty years," Charlie said. "Your scientists are already talking about singularity—where a computer will match the capacity of the human brain. Where do you imagine computers will be in forty thousand years?"

Theo reached out and held on to the autopsy table to steady himself. "I don't think I can. I have trouble imagining what computers are going to be like in twenty years."

The implications were staggering. If the Zeta Greys reached singularity forty thousand years ago, Theo thought, and the neural network brains and the artificial programs were still advancing?

"Well," Charlie said. "That's where *they* are now."

Theo's mind was spinning, trying to grasp the consequences and scope of what he just learned. The Zeta

Greys were about as alien from humans as it got, despite the similarity of internal organs.

"So they're a lot smarter than we are," Theo said.

"That depends," Charlie replied. "Do you understand how to manipulate the subatomic electromagnetic fields to control gravity and the time-space continuum? Can you adjust the subatomic fields so you can pass through supposedly solid walls?"

"No," Theo replied. In our level of science, that's just not possible, he thought.

"Then they're a lot smarter than you are in that area. Earth humans are evolving. Eventually you will have the same level of technology the Zeta Greys have. The difference is the Zetas are *devolving*. They have become an interstellar parasite. Once they lose access to hosts, such as your population, they will eventually die out."

Theo understood "eventually" to mean something that wasn't of any practical use in the near future, which is what concerned him now.

"So why two brains?" Doc asked.

"It's simple," Charlie replied, turning back to Theo. "At its most elementary level of operation, what does a computer use?"

Theo thought for a moment. "Instructions and data."

"Precisely. The front brain contains the instructions and the processing capability . . ."

"And the back contains the data storage," Theo replied. "But if they are essentially a computer, how can they be telepathic?"

"It's a function of biological synapses and the electromagnetic fields it produces," Charlie said. "That's what an EEG records. A neural network is, by definition, capable of telepathic communication. Now you have a better idea of what you're up against."

Chapter 10

Martha Andrews sat with her husband, the President of the United States, in the private dining room in the residential section of the White House as the staff cleared away the breakfast dishes.

"Coffee service for three and that will be all," Andrews said. He waited until they were alone, which worried Martha.

"He's a nice young man. Being telepathic, he can be unnerving to be around, but I think it's important for you to meet him."

She shook her head slightly and looked up at the ceiling.

"I'm not sure I want him knowing my thoughts."

He nodded, clearly sharing her concern. "I know. For him it's as if everything we think we're saying out loud."

She turned, pulling away from him on the couch. "And my feelings?"

"He feels what you feel, just not as intensely."

She shook her head. "That's extremely personal."

"Very much so, I'm afraid. But you can get used to it, at least to a certain degree. I've had to. It's not as bad as you think."

Martha was uncertain at best. "So if I feel this is getting too personal, I can just get up and leave?"

Andrews shook his head. "I wish it were that simple. He's on his way up here with a Secret Service escort. He'll already know what we've been discussing when he arrives. He can hear our thoughts from a distance."

She glanced at the door. "From how far away?"

Andrews shrugged. "I don't know. My best guess is that he can tune in from anywhere on the planet."

A look of alarm appeared on her face. "That's really spooky."

Andrews nodded.

"Look, I'm not comfortable with this." She got up and started to leave.

He reached up and gently held her hand. "Please stay, I think you'll find it worthwhile."

"Is he going to know everything I've ever done or thought or, heaven forbid, felt?"

Andrews shook his head again. "He hears or senses only what you think and feel right now. Nothing else."

A gentle knock on the door interrupted their conversation.

Andrews said, "Enter."

She glanced at the door, sighed, and sat back down. A Secret Service agent opened the door and ushered Charlie in. Andrews stood, shook Charlie's hand, then said to the agent, "Thank you. That'll be all."

The agent nodded and left the room.

"Martha, this is Charlie."

Charlie smiled. "It's not that bad. With me, telepathy isn't an invasive process, and it's selective. I can tune into your thoughts when I need to and ignore them the rest of the time. Consider what being in a room filled with seven billion people all talking at the same time would be like. It would be so loud you wouldn't be able to think. It's more like the three of us, here, in the same room, confiding our thoughts and feelings with each other. It's personal and private, with everything kept in strict confidence."

"So you're proposing this is a privileged conversation, like between doctor and patient?" Martha asked, skeptical.

"Yes, precisely like that. Because the two of you talk things over and discuss what course of action you should take, I need to bring you up to date on what's happening."

Charlie poured himself a cup of coffee.

"I was going to . . ." Martha said as she reached forward.

"I know. It's fine," Charlie replied as he sat down in the chair.

"Many generations ago, in my father's world in the Tau Ceti star system, we were like you. We had our disagreements, our secrets, our deceivers, and our greed. We were a broken civilization, hopelessly divided against ourselves, just as you are now. The Zeta Greys arrived quietly, one or two at a time. They offered us power and advanced technology with the implied promise that we could defeat our enemies and rule the world. Our leaders found the offer irresistible."

He took a sip of coffee.

"They gave each group just enough technology to believe they could have it all—control of our entire planet, plus the ability to travel to the other planets in our star system, and eventually to the stars beyond. We fought among ourselves and struggled for power and control. In the end, when we thought we had won the battle and the world was under our control, the Zeta Greys simply replaced our world leaders with hybrids— beings they made by combining their DNA with ours, and took control. The advanced military we developed to conquer our enemies then became the enforcement arm of the Zeta Greys, coercing us into compliance—a state of slavery in a world we once thought we owned."

"But you're free now?" Martha asked. So far the exchange wasn't as scary and intrusive as she imagined.

"Yes. In our broken world of nine billion lost souls, one man rose against the Zeta Greys. He exposed their hidden agenda and the corruption that allowed them to secretly control us. He inspired our people to unite against a common enemy and to overcome our differences. He showed us that honestly caring for one another and standing united against the Zeta Greys was the only solution."

Martha's clenched stomach relaxed a bit. The idea that honestly caring about each other as a way of overcoming corruption piqued her curiosity.

"Together," Charlie continued, "our people broke down the walls of corruption, secrecy, and greed. We exposed all those who cooperated with the Zetas and all of the hidden agendas that contributed to our downfall. We lost billions of people in the struggle, due to the inequity in technology. The final blow to the Zeta Greys came when we forced ourselves to become an open and completely honest society. When there were no more secrets and no more lies, there were no places left for the Greys to hide and work their deceit and corruption. Through openness and brutal honesty with each other, we gradually became telepathic and eventually joined the other human races in the interstellar community."

Your whole population became telepathic? Martha thought. How could that happen?

Charlie smiled and looked at her, a gentle expression on his face. "If I may?"

He waited until she nodded.

"In your world, children learn various languages, first by being exposed to the sounds, imitating those sounds, then eventually connecting the sounds to words, ideas, and concepts. They learn language slowly, word by word. In a telepathic society, babies learn the same way, based on thoughts rather than spoken words."

But how? Martha wondered.

"Telepathy is a natural ability," Charlie said. "What you may not realize is that your babies are born with both telepathic and verbal capabilities, but because your main system of communication is verbal, and older children and adults have not used their natural telepathic ability, the new child is forced into a verbal language out of a necessity to communicate. Telepathy has to be practiced and perfected, just as a spoken language does."

We're born telepathic? Martha thought.

Charlie nodded. "Every single person is born telepathic. Because that skill is not recognized or used, it never develops, with rare exceptions, of course."

Martha's mind was beginning to spin. "There are people in our world who are telepathic?" she asked aloud.

Charlie finished his coffee and set the cup down on the tray. "To one degree or another, yes. They hide their ability because using it is considered taboo in your society."

How could that be? she wondered. How could we not know?

Charlie gazed at her calmly, patient understanding radiating from his face.

"You said your world used to be like ours," Martha said. "What is it like now?"

"If you will allow me to share my father's world with

you telepathically, you can experience it for yourselves, just as I did when I was there last year."

Martha and Andrews looked at each other, then at Charlie, and both of them nodded.

Chapter 11

"Close your eyes," Charlie said.

Martha found herself standing next to her husband in a strange but beautiful city. The air was clean and fresh, pinkish-white clouds drifted slowly against a turquoise sky. Glowing eclair-shaped craft of different sizes slipped silently through the air between gigantic sculpted structures. They docked periodically against the side of what had to be buildings of some kind to let people on and off.

Martha reflexively put her hand on her chest. This view of the city was breathtaking to her. She turned slowly, taking in the grandeur all around her.

The buildings were large, exotic, sculpted works of art, shimmering in the bright daylight. Where buildings on Earth were mostly shades of gray and black, these were all of the colors of the rainbow. Some were a little on the intense side, especially the rich greens and deep blues, but most were pleasing pastels.

A glowing silver craft set down in front of them and a door opened. They stepped in and the craft moved quickly into the air and through the city. While the tallest building on Earth was just over twenty-seven hundred feet tall, these structures reached more than a mile into the sky.

The portrait of a man looked back at them from the forward wall of the craft. He had light brown hair, tan skin, and light blue eyes. Martha felt drawn to the image. She walked over and touched the face on the wall. His charisma clearly portrayed that he was a natural leader. But who was he?

He's the man who set us free, Charlie's voice came into her mind. *Drufallo.*

That's his name? Martha thought.

Yes. Now, the name means Great Soul. You'll find his portrait everywhere. His image symbolizes the ultimate service to others. We all aspire to be like him.

The craft docked at a tall, spiral-shaped, golden glass tower. They got off and walked through the open space. Martha paused and stepped back, surprised at the appearance of the people. They were much taller than she and her husband were, with men ranging up to nine feet tall. The women were closer to seven feet in height. Their hair was light to medium brown with gray tones present in most of them. She looked at Charlie and quickly recognized the genetic connection: his tan skin and light brown hair color. His eyes, too, were light blue, just like the Tau Cetians.

She opened her mouth to speak, but her mind was still locked on the people. They wore elaborately embroidered tunics in rich colors, textures and styles. Four distinct races were apparent: some had an almost copper colored skin; some a light green tone; some, tan like Charlie; and others with a red colored skin, much like the southwestern Native Americans on Earth. She turned to Charlie.

He smiled. *Yours is not the only racially mixed planet. We overcame our differences a long time ago. Your planet can, too.*

Mounted on the wall of the first intersection they came to was the same portrait she had seen in the transport craft.

There are so many shops, Martha thought. *How do people afford things like this?*

There is no money, Charlie's voice came into her mind. *People create these things because they love doing it.*

But what about food, clothes, homes, water, and utilities? Martha thought. *Who pays for those?*

It's a simple barter system, came Charlie's voice into her mind again. *All people are provided with everything they need: a home, food, health care, transportation, entertainment, and an opportunity to be of service to others.*

The image of large apartment complexes came into her mind. They were tall and spacious, providing, for each unit, a view of the city around them.

This is where some people live. Each apartment complex has its own food and basic needs provided on the ground floor. People can pick out what they like. They do their own cooking and cleaning.

Does everyone live like this?

No, Charlie's thoughts returned. *If you want more, you become entitled to more to the exact extent you are of service to others.*

Where do they work? Martha wanted to know.

All over. Work is voluntary.

So how do you get people to work if it's voluntary? Martha wondered.

We actually have the opposite problem, Charlie's thoughts came to her again. *People do what they love. Farmers love to grow food, chefs love to cook, doctors love to heal, pilots love to fly, athletes love to compete, and some people simply love to help others. We have trouble getting them to take time off.*

And those who serve others?

People who dedicate their lives to being of service to others live in much more luxurious accommodations. Professional cooks and housecleaning services are provided for them.

Martha wandered into the store in front of her. Beautiful bowls, utensils and other objects were fashioned out of different colored crystal materials, each one exquisite in workmanship and design.

But stores like this? Can anyone just walk in and get what they want?

No. In a telepathic society everyone knows the rules. Everyone knows what they're entitled to receive. There's a computer system that recognizes people and identifies them by entitlement. The entire transportation system is connected to the computer database. The transportation system won't take you to a place where you aren't entitled to receive what they have, so there's rarely a conflict.

* * *

This can't be right, Andrews thought. *Where are the poor, the sick? Where are the police and the criminals? Where are the soldiers to keep the peace?*

No one is poor. No one is sick. People are occasionally injured, and doctors work hard to heal them, Charlie's thoughts answered.

What about substance abuse? Andrews wondered. *Drugs, alcohol?*

We don't allow those things on the planet.

A virtuous society? I'm not buying it, Andrews thought. *We have an elaborate planetary shield system in place.*

The image of multiple spheres of protection and a type of customs enforcement appeared in Andrews's mind. No one could approach the planet without being stopped and inspected. *This is where the police and military operate,* Andrews thought. *Off planet—out of sight, out of mind—clever.*

What about criminals? Andrews thought. *What about power hungry maniacs and dictators? Where are they? I know people. Not everyone wants to help. Some people only want to hurt others and take what they have. You can't tell me you don't have any people like that.*

We do, Charlie's thoughts came to him. *We have two societies. Our home world—what you see as a virtuous society—is peaceful and law-abiding. This is our manufacturing and technology base. Our peaceful society is the foundation of our space-based military.*

The scene changed in Andrews's mind. They were standing in a military academy with young people dressed in uniforms, laughing and smiling as they walked down the hall.

What is this? Andrews wondered.

The military colony on a moon in our solar system, Charlie's thoughts replied.

But how do you know? How do you determine who goes here?

The images dissolved. Andrews and Martha opened their eyes.

"You have to understand," Charlie said. "In a telepathic society there are no secrets. Everyone knows. By the time a child is three to four years old, the basic personality has emerged. By the time the child is eight, everything is clearly defined. The psychopaths, the sociopaths, the criminally inclined are all identified. Everyone knows this child's future is in the military. The parents have had several years to adapt to who the child really is, and where he is going and who he really is. Everyone accepts that. The child is removed from the family and sent to the military colony.

"Those children grow up in the military. They live their lives defending our world in space against the Greys, the reptilians, and other violent species. Even though their motivation is service to self, we place them in a situation where they are serving others by protecting our home world. They love the power and the challenge, the violence and the risk. They live for the battle and the glory or the intrigue on other worlds.

"In your world, the psychopaths and the sociopaths seek power, control, and influence. They do everything they can to get that power and control at the expense of other people. This is why you have the poor and the sick. People driven by greed deprive others of resources by taking more and more for themselves. They don't care about other people. That lack of caring about others creates the poor and leaves people sick and suffering. This is why you have crimes, wars, and violent conflicts amongst yourselves. It's also why the Zeta Greys are here. Your world is already divided, waiting to be conquered."

It was a disturbing vision, Andrews thought. Haven't the poor and the sick always been with us? Or have we also had the greedy and power-hungry creating those conditions from the very beginning? "What stops the military from invading your world and taking whatever they want?" Andrews asked.

"The planetary shield is closely controlled by civilians from the surface of the planet," Charlie explained. "The military has no access to the shield or to the planet."

"I take it only the most dedicated and loyal military are stationed close to the planet?"

Charlie nodded. "It's a simple but practical system."

The simpler it is, the better it works, Andrews thought. Charlie smiled at him.

"How many?" Andrews asked.

Charlie looked him in the eyes. "Five and a half percent of our population goes into the military: One out of every ten men, one out of every hundred women."

Andrews breathed out and looked at the floor. "And here?"

"That percentage and the ratio of men to women is surprisingly consistent among human races—yours included."

Andrews shook his head. With a world population of over seven billion people . . .

Three hundred and eighty-five million people would go into a space-based military, Charlie's voice answered in his mind. *If you're going to patrol and effectively defend your solar system, you're going to need that many people.*

He looked over at Charlie. "And on your home planet?" Andrews asked.

"We don't allow psychopaths, sociopaths, and criminals to have access to our peaceful, law abiding population. We keep them forever separate."

* * *

"But don't the parents miss their children?" Martha asked. "Don't they worry about what is happening to them?"

Charlie nodded. "Yes, of course they do. What if you had a child who didn't care if he hurt others and he went into the military where he could do what he really wanted to do to others while defending your world? Would you want him at home, hurting innocent people?"

The question stunned her. She sat, mouth open a bit, unable to form a response in her mind.

"Or if you had a child who was caring, loving, gentle,

and kind. Then he ended up going into the military, fought in a war, and came back physically damaged, emotionally broken, and unable to cope in society, unable to have a meaningful relationship? Which would you choose if it were your child?"

Martha's shoulders slumped. Her mind was frozen on the question of what she would really want for her own child.

"We try to do what's best for each individual," Charlie said. "We don't send the gentle souls into war, and we don't let the violent souls loose in our peaceful society."

"Like tough love?" Martha asked.

She looked into his face, looking for hope.

"It's tough to do, I agree, but it's actually reasoned, caring, and compassionate."

Reason, caring, and compassion, she thought. Three words that rarely make it into the same sentence.

"That's the kind of choice we're going to have to make in the future, isn't it?" Andrews asked.

Charlie nodded. "Sooner rather than later."

She had trouble thinking of sending a child of hers away to a military academy at age eight as caring and compassionate. It seemed much more like abandonment to her. The whole concept troubled her, but conditions here on Earth weren't like that now. Maybe they never had to be.

"And you're here because . . . ?" Martha asked.

"You need to know that you're not alone—that the Zeta Greys have done the same thing to hundreds, if not thousands of other worlds—that you have help from other human races, and that you can defeat the Zeta Greys. You will have to expose and destroy all of the corruption, lies, and secrets in order to succeed. Keep in mind that it is deceit, corruption, and secrecy that allowed the Greys to be here in the first place. It's a hard and brutal process, but it's the only thing that will work. This method worked for us and we are here to help insure it will work for you."

Andrews turned to Martha. She suspected he knew what her next question was going to be.

"What happened to Drufallo, the one who first stood up against the Zeta Greys in your world?" Martha asked.

Charlie glanced at the floor, then back to her. "He was killed before he could witness the success of our battle for freedom. But his life and his ideas inspired others who fought on in his place. Because of him, and his vision for our world, we are free today."

Martha turned and looked at her husband, worried fear filled her chest. "And my husband's place in all of this?"

"He is the first world leader to stand against the Zeta Greys and try to unify your world. We hope his vision and courage will lead others in your world to fight for their own freedom."

She moved to face Charlie. "And if he fails?"

Charlie looked directly into her eyes.

"If he doesn't commit everything to this fight, then there is no hope."

Chapter 12

Elegant simplicity, Rosaq thought. Earth humans loved secrecy and couldn't resist being in on something denied to others. For many humans, secrecy was the equivalent of high social standing, self-worth, and personal importance all rolled into one. Secrecy and compartmentalization became so ingrained in human political and military control systems that it was the obvious choice as a manipulation vehicle.

Human secrecy systems were still elementary in their structure, with three primary levels of access, becoming more restrictive with each progressive level. The lowest level was confidential, followed by secret, then top secret. Not satisfied with those, humans devised a higher level known as special access programs, or SAPs, which were often numbered. Some SAPs were so secret that they were not only officially denied, but were never even acknowledged to exist. That's where Rosaq implemented his plan to subdue the humans.

Through abductees, Rosaq was able to get wireless access to every major computer network on the planet. He became an invisible administrator in every system, creating hundreds of unacknowledged special access programs (USAP) piggybacked onto the existing networks. No trace remained on the servers, as he spliced his communications into current data streams. His messages were unrecognized by all, except his human targets for covert activities. Each human contacted through this USAP network thought he was a part of a government sponsored activity, which was simply unacknowledged. His targets were humans filled with greed, avarice, and loathing for the ordinary person. Some of them he had met, but most he hadn't. It didn't matter. They were what humans called pawns, objects with little intrinsic value, but willing and able to accomplish his designs for the future of humanity.

For the last nine years Rosaq recruited and directed his secret army of humans to create even more division and mistrust in the population. Now it was time to take the next logical step and increase the violence and mistrust on the planet, bringing it one step closer to total collapse. Regional wars and terrorism must be gradually escalated into a global conflict, and he knew exactly whom he could use to accomplish that task.

* * *

Conrad Kaplan met with Harlan Mohr, head scientist for research and development of Valkyrie Research Industries, Limited.

"What did you get from Rosaq?" Kaplan asked.

Mohr grinned. "A potential solution to our speed and

distance problem in the anti-ballistic missile program. An intercontinental ballistic missile is most vulnerable during its boost phase, meaning from the moment it is launched until it is in the upper atmosphere. That's about a five-minute window. We have the interceptor missile that can hit an ICBM within that timeframe, but we currently need to be within a hundred and fifty miles of the launch site."

Kaplan understood the problem. "For a country as large as Russia, that's just not possible."

"Exactly. However, by combining our conventional design with Rosaq's alien technology, we can achieve much higher speeds and a greatly extended range. The new hybrid design should allow us to hit an ICBM within two minutes of its launch at a range of a thousand miles, maybe more."

Kaplan tried to run some quick calculations through his mind. "So what does that mean in plain English?"

"It means that the anti-ballistic missile system we have in place around Russia and China will have the speed and range to become a hundred percent effective against land-based ICBM launches. In its original concept, the ABM program focused on hitting an incoming nuclear warhead falling from sub-orbital space. That was the equivalent of hitting a bullet with another bullet, both fired at each other. With the new system we can take out the ICBMs right after launch, while it's a large, slow-moving target and still within the atmosphere."

Yes, Kaplan thought. This was what he had wanted all along. "How long before we can run a test?"

Mohr ran his hand over his mouth, apparently estimating what remained to be done. "Three to four months. We'll run the first test without a moving target, just to finalize the proof-of-concept."

"We've had problems with technology we received from him before," Kaplan said. This was the problem with Rosaq: He made it seem so simple in the beginning, but the project kept running into one problem after another. Progress that should have taken a month or two was taking years to accomplish. "How confident are you of obtaining reliable results?"

"Fairly confident at this point. In the past we've been working with technology way beyond our level of experience and understanding. I blame our lack of understanding as much as Rosaq's vagueness on details. Basically, we didn't know what questions to ask, so we didn't have enough answers or knowledge. Once we learned enough to pin him down, we finally got the answers we needed."

"I don't know," Kaplan said. "I still don't trust him. He's just plain creepy."

"He's commander of the Zeta Greys. That's what his name, Rosaq, means: commander."

Kaplan shook his head. "I still don't trust him. He's too manipulative and deceptive."

Mohr stepped back a little and grinned. "So he's too much like you?"

Kaplan had to chuckle. "You know what I mean—I hate competition."

Chapter 13

Diane Zadanski woke at 6:00 a.m. as usual, showered, and dressed in her new uniform. They did their homework, she thought. The uniform fit perfectly. She wondered when she'd get a flight suit. Flight suits were typically custom-made to a person's exact dimensions. A weight gain of only two pounds could alter how her suit fit. A five pound gain and she couldn't get into it at all.

She walked briskly down the hall to the cafeteria, weaving between moving construction vehicles. Eight men and one woman sat eating at the long table in the center of the large room.

"Hey," a dark-haired man said, nodding in her direction. "Newbie."

They all turned to look at her.

"Let me guess," a tall African-American man with a shaved head said, looking her over. "No brothers or sisters?"

Why would he ask that? she wondered. "None."

He nodded once. "Parents both dead?"

She flushed with the personal nature of the question. "My dad died before I had any memory of him. I lost my brother nine years ago. Mom passed last week. Why?"

The group glanced at each other.

"Sorry about your mom," the dark-haired man said. "I'm Clay Obers, used to be a captain in the Army Air Corp. I've been here the longest—six months."

"Matt Douglas," another man said, standing to shake her hand.

"Glen Simmons," the African-American man said. "Welcome to the orphan squad."

"The what?" This was the strangest group of pilots she had ever encountered.

"The orphan squadron," the woman said. "I'm Captain Helen Catalano, Air Force. Every one of us is an orphan: no family or close relatives."

Diane frowned. "Why would that matter?"

"We're expendable," Clay said. "No notification requirements. They don't have to even acknowledge we existed, let alone died."

Diane was stunned. She had never looked at it that way before.

"Oh, don't listen to him," Helen said. "He's got this morbid thing going."

"It's pointless to deny reality," Clay said. "We're cannon fodder—expendable people in a hopeless cause."

Helen stood and faced Clay. "It's not hopeless, but your attitude certainly is. I can't understand how they let you into this program in the first place. This is a squadron of winners. How a loser like you got in is beyond me."

Clay stood and moved closer to Helen. "You're still too naive and gullible to see the writing on the wall. We're all going to die. We can't win against the saucers and you know it."

Diane was horrified at the confrontation taking place.

"We can and we will. Just not with cowards like you." Helen shoved Clay back. "Why don't you pack your bags and go back home where you belong!"

Clay stepped nose to nose with Helen. Anger flooded into his face. His hands closed into fists.

"Hey!" Diane shouted. "Are we professionals?" Clay and Helen looked at her. "Because if we are—there's no room for squabbling and disrespect. Admiral Hollis didn't pick us because we're expendable, but because we're the best hope he has for winning." She felt the presence of someone behind her. She spun around, only to come face-to-face with Hollis.

Diane was stunned that no one announced the admiral's presence, or stood at attention. She stood stiff and tall. "Sir."

"Not necessary," Hollis replied as he walked past her. "I understand Captain Obers feeling discouraged about our lack of progress. I feel discouraged, too. It doesn't change the fact that we have a job to do. If you weren't the very best in our military system, you wouldn't be here. So let's focus on that and find a way to shoot down those saucers. Can we agree on that?"

"Yes, sir," they all responded.

Hollis headed over to the breakfast buffet line.

"You two have to put an end to this conflict with each other," Simmons said. "It's bad karma for the entire group. Fighting with the enemy is what we do—it doesn't define who we are. We're not fighters for the sake of fighting—we're warriors in the cause of freedom. In order to succeed, we have to be at complete peace within ourselves and with each other."

Diane approached the nine people at the table.

"He's right," Diane said. "Out there in the sky, our lives depend on unwavering trust in each other. Anger and resentment erode that trust and put all our lives at risk. This has to end, now."

Clay looked embarrassed, but he held his hand out to Helen.

"Clean start?" Clay asked. "Forgive and forget?"

Helen seemed hesitant at first. She glanced at Diane, then nodded. "Clean start," Helen said as she shook his hand. "Forgiven and forgotten."

As some of them began to sit back down, Diane turned to Simmons. "That's quite the insight."

He smiled and shrugged. "It's a Zen thing. Most people wouldn't understand."

Zen, she thought, in a secret space program. Go figure. "Well, I don't necessarily understand," she said, "but I like it."

Clay turned to Diane. "Hollis run you through the simulator last night?"

"Yes." How could she not admit that? The scout saucer, her brother's abduction, finally realizing he was gone. It wasn't her finest moment.

"How much thrust when you crashed?"

This certainly was a strange group. First the orphan squad thing, now the simulator crash. "How do you—?"

"Everybody crashes their first night," Helen said. "You are?"

Everyone crashes? Diane thought. Hollis must push all of the new pilots until they crash, she realized. That would give him a realistic understanding of their skill level. Clever.

"Lieutenant Diane Zadanski, U.S. Navy—well, was."

Clay shifted his weight from one leg to the other, apparently anxious about something. "So how much thrust?" he asked again.

"Only twenty percent," she said, half embarrassed by

the low number.

"Whoa," Glen said. "How many times through the simulator?"

She thought back to last night in the simulator room. "Three." I wouldn't necessarily count the first one, I froze, she thought, but I guess it still counts.

"Ooooh," a sandy-haired man replied. "We got a hot new jockey on board. Watch your back, Obers, she's goin' to take you down."

Clay looked shocked. "No way."

"Way," the sandy-haired man said. He stood and walked over to Diane. "I'm Ryan Atkinson, radar intercept operator." He held out his hand and shook hers. "I'd like to be your scope."

Admiral Hollis brought his breakfast tray over to the table. "I see you've met."

"Sir, I'd like to be her RIO," Ryan said, brimming with enthusiasm.

Hollis looked around at the others. "Objections?" No one said anything. "Zadanski?"

She looked around the room. Apparently he wasn't assigned to anyone yet. "Okay by me."

"All right. That gives us five operational craft teams."

Ryan led Diane over to the buffet line.

"Is he always this casual?" she asked Ryan quietly.

"Pretty much. Get your breakfast and we'll talk."

She picked a tray from the stack on the right and slid it down the rails in front of the glass with steaming hot food behind it. She selected the scrambled eggs, some corned beef hash, skipped the toast and pancakes—too many carbs—and added a cup of coffee. She sat at the long table across from Ryan.

"So talk," she said.

"Born and raised in Des Moines, Iowa. Marine Corp

Officer Candidate School out of college, equipment and electronic countermeasure officer on an EA-6B Prowler out of Cherry Point, North Carolina. You?"

That was short and to the point, she thought. He must like getting to the bottom line quickly. I like that in a guy.

"Minneapolis–St. Paul, then Annapolis. Flew an F/A-18 Super Hornet off the *Ronald Reagan*."

He seemed to be paying close attention. She liked that, too.

"You go to Top Gun?"

This guy knew how the system worked. Another plus.

"Top of my class," she replied with a slight grin.

"I knew it," Ryan said with a quick smile as he slapped the tabletop. "I can pick 'em." He sat back and sipped his coffee as she ate.

This can work, she thought. I have a good feeling about him.

Chapter 14

"We have a special guest," Hollis said as he ushered the flight teams into the conference room. "Please be seated."

The conference room was large for being underground, Diane thought. Ten feet from floor to ceiling, she estimated. The band of dark corkboard mounted to the walls around the room was a good workable height. Someone put some thought into its design.

Diane was intrigued by the tall, slender man with the unruly brown hair who stood at the front of the room. He wore gray dress slacks and a light blue dress shirt. The lack of a suit or uniform indicated to her that he wasn't part of the military or the government bureaucracy. His intelligence seemed to sparkle from his eyes and added to his charisma, which radiated into the room.

"This is Dr. Theodore Shugart," Hollis said. "He is the director of Ceti Research, the company that is building your fighter craft. Dr. Shugart has two PhDs, one in theoretical physics, the other in advanced material sciences. He is here to tell you about your new fighter craft."

Dr. Shugart stepped forward. "Please just call me Theo. I hate pretentious titles. I have the first operational manuals for your fighter craft, the X-1000. We are currently making changes to the simulators in order to conform to the actual craft performance. Top speed in the lower atmosphere will be slower than anticipated, but my understanding is that none of you is there yet anyway.

"The repeat firing of the weapons will also be slower. In the simulator you had one particle beam cannon with an unlimited firing rate. The actual craft has two particle beam cannons, but they require a one-second recovery and recharge time. Consequently, you will now have two choices— alternating guns at a half-second separation, or both guns at a one-second firing interval. A new switch is being added to your control sticks for selection."

Diane raised her hand slightly. "Theo, you said lower atmosphere speed would be slower. What's our ceiling?" Calling him Theo felt personal, but it also lacked any formal recognition of his position. He smiled back at her.

"The X-1000 is the first fighter craft with both atmospheric and outer space capabilities."

Outer space, she reminded herself. The U. S. Space Command. It was starting to sink in. Where astronauts went in space capsules, they were going in fighter craft. This was going to be the most advanced and dangerous unit in the military system. She felt surprisingly at home with the idea.

"What about fuel consumption?" she asked.

"Fuel is an Element 115-based antigravity drive, which will have to be replaced every five years under full time use.

Originally the fighter craft used the main drive to power both the propulsion and the weapon system. After initial test flights, we determined that a second, smaller fusion reactor needed to be added exclusively for the weapons. That is why you are still working with simulators and not your actual craft."

"When will the new craft be ready for us to fly?" Helen asked.

Theo nodded and smiled. "Soon, I hope. Still a few more problems to resolve."

"We can help find and resolve those problems if we can fly them," Diane said. She found him strangely attractive.

Theo turned to face Hollis.

"You don't understand," Hollis said. "Your combat training and experience is more valuable to us. We have already lost seven test pilots in the development process. Keep in mind, when you crash in the simulator, they crashed in real life."

"I'm afraid he's right," Theo said. "When you get to fly your craft for the first time, you'll see what I mean. It's a very different experience from flying an aircraft. Our test pilots have paid a very heavy price to bring you the performance levels you will need in combat."

Hollis said, "Their skill and their lives have gone into the programming for your simulators. When you can fly your craft, engage, and destroy the enemy without crashing, their sacrifice will begin to have meaning. Until then, they will have died for nothing."

Hollis handed out the manuals. "Take the rest of the day to go through the technical information about your fighter craft. The programming revisions and the physical upgrades to the simulators will not be ready until sometime tomorrow."

As Diane and Ryan walked out of the conference room, she nudged him and whispered, "Is that some kind of a guilt trip? That their deaths don't mean anything yet?"

Ryan shook his head. "Hollis isn't like that. Nobody knows if we're going to be able to kill a scout saucer yet. Do you happen to know what the average life expectancy of an Abrams M1A1 main battle tank is in full combat?"

"No." What has that got to do with us? she wondered.

"Four minutes. Do you want to know what our life expectancy is in full combat?"

She stopped, turned, and looked him in the eyes, her heart beating faster.

"Currently two seconds," he said. "That's where Hollis is coming from. It's not guilt—it's reality."

Chapter 15

President Andrews stared at the notice on his desk. The Office of Personnel Management was officially admitting they had been hacked, with something in the range of twenty to twenty-five million records being stolen. Of particular concern were the records of investigations required for security clearances for both governmental employees and civilians involved in classified military projects. Conspicuous by their absence were similar reports from other agencies Andrews knew had also been hacked. He drummed his fingers on his desk, considering the massive changes that had to be made.

He stood, walked down the hall, and leaned into Chief of Staff Doug Franks's office.

"Anything from Charlie?"

Franks looked up from the pile of files on his desk.

"Yes. I was almost on my way to see you."

Andrews stepped into the office and closed the door.

"Charlie's group of Tau Cetians in China were successful in penetrating several of our government databases. It will look like an international hacking incident. He says that from the information collected he can provide us with a list of people in the government, military, and civilian sector who are corrupted and cooperating with the Zeta Greys. That way we know who we can, and more importantly, who we can't trust."

"How can they tell?" Andrews asked. "I mean, we have all of that information anyway, right? What can they see that we can't?"

Franks nodded. "Charlie collected extensive data files on over eight million people, and that's only here, in the U.S. He's doing the same thing in Russia and China. While we would love to have all that data, it would take us months if not years to process it and sort out what was important from what wasn't. Plus, things we would normally take for granted and consider unimportant, his people will flag right away. Keep in mind they're looking at this with hindsight, so they know what the information means. The Tau Cetians successfully revolted and threw off the Zeta Grey influence and control. If we try to do that without knowing whom we can trust, the whole process is doomed from the start. It won't work."

Andrews put his hands on the back of the chair in Franks's office and thought, I wish this were more of a solution and less of a beginning. "So what, exactly, is this going to give us?"

"At least we'll know who's on our side and who isn't. It doesn't give us evidence we can use in court. The information was acquired illegally, so even though we find out who's betraying us, we still can't charge them and drag them into court. No probable cause, no subpoenas, no warrants. We can't do it."

Andrews frowned and looked at the portrait of himself on the wall behind Franks's desk. "Okay," Andrews said. "We can't use the legal court system without more evidence, but there's another court we can use: the court of public opinion."

Franks shook his head, and said, "We can't be tied in any way to leaking this information. That would derail any chance you have of a second term in office."

He looked at the portrait again, deep in thought about how they could get this information into the public media.

"Charlie could leak the information. That way we aren't involved. The fact that we also have the files is moot: They were ours to begin with."

Franks shook his head again. "It's not the files; it's the analysis and identification of suspected individuals that's damaging. That analysis didn't go through official channels."

Andrews stared out the window, thinking. "We could use a reporter we trust."

Franks was being obstinate about the issue, but he was right.

"I hate to disagree, but we can't. If this comes through a reporter who's perceived as being on the inside, we take the fall."

Andrews looked directly at Franks. "Guilt by association."

Franks nodded. "Exactly. This has to come through someone who's perceived as being against us: an outsider, but a reporter with a solid ethical reputation. Otherwise it's not going to be believable."

Andrews patted the top of the chair and walked a couple of steps to the side, deep in thought. "Anyone in mind?"

"I'll talk with Stephanie. She may have some ideas."

Chapter 16

"How's the Zeta Grey doing?" Charlie asked.

Nurse Donatello smiled at Charlie. He smiled back at her, hearing the private thoughts and sensing the feelings she had for him.

"Doc says there's some improvement, but it still can't move on its own."

She couldn't take her eyes off him.

"Can you log me in? I need to check on it." He gave her an appreciative smile.

"Sure," she said as she typed away at the keyboard. "Doc gave you full access."

"Thanks." It felt good to have that kind of an effect on a woman.

"Don't you need a helmet?" she asked. "Doc always

wears one."

Of course he does, Charlie thought. He needs to. I don't. "I think it'll be fine. It's brain damaged."

He entered the outer section of the containment chamber, which isolated the creature from outside telepathic communications. He sensed the scattered functioning of the creature's brain.

Yeah, you can't process properly, can you?

Charlie put on the bio suit and entered the inner chamber. He stood over the Zeta Grey and probed its thoughts with his mind.

He smiled at the Zeta's inability to focus its thoughts. That made the job much easier. He leaned directly over the Zeta's head and stared into its eyes. He followed the optic nerve to the damaged processing center, through the connection to the data storage area, and examined the memories contained within.

That's disturbing, he thought.

He telepathically extracted the information he needed, stood up, and walked out of the inner chamber. He removed the bio suit, placed it in the decontamination bin, and left.

He knocked on the door jamb to Theo's office.

"Got a minute?"

Theo waved him in. "I have the latest and greatest version of the telepathic blocking helmet," he said as he put it on.

Charlie sighed. "Color." Charlie grabbed a sheet of paper from Theo's desk and wrote blue on it.

"Red, definitely red," Theo said.

"Number." Charlie wrote eighteen on the sheet and projected the number into Theo's mind.

"Seventy-two," Theo said, as he took the helmet off.

Charlie handed him the sheet.

Theo grinned. "It's working."

Charlie held out his hand. "May I?"

Theo handed the helmet to him.

The second he put the helmet on silence surrounded him for the first time in his life. From the time he was an infant he could hear the thoughts and sense the feelings of every creature around him: people, dogs, cats, birds. Everything had visual images he could see, thoughts he could hear, and feelings he could sense. Now, all of that was absent. He panicked. He yanked the helmet off and stared at Theo.

"This is what your experience is? Isolation? Separation? Loneliness?"

Theo nodded slowly. "You never knew, did you?"

"Well, theoretically, yeah. But this?"

Charlie always felt compassion for other people. This was the first time an Earth human had expressed compassion and empathy for him. He was shocked.

Charlie looked at the helmet. This changed everything he thought he understood about Earth humans. Now he knew what they actually experienced. It was devastating and depressing. He felt as if every last vestige of hope had been sucked out of him.

"One last test." He put the helmet back on.

"Color." He projected purple into Theo's mind. "Number." He projected fifty-five.

Theo nodded. "Yellow and forty-nine."

"It works both ways: Just as it should. Now your people stand a fighting chance against the Zetas."

Charlie kept the helmet on for a few more minutes. He felt lost, drifting, disconnected, and alone. How do people stand this? he wondered. Not knowing, not connected. There aren't even words to describe exactly how isolated he felt. He pulled off the helmet.

"You don't feel any different when you wear it?"

Theo shook his head. "No different."

Charlie looked down at the helmet in his hands. "I'm so sorry. I didn't understand."

He handed the helmet back to Theo.

"So, what do you have for me?" Theo said, as he motioned for Charlie to sit.

Charlie sat in the chair, still feeling disoriented from his experience with the helmet.

"I've had a chance to do a mind probe of the Zeta Grey in containment. It's damaged to the extent where it can't recover, but I did find some interesting things. We're in a lot more trouble that we thought."

Chapter 17

At breakfast the next morning, Hollis stood at the head of the long table.

"The simulators won't be ready until this evening so I've arranged a field trip for you today. I think getting more personally involved in our situation will help us toward a solution. Please dress in civilian clothes. We'll meet topside at 0800 hours."

"What's going on?" Diane whispered to Ryan.

Ryan shrugged. "No idea. First time out of Peregrine Base."

Just before eight in the morning, Jed Collier began escorting small groups up the elevator and out in front of the mine. Three black SUVs with government plates and drivers were waiting for them. Diane, Ryan, and Glen Simmons climbed into the back of the first vehicle. After the other cars were loaded, Hollis slid into the front seat.

During the six hours in the car, Diane's mind repeatedly drifted to Theo. She wanted to see him again, this time in a less formal or public setting. She was intrigued by him. He was just so different from anyone she had ever known. He was obviously smart, yet disarmingly humble at the same time.

They arrived at a small home on the north side of Pagosa Springs, Colorado. The building was a white stucco bungalow with a brown roof, surrounded by a chain-link fence. A sign was attached to the fence on the right of the gate:

NO VISITORS
NO SOLICITORS
NO REPORTERS
NO EXCEPTIONS

Diane frowned as she read the sign. She turned to Ryan. He shrugged.

"You know, in broad strokes, what we're doing," Hollis said to the flight team. "You're going to meet a few people who can fill you in on why we're starting a war and going after the saucers. Listen to what these people have to say. You may ask any questions of them, but just don't mention anything about what we are doing, or who we actually are."

"Understood, sir," they all replied.

"Just for your information, they know me as Inspector Howard, of Homeland Security."

Hollis led them to the front door and rang the bell. A man answered the door. He was a little shorter than Diane, prematurely bald with a scraggly mustache.

"Inspector Howard, come in, please."

Hollis hesitated before entering the home.

"Mark, I have some people from the Department of

Homeland Security who would like to hear Jamie's story, if she's up to it today."

Mark glanced toward the back of the house.

"She said she is. If it gets too much for her . . ."

Hollis nodded. "Of course. We can leave at any time. Thank you for doing this."

Mark led them into the family room at the back of the home. Jamie sat in a comfortable chair set back against the bay window. She was thin with dark blond hair and green eyes. The lightweight curtains were closed. Diane and Ryan sat on the couch next to Hollis. The rest of them sat in chairs placed in a wide circle.

"Jamie, these are the people I told you about," Hollis said. "I've asked them to listen to your experience and be respectful of your privacy, but they may have some questions. Do you feel up to that?"

Jamie scrutinized the people in the room. "Maybe. I'll have to see."

"We can stop at any time. You just let us know what you need, okay?"

Jamie moved uncomfortably in her chair. "It all started nine and a half years ago. Mark and I were visiting Mesa Verde National Park to see the cliff dwellings. We left when the park closed, at sunset. We were driving east on U.S. 160. It was dark—hardly any traffic."

She pulled a tissue from a box on the table next to her.

"A bright white glowing thing swooped over the road in front of us. The car stalled. We were blinded by an intense beam of light."

Diane swallowed hard, her heart racing. This is what happened to Daniel, she thought.

"The next thing I knew, the thing was gone and two hours had passed. I felt really strange, but didn't know why. We drove on to Durango and spent the night in a motel."

Jamie breathed deeply, broke eye contact, and wiped the tissue under her nose.

"I began having nightmares of monsters—things with gigantic gray heads and horrible long fingers. They had these huge black eyes and a tiny mouth. They did excruciatingly painful things to me. I screamed, but I couldn't hear any sound at all. I thought they were just dreams, you know? But they wouldn't go away."

Mark nodded. "We were confused," he said. "We were both having these strange nightmares. It took us almost two weeks to realize we were having the same dreams—well, almost the same. Jamie's nightmares were worse than mine."

Jamie watched Mark as he spoke, then turned her attention to the group.

"That's right," Jamie said. "The following month I found out I was pregnant. It turned out to be twins. I was so happy. I thought the dreams would eventually go away." She wiped the corner of her eye with the tissue. "They got worse instead. I didn't know what to do. I tried talking with my doctor. He prescribed a mild sedative. It didn't help. I stopped taking it to protect my babies."

Diane's heart was pounding, her hand trembling. She could sense where the conversation was headed and didn't really want to go there. As much as she wanted to get up and leave, she forced herself to sit and listen.

"At five months, I had an ultrasound. Twin girls. Everything was normal. Then I woke up in the middle of the night. Those little monsters were here, in my bedroom. I felt paralyzed. I couldn't move. They took me out through the wall and up into their ship."

Tears flowed from Jamie's eyes. She dabbed at them with a tissue. She glanced out the window, as if the saucer was still there, in her back yard.

"Jamie, do you want to stop?" Mark asked.

She shook her head. "They need to know what these monsters are doing." She took a deep breath and continued, "They took my baby. Those little monsters took my baby and I couldn't move. I couldn't stop them. They hurt me so much with their shiny metal instruments. I couldn't even open my mouth to scream. All I could do was cry. I'm still crying. I can't stop."

Diane glanced at her teammates. Helen was wiping her eyes. A tear ran down Clay Obers's face. Mark sat and stared at the floor, guilt and hopelessness etched into his expression.

"Four months later I gave birth to Julie," Jamie said. "She's eight now. That's her picture on the table over there."

"She's in school today," Mark said, "so she doesn't know you're here."

Jamie's hands began to tremble. Her breath was labored.

"Was there any sign of the second baby?" Helen asked.

Jamie closed her eyes and lowered her head for a moment. She took another deep breath.

"When I gave birth to Julie, there was only one baby, but there were two placentas. The doctor was surprised and said something about it to the nurses." She paused to wipe more tears from her eyes. "After I finally realized everything that had happened to me was real, I went back to my doctor and asked to see the records of Julie's birth. They told me they couldn't find my records. They said they couldn't remember anything about what happened or what was said. They wouldn't even look at me. How could they lie to me like that?"

Jamie was shaking now. Her frustration, fear, and anger barely contained.

"So Julie is normal? She's okay?" Helen asked.

Jamie glanced at the photo of Julie on the small table.

"Yes." She nodded slightly and wiped more tears away. "Julie is the one good thing that came out of this whole terrifying ordeal. I'm just afraid they'll come back for her."

Helen looked horrified at the prospect of the aliens coming back for the child.

"What makes you think they'll come back?" Diane asked.

"They already did—a year and a half ago. They took me from my bedroom and up to their ship. They showed me a small child. She had light blond hair and big blue eyes. She looked a lot like Julie, but her head was much larger than it should have been and her eyes were way too big. They pushed me closer to the child. That's when I realized it was my other baby—the one they took. I could feel it—I could sense she was mine."

Oh god, no, Diane thought, her eyes welling up with tears.

"She didn't recognize me, of course, but I could tell. I think they wanted to see if we would bond or something. I don't know. I just couldn't. I know she was my child, but I just couldn't feel what they wanted. I had been through so many horrible things with those little monsters. I couldn't overcome the pain and the fear. I still have nightmares. I'm still terrified that they will take me and do all those disgusting and hurtful things to me again. Every night I cry myself to sleep, scared to death that they'll come back. I don't know what else to do."

Mark stared at Jamie, trying to be as supportive of her as he could.

Even if you really love someone, Diane thought, how do you overcome something like this?

"Mark and I have discussed having my uterus and ovaries removed," Jamie continued. "Maybe if I'm not fertile, they will finally leave me alone. I don't know. Mark tries to protect me, but we both know he can't. How can you be safe from those little gray monsters when they can take you right through the wall in the middle of the night? We don't have any way to stop them. We're helpless."

Jamie was trembling, losing control over her fear.

"Mark, did they ever take you after the first time?" Clay asked.

Mark closed his eyes and nodded slowly. "Yes, several times after that."

They keep doing this? Diane thought. Can't they leave these poor people alone?

"What did they do to you?" Clay asked.

Mark changed position in his chair, glanced at Jamie, then looked back at Clay. "Not much compared to Jamie."

Clay glanced at Jamie. She looked as if she were falling apart. "What did they want?"

"Genetic material," Mark said, looking ashamed.

Clay appeared clearly shaken. "They took your . . ."

Mark looked up, took a breath, then looked at Clay.

"Yep. Not in a pleasant way, either. It was painful and involuntary."

Jamie was shaking uncontrollably.

Diane was shocked that this experience was still so raw and terrifying to Jamie and Mark. She closed her eyes and lowered her head. It was still raw and terrifying to her, too, and she hadn't gone through anything near what they had endured.

"Jamie, you look really stressed," Hollis said. "Would you like to stop now?"

She nodded as she brought a trembling hand up to dab at her tears. "I have to pull myself together. Julie will be coming back from school."

Hollis stood and said, "Thank you for doing this."

The group got up and walked out to the cars.

"Those poor people," Glen said, once outside. "How many folks get abducted like that?"

Hollis glanced at the flight team and said, "Twenty to twenty-five a night."

Glen appeared stunned. "Every night?"

Hollis appeared to be struggling with the anger swelling up within him. "Yes. Every night. And that's just in the U.S. This is going on in every country around the world and it's getting worse. The number of abductions has doubled in the last year alone." He glanced at his watch. "We're going to have some lunch and then there is another person you need to meet."

Chapter 18

After lunch they headed south on U.S. 84 for more than twenty miles before turning left on a gravel road. Eight miles in, they stopped at an old dilapidated house that looked abandoned, except for a black SUV parked in front with G14 on the left side of the government license plate.

Hollis led Diane and the rest of the group inside. Two agents in dark suits stood in the small central room glancing out the dirty windows. Chairs were placed in a semicircle.

A thin man, a little taller than average, stood in the middle of the room. To Diane, his most notable trait was the level of stress and anxiety he seemed to be experiencing. He couldn't sit or stay in one place, but paced nervously, keeping his hands in motion, occasionally digging at his fingernails.

Hollis stepped before the group. "This is Greg. He is

putting himself at risk in order to talk to you. Use your own judgment regarding what he has to say. Greg?"

"You're going to think I'm crazy. Some days I think I am, too. Other days I know I'm as sane as anyone. Those are the hard days. It's easier to think everything was a delusion, some trick my mind was playing on me. But what I'm about to tell you really happened."

Diane frowned. Whatever this guy went through, he was more traumatized than Jamie and Mark.

"I was an army sergeant, assigned to security in an underground base in northwestern New Mexico. Am I allowed to say it was in New Mexico?"

"For this group, yes, you are allowed," Hollis said.

Greg glanced at the group sitting around him.

"Anyway, there was a large hangar in the center on ground level. The hangar door was kept closed unless one of their vehicles was entering or leaving. There was a huge hole in the center of the hangar that extended down for a hundred and fifty feet. There were seven levels that I know of, could have been more, I'm not sure. Each level was a series of five tunnels that branched off the central section in different directions with rooms off each side of the tunnel. I think the vehicles landed on level five. It was hard to tell. The central shaft was closed off by a wall on levels one through four. I got a look at it once from the hangar."

Greg paced back and forth, stopping to look briefly out the dust-covered window at the back of the room.

"Army security controlled outside access to the base and all of Level One. Our orders were to keep ordinary people out and away from the base. Part of my job was to interact with the aliens on the lower levels. I've been down to Level Four once, Level Three several times, and Level Two a lot."

Greg looked at his trembling hands, then put them in his pockets.

"When I first got there, I thought Level One was amazing. Doctors and scientists were doing experiments on advanced equipment that could measure the human aura and consciousness. I saw devastating diseases cured and severely damaged body parts being renewed, missing limbs literally being regrown."

Diane looked at Ryan, eyebrows raised. His mouth was hanging open.

"They can do that?" Diane asked.

Greg nodded. "That and more, but they don't let us have the machines or the technology. They keep it for themselves."

"Then what are they doing with it, if they're not sharing it with us?" Helen asked.

Greg paced some more and looked out the back window again. "I'll get to that." He looked at Hollis, who nodded back at him.

"Then I was allowed into Level Two, where I saw people and animals in cages. I was told these people were hopelessly deranged and I needed to stay away from them—that they were too dangerous. I gradually learned that they were subjected to gruesome medical experiments. I was horrified at what was happening."

He breathed in and out deeply and looked out the window again.

"Eventually I got to Level Three. There were vats of stinking liquids and some kind of large membranes hanging in the vats. Each membrane contained six, sometimes seven alien bodies growing inside. In another part of Level Three I saw strange creatures. Some looked like combinations of part human and part animal. Some appeared to be part human and part alien. There were all kinds of genetic experiments going on. Some of what I saw I can't even describe to you. I don't have words adequate to give you an accurate idea of what was going on."

Greg's forehead glistened with sweat, even though it was cold in the room. He picked up a small bottle of water and took a drink.

"The one time I was allowed into Level Four I saw large vats where human and animal body parts were being dissolved. I later learned the liquid from the vats was being used to grow alien bodies and was a form of liquid nutrient for the small Grey aliens."

Diane's stomach churned, that sour taste filled her mouth. She struggled to keep from throwing up. Is this what they did with Daniel? She shivered involuntarily.

"That's when I made my decision to leave," Greg said. "I couldn't take it any longer."

Diane couldn't imagine serving under those conditions.

"They just let you walk away from your post?" Clay asked.

Greg shook his head. "Being in security, I had become aware of certain gaps in surveillance. I crawled out through an air vent one night. I've been on the run ever since."

Diane shook her head. This is just too incredible to believe.

"I can't believe our people could be involved in something like this. Our own military?" Helen said. She looked disgusted, shaking her head in disbelief.

"All I can tell you is what I saw and what I experienced," Greg said. "I followed orders. That's all. Over time, from what I understand, the medical experiments grew completely out of control. What was supposed to be a joint operation devolved into our military people either compelled to work for them, or being totally mind controlled. Same thing for the doctors and scientists who started on level one: They were gradually either coerced, or mind controlled to the point of total delusion. By the time they got to the lower levels, they were totally under alien control."

Glen Simmons was shaking his head, too.

"You said you were in security. What type of security is in place?" Clay asked.

Greg looked at the flight team, the corners of his mouth turning down, then looked straight at Clay.

"Hundreds of cameras. The halls and rooms are lined with some kind of sound device. I've seen it used. You can't hear it, but within five to six seconds you lose consciousness. I've seen people just drop to the floor, unconscious. The small Grey aliens come and haul them away. Then you never see those people or hear about them again. They're gone, like they never existed. Even their personnel files disappear from the security office."

Helen's mouth was open as she stared at Greg.

"What about weapons?" Clay asked. "Did you have a weapon?"

Glen glanced at Clay, then focused on Greg, a frown formed on his face.

"Sure," Greg said, looking at the floor. "A standard issue .45 automatic—useless against the aliens."

Clay frowned, too. "Why?"

"Because of the cameras. You do anything suspicious and a device on the ceiling emits a flash of light. Ten minutes later you wake up with a massive headache. That's assuming the Greys don't haul you off, never to be seen again."

Helen looked torn between disbelief and curiosity, and said, "So, genetic experiments?" She shivered and shook her head.

"Worse than any horror movie you could imagine," Greg said. "I threw up the first time I saw them. After a while, your brain just gets kind of numb: You see it, but it doesn't really register. That could be part of the mind control they use in there, too. It's hard to tell the difference."

Diane felt conflicted. The information was intriguing, but difficult to believe. Was this guy for real?

"You saw Levels One through Four," Diane said. "Any idea what happens on Levels Five through Seven?"

Greg shook his head strongly again. "I didn't want to know." He pulled his hands out of his pockets and held them out. "Believe me, this is not something you want inside your head for the rest of your life."

He let his arms down, blinked hard, and looked off to the side.

"You must have heard rumors," Diane said.

Greg turned and looked at Hollis.

Hollis nodded. "You can tell them."

Greg looked around the room and glanced at the window again.

"I heard there are tunnels connecting hundreds of underground bases, all over the world, with a high speed transit system. I heard you could travel from Denver to Paris in less than twenty minutes."

Diane jerked back. How could you ever get from Denver to Paris in twenty minutes without killing everyone with the acceleration and deceleration forces in the process?

"This sounds very extensive," Glen said skeptically. "How many aliens do you think are here, underground?"

Greg pursed his lips together, then answered. "I heard rumors that there were between one and two thousand of the small Greys just at the base in New Mexico. Worldwide, I've heard it could be eighteen thousand, maybe more."

Hollis pulled his buzzing phone from his pocket and read the screen. "I hate to cut this short," Hollis said. "But we have to keep Greg moving, he's being hunted by the Zeta Greys."

Hollis turned to the security detail guarding Greg.

"We have activity in the area. Get him out of here."

Greg looked terrified. The two agents rushed him out the front door and sped off in the black SUV.

* * *

Once they returned to Peregrine Base, Hollis gathered them in the conference room.

"Sir?" Diane asked. "There's an underground alien base in the same state where we are. Isn't that kind of close?"

"It's actually just over two hundred and fifty miles away," Hollis said. "Right now we're not flying any craft in the area. Everything we need moves by truck, so we think it's perfectly safe, at least for training."

"So we're almost right under their noses?"

Hollis nodded. "Yes, we are. Just for curiosity, would you look for an enemy base this close if you thought you were in complete control?"

Diane glanced at the wall and then back to Hollis. "No. I guess I wouldn't."

He held his hands out, palms up. "Well, they haven't either. I took the time out of your training because you need to know exactly why you're being asked to put your lives on the line. Our world is at risk and the future of human life hangs in the balance. I believe in you—all of you. You are the brightest and the best this world has to offer. I have every confidence that if a way to defeat the saucers can be found, you'll find it."

The pilots looked at each other in depressed silence, overwhelmed by the enormity of what had happened to the people they saw today, and the inconceivable task that stood before them.

"It's been a long day," Hollis said. "Get some rest. Tomorrow we go back in the simulators. Find a way to shoot down the saucers."

This really is the evil mom spoke about, Diane thought.

Now I understand. All I have to do is figure out a way to do the impossible.

Chapter 19

Sean Wells took a seat eight rows back and near the aisle in the White House Briefing Room. The regular *New York Times* White House correspondent had promised that Stephanie Peterson, the White House Press Secretary, would call on him. After twenty minutes she walked to the podium and began her prepared briefing. When the time for questions came, Sean raised his hand.

"Mr. Wells, your question."

"Yes, thank you. President Andrews is a huge supporter of global warming research. I have data showing a cooling trend in the Southeastern U.S. and a report from a guy who was a consultant for NASA and an advisor to the White House reporting that the ice in Antarctica has increased, not decreased, over the last fifteen years. The numbers involved aren't trivial, they're substantial. Your comment?"

The entire group of reporters groaned, obviously irritated with the politically incorrect question.

"While we are making some progress in dealing with global climate change, the vast majority of what needs to be done is still overwhelming. This is pulling us off topic. Will you see me after the briefing?"

"Of course."

Okay, he thought. Now that I have their attention, what lies are they going to hand me next?

He waited for the briefing to end and for the room to clear out. Stephanie ducked back in the side door and motioned for him to follow her. She led him across the hallway and into her office.

"This is not for public consumption," she began. "You can use it for deep background—from a well-placed, anonymous source—but nothing beyond that. Understood?"

"Certainly." He knew the routine.

"We have an aerial spraying program in place to increase the reflectivity of the atmosphere and reduce the solar heating effect from the sun. That alone has reduced the rise in global temperature and postponed the devastating effects of global warming. We have managed to hold back, to some degree, the rise of ocean levels. So while global warming is caused by human activity, we are gradually finding man-made solutions to those same problems."

Sean smiled. "This sounds like an expensive program. Is it?"

She nodded. "Yes, but it's nowhere near the cost of displacing billions of people, let alone the political upheavals that global warming will cause. Compared to that, what we're doing is a dirt-cheap bargain."

Sean leaned forward in his chair. "How long has this program been in effect?"

"The program started small, twenty-five years ago. Once we worked out the kinks in the delivery system, we increased coverage. That's why President Andrews is such a supporter of getting the global warming issue in front of the people. We have a potential solution: All we need is broader public support. That is where I think you can help us. Get the message out at the grass roots level that with more public support and funding, we can solve the global warming debacle."

Yeah, Sean thought. Like I'm ever going to be your lap dog.

* * *

President Andrews looked up from his desk to see Doug Franks smiling as he walked into the oval office.

"You hardly ever smile anymore. Good news, I take it?" He relaxed back in his chair, waiting.

"Stephanie thinks she has a reporter for us—Sean Wells from the *New York Times*."

Andrews thought for a moment. "That could work. Would he agree to do this for us?"

"That's the beauty of it. He doesn't have to agree. He's anti-establishment. He'll do it because he can take down part of the inner circle of influence. That's what he loves to do. He won't even question us being involved. It's the perfect plan."

Andrews smiled and nodded.

"I like it. Do it."

* * *

Conrad Kaplan used his encrypted phone to access USAP317, the unacknowledged special access program he had been using for the last six years. He assumed that he had been granted access because of his position in black budget research programs. He didn't know anyone in the USAP and no one had spoken to him about it. The access authorization, Internet address, and login had simply appeared on his encrypted phone one afternoon. The address didn't show up on any Internet searches, leading him to the realization that it was part of the Darknet—sites accessible only if you've been invited in. He had logged in, created a password, and received the encryption key. He sent in a number of questions to the site to find out more about what it was, and what it did, but never received an answer of any kind.

Then, three months later he had a very vivid dream in which he owned two companies and was making millions of dollars in the Middle East and Africa, all with USAP317 protection. He had logged into USAP317, described what he envisioned, and much to his surprise received not only authorization, but contacts who would help him set his plan in motion. His role and position in the Partnership had come the very same way. He suspected that at least some of the other members in the Partnership had access to USAP317, but he had been carefully instructed to never talk about the program and, if questioned, what cover story to use.

Kaplan had recognized early on that some of the activities he was becoming involved in could run afoul of the government, not only here in the United States, but in other countries as well. But every time a situation arose and someone asked about what he was doing, he used the cover story provided by USAP317, and there was never any follow up. He was free to do whatever he wanted, as long as it was authorized through USAP317.

In his mind Kaplan used words like intoxicating and addictive to describe USAP317. The power and control provided by the program was both satisfying and inspiring. At this point, he couldn't imagine life without USAP317.

The other side of being involved in the unauthorized special access program was the actions they requested of him. This request involved adding a new member to the Partnership, a growing organization of highly influential people. The new member, Irwin Gould, was the head of the fourth largest financial institution in the world. Gould's family had been involved in international banking for more than a hundred and fifty years with connections to several central banks across the globe. He would certainly be a welcome addition to the organization.

Chapter 20

"How's life in conspiracy theory land?" Sean Wells asked.

"Business is good," his old friend Patrick Flaherty replied. "The magazine and website are waking up more people every day. You need to get out of New York and take an honest look at what's happening in the world. We're spreading a lot of truth in a world of lies."

Sean nodded. If something unusual was going on in the world, Patrick had an explanation for it. That's why he called Patrick and asked what he knew about aerosol spraying programs. "Well, I can't argue about the 'world of lies' part. What makes you think the other version is actually true?"

Patrick grinned. "Lab results, insider leaks, plus, most of this stuff is going on right in front of people's eyes. You can see it for yourself."

The waiter stopped by and took their drink orders.

"Stuff like what?" Sean asked.

Patrick glanced around the room, then leaned forward. "Chemtrails."

Sean shook his head. "Those are just contrails from commercial aircraft. They fly at higher altitudes, so the contrails last longer."

Patrick settled back and grinned. "You want to bet?"

Sean grinned right back at him. This was the Patrick he knew. "What did you have in mind?"

"Hundred bucks, cash on the barrelhead."

Sean raised his eyebrows. Must be serious, he thought. It's usually fifty.

"And how do we decide who's right?"

Patrick leaned forward again as if what he had to say shouldn't be overheard.

"Simple. Watch the skies over the next few days. When the sky is clear blue, check to see how many commercial flights have been cancelled or altitudes have been changed. If commercial aircraft are creating the extended white trails in the sky, a clear blue sky shouldn't have any planes in it. Deal?"

Sean just had to chuckle to himself. "I know you're wrong."

Patrick had that clever Irish gleam in his eyes.

"Then prove it. If I'm right, buy me dinner as a bonus."

Sean smiled. Neither one of them was going to settle for dinner at a buffet, he thought. This could get interesting.

Sean raised his eyebrows. "And if I'm right?"

Patrick chuckled. "You get a hundred bucks and dinner on me."

"Deal."

* * *

Sean walked out of the Washington Hilton the next morning and looked up at the sky. Not a cloud in sight—nor were there any contrails. The sky was a rich light blue. He used his phone to locate a college nearby with a meteorology department. The University of Maryland was close and it had post-graduate studies in Atmospheric and Oceanic Science.

He hailed a cab and headed northeast to College Park, Maryland. The cab dropped him off on Stadium Drive on the south side of the Computer and Space Sciences Building. He walked north and entered the main doors under the three-story rounded glass atrium of the red brick structure.

"I'm looking for Dr. Raju. Where can I find him?"

He asked three students before he got a response: "Lecture hall."

"Where?"

The student pointed down the hall.

Sean quietly opened one of the double doors and stepped inside. The lecture hall was built on a sloping floor with approximately two hundred seats, of which only eighteen were in use. Dr. Raju stood at the podium pointing to a display behind him.

"Human contribution to carbon dioxide levels in the atmosphere is significant. As people burned more and more coal for heating and power generation, the cooler oceans acted as a carbon dioxide sink, absorbing ninety thousand million tons of carbon dioxide each year. As the oceans warm during the summer, eighty-eight thousand million tons of carbon dioxide is released back into the atmosphere. The two thousand million tons of carbon dioxide retained by the oceans each year accounts for approximately one quarter of the carbon dioxide produced by humans. Colder ocean water holds more carbon dioxide, while warmer water releases more."

Sean took an aisle seat in the middle of the lecture hall.

"Right now, the ocean absorption is helping us, but as the climate warms, the oceans will turn against us, releasing more carbon dioxide into the air than we produce. That will make the overall situation worse, creating a carbon dioxide cascade effect and warming the planet even more. As you can see, we are on the verge of catastrophic climate change. If we wait any longer, it may be too late to do anything at all to alter the global impact of greenhouse gasses."

A bell rang, ending the class. Students filed past Sean as he waited for their teacher.

"Dr. Raju, I'm Sean Wells from the *New York Times*. I'm doing an article on climate change and need some information from you on certain aspects of controlling global warming. Do you have a few minutes?"

"The *New York Times*?"

Sean showed him the press credentials.

"Would I and the university be mentioned in your article?"

Sean smiled. "Certainly, if you would like. The public recognition could help both you and the university."

Dr. Raju glanced at his watch. "I could spare a few minutes. My office is on the third floor."

Sean followed him up the stairs. Dr. Raju's office walls were stuffed with books and research materials. Stacks of research papers crowded the floor space, leaving a small and unsteady path between the piles. Sean sat in the only chair in front of the overloaded desk.

"Now, what is it that concerns you?" Dr. Raju asked.

"Aerial spraying to reduce heating from the sun. Ever heard of it?"

Dr. Raju grinned and nodded. "Of course. Cloud reflectivity modification and solar radiation management. The other approach is carbon dioxide reduction. Both can be used in conjunction for better results."

Sean flipped open his small paper notebook. "So what are they spraying?" He clicked his pen, ready to write.

"Mostly sulfur-based compounds have been proposed. Sulfur scatters sunlight, thus reducing the heating effect on the surface of the planet. It amounts to creating more clouds and making existing clouds whiter."

Sean frowned. Something that was proposed didn't sound like a twenty-five year-long project. "I assume there's a down side?"

Dr. Raju nodded. "Acid rain. The sulfur combines with oxygen and hydrogen to form sulfuric acid. Reducing acid rain is the reason we reduced the sulfur content of fuel oil for use in diesel engines and why coal-fired power plants require sulfur scrubbers."

Sean shook his head. "I came from the White House where I learned they have been doing aerial spraying for the last twenty-five years. That doesn't sound like sulfur and acid rain to me. What is really going on?"

Dr. Raju got up, walked over, and closed his office door.

"You can't quote me or mention the university. This is an issue where publicity is seriously discouraged."

Now we're getting somewhere, Sean thought. "I understand. What are they spraying?"

Dr. Raju sat down, took a deep breath, and looked directly into Sean's eyes.

"A combination of aluminum and barium, converted to very small particles. The metals stay floating in the atmosphere for eight to ten weeks. The stratospheric aerosol injection program creates a light cloud cover. By spraying in the early morning, sometimes before the sun comes up, we can increase the reflectivity of the atmosphere and decrease the heating from solar radiation. The clouds generally dissipate by night, allowing the earth to radiate heat back out into space. The combination of the two lowers the global temperature. This is all part of the new science of geoengineering. We watch the temperature trends in various areas and apply the aerosols appropriately. If an area is in a cooling trend, we let it alone. If temperatures are climbing, we spray."

Sean scribbled in his notebook, then looked back up at Dr. Raju. "Would I be able to see these aerosols in the sky?"

Dr. Raju shrugged. "Maybe, if you looked at just the right time. The spray disburses quickly into light clouds or a haze."

That's not what Patrick was indicating, he thought. Sean nodded and made some more notes. "So if you have a system that's working to control the climate, why not tell everybody?"

Dr. Raju breathed out deeply and looked Sean straight in the eyes.

"It's not that simple. Solar radiation management has to work hand-in-hand with carbon dioxide reduction, and we're nowhere near close on that, yet. We need the global carbon tax in effect to cut down on carbon dioxide emissions and finance the solar radiation management costs. Eventually, the program will pay for itself. That's the goal: a self-sustaining geoengineering program where we can control the climate worldwide."

It always comes down to this, doesn't it, Sean thought. "So, it comes down to money?"

"Of course. It always does. We can't afford to keep dumping unlimited funds into a project like this. We all have to pay our fair share to save the planet."

Sean walked down the hall deep in thought. There has to be more to this than Dr. Raju is telling me. Storms are worse now than in the recent past. But if I go back far enough, there are larger storms than we're having now. What have the carbon dioxide levels been and how far back do the records go? Who would I even ask?

* * *

Sean headed back to the Hilton, and checked out the sky once more. It was still clear light blue. No clouds and no contrails.

In his room, he went through the EDGAR files for corporations on the Securities and Exchange Commission website. He cross-referenced the corporations on the list he had from Charlie, checked the stock filing reports, and compared the members of the board of directors for the companies. A tight network of names was emerging, and those same names were at the top of Charlie's list of corrupted individuals.

He checked the sky once again. Still clear blue. His curiosity was getting the better of him. He checked for flight cancellations. There weren't any. He called a contact he had at one of the major airlines. There were no changes in flight altitudes. He called the National Weather Service. There was no significant change in humidity, temperature, or atmospheric pressure from yesterday to today. There was nothing to explain why the sky was clear today when it hadn't been yesterday.

Sean spent the rest of the day in his hotel room working on his exposé of three interlocked corporations. At five in the afternoon, he checked the sky one last time. It was still clear blue. He pulled his phone and invited Patrick to dinner.

Chapter 21

President Andrews listened carefully to the discussion taking place in the White House conference room. The Secretary of Defense, the Joint Chiefs, and the commanding officers of all the military branches were present. He felt uneasy about the direction things were headed.

"Our unanimous opinion is that our advantage over the Russian Forces in Eastern Europe needs to be pushed forward," Secretary of Defense Farnsworth said. "NATO is fully aligned with us and we have sufficient support from pro-western elements within Ukraine and Belarus."

Farnsworth used the remote to turn on the main display, then zoomed in showing Ukraine and Belarus full screen.

"We have rising political operatives in place in each country ready to insure a referendum vote in favor of NATO membership. This is the culmination of two decades of funding covert political figures and their agendas. By bringing Ukraine and Belarus into the NATO sphere of influence, we will be able to place anti-missile installations literally on the border of Russia."

Farnsworth zoomed the screen view out to show Russia and the anti-missile facilities already in place. Existing placements were in red; proposed sites in Ukraine and Belarus were in blue.

"That will place us within reach of more than seventy percent of Russia's ICBMs on the ground. By adding these anti-missile units to the bases already in Greenland and Northern Canada, our high-speed missiles will be able to destroy ninety percent of all Russian ICBMs launched against our country before they can leave Russian airspace. This is a necessary step in creating a much higher degree of national security."

He seems to think being ready and able to blow everyone up makes us more secure, Andrews thought. Isn't that the same thinking that got us into this mess in the first place?

"What about Russian submarine-based nuclear missiles?" Andrews asked.

Farnsworth turned and nodded to Admiral Dosinski, who typed on his tablet bringing the position and status of all Russian subs onto the main screen.

"Russia hasn't had the financial resources to maintain their full submarine fleet. Currently only three ballistic missile submarines are on patrol at any given time. With our advanced submarine technology, we are able to follow them and remain within striking distance at all times without their knowledge." Farnsworth pointed to the three submarine locations on the screen. "Those subs are currently here, here, and here. We have a nuclear fast attack sub tailing each of them. You can forget about any threat the Russian subs pose to us."

Andrews leaned to the side in his chair and studied the screen. He frowned.

"This sounds as though we're developing a first-strike nuclear plan against Russia. Is that where this is going?"

Farnsworth shrugged. His expression and hand gestures seemed a little too rehearsed to Andrews.

"It's not entirely out of the question, world tensions being what they are. Obviously, it's not our first choice, but with the recent increase in Russian military actions in Crimea and Syria, something has to be done to counter the Russian president's provocative actions."

Farnsworth turned to face Andrews directly.

"We need to take a firm and decisive stand against them. The American people and our allies are waiting to see if you have the resolve to do what needs to be done with the Russians. You've been in office for ten months. Now is the time to demonstrate the world-class leadership qualities we know you possess."

Andrews ignored Farnsworth's blatant attempt at manipulation painted in flattery. They had known each other much too long for him to take it seriously. It was just Farnsworth being Farnsworth; that was all.

"Timetable?"

Farnsworth skipped back with the remote to show Ukraine and Belarus on the main screen. "Our people can force a referendum in Ukraine within two months. Belarus will take another six months."

Okay, Andrews thought. It *is* where they're going with this. "And you're certain of the outcome?"

Farnsworth seemed to relax a little.

"Hundred percent," Farnsworth replied, as he showed more enthusiasm. "Barring any unforeseen incidents, of course." Farnsworth's smile wasn't reassuring at all.

"Of course," Andrews said. "I'll let you know what I

decide to do with Russia. Thank you for your input."

Andrews stood, left the conference room, and leaned into Doug Franks's office.

"Walk with me."

Franks looked up. His expression revealed that this was one of those "we've got to talk" moments no one likes. He followed Andrews through the White House and into the personal quarters for the First Family.

"I need an off-the-books sit-down with Pasternov in three weeks. No press, no military, minimal security, and face to face. Can you make that happen quietly?"

Franks looked stunned, yet curious. "I can. What's going on?"

Andrews set his lips tight together and looked around the room.

"I need to invite him into the circle."

Chapter 22

"Okay, I'll bite. How did you know?" Sean's curiosity was piqued. It wasn't often he got something wrong, at least not something he considered this basic. Dinner could go on the expense account, but the hundred bucks would come out of his pocket. It just might be worth it.

"When you understand how a system works, the results become more predictable," Patrick said with a self-satisfied smile.

Sean let a half smile show. He liked how Patrick was always so careful about his documentation.

"Which means something happened so you knew what was going to happen next?"

Patrick was deep into conspiracy theories and far out stuff, but he usually knew what he was talking about. That's why Sean called him in the first place.

"Exactly," Patrick said. "I knew from the weather forecast that we didn't have a storm front anywhere close to us. Plus, the day before, Iran fired off a new ballistic missile."

Sean nodded. He remembered the news item from the previous day.

Patrick used his hands to emphasize different parts of the globe as he said, "When Iran or North Korea does something provocative like that, the U.S. puts its military pilots on alert."

Sean tipped his head, frowned, and wondered what the connection was going to be.

"The planes that spray the chemtrails are flown by military pilots. When they're put on alert, no chemtrails. The pilots aren't available."

The waiter brought their salads and drinks. Sean took the opportunity to study Patrick for a moment. So far this wasn't making a lot of sense.

"Why do you call them chemtrails instead of contrails?" Sean asked, as he started in on his salad.

Patrick beamed. "Contrails are the result of burning jet fuel, which is high-grade kerosene," he said, holding his left hand over the table. "So what you get is partially consumed hydrocarbons and water vapor. The white part you see from the ground is the water vapor, which freezes and then dissipates in thirty to sixty seconds." He held his right hand out to balance the left. "Chemtrails are composed of a mix of metals and other chemicals that remain suspended in the air, at least for a while. These chemicals gradually settle to the ground. We collected samples of the residue and sent them to a lab for analysis."

Sean nodded. He could see where Patrick was going with this, but said, "How do you know people aren't jiggering the results by doping the samples?"

Patrick's face flushed. He didn't like being challenged.

He's probably emotionally invested in being right, Sean thought.

"Here's a packet of different lab results from various parts of the U.S. and Canada," handing a buff envelope across the table. "You may find the analysis from the State of California particularly interesting. Because of their high level of environmental regulations for air and water quality, they test and report the contamination levels and components in the air and water every year."

Sean took the envelope and set it to the side. There would be plenty of time to go over it later tonight.

"I take it you believe these so-called chemtrails are the solar radiance management program and that only military pilots fly the planes?"

Patrick shook his head, trying to stay calm.

"It's not that simple. Solar radiance management is just a small part of what's being done, and it's actually a large part of the plausible deniability scheme of lies designed to cover the real reason for the chemtrails."

Plausible deniability, Sean thought. The unofficial motto for every covert agency he ran across. "Which is?" Sean pressed.

"To make the upper atmosphere electrically conductive."

The waiter arrived with their dinners. Sean waited as Patrick cut into his steak.

"Electrically conductive? For what purpose?"

Patrick nodded, swallowed, and took a sip of his drink.

"Chemtrails suspend nanoparticles in the upper atmosphere, primarily aluminum and barium, in order to make the upper layer electrically conductive. High frequency radio waves are then used to heat the upper atmosphere, which expands, and in turn pushes and shapes the ionosphere above it," Patrick said, making an umbrella shape with his arms.

"The ionosphere reflects radio waves. The end result is a type of concave radio-frequency mirror that can be used to reflect and focus electromagnetic energy back down to any spot on the planet."

Sean shook his head. "From my understanding of radio waves, they dissipate rapidly, so the energy at that distance is very small."

Patrick nodded with a knowing smile.

"That depends on the antenna. One of the early experiments used the huge dish antenna at Arecibo, in Puerto Rico. That antenna was able to focus several million watts of electromagnetic energy into a very small area in the upper atmosphere."

"Okay," Sean said. "That means whoever controlled the antenna could project the destructive power over a large target area."

"That's exactly correct," Patrick continued. "Since then we have developed phased array antennas, which can direct and focus tremendous amounts of electromagnetic energy anywhere on the planet."

Sean nodded as he cut another piece of steak.

"To do what?" he asked, his reporter instinct urging him to push harder. He didn't like doing this to Patrick, but if he was going to get to the bottom of this issue, he needed to push. "This is beginning to sound like some long, involved, science fiction thing," he said, waving his steak knife over his plate. "What are they—whoever 'they' are—doing with this energy?"

Patrick put down his utensils and looked directly at Sean.

"It's a weapon system," Patrick said. "And like all weapons, it's been used for good purposes and for bad. Heating the upper atmosphere can move the jet stream, change the weather, create and steer storms, and create droughts or floods.

It has been used as a strategic weapon against other countries. Electrifying the upper atmosphere can destroy the electronic control system on intercontinental ballistic missile warheads, creating an invisible shield against incoming nuclear bombs." Patrick looked up, his arms following his gaze. "With the billions of watts of electrical power that can be generated and focused in small areas of the upper atmosphere, you could melt an incoming warhead before it got anywhere near its target."

Almost there, Sean thought. "That sounds like a *good* thing—protecting us from warheads."

Patrick shook his head again.

"But it's a bad thing when it's used to create floods, droughts, hurricanes, and record-breaking tornados that kill people and destroy property for hidden political purposes." Patrick's anger flared, his face turning red. "That's the problem. It's a military grade weapon that looks like an Act of God, a natural disaster that just happened by itself. It has plausible deniability built right into it because so very few people either know about it, or even believe it's possible to do these things."

Sean nodded as righteous indignation took over Patrick's body language, and his voice became louder.

"That's why I'm publishing the information: to educate people. You think this is just some fantasy conspiracy theory and that only stupid people would believe anything like this could exist. Well, you're wrong. It does exist. It's real!"

Sean sat back in his chair to give Patrick a chance to cool down. This was clearly an emotional subject, but he needed the facts. In his experience, people believed a lot of things that just weren't true. It didn't matter what Patrick believed, it only mattered what evidence and research materials he had collected. That's what he wanted.

"It's a lot to take in," Sean said calmly. "Especially in a short time frame."

Patrick glanced furtively around the restaurant.

"Didn't mean to make a scene. The aerial spraying program is a piggyback operation."

Sean slowly looked around. The waiter had a worried look on his face, probably wondering if he needed to ask them to leave. Other people were looking at them with suspicious eyes. He needed to cool this down. He leaned forward and spoke softly.

"Piggyback? As in?"

Patrick followed his lead and leaned forward as well.

"The government offsets the cost of the program by collecting fees from companies that want to put other things in the chemical mix."

Sean glanced at the waiter, who turned away.

"Such as?"

Patrick leaned in more.

"Polymers, viruses, toxins, bacteria, and a number of other things."

Viruses? Bacteria? Toxins? Sean thought. That was a shock.

"They're spraying toxins?"

Patrick nodded. "If you disburse a toxic substance over a wide enough area, it's no longer considered a toxin."

"You're kidding." Sean had never heard of such a thing.

"No, I'm not kidding. They also spray polymers that absorb ultraviolet radiation from the sun—part of the solar radiance cover. The program is open to all kinds of experiments. You'd be surprised at who's involved in some of these tests."

Sean wrinkled his lips and paused. "Okay, try me."

Patrick named several major corporations, the first three of which Sean was already studying because of their placement at the top of Charlie's list.

"This is geoengineering we're talking about?" Sean asked.

He glanced around the dining room. People had refocused on their dinners.

"Yes. The spraying is going on all over the globe. What started out as an essential part of a military weapons system has slowly morphed into a vast experiment to modify and control the climate."

Patrick shook his head, disgust showing on his face.

"Some scientists are swooning over the ability to transform the climate on the planet. And to think I was worried about the threat of nuclear weapons incinerating millions of people during the cold war. Now we've got people playing God with the climate and the power to end life as we know it on planet earth."

The waiter returned and refilled their drinks.

"So how did all of this get started?" Sean asked.

Patrick nodded and cut open his baked potato.

"Nicola Tesla and Tunguska, Russia, June thirtieth, 1908."

Tesla? 1908? Patrick was certainly full of surprises tonight.

"Tunguska," Sean said. "That was a meteor or an asteroid."

Patrick smiled and shook his head once more.

"No. It wasn't. It was Tesla's demonstration of the projection of electromagnetic energy from his Wardenclyffe magnifying antenna tower on Long Island, New York."

This was the first Sean had heard anything like that.

"What evidence do you have?"

Patrick waved his fork over his plate.

"There's a website—" Patrick said, pausing to take another sip of his drink—"dedicated to all things Tesla. They have the documents and some of Tesla's letters and notes. It's all there."

Patrick took back the envelope he had given to Sean and scribbled the web address on it.

"Take a look. You'll be surprised."

Sean looked at the address. Just because it was on a website didn't make it true. People can, and do, put anything on websites.

"That devastated a huge area," Sean said.

Patrick looked him in the eyes again.

"It did. The demonstration flattened a thousand square miles of trees. Fortunately, it wasn't in a populated area. You see—and this is the part people don't understand—the power you put into the transmitter is magnified through the antenna. This is what makes it an effective military weapon."

Patrick paused as he finished his baked potato.

"You put ten million watts into the transmitter and when it gets focused at the target, you have billions of watts of energy released. The military weapons use Tesla magnifying antennas. The energy released by Tesla over Tunguska was greater than our most powerful hydrogen bomb, and it was projected a quarter of the way around the globe, in 1908, by one individual. You can't *imagine* the power these modern facilities have."

Sean sank back in his chair. This whole conversation went way beyond what he was thinking when dinner began. If what Patrick said was true, the consequences could be profound.

"How many of these places are there?"

Patrick sat back and finished his drink.

"Right now? Two dozen or so. Ten of them are in Russia. The thing is, Tesla did that without any conductive materials in the atmosphere. With the metals from the chemtrails, the power that can be projected is horrendous."

Sean picked up his glass and looked down into the

amber liquid. If Patrick was right, and he just could be, these facilities were very dangerous places.

"So where are these facilities and who owns them?"

Patrick tapped on the buff envelope. "I have a 'members only' section on the website. Membership costs a hundred bucks. I took the liberty of assigning you a user name and an initial password. That's where you'll find all of the research documents, sources, and scientific references. That way you can expense our bet as research. Receipt is in the envelope."

Sean nodded and smiled. Some sources, like Patrick, were worth cultivating. "Facilities?"

"The more powerful transmitters are inside the Arctic and Antarctic Circles, where they have access to the electrojet—naturally occurring electrically charged particles flowing in from the north and south magnetic poles."

Sean wrote the word electrojet on the envelope under the web address so he could research it later.

"Take a look at Poker Flats in Alaska, Tromso in Norway, and the phased antenna arrays in Antarctica," Patrick said.

"Antarctica?" Sean looked up at Patrick. "I thought it was all ice and research stations."

Patrick shook his head. "The United States, Russia, and China all have HAARP transmitters in Antarctica. They claim it's for research, but it's a weapon system, plain and simple."

Chapter 23

"Dr. Schambrect?" Sean called out.

Hundreds of sliding drawer cabinets filled with tens of thousands of fossils formed a virtual maze in the basement of the Earth Sciences building.

"Back here."

Sean followed the sound of Schambrect's voice as he worked his way around rows of gray metal cabinets.

Dr. Schambrect stepped out of an aisle. "Welcome to Virginia Tech. How can I help you?"

Sean pulled out his notebook and flipped through several pages before he found it.

"You wrote a paper on paleoclimatology."

Dr. Schambrect grinned. "Not every day I get reminded of that. Don't tell me you actually read it."

"Still trying. I'm Sean Wells from the *New York Times*. I've heard a lot of talk about carbon dioxide and climate change, but everything is very recent, time wise. I hope you can translate the gist of your paper into my level of English so I can get some perspective."

Dr. Schambrect led the way to a small table with chairs in the corner of the room.

"You mind if I bring a friend into this? I think his opinion can help you."

"Sure, why not." Two for the price of one, Sean thought.

Dr. Schambrect punched in a number on his cell phone. "Yeah, Daryl. I've got a live one. You want to join the conversation?"

He glanced at Sean, then added, "Yeah, I'm in the tombs."

He hung up.

Sean grinned. "So, I'm a live one?" He was amused at the term, especially in regard to himself.

With a smile and a shrug, Schambrect said, "You're willing to listen and look at the facts. Too many people are so afraid of being politically incorrect that you can't even have a conversation with them."

"Well, political correctness and I aren't exactly on good speaking terms," Sean replied, returning the scientist's smile.

"I can tell—you're here—talking to me."

The door opened and a short, chubby man walked in.

"Daryl, this is Sean Wells from the *New York Times*. Sean, Dr. Daryl Rathbone, head of anthropology. Sean is asking about the role of carbon dioxide."

Sean and Daryl shook hands. Daryl took a seat as he said, "Aaah. The industrial revolution bogyman."

Sean chuckled. "Bogyman?"

Daryl nodded. "Short version: The industrial revolution

started around 1760 with a world population of about seven hundred and twenty million people. Over the last two hundred and fifty years the human population has grown to ten times what it was, and much of the human diet has shifted toward meat consumption. The end result is that the number of animals—humans and food animals, such as cows, sheep, pigs, and chickens, have exploded all the while trees and oxygen producing plants have been cut back. Where there used to be grass and farmland, now we have cities, with concrete and asphalt."

Sean wrote a quick note. "Which don't produce oxygen, I take it?" Sean asked.

"Exactly," Daryl said as he shuffled his chair closer to the table. "We have ten times the people and more than ten times the amount of food animals converting oxygen into carbon dioxide, plus all of the jet aircraft in the air producing even more carbon dioxide."

Sean nodded as he wrote more notes. "So the carbon dioxide level has gone up by ten times?"

When he glanced up, the two of them were staring at him, a serious look on their faces.

"Human produced carbon dioxide, yes," Daryl said. "The overall increase is thirty-two percent."

Sean frowned. So far this wasn't making a lot of sense. "If the carbon dioxide levels have increased that much, why hasn't the temperature gone up by that much?"

"As you might be aware," Dr. Schambrect said, "there's a lot of disagreement on the climate change issue. Historically we have been in a prolonged cooling period, so if the climate is warming up again, it shouldn't come as a surprise to anyone."

These guys are holding something back from me, Sean thought. What is it, and why?

"How much does the temperature actually change over time?" Sean asked.

Dr. Schambrect tilted forward in his chair. "Over the last billion years, or something shorter?"

A billion years, Sean thought. How would they even know? "Sure, let's go for the billion year range."

Dr. Schambrect seemed to be loosening up a little. "The average surface temperature has gone up and down through a limited range of ten degrees Celsius, that's eighteen degrees Fahrenheit for most people in America."

Eighteen degrees didn't seem that drastic. "Really? That doesn't seem like a lot. So what role does carbon dioxide play?"

Now they both appeared more relaxed.

Dr. Schambrect chuckled. "Water in the form of humidity, rainfall, and clouds has a major effect on both life and the climate. Water vapor is the primary greenhouse gas, not carbon dioxide."

Then why the big fuss over carbon dioxide? Sean wondered.

"Water creates clouds," Dr. Schambrect continued, "which moderate the amount of sunlight that reaches the surface of the planet through reflection. Water also stimulates green plants, which absorb the sunlight and release oxygen. When water evaporates it absorbs a huge amount of heat."

The shift in focus from carbon dioxide to water was unexpected.

"Right," Daryl said. "Ninety-five percent of the climate is controlled by water vapor, not carbon dioxide. Besides, almost ninety-seven percent of carbon dioxide is produced by nature, only a little over three percent is actually man-made."

Ninety-seven percent, Sean thought. Where have I heard that number before? "Meaning what?" He shifted forward in his seat.

"Meaning the man-made contribution to the greenhouse effect is less than one percent."

Less than one percent? The climate change people were convinced the whole problem was human-produced carbon dioxide. Why weren't they even mentioning water vapor? What was going on?

"My point is," Dr. Schambrect said, "that climate change is most often caused by tectonic plate movement, volcanic eruptions, and changes in solar activity, not carbon dioxide."

Sean put his pen down and straightened up in his chair. This was getting interesting.

"The two basic gases of life are oxygen and carbon dioxide," Dr. Schambrect continued. "Animals breathe in oxygen and exhale carbon dioxide. Plants, through photosynthesis, take in carbon dioxide and release oxygen. More plants, higher concentrations of oxygen in the atmosphere. More animals, higher amounts of carbon dioxide. The balance between plants and animals seesaws back and forth."

This was a completely different take from what was being promoted to the public.

"I'm confused," Sean said. "Isn't there a direct relationship between carbon dioxide levels and temperature?"

Dr. Schambrect shook his head. "Not really. Warmer temperatures and higher levels of carbon dioxide encourage higher rates of plant growth, resulting in more oxygen, which encourages more animals to grow."

Sean was uncertain as to how seriously he should take all of this. These two could be trying to put one over on him. "So what kind of a swing in carbon dioxide levels are we talking?"

Sean watched Dr. Schambrect closely.

"We've had carbon dioxide levels of less than one hundred parts per million and as high as six thousand parts per million."

Sean's eyebrows rose. That's quite a spread, he thought. "Where are we now?"

Dr. Schambrect didn't have the intensity, or elevated emotional level, typical of people who fanatically believe in something. He seemed more reserved, calm, more comfortable with his facts and knowledge level.

"Somewhere in the range of three hundred eighty to four hundred parts per million."

That figure Sean had seen before. If carbon dioxide levels have been as high as six thousand, why were the environmentalists panicking at the prospect of five hundred parts per million? "So, near the lower end?"

"Yep. I'll give you an example. Four hundred fifty million years ago, near the end of the Ordovician period, carbon dioxide levels were around forty-five hundred parts per million. Twelve times higher than they are now."

Sean glanced at the two scientists. They seemed calm and confident.

"How hot was it then?"

Dr. Schambrect smiled. "It was an ice age."

Sean was shocked. How could that be? "Glaciers?"

Dr. Schambrect nodded. "All over the place. That was the problem. Plants and animals don't grow very well in the cold. Carbon dioxide levels soared. Oxygen dipped to the lowest levels in history."

We die without oxygen, Sean reminded himself. "So what happened?"

Dr. Schambrect breathed out and looked him right in the eyes.

"Second largest extinction event—ever. With low levels of oxygen, the sea animals died off until the balance of plants and animals was restored by a warming climate."

Incredible. How could this not be part of the media conversation? "You seem fairly certain about all of this. How do you know?"

Evidence, Sean thought. Where's the evidence?

"Radioisotopes," Dr. Schambrect said. "We have accurate ice cores from east Antarctica that take us back eight hundred thousand years. We can infer the climate from pollen and other particulates in the layers of the ice. That sets the pattern."

Okay, now we're getting somewhere, Sean thought.

"By following the established relationships of carbon-14 and oxygen-18 isotopes, we can take the climate pattern back for a billion years," Dr. Schambrect explained.

So there's a well-defined scientific basis for what they're saying. Sean wrote the name of the isotopes in his notebook. "Then it's not really about temperature, but the balance between oxygen and carbon dioxide? Plants and animals?"

He glanced at the two scientists.

"In a nutshell? Yes. Carbon dioxide isn't a primary cause of climate change, as some people insist. It's an indicator of the plant and animal balance."

Okay, Sean thought. Now I can clearly divide the political propaganda from the scientific facts.

"Swell," Sean said softly, then thought, Now I remember . . . "I've read that ninety-seven percent of scientists agree that global warming is real and that it is caused by human activity. Any comment?"

They both laughed.

"What's so funny?"

Daryl was shaking his head.

"Who did you talk with?" Dr. Schambrect asked, a wide smirk forming on his face.

"Dr. Raju, University of Maryland."

Dr. Schambrect nodded. "Guess he didn't bother to explain."

If you wanted to know what someone's motivation was, or what they were hiding, you just had to ask their competitors, Sean thought. "Explain what?"

"Dr. Raju submitted the results of his research to NOAA and several U.N. non-government organizations demonstrating that the so-called warming trend was from data in the early 1990s, and that the planet has actually been cooling off ever since then."

Dr. Schambrect looked over at Daryl, then back to Sean.

"They brought his research paper back to him and told him to change his conclusions and resubmit it to them."

Sean's shoulders dropped. It was the same old story of corruption and influence he had encountered so many times before.

"Did he do that? Did he change the conclusions on his own research?"

Dr. Schambrect nodded, a sad expression on his face.

"They told him if he didn't, he and his whole department at UM would never receive another dime in federal research grants or federal support in any form. It was a career-breaker, so he made the changes."

Sean nodded. It was the political hacks and money again. "And the rest of the ninety-seven percent?"

Dr. Schambrect shook his head. "It's actually more like one percent, not ninety-seven. If you get federal grants or federal financial support, you support the climate change agenda. It's a package deal."

This was why Sean hated political agendas: It was all about money and influence, never about truth and honesty.

"You two obviously don't support the global warming premise. Why not?"

Daryl shook his head slowly. "Well," he said. "First of all, the real science just isn't there, and secondly, we don't have any grant money at stake."

Sean tapped his pen on the table. "And if you did?"

The two PhDs glanced at each other. "Fortunately, we haven't been required to choose. That's one of the really difficult parts of university employment: being forced to choose between your own ethics and your career. So far, we've managed to avoid that dilemma."

On the drive back to DC, Sean kicked the whole argument back and forth in his mind. Could it really be that simple? The balance of plants and animals on the planet? It certainly makes more sense than carbon emissions, or cow farts. This can't be that complicated. If the whole problem in the environment is the balance between plants and animals, why are they spraying aerosols into the atmosphere? Wouldn't that just make things worse? It doesn't make any sense! This geoengineering thing is taking place for a reason, but why?

Chapter 24

"Close your eyes," Dr. Cowen said softly. "Take three deep breaths and release them slowly."

He was wearing a U.S. Space Command uniform instead of the regular Navy uniform he wore on their first encounter. Diane hadn't seen him since the interview in San Diego.

She breathed in and out slowly.

"Relax," he said slowly. "Breathe deeply. Let go of all of your thoughts. Just relax."

Ryan had told her about Dr. Cowen's exercise and how valuable it was in the simulators. She was skeptical, but if it was going to help her kill Zeta Greys, she was willing to try it. She let the tension drain from her body.

"In your mind, picture your last flight in the simulator,"

he said. "Visualize how everything seemed to move so fast. Now slow the motion down in your mind so everything moves in slow motion. Notice all of the detail. Draw everything from your peripheral vision into your awareness and remember all that is there."

Really? she thought. It actually happens that fast. How is my mind going to slow that down?

"See the trees, the rocks on the mountainside, the light, and the shadows. In your mind, imagine where you are in three dimensions: your distance from the ground, the mountainside, and the scout saucer. Keep yourself aware of your surroundings at each and every moment. Feel the motion of your craft. Make that motion part of your being, an extension of your own body. Sense the connection you have with your craft, how it banks and rolls. See your craft as the outer extension of yourself. Expect your fighter to function as your mind does, an integral part of you, naturally and smoothly."

She moved her fighter craft through the air, and imagined it as an extension of her own self: No division, no delay, just slow, smooth, flowing motion. Interesting, she thought. It seems to be working.

"Bring your fighter so it directly faces the scout saucer. As you are centered on the target, pull the trigger. See the light beam strike the scout saucer. Imagine your shot disabling the craft, knowing it will go down. Feel the satisfaction of confronting and destroying the scout saucer."

She imagined her shot penetrating the scout saucer, damaging the controls inside, and bringing it down. If only it worked this way in real life.

"Now begin again. This time make everything even slower. Bring in more detail, become more aware of your position in three dimensions. See each separate item within your field of vision clearly and distinctly, placed exactly in the space around you."

This seems to be more of a distraction, she thought. How is bringing in more detail going to slow things down?

"Become instinctively aware of every particle, each movement, and anticipate where each thing is going. See it move—feel its direction and speed, sense where it will be next and verify it is all happening in three dimensions, all around you."

She completed the exercise and slowly opened her eyes as he waited in silence.

"The human mind is amazing," he said. "A study at a university in Arizona determined that words and pictures flashed on a screen for as little as six-millionths of a second are recognized and processed by the mind, even though we don't consciously see the image with our eyes."

That's six microseconds. she thought. If that's really true, this might actually help. "And by slowing everything down in my mind?"

Dr. Cowen smiled. "We make our mind more aware of every detail around us, physically and spatially. As long as our eyes are open, we will see with our brain and not just our eyes. Take fifteen minutes after every simulator session and do this exercise. Re-experience your flights in exact detail and you will begin to fly your fighter craft with a precision and dexterity you cannot imagine."

That I will have to see for myself, she thought.

"Thank you, Dr. Cowen. I will do the exercises."

He nodded. "Each week we will meet to review your results and fine tune the process." He glanced at his watch. "Meanwhile, I have another pilot and RIO to interview. Remember to do the exercise after every simulator session."

"Will do."

Chapter 25

President Andrews looked up as Doug Franks entered the oval office. Franks looked both satisfied and concerned at the same time.

"We have the analysis of the hacked files from Charlie," Franks said.

Andrews closed the file on his desk and motioned Franks into a chair. "And?"

"Two files. Fortunately the list of corrupted officials and crooked corporation officers is smaller than the un-co-opted file. Each list is prioritized by level of influence." He handed the printout to Andrews and waited as the president flipped through the pages.

"Wow! Some of these names I can see as being more interested in their own advancement, but some of them are a real shocker."

Farnsworth, for example, was near the top of the corrupted list. That was unsettling.

"That's what I thought, too," Franks said.

Andrews continued down the list a ways, then looked up at Franks.

"We think of ourselves as shepherds, guiding a flock of sheep, and now we find out we're surrounded by wolves instead."

Wolves, Andrews thought. These are the same kind of people who, in Tau Ceti, are removed from the population and raised in their military academy on a moon.

"Exactly. Now what do we do?" Franks asked.

Andrews sat with his right hand over his mouth, his index finger resting under his nose, deep in thought. He slapped his hand on the desk and said, "Two things. First we flush the wolves out of our inner circle. Once that's done, we restructure and go after the rest."

Franks raised his eyebrows; apparently he expected something less drastic.

"When do you want Charlie to leak the list to Sean Wells?"

Andrews studied the printout for a few more seconds. This was extensive and was going to require an in-depth plan, which he currently didn't have.

"Let's do that now. Wells is going to want to verify everything before he does anything else. That'll give us a chance to get ahead of the curve."

When Franks left the room, Andrews walked slowly over to the window and gazed out, deep in thought. Wolves among the sheep. They seek power at the expense of others. Have I been any different? Wasn't it my desire for power that led me to seek the presidency? The only thing that changed the course of events was my meeting with Charlie and the realization that not only are we not alone in the universe, but we are under a covert assault by an alien race. Would I have been part of the problem, through my ignorance, if it weren't for someone sharing highly restricted information with me? Am I capable of doing what needs to be done to save our world?

He walked back to his desk and opened the small drawer on the top right. He retrieved the personal letter from the previous president, which had been waiting for him on his desk the day he was sworn in. He reread the letter, as he had numerous times since then. The advice wasn't political or partisan, but spoke of the soul-searching that must be done if he were to become an effective leader. "Your mind can be deceived," the advice said. "If you are to lead, it must be done through your heart. If your heart and soul are not in what you do, only failure can come of it. Whatever path you choose to pursue, send your heart there first. If it is at peace in that place, then commit everything you are, have, and do to make that destination a reality."

Chapter 26

Conrad Kaplan stood in front of the two-story-tall glass window complex that formed the south wall of the great room of his log and stone mansion in Jackson Hole, Wyoming. Large flakes of snow fluttered down in a lazy zigzag pattern, illumined in the night by the light radiating from his mountain get-away. He took another sip of Bourbon and turned to greet his most recent arrival.

Senator Roger Whitcolm, chairman of the powerful Senate Armed Services Committee was the last to arrive. Secretary of Defense Oliver Farnsworth sat on the plush couch, slowly puffing on his cigar, while Speaker of the House Joel Metzner stood in front of the blazing fireplace, warming his backside. U.S. Ambassador to the United Nations Ruth Poulton slowly paced the perimeter of the room.

"If you haven't officially met, I assume you are all familiar with Irwin Gould."

"Only by reputation," Whitcolm said, shaking the man's hand. "I believe I know your son, Ira, a VP at Malthus Investment Bank. Very astute young man."

Gould smiled at the compliment. "Yes, thank you."

Kaplan cleared his throat. "Shall we get down to business? Where are we on Bob Harper?"

Whitcolm nodded and took a seat. "The vice president is fully committed to the cause. We made sure Harper was on the ticket with Andrews just in case we needed a change in leadership. Andrews is well liked and was the most electable candidate in the presidential field, so we backed him as long as he went along for the ride."

Always have a plan for every contingency, Kaplan reminded himself.

"Andrews is under control?"

Farnsworth set his cigar down in the ashtray.

"He's been cooperating with the program so far," Farnsworth said. "I don't see any reason for that to change."

Kaplan took another sip of his drink, mulling things over.

"If you are not aware, after our demonstration of nuclear weapons in Japan in 1945, President Truman ordered General Eisenhower to come up with a plan to use nuclear weapons on Russia, and then to use Russia as a platform to defeat China. Russia was, and still is, considered the critical pivot point."

He paced in front of them, much as a university professor might do. He liked that image of himself.

"The problem was an effective delivery system. Russia was so large we couldn't fly our bombers over land to get on target without refueling or being shot down."

He took another sip of his drink.

"The race-to-space between the U.S and Russia was about the development of inter-continental ballistic missiles capable of delivering nuclear warheads half way around the world."

He paused and faced the group so they didn't miss the point.

"We came in second, in case you missed it."

He turned and continued his pacing.

"That morphed into the Cold War and a nuclear standoff with mutually assured destruction. The collapse of the Soviet Union changed the dynamics of that standoff, giving us the advantage we needed in our quest for full spectrum dominance. History has selected us as the inevitable dominating force on the planet, and I intend to see that selection through to its successful conclusion."

He swallowed the last of his drink and set the empty glass on the bar.

"The recent rise of Russia under their new president is troubling and poses a direct threat to our influence and status as the world's only superpower. We cannot allow this threat to materialize or to continue its growth. Russian power is a cancer in the world that must be removed."

He grinned, full of self-satisfaction.

"I am pleased to report that we will soon have a one hundred percent effective anti-ballistic missile system that can be launched from the border of Russia, eliminating the threat of ICBM retaliation. This is the last step before we neutralize Russia and coerce China into full submission."

Seventy years of planning and preparation, he thought, and finally Truman's vision of a unified world under U.S. direction and influence was coming within our grasp.

"This development will not only make us the preeminent military force on the planet, but it will elevate our commercial corporations to world dominance, opening the entire Russian and Chinese markets to us and our control. With the fall of the Russian and Chinese governments, their businesses will also fall to us. We will own the world market for everything."

What a rush, he thought, to be an instrumental part in making it all happen.

"I have brought Irwin Gould into the Partnership so his banking family will become the world's largest and most dominant financial organization in the history of the world. Each of you is currently in a position of power and influence within the United States. I am about to transform your positions from national to global. I just need to be assured that each of you knows your role and responsibilities."

Irwin Gould sat forward on the seat. "I will guarantee the private funding for our plan. With leveraged buyouts of ownership in natural resources and infrastructure, as we're doing in Ukraine, members of the Partnership will acquire these assets for a penny or two on the dollar."

Kaplan nodded and looked at Farnsworth.

"President Andrews has followed our lead," Farnsworth said. "He has ordered an extensive increase in the number of cruise missiles based on our nuclear powered submarines. He believes the warheads are conventional in nature. I have taken the liberty of upgrading those warheads to full thermonuclear status. Because of Russia's ten phased-array antenna facilities, we can no longer use ICBMs or space-based warheads without having them destroyed before they get to their targets. Only cruise missiles, skimming under the radar system, are an effective means of attack."

Kaplan gave him a knowing nod. "Initial targets?"

Farnsworth moved forward on the soft couch.

"Military bases, ICBM silos, and the phased array antenna systems. Once those are neutralized, we can use our ICBMs to finish the job."

Kaplan stopped and looked straight at Farnsworth.

"If Andrews believes the cruise missiles are conventional, how are you going to issue the nuclear arming codes?"

Farnsworth smiled. "Andrews will be incapacitated. Harper will authorize the nuclear option."

Kaplan nodded. Farnsworth was good. He thought things through and had a plan for contingencies. He liked people with initiative.

He turned to Whitcolm. "Funding for the military?"

Whitcolm grinned and leaned forward.

"I will make sure Congress provides the funding for our great armed services," Whitcolm said. "With the increased tension in Ukraine and Syria, plus the expanded terrorist activities, it's an easy sell."

Kaplan plopped two ice cubes into his glass and added some more Bourbon.

"Sanctions?"

He turned to face Ruth Poulton.

"President Andrews has supported sanctions against Russia and I am pushing those through the U.N.," Ruth said. "I will also use our Security Council veto power to prevent the U.N. from limiting our future actions."

Last piece of the plan, Kaplan thought, as he faced Metzner.

"We have the votes in the House to expand the trade agreements to legalize the takeover of Russian and Chinese businesses," Metzner said. "Part of the legislation is already in place as subsections of existing trade agreements. We just need to add connecting phraseology in the new trade bill to vastly expand the interpretation. No one will connect the dots before everything is in place."

Conrad Kaplan raised his glass into the air. "To the world, under our control."

Chapter 27

Sean Wells was going through a paper entitled "Solar Radiation Management by Stratospheric Aerosol Injection" online when he was interrupted by a knock on his hotel room door. He closed his laptop and looked through the peephole lens in the door. The guy standing in the hall was tall, and on the thin side, with light sandy hair and light brown skin. He appeared to be in his early twenties, and didn't seem to be particularly dangerous, so Sean opened the door.

"Mr. Wells, my name is Charlie. I have some information that I think you'll find interesting."

Okay, Sean thought, another citizen in search of money for information.

"You have a last name, Charlie?"

Charlie paused, calmly gazing at Sean. "I need to

remain anonymous."

Sean studied him for a moment. "How did you come by the information you have?"

Charlie glanced around at the hotel room in back of Sean.

"I can't really explain that to you at this point."

Sean smiled. Another version of the shuck and jive routine. How original! "So the information is either entirely bogus or it was obtained illegally."

Charlie smiled at him. "I'm prepared to let you be the judge of whether the information is real or, as you say, bogus. I'm confident you will find it interesting, either way."

Fair enough, Sean thought. Now for the bottom line. "How much?"

Charlie glanced up and down the hallway.

"Money?" Charlie said. "I have no need for money. Let's say the information is being provided in the interest of the good of society."

Sean tipped his head and grinned. "So you're a whistleblower?"

Charlie gazed at him again. "Yes, a whistleblower."

Uh-huh. We'll see. "Who do you work for?"

The hint of a smile played across Charlie's face.

"I don't work for anybody, at least no one I can discuss with you."

Probably not true, Sean thought. But what else did I expect?

Charlie grinned at him again. So what did he find so amusing?

"So who *did* you work for?"

This feels a little more like mental fencing and less like a negotiation, Sean thought.

"Mr. Wells, if you're not interested in the information, I understand. I won't waste any more of your time."

Charlie turned to leave.

"Hey, Charlie? Look kid, I just want to know the background, the history, where the information came from, who had possession of it. That helps me evaluate the importance of what you have."

Charlie turned slowly to face Sean.

"Oh, I think that will be self-evident."

Sean glanced up and down the hotel hallway. No one else was there.

"Okay, come on in. Let's take a look at what you've got."

Charlie sat patiently as Sean scanned through the files on the USB drive for the next two hours. Most of the documents were official reports on FBI and NSA letterhead, all signed, dated, and file-stamped by the Office of Personnel Management. Some of them were a condensed analysis of the corruption and illegal dealings of people in very high positions of power and authority, all with the associated evidence trail and the supporting documents, including financial records.

The OPM hacking story, Sean thought. These are the files. "When do I get the rest of it? These files have been scrubbed."

Charlie gazed at Sean in the same relaxed manner. "The code word operations."

The kid caught on fast. "Yes. That's what ties everything together."

Charlie nodded. "That will require a certain level of trust, which has not yet been developed."

Sean smiled. This kid was good. "So how much is the rest of the information going to cost me?"

Charlie smiled. "Trust cannot be purchased, Mr. Wells. It has to be earned."

That was refreshing, Sean thought. Maybe he means it.

"Everybody has an agenda, kid. What's yours?"

Charlie's expression turned serious. "Let's leave the details for a while, until you can fully appreciate my motives. For now, I can tell you my motivation is compassion with an element of revenge. Will that suffice?"

"For now."

* * *

As soon as Charlie left, Sean called his editor.

"I just got a ton of documents dumped in my lap. We're talking corruption and illegal activities at the highest levels of government, defense contractors, and international corporations. It's all here—well *most* of it's here. I have evidence, document trails, investigations, financial transfers, bank statements—the whole nine yards. I just need time to verify everything."

It was hard to contain his excitement for a story like this.

"What about the global warming story?" Ed asked.

He can't be serious. "You can forget about that. This is important."

Here was that pregnant pause he hated so much. Why did editors always do that?

"Unfortunately, I can't forget about it. Global warming is the general manager's pet dog and you're my only pit bull."

Sean shook his head. The dog-eat-dog analogy again.

"So, you don't want the new story?"

Sean closed his eyes and waited.

"Don't pull that crap with me, Wells. I want both stories. Now find a way to make that happen."

Sean looked at the receiver in his hand. He hung up on me again. Well, I guess some things will never change.

Sean's thoughts returned to Charlie. I've got no way to contact him. All he said was he would know when I needed to see him. What a strange kid.

Chapter 28

Diane woke and quickly sat up in her bed. She looked at the clock: 1:48 a.m. She dressed in a hurry, left her room, and walked down the hall to Ryan's room to knock quietly on his door. As she was about to give up, he opened the door, still half asleep.

"What?"

"I've got something I have to try in the simulator. You coming?"

Ryan rolled his eyes. "Can't it wait until tomorrow?"

She put her hands on her hips. "No."

He closed his eyes and breathed out slowly. "Okay, okay. Just give me a few seconds."

"Meet you there." Diane rushed through the hall, down the stairs, and into their simulator room. She flipped on the lights, powered up the equipment, climbed into the pilot seat, and strapped in. Ryan entered the room, hopped into the RIO seat, and fastened his harness.

"Okay, what are we doing?" he asked.

He activated the simulator program and turned on the screens.

"Something came to me in a dream. I just want to try it out before I forget what it was."

Ryan stopped and tilted his head.

"A dream? You woke me up in the middle of the night for a dream?"

She breathed out quickly. "Hey, most of our best inventions have come from dreams."

Ryan shook his head. "Unbelievable." He sighed, then said, "Okay. Let's try it."

"This is going to be rough, so hang on tight."

The simulator started at normal speed. Diane turned off the weapon lock system, pushed the thruster to forty percent thrust, and banked into the valley. As soon as she saw the scout saucer she started firing at it in alternating mode, one shot every half second. She started jerking the control stick randomly to each side, forward and back. The simulator banged violently in response, side to side and up and down. The scout saucer lifted off the ground and fired its light beam at them. It missed for the first time ever. She kept jerking the controls as her intuition guided her and continued firing at the scout saucer, as it bolted up into the sky. She pushed the thrust to sixty percent and flew straight at it. The next light beam from the scout saucer hit them and the simulator screens went dark.

"You stopped jerking," Ryan said.

"It's jinking, not jerking." Jinking is what you do with the controls, she thought.

"Whatever. It was working, so keep doing it. You ready

to go again?"

She took a deep breath. "Yep."

Ryan started the simulator and the screens came on again. She pushed to forty percent thrust and flew into the valley. Again, as soon as she saw the scout saucer she began firing and jinking the control stick. The saucer lifted off the ground and fired at them, missing with every shot. This time as the saucer shot up, she continued jinking the control stick and accelerated to sixty percent thrust. The scout saucer was going even faster, so she pushed the thrust to seventy percent. The jinking became even more violent, slamming them against the side restraints of the simulator and bouncing them roughly in their seats. She switched from alternating fire to using both particle beam cannons together. The scout saucer was still accelerating away from them into the upper reaches of the atmosphere, so she pushed the thrust to eighty percent while continuing to fire. The light beams from the saucer continued to miss them.

One of her particle beam cannon shots connected with the scout saucer, causing it to tip to the side and start a slow arc back down to the earth. She continued the jinking and let her intuition guide her finger on the trigger. The particle beam cannon hit the scout saucer a second time, sending it into a tight spin. No light flashes came from the damaged saucer as it fell to the earth below. Diane decreased the amount of thrust and jinking and followed the saucer down. With the smoother flight she was able to aim more accurately, hitting the scout saucer three more times with both cannons. Smoke streamed from the damaged saucer as it plunged into the denser air below. She slowed her speed and watched as the scout saucer eventually crashed into the side of a mountain.

Ryan powered down the simulator, released his harness, and jumped from his seat. "Oh my God!" he shouted. "You did it! First kill!"

He was dancing around, waving his arms, acting as if he had just scored a touchdown in the Super Bowl. She shook her head. Guys! she thought.

She released her harness and slowly climbed out of her seat. "It worked," she said, her heart still pounding in her ears. Dizzy and disoriented, she leaned against the side of the simulator.

"So what was in your dream?" Ryan couldn't contain his enthusiasm.

"Every time the saucer fired at us, it was a direct hit. They never missed. Their aiming system had to lock onto us for every shot. Their firing lock is faster than ours, but it still takes time. Jinking our flight path alters where we are when their weapon fires, so they miss. They can't compensate for rapid random movements."

She glanced up. Admiral Hollis stood in the doorway, mouth open, staring at her.

"Sir, how long . . . ?"

"Long enough." The expression on his face was pure excitement. "This is the breakthrough we've been waiting for. I've got to call the president." He turned and raced down the hall. "And congratulations!" he shouted from the stairway.

* * *

Diane couldn't sleep. She slowly paced a semicircle around her bed, her heart still pounding. It's just a simulation, she reminded herself. A real life encounter could be entirely different. The disorientation remained and she still felt dizzy. Why do I feel like crap?

A soft knock on the door drew her attention. She opened it, thinking Ryan would be there. Instead, Dr. Cowen stood there, looking her over closely.

"You feel up to talking?" he asked. She stepped back

and motioned him in. "I assume you heard."

"Hollis. He's concerned about how you're doing."

She held on to the doorknob as a wave of nausea swept over her.

"I'm okay. I just feel a bit strange is all."

Dr. Cowen nodded. He pulled a small light from his pocket, shined it in each of her eyes, moved it away and then back at her eyes again. "Hollis described what you went through in the simulator. The human body isn't designed to take that kind of shock. The jolting must have been severe."

"It was." She took a deep breath, trying to stabilize the growing nausea. "So why was Ryan able to stand that? It didn't seem to affect him like it did me."

Dr. Cowen shook his head. "Actually, I just came from Ryan's room. He's throwing up with a severe migraine headache."

Her shoulders slumped. "Swell. Not much of a breakthrough if it makes everyone sick."

Dr. Cowen listened to her heart with his stethoscope.

"Well, it is. Do you know what it took to develop the flight suit you wore in your Super Hornet?"

He wrapped the blood pressure cuff around her arm.

"I just know it was custom-made and skin-tight."

He pumped the cuff bulb and applied the stethoscope to the inside of her elbow.

"That was to keep your internal organs and bones in place and minimize the G forces on your body. Decades of refinement went into the design of that suit. We didn't know what we would encounter in the new fighter craft, but just assumed the simulator wouldn't cause any damage to anybody."

He watched the gage as she felt her pulse pushing through under the pressure of the cuff.

"We just never imagined someone would do what you

did. The jarring forces overwhelm the nervous system, causing dizziness, disorientation, painful joints, severe headaches, and nausea. Frankly, I'm amazed you're still upright."

So was she. "So it's of no real use to us, is it?"

"No, no, no," Dr. Cowen said as he recorded her stats. "These are solvable problems. We already know how to fix them. Hollis is on the phone right now with Ceti Research. They're adding shock absorbers and padding to the sides, top, and bottom of the seats. Now that we know what we're dealing with, we can complete the design of the new flight suits. This *is* the breakthrough we needed—don't you ever doubt that for a second. We just need to adapt the fighter craft, that's all."

She started feeling nauseated again and ran for the bathroom, retching into the toilet.

"It's okay," Dr. Cowen said softly. "It'll pass. I gave Ryan some meds to help him cope and get some rest. I have some for you, too."

She nodded as he handed her two small yellow tablets and filled a glass with water. She swallowed them and moved slowly over to her bed.

"Sleep as long as you can. You and Ryan are off duty until further notice."

* * *

She woke at 10:14 a.m. feeling exhausted. The disorientation was gone along with the dizziness. Her joints ached, though they hadn't before. Diane took a long hot shower and dressed. She slowly walked down the hall to the cafeteria, moving to the side to avoid moving construction vehicles. She didn't expect anybody to be there at this hour, but all the other officers, except Ryan and Hollis, were sitting at the long table. When she entered the room they all stood and saluted.

"Guys, you shouldn't be doing that." She didn't expect

their recognition.

"Honors for first kill," Clay Obers said.

She shook her head. "It was just in the simulator. It could be a computer glitch. The whole thing may not work in real life."

She sensed someone behind her again and turned to see who it was.

"It's not a glitch," Hollis said, walking into the room. "First thing I checked. I sent the data from your simulator flight to Ceti Research. They're incorporating your 'jinking' into the control system."

"Sir, I—" This was embarrassing for her.

"In your honor, we're adding a new control switch to the fighter console, labeled JINK. You're getting credit for this breakthrough whether you want it or not, Lieutenant. I suggest you get used to it."

Clay smiled. "I like it. Jink Zadanski. Has a ring to it."

She rolled her eyes. "Come on guys, it's not that big a deal."

"It is to me," Ryan said from the doorway. "And I like the call sign, Jink Zadanski."

"As I said," Hollis added. "Get used to it, Lieutenant."

She closed her eyes. "Jink!" She couldn't think of a worse call sign.

"So how much thrust?" Obers asked.

It's always about thrust with him. Doesn't he think about anything else? "When I finally shot the scout saucer?"

He nodded and stepped a little closer to her. "Yeah, how much?"

Okay, hot shot, you wanted to know, she thought. Try this on for size: "Eighty percent."

Obers staggered back momentarily. "Eighty?"

"Holy cow," Simmons said.

Ryan nodded, "It was eighty percent, all right."

Finally got to him, she thought. "It's less disorienting when you get away from the ground," Diane said. "And it helps when you're chasing a scout saucer that's trying to get away."

She smiled at his discomfort.

"Still," Obers said, "it puts a whole new meaning to high speed chase."

"It does," Hollis agreed. "In the meantime, it's going to take two or three days to make all the modifications to the simulators, so you have some down time. I suggest you get some rest, because when we get back to it, I expect a hundred hours a week of simulator time. Understood?"

"Yes, sir," they replied together.

As Hollis turned away, Diane interrupted. "Sir?" she asked. "Can the simulators be cross-connected? What I mean is, can we fly the simulators in a coordinated attack and be able to see each other, like real life?"

Hollis grinned at her. "Technically, yes, we just hadn't gotten that far before. I'm putting you in charge of coordinating attack strategy, Lieutenant. Make it happen."

"Yes, sir."

* * *

By late afternoon crews from Ceti Research were arriving with their equipment. Diane stood in the doorway and watched them remove the screens, seats, and controls from the simulators. Then they began cutting away portions of the metal frame.

She wondered if Theo might make an appearance again at Peregrine Base. She hoped he would.

"Jink?" Ryan spoke from behind her. "You're needed upstairs for flight suit fitting."

She cringed; irritated that everyone had shifted so

quickly to calling her 'Jink.' There wasn't anything she could do about it now. She was stuck with it.

"It's getting real, isn't it?" Diane said. Nervousness filled her chest. Would the jinking work in real life? Was she going to be able to extract her revenge on the Zeta Greys? Would she finally get justice for her brother's death?

"Yep," Ryan said. "From this point on, it's about combat readiness. In the end, we win or we die. This training and practice will be the deciding factor. If we do it right, we win. Otherwise . . . ?"

* * *

After dinner Diane wandered down to the simulator rooms, hoping that Theo would be there. She slowly worked her way down the wide hall, zigzagging so she could check in every room. She sighed as she looked into the last room. He wasn't here. She turned abruptly to leave and collided with someone in the hallway.

"I'm sorry," Theo said. "I guess I should have made more noise—or something."

She tried to steady herself by reaching for the wall. He reached out and held her arm for support. She grabbed on to him and looked up into his eyes.

"You're here," she said.

He nodded. "I wanted to meet you. What you came up with is amazing."

She glanced away, feeling a bit self-conscious.

"When I asked where you were, everyone kept calling you 'Jink.' "

Her face flushed and her shoulders slumped. "Please don't call me that."

He smiled at her and waited.

"Diane," she said softly.

He nodded. "Diane. I like that. I'm—"

"Theo," she said, "I know." She blushed again. "Everybody knows your name."

Now he was blushing. "I guess they do. I just—I mean . . ."

They began chuckling together.

"So, coffee?" he asked.

She smiled and nodded.

They sat in the cafeteria, slowly sipping their coffee.

"You're different than I thought you'd be," Theo said.

Diane found that amusing. "Really?"

"You know," he glanced around, "with the nature of this unit. I kind of expected everyone to be hardened macho warriors, that sort of thing."

She smiled. "And now?"

"You're more like a real person." He seemed excited about that.

I *am* a real person, she thought. The expression on her face must have startled him.

"That's not what I meant." His face was red again. "I'm really messing this up, aren't I?"

For being such a brilliant person, he was certainly stumbling for words around her. She tried to think of a clever comeback—something to put him more at ease. Her mind wasn't cooperating much, either. She was drawn to him in a way she hadn't experienced before. Strong physical urges that surprised her with their intensity. That's when she realized he was struggling with the same kind of feelings himself.

"It's okay," she said. "I'm feeling it, too."

He smiled and relaxed a bit. "So: brilliant, beautiful, and intuitive. How could it get any better than this?"

She laughed. "I was thinking the same thing."

He looked puzzled. "That I'm beautiful?"

She shook her head. "Okay, handsome. Is that better?"

He nodded.

"In a beautiful person kind of way," she added, a sly grin on her lips.

Now he was embarrassed again.

"Look, I . . . I really like you," he said. "With our jobs and the upcoming war, we may not have many opportunities to get to know each other in the usual way. I don't want to waste any chances we may have."

Bold, but practical, she thought. What's not to like about him?

She glanced at her cup, then back at him. "I really like you, too. It's just that there's no privacy here at all. Peregrine Base is under constant surveillance."

He nodded. "Ceti Research is like that, too. But, because of my position, I do have some privacy there. Maybe I could arrange for you to visit, if you would like that?"

She grinned. "I would like that."

Chapter 29

Diane and Ryan stood examining the simulator as the work crew carried the remaining equipment out of the small room. After three days of twenty-four-hour work crews climbing all over them, the simulators were finally back together. Short shock absorbers surrounded the inner frame of the two-seat control section. Stiff foam padding had been added above, below, and all around the control seats, form-fitted to each occupant.

"It looks like half a cocoon," Diane said. She pushed on the new foam padding. It was a little stiff, but it did give. She smiled and nodded. This was going to work. Her mind drifted back to Theo, wondering when she would get to see him again.

"So how are we supposed to see out of the side window?" Ryan asked. "The foam comes around the sides up to our face-shields."

Diane leaned into the simulator and smiled. "The part where our helmet fits is mounted on some sort of a swivel system. The padding will move with us, protecting our head and neck, see?"

Ryan reached in and moved the head restraint system. "Clever."

"Now all we need are our flight suits and we can get back to work."

Jed Collier poked his head through the doorway. "Hollis wants everyone up in the conference room."

Diane and Ryan were the last to arrive.

"Your flight suits are here," Hollis said. "From this point on you will be in your suits, wearing your helmets in the simulator at all times. Get used to real-life conditions, people; your fighters are a week away. Each helmet is equipped with a communications connector, which you will have to plug in before you can talk with one another. Your helmet and flight suit are fully shielded from outside electromagnetic waves and telepathic influence. The comm connector also grounds your suit, so make sure it is properly connected."

Hollis handed out single sheets with the communications protocol printed on them.

"You will have new digital encryption algorithms installed before each flight," Hollis said. "Forty comm channels, forty different algorithms. If you suspect the Zetas are getting through the algorithm, change channels."

Clay Obers raised his hand. "How will we know if they are getting through?"

Hollis acknowledged Clay's question with a nod. "If you think you have the upper hand in a fight, they're probably getting through, so change channels. Any other questions?"

Glen Simmons waved his hand in the air. "How bad is the jinking? We all saw what it did to Zadanski and Atkinson."

Diane thought it was a good question. She wanted to know, especially after what she and Ryan went through.

"Jinking in the simulators will be progressive," Hollis said. "We're starting at ten percent movement and gradually increasing it by one percent for every hour of training time. By the time you finish this week you'll be ready for the real thing in your fighter craft. Come get your flight suits. Simulator work begins right after lunch."

* * *

Sean began going through the lab reports he got from Patrick. He started with the California air and water analysis looking for aluminum and barium. The reports went back to 1980. A few minerals and other contaminants were present in the air: mostly lead, cadmium, sulfur, and hydrocarbons from incomplete combustion of gasoline and diesel fuel—that and an extensive list of volatile organic compounds listed by the California Environmental Protection Agency's Air Resources Board. The amount of aluminum and barium on each report was zero. Then in 1991, both aluminum and barium showed up for the first time. How long did Stephanie say they had been doing aerosol spraying? He checked his notes and thought, Twenty-five years, which would bring us back to . . . 1991.

The amount of aluminum and barium increased each year. By the new millennium, the levels rose above the maximum allowable set by the U.S. Environmental Protection Agency. He got on his computer and began going through the laws and regulations for the State of California regarding aluminum and barium remediation. Nothing. California had aggressively gone after all kinds of pollutants, but not aluminum or barium. Why?

Chapter 30

Diane was the last one to join the others in the conference room.

"We have a very special guest with us this morning," Hollis began. "He said we should call him Etnar. He has been helping us with the technology for the fighter craft and the particle beam cannons. I don't want you to be shocked by his appearance. He is a bit taller than we are, and has to duck to get through our small hallways and doors. Etnar is actually from the Zenetae star system in the Andromeda constellation. Although he is a member of the one hundred and thirty-nine star system Andromeda Council, he is here in an unofficial capacity, so his existence and presence is highly classified. Etnar also has a telepathic human with him, by the name of Charlie, who will help with communications."

Jed Collier, head of security, opened the door to the conference room. Everyone in the room moved back slightly, partially from the initial shock but also to make room. Etnar was bent over as he squeezed through the doorway. He stood up straight, taking up most of the height to the ten foot ceiling. Charlie walked in behind Etnar.

Diane's heart began beating rapidly. She had talked with Hollis and a few of the other pilots regarding extraterrestrials and what an encounter might be like, but she found herself quite unprepared for the reality of actually being in the presence of such a being. It was one thing to intellectually accept the existence of extraterrestrial life, but a direct encounter was unexpectedly both emotionally and physically shocking.

She could feel the serene emotional power of Etnar's presence in the room, as if his consciousness and the strength of his mind pushed everything else back out of the way. A feeling of deep peace and calmness surrounded her. As nervous as she may have been, Etnar's energy brought a quiet confidence to her. Etnar's physical appearance still generated a fear-based reaction in her body and some nausea, partially at least from his size, color, and shape. Seeing a photograph or drawing of him standing next to a human before a personal meeting took place might have eased her reaction, but that hadn't happened. The combination of emotional stillness and physical shock she was experiencing felt both empowering and somewhat devastating at the same time. She just had to do the best she could under the circumstances.

"Etnar is telepathic," Hollis said. "He knows your thoughts and emotions. You can ask him any question you may have. Charlie is here to convert the telepathic messages from Etnar into words, so there are no misunderstandings."

Diane stood. "How much of our thoughts and feelings does he know? I mean, does he know what we are thinking now, or does it include everything we have ever thought and felt?"

Others nodded in agreement. They wanted to know, too.

Charlie smiled. "I understand your concern. Telepathy is limited to the current moment. Your secrets are safe."

Diane sat down wondering just how truthful Charlie was being. For now, she would have to accept what he said at face value.

"I wish to communicate my admiration for your courage in choosing to fight against the Zeta Greys," Charlie said, speaking for Etnar. "The interstellar community is not unified. There are alliances and conflicts. We seek to minimize the conflicts within the accepted law of our galaxy. That law is simple, in that it recognizes a civilization's freedom to form treaties and contracts with any other group. Members of the various alliances normally do not interfere with established treaties or contracts, but under our galactic law, the more powerful party to a contract has a higher standard of duty to honor the terms of the treaty and must not abuse its position in the relationship.

"In your year of 1954, a peaceful alliance approached your President Eisenhower, offering advanced technology and medical assistance. They offered to cure all of your diseases and extend your life span to more than two hundred years. Their only requirement was that your world cease the development of nuclear weapon technology. Your president declined that offer, as did the leaders of two other dominant countries. Six months later the Zeta Greys met with your president, offering advanced weapon and propulsion technology in exchange for access to animals and a small percentage of your population for medical and genetic experimentation. Your president and the leaders of the two other world powers at that time agreed to those terms.

"We have allowed that treaty to stand based on your freedom to create and maintain contracts. However, as is often the case with the Zeta Greys, they have abused that treaty to your detriment. We will not interfere directly, but have decided to provide assistance to you so you can break free from your agreement with the Zeta Greys. This is not an easy process and should not be taken lightly."

Etnar pointed at Diane. "What is your question?"

"Why are they here and what do they want?"

"The Zeta Greys are part of the Corporate Alliance. Their primary purpose is to obtain natural resources and trade those resources as finished advanced technology for a profit. They have been mining the minerals on your moon, and other moons in your solar system for thirty-five hundred years. They became annoyed by your landings and exploration of the moon and ordered your leaders to stop any attempts to take possession of the moon. They consider it their property, not yours."

What do you mean "their" property? Diane thought. "They're operating on our moon?" she asked. "Does this explain why nobody's been back to the moon in over forty years?"

"Yes. They have established a large base on the far side of the moon. Interference with the Zeta Greys always results in continuous war."

Well, she thought. So it comes down to the last one standing; a human or a Grey? Maybe it doesn't have to be all or nothing . . .

"I believe the Zeta Greys are some kind of a drone. Is somebody controlling them? Maybe remotely?" Diane asked.

"No. Before you engage them you need to understand a little more about them. Forty thousand years ago, they were created by a human-type race. Those humans were very passionate and emotionally unstable, not too different from the way you are now. They fought constant wars among themselves, with devastating results."

That feels a little too close to home, Diane thought.

"In an effort to end the wars, two competing corporations merged. The first corporation had developed a very sophisticated artificial intelligence computer system. The second developed a biological neural network from brain tissue that could function as a computer. The combination of the two technologies produced the first drones, as you call them."

Diane frowned. "So nobody controls them? Doesn't somebody have to be in charge?" she asked.

"Not directly, no. Their bodies are created from synthetic material connected to muscle, nerve, and circulation system cells to form a functioning being. The neural network computer that forms their brain communicates by way of an electronic interface with an extended computer system. The Zeta Greys have a limited sense of self consciousness, preferring to function as a group or communal consciousness."

Like bees or ants? she wondered.

"What happens when we kill one of them?" Ryan asked.

Yeah, good question, she thought.

"The body dies, but everything they were and learned is retained within their massive computer system. Their identity and knowledge is downloaded, through the electronic interface, into a new body. They do not fear death. It is essentially meaningless to them."

Etnar pointed to Helen Catalano.

"You mentioned medical and genetic experimentation. What exactly are they doing?"

Is that why they took Daniel? Diane wondered.

"The Zeta Gays have no reproductive system. They clone new bodies. The problem they face is that the cloned cells degrade over time and become genetically useless. They

183

solve that problem by splicing new genetic material into the stem cells to grow new bodies."

Diane's shoulders slumped. That's all Daniel was to them? A source of genetic material? Like a lab rat?

"Doesn't there have to be some genetic similarity for them to use the new stem cells?" Helen asked.

Diane looked over at Helen. She felt her frown deepening.

"There does. The original human-type population of their home planet is genetically connected to your human race on this planet. You and the civilization that created the Zeta Greys are, in a sense, cousins."

Anger began rising in Diane's chest. The injustice of it all was getting to her.

"After the corporate clones were developed, the humans on their planet became afraid of them. They tried to destroy the clones, but succeeded only in driving them underground. The clones developed smaller bodies and larger eyes to cope with living underground. They wanted more intelligence and mental capacity, so they enlarged the head and cranial volume in successive generations."

These things really are disgusting, Diane thought.

"So what happened to the human population?" Glen Simmons asked.

The same thing that happened to Daniel, I'll bet, Diane thought.

"Eventually, through advanced technology, the clones subdued the human population on their home planet and used them for a supply of genetic material for more cloned bodies. When they exhausted the human supply of genetic material, they expanded to other human-based planets, initially trading technology for genetic stem cells. They gradually introduced AI and neural networking technology to each human population and used it to create a new cloned species. Each human world inevitably suffered the same fate: extinction due to genetic harvesting."

Diane was fuming over the injustice. "And you didn't save them?" she asked.

She glanced around the room. Was she the only one who was feeling this angry?

"First, we do not directly interfere with the treaties, but more importantly, the human populations were not capable of fighting back against the Zeta Greys."

No, she wasn't the only one. Diane could feel the level of anger rising in the room.

"But you're helping us. Why?"

Etnar made eye contact with her. He nodded slightly then continued, "You may not understand this at first, but you are considered a very violent and unpredictable species. Two different alliances have quarantined your planet in an effort to keep you from developing advanced capabilities, then invading and waging war on your galactic neighbors. The Zeta Greys did not agree with the quarantine and saw it as an opportunity to exploit your planet and its population."

"We're violent and unpredictable?" Helen asked.

Look who's talking, Diane thought as she looked at Helen. She was the one who shoved Clay on my first day here.

"Consider your own history. It is essentially a continuous series of wars and conflicts. You have little regard for your own species, abusing and killing your own populations with more and more efficiency. Your violence and disdain for each other made you ripe for intervention by the Zeta Greys."

Diane glanced at the floor and nodded. He's right. We're a large part of the problem.

"You were offered peace, health, and prosperity in exchange for the elimination of nuclear weapons. Your leaders chose the path of power and destruction over peace, health, and prosperity. Now that your current president sees what your choice has brought, he has decided to break with the Zetas and fight for your survival as a species."

So this is why Hollis and the rest of us are here. We may be humanity's last chance.

"Some of us believe you have the potential to not only survive, but to mature into a productive civilization that can live in peace with your galactic neighbors. You will have to prove yourselves.

"First, defeat the Zeta Greys and drive them from your solar system. Second, you must stop the violence and abuse on your own planet. Live together in harmony for a hundred of your years. Eliminate poverty, disease, and intolerance. Only then will other worlds begin to trust you."

Okay, Diane thought. I can see us defeating the Zeta Greys, but stopping all violence, poverty, and disease? Eliminating intolerance? I don't know. Maybe we can't. Then what?

"We do not know if you will survive the process, but we are willing to give you a chance by introducing you to a certain level of technology. Your risk is survival, which is tenuous at best. Our risk is that you will succeed against the Zeta Greys, then continue to use that technology to wage war against your neighbors. The future is in your hands. There are consequences and costs for each path you take. Choose wisely."

Etnar made eye contact with each individual in the room. He turned and left. Etnar ducked through the doorway and Collier closed the door behind him. Charlie stepped to the front of the room.

"I'm sure you have a lot of questions," he said. "Etnar has to keep moving to hide his presence on our planet. He's not supposed to be here at all."

"His people have shared an amazing level of technology with us," Diane said. "If, as he says, we are so unpredictable and violent, why does he trust us with so much capability? Doesn't this also put his people at risk?"

Charlie smiled and shook his head. "You misunderstand what we have," he said. "Compared to the Andromedans, what Etnar has given you is the equivalent of giving fire to cave dwellers."

Diane frowned at the comparison. Cave dwellers? Really?

"Hollis said Etnar comes from the Zenetae star system," Diane said. "How far away is that?" I've never even heard of that star before, she thought.

"Something in the range of four thousand light years."

Diane sat with her mouth open. "Hollis said that at a hundred percent thrust our fighter craft could exceed the speed of light. How long does it take them to travel four thousand light years?"

Charlie glanced at Hollis. "Actual flight time?" Charlie asked. "About two hours, your time. As I said, all they have given you is a little fire. It's actually a very small gift from their perspective. They consider their help as little more than a scientific experiment. You still have to prove you can use it responsibly."

Diane was feeling overwhelmed. If faster than light fighters were like a little fire, how advanced were some of their other technologies?

"Etnar talked about artificial intelligence and neural networks. Aren't those cutting edge technologies our scientists are just now developing?" Ryan asked.

Diane looked at Ryan, impressed with his questions.

"It depends on where you look," Charlie said. "AI and neural networks have been around for millions of years, it's new here in your world, in this current evolution of your civilization."

Current evolution? Diane wondered. What else aren't

we being told?

"I don't understand," Ryan said. "These technologies hold so much potential for us as people. Etnar spoke of them as if they're evil."

Charlie nodded. "The technology, in and of itself, isn't evil. It's what people do with that technology that matters. Right now AI is a new reality in your world and neural networks are not far behind. But for the Zeta Greys, they are life itself. As early clones, they were programmed in the corporate ethos, ethics, and goals—all logic was driven by profit and loss. The first clones were used for deep space exploration and moon mining operations."

Which they're still doing, Diane thought.

"The present evolution of Zeta Greys have retained a large part of that early corporation level programming. They still mine for natural resources and closely consider profits and losses."

"And their treaty with us?" Glen Simmons asked.

Charlie turned to face him. "Amounts to a covert corporate takeover."

Jeez, Diane thought. It sounds like interstellar relations aren't much different than how things work here. "Leaving us where, exactly?" she asked.

Charlie nodded slightly and smiled at her.

"The Zeta Greys consider you assets of Corporation Earth. Once the takeover is complete, Zeta-human hybrids will control the planet and the rest of you will be relegated to the role of genetic stem cell production."

Like animals on a farm? Diane thought. Not after what they did to Daniel. Not if I can help it.

"If opposition to the Zeta Greys results in endless war," Clay said, "how can we ever expect to win? How do we drive them from our solar system?"

Charlie grinned. "Profit and loss. In today's world, you

defeat a hostile corporate takeover in business by taking all of the profit and assets out of the operation, leaving only losses. We will use the same basic strategy with the Zeta Greys. When their short-term losses exceed their long-term gains, they will leave—not before."

If loss of Zeta Grey lives has little meaning to them, what's it going to take to create significant losses? Diane wondered.

"This isn't a fair fight," Helen said. "We're going into this with a huge deficit of fighter craft and people. They have thirty-five hundred years' worth of experience and equipment. We have only six fighter craft and twelve people. It isn't fair."

Hollis stepped forward. "No, it isn't. But right now, fair or not, this is the only chance we have."

Clay was shaking his head. "This sounds like long odds to me," he said. "How do we even up our chances against them?"

Hollis nodded. "That's actually one of the advantages we have from our long history of warfare. We know how to fight against overwhelming odds."

Ryan smiled and said, "Guerilla warfare tactics."

Hollis nodded. "Precisely. Hit and run attacks. The Zeta Greys have deep underground bases spread out all over the world. It's difficult for us to get into those bases, but the basic weakness of long Zeta Grey supply chains remains. If we can cut off their supply of material and means of escape, eventually we can win. It's all a matter of time and persistence."

Diane looked at Ryan with new respect. She was impressed.

"So how do we keep the Zeta Greys from swarming all over us with hundreds of saucers and simply wiping us out?" Simmons asked.

Hollis gave a slight smile. "We also are developing the means of limiting their saucers from accessing our planet. Once in full operation, our Planetary Shield will destroy all saucers attempting to enter or leave our atmosphere."

Diane smiled. A planetary shield would give them a fighting chance. "Won't that also affect our fighter craft? It would mean we are stuck here along with the Zeta Greys."

Hollis shook his head. "It's selective. We can target individual sections of the upper atmosphere at any given time. If you are flying neck-and-neck with a scout saucer we can't hit one without destroying the other. If the two craft are ten miles apart, no problem."

Diane could see where this was going. "So if we flush them off the ground and into the upper atmosphere?"

Hollis grinned. "Then we can bag 'em."

Chapter 31

Psycon Industries, Inc. was a small corporation, comparatively speaking, but it was run by close associates of Conrad Kaplan. Sean discovered that each one of the five-member board of directors was a mid-level executive in a different company controlled by Kaplan. Psycon Industries was a privately held corporation, so very little information was publically accessible. No stock was available and there were no EDGAR listings. There were no customers listed in any public database, nor were any sales figures available—except in the files Sean had received from Charlie.

Psycon Industries produced one product: a synthetic polymer microfiber made from modified organic compounds. This had to be the microfibers Patrick said were in the chemtrail mix. Psycon owned two manufacturing facilities: one in Spain and one in India. According to some of the lab reports from Patrick, these polymer microfibers were showing up in residue samples from Italy, Greece, Turkey, Lebanon, Syria, and Iraq. Sean checked the wind patterns for the area and found that they were all in a prevailing westerly wind zone, which meant that if the microfibers were sprayed from planes as part of the chemtrail mix over the Mediterranean Sea, the winds would carry the polymers generally to the east over the list of countries on Patrick's lab samples. But what would prevent the polymers from spreading out over North Africa? Nothing, apparently.

Sean went back to the chart of chemtrail spraying areas. The Mediterranean Sea was being heavily sprayed. International boundaries extend out twelve miles from the coast, which left most of the Mediterranean Sea as International Waters, unregulated by individual countries, but under the supervision of the U.N. So what else did these countries have in common? After a dozen different search parameters, several answers emerged: drought, food shortages, water shortages, political unrest, armed conflicts, and regime change; especially across Northern Africa and the Middle East.

Sean reviewed the properties of the polymer microfibers: ultraviolet light and water vapor absorption. In other words, the near elimination of clouds and in particular, rain. He stood and walked slowly over to the sliding glass door to the balcony of his hotel room, deep in thought.

This has to be a deliberate act, he decided. And if it is being done deliberately, for what reason? *Cui bono?* Who benefits?

He went back to the records for Psycon Industries. What an unusual name. It almost looked like an abbreviated combination of psychology and control, maybe psychological control?

What kind of warped egomaniac would be so blatant

and yet cryptic in what he did? He looked back at the connections to Conrad Kaplan and asked himself what other companies did Kaplan own or control? As he went down the list, another name stood out: Mersec, Inc. He dug through the files provided by Charlie. Mersec, Inc. provided mercenaries as security and protection for wealthy business people in the Middle East, the Saudi Arabian peninsula, and parts of Africa, specifically in the Horn of Africa region: Somalia, Ethiopia, Kenya, Southern Sudan, and Uganda. The search parameters for what these countries had in common turned up the same results: drought, food shortages, water shortages, political unrest, armed conflicts, and regime change.

He went over the wind charts for Africa. Eastern trade winds, which meant if chemtrails were being used the aerosols had to be disbursed over the Arabian Sea. International waters, again. But where would the planes be based? He reviewed his map of the world. India. Psycon had a production facility in India. He examined the satellite photos showing the global chemtrail patterns. There they were—spread out directly east of the southern coast of the Saudi Arabian peninsula and the Horn of Africa, making Oman and Yemen targets as well.

Sean reviewed the financial records provided by Charlie. Psycon produced the microfibers and sold them to a distribution company, also under the control of Conrad Kaplan. The distribution company paid a hundred and forty-seven million dollars last year to another company involved in aerosol spraying. Crops had failed in Ethiopia for the second year in a row, forcing the country to import the majority of its food, which drove the prices ever higher. With a faltering economy, starvation was becoming more common and food riots were taking place in protest, demanding that the government do something to make food and water more available to everyone, which wasn't happening. It was the same pattern that led to the Arab Spring starting in Tunisia and spreading across North Africa, through Libya, and into Egypt. The same forces were at work in Yemen and Ethiopia as well. Could the underlying conditions that created the Arab Spring have been deliberately created through the use of chemtrails?

In the media, the conflict was portrayed primarily as a religious war, which was at least partially true, Sean thought. Religious fanatics were promising people they would get them food and water. The conflict wasn't about religious ideology; it was about the basics of life. And smack in the middle of the cause of the lack of food and water was Conrad Kaplan and his use of chemtrails. He spent a hundred and forty-seven million dollars so it wouldn't rain. What did he get in return?

Sean pulled the financials for Mersec. Annual income: $1.7 billion. Quite the return on his investment, he thought, considering the protection wouldn't have been necessary if the people had enough food and water. So this was one of the piggyback programs Patrick had described.

Sean walked back over to the balcony door and looked at the skyline of Washington, D.C. If Conrad Kaplan were your everyday Wall Street manipulator, his crooked dealings would be understandable: another simple case of greed. But it *wasn't* so simple, was it? Conrad Kaplan was also vice president in charge of research and development for the nation's largest aerospace and defense contractor, heavily involved in deeply classified aircraft development. Sean knew he couldn't expose Kaplan's role inside the defense industry without being accused of violating national security. That kind of public attention would distract people from the real point of exposing Kaplan, too. But the chemtrail angle just might do the job. It's not like he needs the money, Sean thought, so what the hell is he doing?

* * *

One name kept finding its way to the top of Sean

Wells's investigation: The Partnership. The organization first showed up connected to Conrad Kaplan and his nefarious ventures in the Middle East and Africa. Now, on his third day of digging through Charlie's files and verifying what information he could, the Partnership connections were spreading through large defense contractors, military leadership positions, and into the political spectrum. Six of the fifteen members of the president's Cabinet were connected to the Partnership, plus the Secretaries of the Navy, Army, and the Air Force. The most powerful positions: Secretary of State, Treasury, Energy, Defense, and Homeland Security, were all connected to the Partnership.

For an organization like this to operate under the public radar and bend or break the law the way they were doing, required protection from prosecution. That protection came from the Department of Justice. No one was charged and prosecuted on the federal level without the Attorney General's office signing off on it, and the Attorney General was a member of the Partnership.

President Andrews didn't seem to have any direct connection to the Partnership, nor did the vice president, but leading members of Congress certainly did. He hadn't known the organization existed before he went through Charlie's files, but he did recognize the criminal rat's nest it represented. That much he had seen too many times before as an investigative journalist. The question was: What were they after? Money was the easy answer, but for people with this level of access, influence, and power, money wasn't an end result; it was a means to an end. If Conrad Kaplan were any indicator, the Partnership's goals were global in nature, and any means available were well within their consideration. In Sean's experience, criminals with access to automatic weapons were dangerous. Criminals with access to military force and nuclear weapons were terrifying.

Chapter 32

Diane and the rest of the flight crew put on their flight suits and followed Hollis to a bank of six elevators deep inside the granite mountain. Five of the elevator shafts were boarded up, obviously still under construction. Each elevator would hold only eight people, so half the crew had to wait. Hollis led Diane, Ryan, and her wing crew up to what he called the preflight deck. They stepped into a wide stone room and followed Hollis down a stone hallway.

"To the sides are your ready rooms. You will keep your flight suits here. The debriefing room is over there."

The ready rooms were small, with eight lockers in each room. Six rooms gave them enough for two full squadrons.

"I assume we are still working with simulators," Diane said. "When will our fighter craft arrive?"

Hollis paused as the elevator dinged and the next group emerged.

"Your assumption is partially correct," Hollis said as Clay's group joined them in the hall. "You will have a lot of simulator time while you're here. Keep in mind that even though you shoot down a Zeta Grey saucer, everything that you do to take that saucer down is sent through the Zeta Grey computer system. Every one of them will know the tactics you used, so every flight needs a new approach and new thinking. Now, to answer Zadanski's question, your fighter craft are here."

Excitement rippled through the members of Squadron One. Diane couldn't contain her enthusiasm any longer.

"Can we fly them now?"

Hollis nodded and beamed with pride. "Yes. But only in a limited area. We don't want to advertise our presence or capabilities to the Zeta Greys before we're ready to strike. If you will follow me."

He led them into a wide rectangular hall. Six fighter craft sat on the right half, resting on their landing pods. The craft were generally oval in shape side-to-side, light gray in color with rounded wings on each side. The twelve-foot wings arched downward slightly on each side. They were thick and tapered to a sharp line only at the very edge. The middle was eight feet from top to bottom and gracefully rounded underneath. The top had a clear canopy mounted slightly forward of the center of the craft. The canopies were standing open, hinged at the back, waiting for them.

Wow, Diane thought. This is nothing like an aircraft. She had seen the drawings of the craft in the manual, but being able to touch one was exhilarating.

"Which one?" Diane asked.

Hollis smiled. "I've taken the liberty of putting your names on them. I've also converted your ranks to the new system. You are free to fly them in the immediate area. Please stay under five thousand feet and within a hundred miles of this base. I don't want any undue attention from the Zetas or our own people. The vertical shaft on your left will take you up to the main flight deck. Wait there until I open the main door."

Diane and Ryan rushed from craft to craft with the others spreading out to find their fighter. The name of the pilot was marked in black letters next to the canopy, followed by the name of the RIO. The first craft had "Lt. 'OB1' Obers" next to the open cockpit. The second had "Lt. 'Hellcat' Catalano," and the third had "Lt. 'Buddha' Simmons" followed by "Lt. 'Mad Dog' Douglas", "Lt. 'Silver' Silverstein", and finally "Lt. 'Jink' Zadanski." Diane and Ryan climbed in, donned their helmets, connected their communication cables, and strapped in. Ryan powered up the craft, closed the canopy and checked all of the meters, indicators, and navigation displays.

"Pre-flight check complete," he said. "We're good to go."

Diane was breathing rapidly and shaking slightly from the excitement. She closed her eyes briefly, trying to calm down. It wasn't working.

She nudged the thruster controls and their fighter craft turned bright white and gently lifted off the stone floor. She was closest to the vertical shaft, so she slowly moved her craft into the opening and rose the two hundred feet to the main flight deck. The main door was closed, so she moved to the left side to make room for the other five craft. Buddha was next. He moved to the right, taking his place as her wing man. OB1 slid over behind Diane with Hellcat behind him, each with his wingman on the right side. Once all six craft were hovering in place, Admiral Hollis walked through the round blast door protecting the hall, and hit a large button on the side wall. Large red lights strobed on each side of the flight deck door. The massive main blast door was twenty feet high, a hundred feet wide, and six feet thick. It slowly rose into the ceiling. The bright New Mexico sunlight flooded into the flight deck.

"These craft are very different from aircraft. Please take everything very slow until you get used to the new conditions," Hollis said.

Slow, Diane thought. Got it.

"Okay," Diane said over the comm system. "Straight, left, or right?"

She couldn't contain her excitement any longer. She longed to see what this thing could actually do in the open sky.

"OB1, dibs on right."

She was grinning so hard, her face started to ache.

"Hellcat takes left."

Okay, she thought. "Which leaves Jink with straight out. See you all in the wild blue yonder."

When the blast door reached the full open position the red strobe stopped and solid green lights came on. Diane bumped the thrusters to ten percent. Her fighter craft shot out of the flight deck with Buddha close on her right side and slightly behind.

The sensation of flight was very different from what she had anticipated. In her Super Hornet the G forces had been strong during takeoff and severe during high-speed turns. Now, during takeoff, the only thing she felt was weightlessness. It disoriented her.

The distant mountain rushed at her. She was alarmed that she was falling into the ground on the other side of the valley. She pulled back hard on the control stick without thinking. Her craft shot upward. She glanced at the altimeter, shocked to see that she was at thirty thousand feet, five miles above the upper limit that Hollis had set. She glanced around. Buddha was nowhere to be seen. Neither was anyone else.

Pushing the control stick forward, now her craft pointed straight down. The sensation of weightlessness panicked her already disoriented sense of where she was. She had lost her situational awareness and position. She glanced at the thruster control. It was still at ten percent. She backed the thruster down to around two percent. The craft slowed, and gave her a chance to think, not just react.

These are rookie mistakes, she thought. How could I be making such dumb moves? I'm better than this! The radio was silent. She was shocked that no one was reporting in.

"Buddha? OB1? Hellcat? Anyone, this is Jink, come in."

The momentary silence caused her mind to jump to the worst-case outcome—that everyone had crashed.

"Jink," Buddha said. "Where did you go? I blinked and you were gone."

Did it really happen that fast? she wondered. When she pulled up, had she disappeared in the blink of an eye?

"Status check. Everyone report in with your position and condition," Diane said.

It wasn't supposed to happen like this. This was crazy!

"I've got them on the screen," Ryan said. "Everyone's still in the air."

Diane sighed in relief.

"Buddha reporting. I'm east of the base. I crossed over three mountain ridges before I realized I was going too fast. Hovering now. Craft and crew are good."

Three mountain ridges? She was shocked.

"OB1 reporting. I'm outside our operating range, approximately two hundred and fifty miles from the base. Craft and crew are good."

She shook her head. This was incredible.

"Mad dog reporting. Also out of bounds to the south. Craft and crew good."

Diane checked the list in her mind. So far no word from Hellcat.

"Hellcat. Check in. Hellcat, do you copy?"

The pause seemed to last forever.

"Roger, Jink. Craft sustained some damage. Cracked canopy. Crew good. My craft started dropping in altitude. Sluggish response. Flew through a danged tree. Still airborne, but limited control. Working my way back to base."

Diane closed her eyes momentarily and breathed out. At least no one died, she thought.

"I've got Hellcat on the screen," Ryan said. "She's fifty miles north of the base, moving slow, altitude low."

This was not the joyous experience she had anticipated. This was frightening.

"Rally around Hellcat," Diane said. She bumped the thruster slightly higher and angled to Hellcat's location.

Diane and Buddha arrived together. Mad Dog escorted Hellcat low and slow over the rolling hills. OB1 and Silver slipped in behind them a few minutes later.

"How you doin' Hellcat?" Diane asked as calmly as she could. At least her voice didn't sound as shook up as she felt.

"I think I can get this thing back to the base," Hellcat replied.

Diane looked at the terrain below them. "You could set it down here."

There were open spots with nothing but sand down there.

"Not giving up," Hellcat said. "Goin' to fly this baby all the way home."

Diane smiled. That's the Hellcat I know, she thought. Pilots and their egos wouldn't admit any kind of weakness. "Roger that."

The approach to the flight deck was slow and careful.

"Let Hellcat go in first," Diane said.

The blast door to the flight deck was standing open, ready for them to enter.

"Negative," Hellcat responded. "If I screw this up, none of you is going to have a place to land. I go in last."

She's right, Diane thought. "Roger that."

Diane swooped into the flight deck, hovered momentarily over the vertical shaft and dropped down to the hangar deck. She deployed the landing struts and set down in her assigned position. Ryan opened the canopy and shut the craft down. In just over a minute, four more craft were resting in place. They bolted from their crafts and crowded into the elevator, repeatedly punching the button for the flight deck.

As the elevator door opened, Hollis stood there, arms wide. "Whoa, whoa, whoa," he said. "The access blast door is closed. You can't go in there."

Closed? "Why can't we go in?" Diane demanded.

Hollis shook his head. "The Element 115 drive system on your craft produces antimatter. If the magnetic containment tube breaks, the result will be nothing short of a nuclear level detonation."

Diane had read about the antimatter section in the fighter craft manual, but it just didn't seem that dangerous at the time.

"Hellcat?" Clay asked.

He seemed to be on the verge of panic.

Hollis held his hands out in front of them, palms forward to stop them. "I have a landing officer in there from Ceti Research. He's guiding her through the process. If this goes sideways, it's going to take out the entire flight deck and part of the mountain."

Diane's shoulders slumped. She took a small step back. "Does she know that?"

Hollis lowered his arms. "I believe so, yes," he said. "I ordered her to land on the ground. She won't do it. She's determined to bring her craft into the flight deck."

Of course she is, Diane thought. I would be, too.

"Did you tell her it could blow up?"

Hollis looked her in the eyes. "I did."

Clay slumped against the wall.

"The guy from Ceti Research is the best there is," Hollis said to Clay. "You have to have faith."

Diane looked at Hollis, then at Clay

What's going on? she wondered. What am I missing? Clay and Helen don't even like each other.

* * *

Hellcat struggled to keep the craft steady. It drifted down. She pulled back gently on the control stick. No response. She pulled back a little more, only to have the craft surge upward, well above the entrance to the flight deck. I'm not going to let this thing defeat me, she thought. Landing on the ground might be safer, but it'll make me look weak. I can't tolerate that.

A man wearing a headset and a bright yellow vest walked to the center of the stone flight deck.

"Hellcat, my name is Steve. Can you hear me?"

She was angry enough without someone interfering.

"Yes, I can," she said in a frustrated tone. "What are you doing? I need to get in there. You're in my way."

She glanced to each side to see if there was enough room to go around him.

"I'm from Ceti Research, Hellcat, I've helped pilots in damaged craft land safely. I'm here to help you bring your craft in. This will be just like a carrier landing."

Like a carrier landing? "Swell," she said sarcastically. "I was Air Force. I've never been anywhere near a carrier."

She was already shaken up from flying through a tree. This wasn't helping.

"It's okay. I'll lead you through the whole thing.

Remain as calm as you can."

Calm? She thought. You've got to be kidding.

"Yeah, right," she replied. Her heart pounded in her temples, her breath was ragged, and her hands were shaking. Remain calm? she thought. Sorry, buddy, this is about as calm as it's going to get.

Steve held out two flashlight type things with glowing red extensions on them.

"When I raise the lights like this . . ." He held the lights up at an angle above his head. "I want you to pull back on the control stick. It means you're too low and you need to increase your altitude. Down, like this, means for you to move down." He lowered the lights, angling out to the floor. "Lights wide apart, like they are now, means you are too far out. You'll need to move forward. The closer you get, the more I'll move the lights together. Do you understand?"

"Yeah, sure," she replied, anything but certain of the outcome.

"You can set it down on the ground, or you can pull the ejection levers. Either way is fine with me," Steve said.

Hellcat shook her head. "I've come all this way, I'm not quitting now."

"Okay," Steve said. "Slide your thruster control back down a tiny bit. Your craft will start to drop. Compensate by pulling back on the stick."

Hellcat nudged the thruster control back. Her craft started dropping to the ground. She pulled back on the stick. Her craft was still dropping, so she pulled back more. The fighter slowed its descent, so she pulled back even more. Finally it stabilized. She was a hundred feet below the flight deck, still well above the ground at the base of the mountain.

"You're doing great," Steve said. "With lower thrust, the response of your craft will be even more sluggish, but the fast jerking should stop. Pull back on the control stick a little more."

Hellcat pulled back more. Her craft drifted from side to side. She tried to compensate, but the response was aggravatingly slow. Then her craft started to rise.

"Good, good," Steve said. "Keep coming up. I want you to go above the entrance to the flight deck by about thirty feet. You are about fifty feet out from the entrance, which is good."

"Should I deploy the landing pods now?" Hellcat asked, still trying to slow her breathing down.

"No," Steve said. "Don't worry about the landing pods. I want you to land this thing on its belly. You understand?"

Hellcat closed her eyes. "Belly landing. Got it." She opened her eyes, hands still shaking badly. "I don't know how steady I can hold this thing. My hands are shaking."

"That's fine," Steve said. "With the thruster this low it won't matter. Can you see me now?"

She looked up. Steve was standing on the edge of the flight deck, his red lights raised at an angle above his head.

"Yes, I see you."

She was beginning to trust him. He sounded confident, like he knew what he was doing.

"Good. Continue up. When my lights are straight out to the side, I want you to nudge the stick forward until you hover in place, okay?"

"Okay," she said. She took a deep breath and breathed out slowly, trying to calm her jangled nerves.

"Okay, good," Steve said. His lights were straight out to the side. She could just see him over the forward slope of the front of her craft, standing on the edge of the flight deck below her.

"I need you to keep your eyes on me. Nothing else. Just me. You understand?"

She glanced around the flight deck embedded in the

side of the stone cliff.

"Just you," Hellcat repeated.

Somehow the deck seemed so much smaller than it did before.

"Just listen for a minute. I'm going to have you nudge the thruster control forward, just a hair, and push the control stick forward at the same time. That should move your craft forward. Then I want you to follow my lights, moving the control stick forward and back as I lower and raise the lights, respectively. I will guide your craft into the flight deck. Once you're inside, I'll lower my lights and cross them, like this . . ." He swung the lights down, crossing them by his knees. "You got it?"

"I got it," she said. She reconsidered setting her craft down on the ground, but that seemed too much like admitting defeat.

Steve returned the lights to the horizontal position. "Okay. Nudge the thruster and watch me!"

Hellcat barely touched the thruster control and encouraged the control stick forward. Her craft slipped forward, dropping too fast.

"Watch me!" Steve shouted.

She moved the stick as she followed his movements. He raised the lights, lowered them, then raised them again. She was drifting into the flight deck. Steve shuffled backward fast, raising and lowering the lights. She followed his lead, fully in sync with his movements. The bright sunlight in the cockpit dimmed dramatically as she entered the shadow of the enclosed area. She couldn't see Steve anymore, but the red lights stood out against the darker background. The red lights moved rapidly down and crossed. She jammed the thruster control into the off position. Her craft thumped on the stone flight deck, slid toward the back wall, and turned as it came to a stop.

"Perfect!" Steve shouted. "Shut everything down and

open the canopy."

He really didn't need to tell her that. Her RIO was already halfway through the procedure before he heard the directions. The two of them climbed out of the cockpit, removed their helmets, and looked the damaged craft over. The leading edge had a dent in it from the tree she had cut in half. The crack in the canopy ran from just right of center all the way back to the hinges. Beyond that, it didn't look too bad.

The round blast door opened and her teammates rushed in.

"You made it!" Diane said. "I thought you should have landed out on the open ground."

Hellcat looked at Diane calmly. "Why walk when you have a ride?" She and her RIO walked nonchalantly to the elevator.

"Debriefing room—ten minutes," Hollis said as he stormed down the hall.

* * *

"I told you to take everything very slow," Hollis said, barely containing his anger.

"When you've been flying at eighty percent thrust in the simulator, ten percent *is* very slow," Obers said.

"I didn't expect the feeling of weightlessness during acceleration," Zadanski said. The others nodded in agreement. "It's more distracting than I could have imagined. All of our reactions are based on the physical feelings of movement in regular aircraft. That no longer applies. It's like we have to learn to fly all over again."

Hollis closed his eyes momentarily, shook his head, and breathed out. "All right, all right," he said, gradually calming down. "That is a function of the anti-gravity drive system. I know this is all new to you. If we have to take time for you to learn how to fly these things from the beginning, then that's what we'll do. You're going to have to get used to this, people, and soon. We're running out of time."

Zadanski nodded. "We're well aware of that, sir. We'll get it done."

Hollis shook his head. More delays, he thought. How much longer before it's simply too late?

"We still have a lot of construction workers," Catalano said. "How long before the base is completed?"

Hollis looked at her. Maybe a change in subject matter was in order.

"Several weeks, I'm afraid. Our Seabees are very good, but it all still takes time. The particle beam cannon defense system has been a priority, so you are going to have to forgo some of your creature comforts for a while longer."

Zadanski seemed uneasy in her chair. "Are the defense cannons the same as we have in our fighter craft?"

Hollis grinned. "Would you like to see for yourselves?" He stood and waved them out the door. Zadanski and the rest of the flight crew followed Hollis down a hall to several staircases. They climbed one set of stairs after another until they reached a long hallway. He led them into the first short hall on the left and through a blast door.

The chamber was fan-shaped with a small hole to the outside near the top of the narrow section of the room. The particle beam cannon was approximately three feet in diameter and twenty feet long. It was mounted on a hydraulically driven swivel platform which could raise or lower the cannon, keeping the end of the barrel located right in front of the hole.

"Holy cow," Atkinson said.

That had also been Hollis's reaction when he saw the cannons for the first time at Ceti Research several months ago.

"The effective range of the particle beam cannons on your fighter craft is about three miles. These can destroy anything within two hundred miles and damage objects out to three hundred miles. There are forty-two cannons embedded in the mountain, providing a full hemisphere of protection for the base. The gunners will be joining us this weekend."

Clay Obers stepped forward and touched the cannon. "I thought the main defense of the base was its secret location."

Hollis walked next to the cannon. "It is, from people on the ground, but it's not going to take that long for the Zetas to figure out where we are. After that we're going to have a real battle on our hands."

Zadanski stepped forward. "I assume the targeting systems are IFF equipped?"

Hollis nodded. "All cannons are equipped with identification, friend or foe systems. We're still working on keeping them secure from Zeta Grey mind control. The electronic systems are fully protected. It's the operators that concern me. For that, we'll have to wait and see."

* * *

"So what happened to it?" Helen asked.

Theo turned to face her on the flight deck as his crew dismantled Hellcat's fighter craft.

He raised his eyebrows. "I'm not sure. Did it start acting unusual before you hit the tree?"

Helen put her hands on her hips. "Is this a woman driver thing?" she asked sarcastically.

Theo started to laugh. "No," he said. "I didn't mean it to sound like that. I just need to know if the command module was malfunctioning."

Helen looked at her damaged craft. "I don't know what usual is supposed to be. I was inflight for less than a minute before my unfortunate encounter with . . ."

Theo looked at her. "Was the craft responding to the

controls the way you expected?"

"No," she said. "It would drop and I would have to correct for it. Then it would be fine for a while, then it would speed up on its own."

Theo nodded. "Steve, make sure the entire control module is replaced, and check the wiring to the gravity wave coils."

He turned to face her. "Anything else you can think of?"

She shrugged. "I don't know. Everything kind of went into the crapper after that."

Theo looked at Steve working on the damaged craft.

"We'll have you back in the air again, soon. I'm sorry you had so much trouble with it."

Hellcat turned and walked away, feeling discouraged.

Later in the day the other five pilots flew out for slow-speed maneuvers, getting used to how it felt to fly weightless. All Hellcat and her RIO could do was watch the repairs progressing on her craft. She watched in heartbreaking isolation as the other pilots returned.

Finally, her craft was back together and she joined her teammates for the next trip out into the air. At the slower speeds she was able to adapt to the weightlessness. Soon her old reactions and moves were adapting to the new conditions.

She tried a higher speed in formation with her squadron. It felt good. She was adjusting to the craft's performance. It felt so good to get her confidence back.

Chapter 33

Air Force One landed in Oslo, Norway early in the morning of December 10th for President Andrews's first international good will tour. Andrews had the jitters and a knot in his stomach. He politely endured the photo ops and public handshaking, smiling and acting as if he really wanted to be here. By a little after ten, Andrews's entourage proceeded on to Stockholm, Sweden for the presentation of the Nobel Prizes. This was the first time in over twenty years that an American had received the Nobel Prize in Literature, although, as usual, American scientists were well represented in chemistry, physics, and physiology.

Andrews and Martha attended a state dinner in Helsinki, Finland with the Prime Minister, the president of Finland, and the other eleven ministers who governed the country. Formalities completed, Andrews and his wife entered the armored limo that would return them to Air Force One for the trip home. Once the limo was in motion the forward bench seat opened and Secret Service Agent Sidney Dodd crawled out.

"Let me check your makeup," Martha said. She examined Dodd's face and compared it to the president's. Sidney Dodd was a close look-alike to the president, although thinner. He was always kept away from the president to reduce the possibility of someone making the connection. The critical biometric markers of eye distance and mouth were the same between Dodd and the president, but theatrical makeup was needed to widen the cheek bones, nose, and chin in addition to reshaping his ears.

Andrews's emotions were churning. Martha used to be so attentive to all of the minor details about him when they were together on the campaign trail for so many months. Now, she seemed distant to him. She just didn't seem distant with Sidney Dodd. She sparkled when she was around him. Is this what we looked like when we were out? he wondered. He felt weird, almost dispossessed when he looked at Dodd made up to look like him. It was disconcerting at best. He wouldn't have any part of it if he could help it, but what he had to do was critical, and people had to believe he was on his way back to Washington. His Cabinet and the Chiefs of Staff could not be allowed to know what the president was about to do. Too much hung in the balance.

Was it his imagination, or was something going on between them? Was he jealous? Was that the feeling he didn't like? He looked out the window of the limo and tried to focus his mind on the upcoming meeting with Yuri Pasternov. It wasn't working. He returned his attention to his wife. Martha noticed a small spot on his shirt where a tiny bit of gravy had dripped. She took out an eyebrow pencil and marked Dodd's shirt to match.

As the limo approached Air Force One, Andrews reluctantly climbed into the compartment under the bench seat and Dodd took the president's place next to Martha. According to their plan, Dodd and Martha would exit the limo and walk to the steps leading up to the door of Air Force One. They would turn, wave to the crowd and photographers, then board the plane.

Andrews waited impatiently in the cramped compartment until the limo stopped and his driver told him it was clear. He crawled out slowly and did a quick visual check of the surroundings. He was in a small, empty hangar. The large folding door was closed and there were no windows. This was where the limo would remain until it was loaded on a C-130 by the Secret Service and flown back to Washington, D.C.

Three members of the president's personal military unit entered the personnel door. The officer-in-charge (OIC) tossed a long, dark, bulky hooded coat to Andrews.

"It's cold out there, sir. Twenty-eight below zero with a damp wind coming in off the ocean, so wrap up tight."

Andrews zipped the coat up and tied the fur-lined hood around his face. The soldiers walked him out to an older car with Finnish plates. They left the airfield and headed west as the darkness closed in around them under a heavily clouded sky. Andrews tapped his fingers on his knee as his anxiety kept building. He had to keep his mind focused on the meeting with Yuri Pasternov.

His mind drifted back to Martha and Agent Dodd. Were they involved? It was a six hour flight back to Washington. Too much time and too little to do? he wondered. He had trusted her completely. Was that a mistake? What would he do if Dodd and Martha . . . ? Realistically, he could fire Dodd, but what would that accomplish? For political reasons he wasn't going to divorce her. He felt powerless in the middle of what he imagined to be a love triangle. How ironic, he thought. The most powerful political figure in the world: powerless.

Two hours later they turned north and followed a plowed dirt road through the forest to a clearing with a small cabin near the eastern edge. The border between Russia and Finland ran through the middle of the clearing. The driver pulled the car up to the cabin and all four of them got out into the stiff, freezing breeze. They stepped back from the car as two Russian soldiers with a canine searched the vehicle while two others stood guard. When the Russians were satisfied that there was no bomb, or other weapons present in the car, they swept Andrews and his men with security wands. They compared Andrews's face to the biometric markers they had on file to verify his identity. The Russian soldiers used a blue-green laser to signal that everything was okay.

Three men walked out of the western edge of the forest and over to the cabin. President Andrews shook hands with Russian President Yuri Pasternov.

"Thank you for meeting me under these circumstances," Andrews said.

Pasternov didn't say anything. He simply extended his arm toward the cabin doorway.

The inside of the cabin was warm and cozy, the fireplace blazing. Two comfortable chairs waited beside the hearthstone.

"It's too cold to stand on formalities," Pasternov said as he removed his heavy coat. "So why all of the secrecy?"

Andrews handed his coat to his OIC. The two presidents sat in the chairs provided, facing each other. Andrews had rehearsed a number of opening lines over the last two days, but none of them seemed right. He decided instead to speak from his heart.

"The military leaders in my country are a formidable force," Andrews said. "I'm sure they are in yours, as well."

"I'm satisfied with the arrangement," Pasternov said. The look of distrust in his face seemed like an impenetrable wall.

"We can't afford to be any longer," Andrews said. "The Joint Chiefs of Staff and my Secretary of Defense are pushing for a nuclear first strike against your country."

Pasternov appeared unfazed by the statement. "I know this already. For decades your CIA spies have infiltrated the former Soviet republics, turning one after another against Mother Russia, buying their leaders and bringing them into this NATO farce. I know all about your missile bases and your subterfuge in Ukraine and Belarus. My friend, the president of Belarus, is old and sick. You can't wait to take his country from him and turn it into another member of NATO, just as you have done with all of the others. The only surprise is that you are willing to say this to my face. Why say this now?"

"Because we can't afford to be enemies any longer." Andrews expected a firm response, but Pasternov's inside knowledge of U.S. strategic thinking startled him. He nodded and smiled as if the response was fully expected. At least it gave him the opportunity to approach the real issue at hand. "If we do not stand side-by-side and fight to protect our world, there won't be anything or anyone left to fight over. We have a common enemy and we must join together and fight them if we are to survive."

Pasternov leaned back in his chair, disgust deepened in his expression. "And who do you propose to be our common enemy, China?"

Now the conversation was getting back on track to where Andrews needed it to go. He shook his head. "No. We will need China to join us. They are in the same danger we share."

"And what is that?" Pasternov folded his arms across his chest.

He doesn't want to hear what comes next, Andrews thought. Best to slide into the subject carefully.

"There is a very small group of people in my country who share critical information with a similar group within Russia. They told me very little. In their opinion, I didn't have a need to know. I suspect the situation is the same for you. But I did need to know and so do you. Once I found out, I had to force the rest of the information out of them. You may have to do the same."

"What is it you think I need to know?"

Pasternov relaxed his arms and placed them in his lap. Partially open, Andrews thought. Now is the time.

"The Zeta Grey extraterrestrials supposedly working with our military and select defense corporations are deceiving us and using us. They have not kept any of their promises. The limited medical experiments and use of animals has grown way out of control. What they are doing threatens the survival of the human population on our planet. We have to stop them."

Pasternov glanced around the room in dismay. "You are insane. You come to me as a madman, telling me we have to do things that cannot be done. Why should I spend any more time listening to you? Why?"

He didn't blame Pasternov for not believing. He didn't believe it at first, either. But conditions have changed, he thought. It was time to put everything on the table and see what happened.

"Because I have the ability to stop the Zeta Greys. I have the technology to shoot down their saucers, and I will share that technology with you, if we can stop being enemies."

Pasternov shook his head.

"Now I know you are mad. That technology does not exist. Even if it did, you would never withdraw your missile bases from our borders. Your generals would not allow that to happen, ever."

He's ready, Andrews thought. He just needs another small shove in the right direction.

"You already have half the technology we need: your woodpecker system, ionospheric heaters, and your phased array antennas. You need to increase the nanometal content in your atmosphere, just as we have been doing, so you can selectively electrify portions of the upper atmosphere. That will stop the Zeta Grey saucers from entering and landing on our planet. If you will coordinate the atmospheric electrification with us, together, we can protect eighty percent of the planet from intrusion by the Zeta Greys."

Pasternov shook his head again, but Andrews could see his resolve starting to wane.

"Why should I believe you?" Pasternov asked again. "My people tell me the Zeta Grey problem is not significant, that it is all under control,"

Andrews smiled and nodded.

"Three reasons. First I can demonstrate the technology to you, personally. Second, once you see the technology, you will want to get the truth from your own people. They are lying to you. Third, I am prepared to demonstrate to you in no uncertain terms that we are no longer enemies. Do you want to see the technology?"

Pasternov turned his head slightly away, but still maintained eye contact. This is like fishing, Andrews thought. He's hooked. Now all I have to do is reel him in.

"Do I want to see what? Photos, drawings, or some video? No. Such things are worthless."

Of course they are, he thought. "I can do much better than that," Andrews said. "Are you willing to step outside for a few minutes?"

"For what? Lights in the sky? I have already seen those."

Okay. Now it's time, he thought.

"Have you been inside one?"

Pasternov's expression turned serious. Andrews turned and nodded to his OIC, who spoke briefly on a small radio.

"You ready to go for a ride?"

They stepped outside and watched as a glowing white oval craft glided silently over the trees and settled into the clearing fifty feet from the cabin. The white glow faded once it landed and the clear canopy opened from the front.

* * *

Diane Zadanski leaned forward and removed her helmet. She stood up in the narrow cockpit and looked at the group of men standing in front of the cabin. She recognized President Andrews and President Pasternov, of course. From her briefing with Admiral Hollis an hour ago she had an intellectual understanding of the situation, but an intellectual understanding was one thing. She was unprepared for being up close with people she was trained to think of as the enemy. It was unnerving, dangerous, and unpredictable. Those emotions swirled inside of her, barely under control.

"Lieutenant Zadanski, this is Yuri Pasternov, the president of Russia. Yuri, you ready to see what this thing can do?"

She took a deep breath. They were really going to do this, weren't they.

President Pasternov glanced at Andrews and then back at Diane. He walked swiftly over to the fighter craft and climbed up onto the wing. Diane handed him a helmet and motioned to the rear seat. Pasternov put the helmet on, climbed in, and strapped into the harness.

"It's cold Lieutenant. Let's go."

His eagerness made her even more nervous. She glanced at Andrews, who simply smiled and nodded back at her. She had to trust something, she thought, and right now Andrews was the only thing available.

Diane leaned back, attached the communications cable to Pasternov's helmet, checked his harness, and pushed his head back into the padding. She turned forward, put her helmet on, and strapped in. She took another deep breath as the clear canopy closed. She powered up the thrusters. The craft began to glow bright white and then bolted up into the air.

"President Pasternov, can you hear me all right?"

What she wanted right now was a rearview mirror, so she could see Pasternov's reactions. Flying blind was as dangerous as it got. She wasn't blind, but having someone she didn't know or trust sitting right behind her, where she couldn't see, felt like the same thing.

"I can," Pasternov said. "Where are you taking me?"

That was an interesting shift, she thought. The president of Russia was deferring to her. If he was willing to trust her, what did that mean about the situation?

"Where did you want to go?" she asked.

"Up."

Well, she thought, that was simple enough. She banked into an upward angle and hit the thrusters. Within six seconds they cleared the lower atmosphere and entered the edge of outer space. Diane slowed and rotated the craft so President Pasternov could view the planet below through the canopy. The lessened gravity didn't seem to slow the Russian down at all.

"This is amazing. It's so beautiful, I could sit here forever."

She understood. This was the first time she had been this high above the planet. The view was exquisite and breathtaking. But the reality was that this was also where the Zeta Grey saucers were.

"I'm afraid we can't stay. We'll attract too much attention from the Zeta Greys."

"Of course." He sounded disappointed. "Where to now?"

"Flying is one thing, weapons are another," she said. "I understand you were asked if you have an old bunker, or heavily armored facility, that is no longer in use. Something we could use for a demonstration?"

"Yes."

He seemed reluctant to get to the business part of the assignment. Personally, she didn't fault him for that. It was so beautiful up here it was inspirational.

"In the north, just above the Arctic Circle, a little west of sixty degrees east longitude. Can you find that?"

"I can." She dived back into the atmosphere and streaked east-northeast. "What are we looking for?"

She was actually starting to like this guy. Too bad he was the president of Russia.

"A low building, nuclear blast proof. It will be covered with five meters of snow. There are old radar domes around it."

Diane tapped her interactive screen and quickly located the building. "You sure nobody's in there? It's about to get two holes punched through it."

She heard him chuckle softly.

"That, I will have to see for myself."

She smiled. For never meeting a Russian before, this was going remarkably well. No wonder the Russian people admired their president.

"Okay. Center top agreeable with you?"

Now she really wished she *could* see his expression.

"Why not," he said.

She flew in at thirty miles up, dived quickly, fired both particle beam cannons together, pulled up, and banked to the left a mile above the ground. A grin crept across her face as she imagined the Russian president looking up through the two holes in his armored bunker. She returned to the cabin on the border of Russia and Finland, landing in the same spot as before. Pasternov unbuckled his harness, removed his helmet, and stood as the canopy lifted into the air.

He checked his watch. "All of that in three minutes. Very impressive, Lieutenant. Very impressive."

She smiled and nodded, acknowledging his praise.

* * *

President Andrews followed President Pasternov back into the cabin.

"I have twelve flight simulators sitting on two C-130 cargo planes. You'll need an underground facility to escape detection by the Zeta Greys and train your pilots. Those simulators and the technical specifications for the fighter craft are yours if you agree to look at the truth regarding the situation with the Zeta Greys."

Andrews pulled a USB drive from his pocket. "This drive contains three large files. The first has the names of those individuals and organizations in Russia who are corrupted and cooperating with the Zeta Greys, including the evidence against them. A second, much smaller file, names the people you can trust. The third file is the complete design and material specifications for a large particle beam cannon with an effective range of two hundred miles. You will need to build enough of them to protect your transmitter sites from the Zeta Greys. Will seventy-two hours be enough time for you to evaluate that information and make a decision?"

Pasternov was smiling for the first time since they had met.

"It will," Pasternov said. "You are offering me a lot. I assume you need something substantial in return."

He understands exactly how the political system works, Andrews thought. The rest is going to be straight forward from here.

"I do. I need your incoherent backscatter arrays tied in with our network so we can detect and track all of the Zeta Grey saucers, plus I need your transmitters in Novgorod, Irkutsk, Nakhodka, and Antarctica tied in under our operational control."

The look of distrust was back on Pasternov's face.

"You are asking me to trust you, but you do not trust us to operate our own sites?"

"I know." Andrews nodded reluctantly. "But, it's actually a matter of timing and communications. By the time we can notify you of a saucer intrusion and you can focus the transmitter, the saucer will have come and gone. They're that fast."

"And what if we share detection and tracking signals? Can you trust us to respond in a timely manner?"

This was how he was going to close the deal—autonomy and local control.

"I can. As soon as you have your command facility built, I will turn over operational control for your part of the globe to your people. I will send you all of the technical specifications that will be needed."

Pasternov studied him for a minute.

"So what happens in seventy-two hours?"

Andrews leaned closer to him. "I will demonstrate to you and the rest of the world that we are no longer enemies. If you will reciprocate in kind, I will send you twelve fighter craft and four large particle beam cannons as a sign of our friendship."

Pasternov pursed his lips and nodded slowly. "And if I don't?"

He may anticipate a threat from me, but he's not going to get it. All I have is the new reality. "Then every human being on the planet will become the disposable property of the

Zeta Greys."

Pasternov settled deeper into his seat. "There is not a lot of trust between our countries. You are asking a great deal."

I am, Andrews thought. "We both have a great deal to lose. If we can't learn to trust each other there won't be anything left, anywhere."

Pasternov looked as though he were in agreement. "I will seriously consider what you have said. In seventy-two hours, we will see."

"Until then," President Andrews said. They stood, shook hands, and Andrews walked out into the cold and climbed into the back seat of the fighter craft.

"Take me home, Lieutenant."

"Yes, sir."

Chapter 34

The scramble alarm woke Diane at 12:57 a.m. She grabbed her robe and tied it as she raced barefoot from her room to the elevators. Ryan was right behind her as they crammed into the elevator with Helen, Clay, and their RIOs.

"Saucer intrusion! Saucer intrusion!" came over the PA system. "This is not a drill! Repeat: This is not a drill!"

Diane stared at the elevator display as they ascended to the ready deck. She glanced at Ryan. He was standing there in his boxer shorts, hands trembling, breathing hard. The door opened and they all sprinted to their ready rooms. Diane threw off her robe and put on her uniform and flight suit. She was tying her boots before she even thought about looking at Ryan again. He was dressed, helmet in hand and running out the door as she finished.

She ran to her fighter craft. Ryan was already seated and powering up the craft as she jumped into the pilot seat.

"Wiggle your controls," Ryan said.

She moved the control stick through its movements with the thruster control in the off position and scanned the control panel. The canopy closed. She heard the motorized screws securing the canopy to the cockpit, sealing it from the outside atmosphere.

"All displays and indicators normal," she said.

"Roger that, preflight check complete. All systems are go."

She nudged the thruster control and the outer surface of the fighter craft took on a bright white glow. She lifted off, raised the landing struts, slipped into the vertical shaft, and up to the flight deck. Hollis stood next to the main blast door button with his comm headset on.

"Comm check," Hollis said. "All units report in."

Diane took a deep breath and exhaled before keying the radio. "Jink ready."

Her heart raced as she glanced to her right at Buddha.

"Buddha ready."

He nodded to her and grinned.

"Hellcat ready."

On through the squadron it went. Everyone was good to go.

"Single saucer intrusion. It entered from space over southern Mexico and is headed north at high speed. Target will pass our location in the next ten seconds." He hit the button to open the blast door. The red lights flashed. "You will be approaching from behind. Saucer is expected to go to ground in northern New Mexico. Good hunting."

The last three days of flight time had brought them up to full speed. Their new confidence brimmed in their chests.

The flight deck lights turned green. Diane and the other

five pilots bolted into the air.

"Stay close to the ground," Diane said. "It'll make it harder for the scout saucer to pick us up."

"Copy," came from the other crews.

Diane's heart raced, her adrenalin flowed, and her mind felt especially focused. This was what made flying such a rush.

"OB1 on the right."

She placed where each team should be in her mind. "Jink left."

"Hellcat on center."

Good choice, Diane thought. Best place for the kill shot. Hellcat needed an emotional boost after her encounter with a tree, maybe this would help.

They spread out with OB1 sweeping fast to the east of the scout saucer on their navigation displays. Diane and Buddha slowed slightly to let OB1 and Hellcat move into position.

"Target is slowing and dropping below ten thousand feet. Range closing fast. Initiate jinking and commence firing upon visual contact," Diane said.

"Roger that."

Hellcat made first contact as she and her wingman, Mad Dog, opened fire. The scout saucer was caught by surprise with a particle beam cannon hit to the left edge. It shot up and to the right, firing back, only to be engaged by OB1 and his wingman, Silver. Diane and Buddha pulled up sharply to engage the scout saucer, which shot higher and moved away to the left over Colorado at high speed. She and Buddha pushed the thrust to seventy percent, closing in on their target. The scout saucer continued firing as all six fighter craft moved in on it. Diane was closest. Her second shot hit the scout saucer on the underside, near the middle. The light beam flashes from the saucer ceased as it began to tumble in the night sky, falling to the ground. Each team zoomed in, hitting the scout saucer repeatedly with their particle beam cannons.

As the scout saucer fell into the lower atmosphere over Wyoming, the three teams slowed and followed it down, each confirming where it crashed.

"Target is down," Diane reported. "Return to base."

Hellcat started to lag behind the rest of the squadron, then she shot out in front.

"Hellcat, what's going on?" Diane asked.

She heard Hellcat swear under her breath.

"My craft is acting up again. It's not right."

Not again, Diane thought. "Can you make it back all right?"

"Affirmative," Hellcat replied.

Diane could hear the anger in Hellcat's voice. Who could blame her? Flying these craft was dangerous enough when they worked right. When they didn't operate properly . . . ?

* * *

"Good job," Hollis said as he entered the debriefing room. "First kill honors go to Lieutenant Zadanski with contributing credit to everyone else. Special mention to Lieutenant Catalano for first hit on the enemy scout saucer. Ceti Research ground crews are recovering the debris in the Wind River region of Wyoming as we speak."

Helen Catalano stood. "Sir, my craft is acting up again. It's undependable."

What now? Hollis thought. "I'll call Ceti Research. They'll have it fixed sometime this morning."

Catalano shook her head. "With all due respect, sir, I'm not getting stuck with a hangar queen. Send this one back to the taxpayers. I'm not flying it."

He read her defiant attitude and resolve clearly enough.

Prima donna? he wondered. He leaned back in his chair and tipped his head slightly. Dr. Cowen looked for prima donna attitudes carefully in his initial interviews. It was a disqualifying personality trait, although her concern was probably fact-based, and accurate.

"All right," he said. "I'll make the call. You'll have a new craft tomorrow."

She nodded. "Thank you, sir." She sat down.

The flight crew's mood appeared sullen, except for Zadanski, who grinned from ear to ear. This was not what he expected to see. Simmons was his usual peaceful self.

"What's going on?" Hollis asked.

"I'm happy," Zadanski said. "I don't understand why everyone else is so bummed, well, except for Simmons, of course."

Hollis looked around the room. "Obers? Catalano? Silverstein?"

No one would make eye contact with him, nor would they say anything.

"Clay? What is it?" Zadanski asked.

Obers was clearly uncomfortable. "Nothing."

He looked away, and then at the floor.

"It's obviously not nothing. Talk to me," Zadanski demanded.

Obers glanced at her, then returned his gaze to the floor.

"Tell me," she said with an understanding tone.

"I don't know. Well, I do, kind of, but I don't understand it." He twisted awkwardly in his chair. "All of these months we've trained to shoot down a scout saucer, and now that we have, it just feels too strange."

The others nodded, except Simmons. He just sat there watching everyone else.

"It feels good to me," Zadanski said. "What are *you* feeling?"

"It feels surreal to me, like it didn't really happen," Obers said.

"We were all there," Zadanski replied. "We all shot and hit that scout saucer. It went down and crashed. We're recovering the debris. It happened."

Hollis was baffled by their response. "What did you think we were doing here?" he asked.

Zadanski had a puzzled look on her face. "Clay? Have you ever seen a real UFO before?"

He shook his head.

"Have any of you?" she asked.

"I've seen two on the radar scope," Atkinson said. He looked directly at Zadanski. "But I've never seen a real one . . . until now." Atkinson looked away.

"Clay?" Zadanski asked.

"I guess I didn't believe they were real," he said quietly.

"And now?" Hollis asked, surprised by their reaction.

"I feel like they are overwhelmingly real," Catalano said. "Now, at least."

"And before?" Hollis asked, trying to understand why they were feeling this way.

Catalano shrugged. "Not so much. I guess I bought into the theory that they were real, but not the actuality, you know?"

"I understand," Zadanski said softly. She looked at Hollis. "If I may, sir?"

He nodded.

"Seeing a real UFO changes you," Zadanski said. "It alters your perception of what is real and what isn't. It turns everything you know upside down and inside out. I know that because it happened to me, nine years ago, when my twin brother was abducted by a UFO and killed. This is no longer the same world you woke up in this morning. This is a new reality—in many ways a terrifying one, but a real one, nonetheless. You are going to have to adapt to the new reality, soon. Your life depends on this shift in perception, because these things are dangerous and deadly. They will not hesitate to kill you."

Her explanation made sense to him. Finally Hollis understood their response.

"We are now officially at war with the Zeta Greys," he said. "I just want to remind you that picking a fight is a long way from winning that fight. Stay vigilant, stay situationally aware, and stay alive. I have four bottles of champagne on ice in the cafeteria for all of you to share if you feel up to it. Then get some rest. You're going to need it."

"Champagne anyone?" Zadanski asked. "Ryan? Clay?"

Atkinson shook his head. "I'm going to bed."

"Me, too," Obers said as he stood up.

One by one they got up and quietly went to their quarters.

*　*　*

Diane looked at the champagne on ice. There wasn't any point in celebrating by herself, now, was there? she thought. She returned to her quarters. As she rounded the corner she got a glimpse of Helen slipping into Clay's room.

She froze. What the hell's going on? she wondered. She scurried down the hall to Ryan's room. He's probably still up, she thought. She knocked gently on the door. After a pause, he opened up and looked at her.

"I just saw the strangest thing," she whispered.

He looked intrigued.

"Helen just slipped into Clay's room."

Ryan looked up and down the hall and sighed. "I guess it's time. Follow me." He walked down the hall and knocked gently on Simmons's door. When the door opened, Simmons was wearing a brown floor-length robe.

She glanced inside his room. An eighteen inch high hand-carved wooden Buddha sat on his dresser.

"What . . . ?" This was the second shock for Diane in as many minutes.

"She needs to know," Ryan said softly.

Simmons nodded and motioned them in.

"So the Zen thing is serious?" Diane asked.

Simmons nodded. "I'm a Zen Buddhist monk."

"But isn't that a non-violence kind of thing?" Diane asked. "What are you doing flying a fighter craft?"

A half smile played across his face. "Buddhists have known about extraterrestrials for more than a thousand years. We train in martial arts for a reason: life is precious, especially innocent lives. We defend those innocent lives with our skill and by placing our own lives on the line. That's what I'm doing here. This is my karmic path."

Diane's mind struggled to grasp the reality of what he said. Then she smiled. "This is why Hollis put Buddha on your fighter craft."

Simmons nodded.

"She saw Helen going into Clay's room," Ryan said.

"Ahhh, that," Simmons said.

Diane looked over at Ryan. "There's a code—no fraternizing."

Ryan nodded.

"It's not fraternizing," Simmons said. "They're married."

Diane stepped back, her mind reeling. "What? They . . ."

Simmons nodded. "I was a witness for them. They tied the knot on leave in Vegas about a month before you got here."

"But—" She was flabbergasted. She hardly knew what

to say.

"We try to help keep it quiet," Simmons said.

Diane sat on the bed. "There are surveillance cameras all over the place. Someone has to know."

"Well," Ryan said, "Collier obviously has to know; he runs base security."

"And he hasn't said anything? Does Hollis know?"

Simmons raised his eyebrows. "Probably. But I doubt it went any further than that."

Diane shook her head. "The argument they had on my first day here?"

Simmons chuckled. "We try to make it convincing."

She looked up at the ceiling. "You were in on it?"

Simmons nodded. She looked at Ryan. He shrugged and smiled. "They're good people. We protect them however we can."

Diane breathed out hard and looked down at the floor.

"Can we count on you?" Simmons asked.

She looked at the two of them and chuckled. "All this time, and I never had a clue."

"Well?" Ryan asked. He stepped a little closer to her. "We'd like to keep it that way."

She laughed out loud. "Yes, you can count on me."

* * *

Hollis walked into his office and picked up the receiver of the red phone that sat on his desk. There were no buttons on the phone. It went to only one location.

"This is Admiral Hollis. I need you to wake him up. National security."

"Yes, sir," a Marine major answered.

Hollis waited patiently. Then he heard the president's voice. "Howie, do we have confirmation?"

"We do, sir. First scout saucer has been shot down, no casualties on our side."

"Okay, now the hard part begins."

Hollis closed his eyes and nodded to himself.

"Yes, sir, it does."

Chapter 35

President Andrews handed the phone back to the Marine major.

"Notify all senior military staff officers that I need them in the Situation Room ASAP."

"Yes, sir."

Andrews called his chief of staff, dressed, and walked to the elevator that would take him down to the underground Situation Room. He paced back and forth, rehearsing in his mind what he was going to say. *I can do this, I can do this,* he repeated to himself. Confrontations were never easy, but they were an essential part of leadership, especially in the political arena. Tension built in his chest as generals and admirals filed, one-by-one, into the room. Also present, at Andrews's request, were officers from each branch's military police and three members of the president's own personal military unit. Those additions to the group left the generals and admirals nervous and skeptical.

When everyone was seated, Andrews stepped to the head of the long oval table and put his hands flat on the surface. That posture had the appearance of strength and power in it, but it also helped keep Andrews's hands from shaking.

"I'm changing our nation's priorities. I have met with the Russian president. Russia is no longer our enemy. You will withdraw all military assets and personnel from Europe. Move all of our armored units to transport ships, fly all of our bombers and fighters back to the U.S., and dismantle every missile installation. I want every nuclear weapon removed from all European countries, and I want it done now."

"That's insane," Secretary of Defense Farnsworth said as he stood. "You can't believe a word the Russian president says. You're starting World War Three. The Russians will drive their tanks right over Europe. Those people won't stand a chance without us there. The whole purpose of NATO is to defend Europe from a Russian invasion. We have contractual obligations that we have to honor. You can't leave Europe defenseless."

"There's nothing to defend them from," Andrews said forcefully. "Russia is not going to attack Europe."

Farnsworth shook his head. "They will. This has been Russia's plan all along: to take Europe."

"I am giving you a direct order. Withdraw all military assets and personnel from Europe, now," Andrews said. His stomach tightened as the tension escalated.

General McHenry, Commander of the Army Forces Command stood and faced Andrews. "Sir, with all due respect, I cannot, and will not follow such an obviously illegal order. We are contractually bound to defend all NATO countries, and I will not shirk that responsibility."

Andrews stared into McHenry's eyes. "Are you refusing my direct order?"

McHenry glanced away. "It's an illegal order, sir. I have every right to refuse to follow it."

Andrews turned to an Army MP.

"Major, arrest General McHenry for refusing to obey a direct order."

The major nodded. "Yes, sir."

The Army major walked over to General McHenry and placed him in handcuffs.

"General McHenry, you are under arrest for insubordination and refusing to obey a direct order."

"You can't do this," General McHenry said. "The order is clearly illegal."

Andrews placed his fists on his hips. "Answer me this, General. Which NATO country has been attacked?" General McHenry stood silent and stared at Andrews. "Our obligation within NATO is to defend any and all NATO members who have been, or are being, attacked. We have no obligation, legal or otherwise, until an attack actually takes place. My order is legal on its face. Will you, or will you not, obey my direct order, General?"

McHenry stiffened, defiance in his posture.

"I stand by my position that this is an illegal order, which I am legally justified in refusing, sir."

Andrews shook his head slightly. "You may argue that defense at your court martial. Take him to the brig."

The MP removed General McHenry from the Situation Room.

"Who's next?" Andrews asked, trying to sound as bold and in control as he could. He stood firm and stared at the remaining military officers in the room. This is the moment, he thought. Either they back down, or I have a full-fledged mutiny on my hands.

Marine Corp General Parsinian stood. "Sir, what are your plans when Russia invades Europe?"

Andrews turned to address Admiral Dosinski. "Admiral, does the Navy have sufficient resources in place to neutralize a Russian attack on any European country?"

Dosinski leaned forward. "Yes, sir, per your order, we have all the cruise missiles we would need in submarines off the coast of Europe and in the Mediterranean."

Andrews glanced at Parsinian and then looked at Dosinski. "Are these forces in Europe?"

Dosinski shook his head. "No, sir. All of our submarines are in international waters."

Andrews turned to face Parsinian. He needed to see his reaction.

"Admiral, is it your understanding that an order that covers all of Europe would not apply to our submarines in international waters?"

Parsinian tightened his lips and stared at Dosinski.

"Such an order would not apply, sir."

General Parsinian glanced around the room and returned his gaze to the president.

"Sir, the United States Marine Corp stands ready to follow your orders to the letter, sir."

"Thank you, General." Thank God, Andrews thought. He then turned to the second in command of the army. "General Lansdale, are you prepared to withdraw all military assets and personnel from European bases and locations?"

Lansdale stood and glanced around the room. "I am, sir."

Andrews nodded. "You are hereby promoted to Commanding General of the United States Army Forces Command. I expect to see equipment and soldiers being removed within the hour. Are we clear?"

Lansdale stood at attention. "Yes, sir, perfectly clear."

"Sir," Secretary of Defense Farnsworth said. "This is a very ill-advised and dangerous move on your part. You need to seriously consider the consequences of what you are doing."

Andrews turned to face Farnsworth, thinking, This is a threat, and not a well veiled one at that. "Need I remind you that you serve at the pleasure of this office?"

"No, sir," Farnsworth replied. His hands were trembling slightly.

"Then begin withdrawing our military forces, now."

Andrews stared firmly into Farnsworth's eyes, who looked away as he answered, "Yes, sir."

Andrews breathed a sigh of relief as he and Franks, his chief of staff, left the Situation Room and walked swiftly to the elevator.

"There will be reprisals," Franks said.

Andrews glanced behind them to make sure they were alone.

"Are we recording everything that takes place in the Situation Room?"

The expression on Franks's face was determined but grim. He understood the risk involved. "We are. You can view it in the Secret Service office."

Andrews was still feeling the adrenalin rush from the meeting when he said, "Then let's go see who's plotting against us."

* * *

Andrews and Franks arrived at the Secret Service security office three minutes later.

"As you suspected, sir, Farnsworth, Lansdale, and General Tessier of the Air Force are conferring quietly in the corner of the room. They're whispering, so we're going to have to enhance the sound to get a clear record of what's being said.

But, from what I've heard so far, their opinion is that you need to be replaced."

Of course, Andrews thought. "Any hints at how they plan to do that?"

"No, sir," Secret Service Agent James said. He looked up at Andrews, concern etched into his expression.

"Okay, I want all of them under long-range surveillance—nothing they can see—and put all their communications on full monitored status."

James nodded in acknowledgement.

"They have to figure all their electronic devices will be monitored," Franks said. "I don't think we'll get anything that way."

Andrews put his right index finger over his mouth as he thought. He lowered his hand then said, "Agreed. I'm more interested in seeing if there's a change in their communications habits. That'll tell me more than their carefully selected words might reveal."

"Pull all recorded communications for those three from the last six months," Franks told Agent James, the head of the president's Secret Service detail. "We're looking for small variations. They're too smart to make sudden and noticeable changes."

Chapter 36

Who could it be? Rosaq wondered. The speed and maneuverability of the craft attacking the scout saucer indicated off world interference, but who would be that bold? Earth human technology wasn't capable of anything near this level of sophistication, so it had to be an outside force. But even with the dozen or so civilizations Rosaq was familiar with, none of them could prevent the weapon system from locking onto the targets. That hadn't happened in eons.

Rosaq realized that whoever this new enemy was it was dangerous. From the data, only six craft were involved in the incident. Maybe that's all there are. What if it were some rogue group? There were certainly some of them around, but they usually steered clear of the Zeta Greys. Plus, no one was able to defeat the weapon lock system. That was tried and true technology—had been for thousands of years. Why was it failing now?

Rosaq took the next logical step. Whatever it cost in scout saucers and pilots, recovering one or more of these enemy craft, preferably with its crew, was imperative.

* * *

Diane and the rest of Squadron One were eating dinner when the next scramble alarm sounded.

"Saucer intrusion! Saucer intrusion!" came over the PA system.

They ran for the elevators and from there to their ready rooms. With flight suits on and helmets in hand they hopped into their fighter craft and took their positions on the flight deck.

"Single saucer intrusion over the Pacific Ocean," Hollis said. "Target is heading east at high speed, toward L.A. at this time. They will be expecting you, so be careful out there."

He hit the large button and the blast door slid into the ceiling.

They flew east off of the flight deck and hooked left into a westerly flight path, keeping close to the ground as they skimmed over the low mountains of Arizona.

"Target acquisition in sixty seconds," Ryan said.

The familiar adrenaline rush sharpened Diane's mind and amplified her senses.

"Something feels strange," Hellcat said. "I don't know what it is. I can't describe it."

Diane could feel it, too. "Commence jinking," she said. "Bumping to next comm frequency." She could feel the hairs on the back of her neck stand up.

"Six bandits just appeared behind us," Ryan shouted, using the military slang for enemy aircraft.

"Break, break," Diane said—the command to break formation and scatter. She broke left and down, clipping treetops as she followed the slope of a mountain.

"I now count ten bandits, two behind us," Ryan said. "They're not firing at us."

"They can't get a weapon lock with the random jinking. They're going to have to aim and shoot manually. Sharp ridge coming up, hang on!"

As she flew over the ridge she continued up for a second instead of following the downward slope of the mountain. One scout saucer trailed her up while the other took the downward path of the rocky slope. Diane jammed the control stick full forward, looping down and back, now upside down at the lower scout saucer. She fired the twin cannons, hitting the lower saucer with one shot, the other beam a near miss. She continued her tight vertical circle coming up under and behind the higher saucer.

The other scout saucer made a ninety degree turn to the right, trying to get away. She banked hard and pushed the thruster control higher, thinking, Oh no you don't. She closed in on the scout saucer. Right again, her intuition whispered. She banked right an instant before the scout saucer made another sharp right turn. She fired both cannons instinctively, hitting the saucer dead center with both beams. The saucer tilted and fell to the ground.

"First target moving away at your five o'clock low," Ryan said. "Slow speed, probably damaged."

Diane smiled. "Not for long."

She swung around and nudged the thruster higher. The other scout saucer fired back at her, missing. She used both cannons together and hit it with both shots. It, too, started dropping from the sky to the mountains below.

"Targets are gone from the screen again," Ryan said.

Diane glanced around as she heard "bumping," over the

headset in OB1's voice.

"Bumping," Ryan confirmed. "Images are back. Dog fight, at your seven."

Diane banked to the left. "Roger that."

She swung around the mountain ridge, and through the canyon. OB1 scrambled above her with a scout saucer tight behind him. The saucer fired, hitting OB1's right wing. Buddha fired and hit the saucer from above with both shots. OB1 went into a slow downward spiral.

"Your four!" Ryan shouted.

She pulled up sharply, banked right and fired at another scout saucer going after OB1, missing with both shots. She flipped the firing control to single shot mode and swung to follow her new target. The saucer fired at OB1, hitting the back of his fighter craft. The bright white glow of OB1's craft dimmed dramatically.

"His jinking control stopped."

She held the trigger down, firing shots at half-second intervals. After the second shot, the scout saucer pursuing OB1 broke sharply to the right and up. She followed while continuing to fire, missing twice and connecting with the saucer on her third and fourth shots.

"OB1, status!" Diane shouted.

"Power at ten percent, limited flight control, craft is not stable."

Diane checked the sky behind OB1. "Are you hurt?"

So far, no saucers were closing in on him.

"Negative. No injuries. Trying to make a controlled landing."

Controlled *crash*, Diane thought.

"Six o'clock high!" Ryan said.

Diane banked left and dived evading a scout saucer right behind her. Silver was closing in on the same saucer, firing every half second. He hit the saucer just as it was breaking away, sending it into a slow spiral to the ground. Two scout saucers closed in on Silver from behind.

"Silver, six!" Diane shouted.

Silver broke right as Buddha swooped down from above, firing at the nearest saucer on Silver's tail. That saucer broke away to the left. Hellcat swung in from the side, firing at the second scout saucer, hitting it as it, too, tried to break away in an upward direction.

"Bumping!" Ryan shouted as he switched frequency again.

Diane followed the scout saucer that was on Hellcat's tail, maintaining a stream of shots after it. The saucer bolted upward at high speed. She pushed the thruster control higher again, firing at the saucer as she closed in. She hit the saucer once, and then again as it reached the upper atmosphere. The saucer tipped and started a slow arc back down to the earth. Diane banked back down to rejoin the dogfight below.

"No bandits on the screen," Ryan said. He called for a frequency change again. "Still no bandits. Status check!"

"OB1 is on the ground," Hellcat said. "Both okay. His wingman, Silver, took a direct hit to the canopy. No chute, crash confirmed. Missing one other craft, anyone see what happened?"

Diane searched the sky, looking for any movement.

"Mad Dog was hit," Buddha said. "I saw a chute. Locator beacon is active."

She pulled back on the thruster control.

"Any other saucers on the long range screen?" Diane asked. Her heart pounded as she waited for an answer.

"Nothing," Ryan said.

Diane took a deep breath and relaxed. "Then we stay in place and guard our own until ground support arrives."

* * *

The debriefing with Hollis went on for three hours and covered every detail of what had happened. Mad Dog, OB1 and their RIOs had been picked up by an Osprey and were on their way back, compliments of the 27th Special Operations Wing at Cannon Air Force Base, New Mexico.

Hollis suspended the meeting until the four remaining members of the squadron could join them in the morning. The six who had returned went down to the cafeteria and got something to eat, then retired for the night.

Diane couldn't sleep. Her hands were shaking. She paced a U-shaped pattern around the bed in her room, reviewing every detail of the battle. Helen had been the first to sense that something was wrong. The Zetas had gotten through the encryption on the communications system and blocked their awareness of the scout saucers on the tactical screen in their fighter craft. The saucers had disappeared a second time from their screens and their sight when Clay had issued the bumping command. Evidently Ryan had taken note of the time it took the Zetas to get through the encryption and bumped to the next frequency before they got through the third time. That was a valuable piece of information.

There was a soft knock at her door. She wondered if it was Ryan, but opened the door to find Dr. Cowen standing there.

"I see you're still up," he said.

She motioned him into the room. "Couldn't sleep."

He looked her over carefully as he walked in.

"Neither could anybody else. Adrenaline rush. Hollis authorized something to help get you to sleep." He looked at her hands. "You've got the shakes. Happens when your adrenaline crashes. You'll feel tired, exhausted even, but not sleepy. You want something? It's optional."

She tried to evaluate how much help she needed to get

to sleep. "The others take any?"

Dr. Cowen nodded. "So far, three yes, two no."

She shook her head. "I'll pass."

Dr. Cowen smiled. "Half and half. Matches my experience. Sleep till you wake up, okay?"

Diane couldn't stop worrying about the other pilots. "Any word about Obers and the others?"

Dr. Cowen reached out and touched her arm. "They're here. Just get some rest."

Yeah, she thought, wondering just how that was going to work.

* * *

Diane woke around 9:30 in the morning. She showered and dressed, feeling stiff, sore, and physically exhausted. Maybe she would take the help sleeping next time. Hollis was waiting in the cafeteria.

"How are Obers and the others doing?" she asked.

"Still sleeping. Obers shot down three saucers. All together we have sixteen confirmed kills. Fifteen crash sites. We're recovering everything except the one you shot down in the upper atmosphere. It crashed in the ocean."

She sighed. "We lost three craft and two people. Not a good day."

"I understand," Hollis said. He motioned her over to a chair. "But overall, you and your squadron proved yourselves capable against the Zeta Greys."

She sat, still feeling overwhelmed. "It's not my squadron, sir. I'm just one member."

Hollis sat in a chair next to her. "Not any more. I've promoted you to lieutenant commander. It's officially your squadron. Keep in mind that none of the saucers came away from the battle. Six of our craft went up against sixteen saucers. Losing only three craft and two people? That's impressive in my book. We could have lost everything. Then where would we be?"

Silver and his RIO: killed, she thought. But Hollis is probably right. It could have been a lot worse.

"Look," she said. "I've been thinking about something. The Zeta Greys were getting through our communications equipment. Ryan figured out the time interval and bumped the frequency before they could get through again. If we expand the encryption algorithms and set the radios to change encryption on the shorter time interval, I think we can keep them out of our heads."

Hollis raised his eyebrows. "Sounds like a good plan."

Chapter 37

Conrad Kaplan threw his cell phone across the room.

"I'll kill him! He can't do this to me!"

He called his specialized operatives and put his plan in motion.

Next he called Harlan Mohr.

"I need that new missile technology moved up. I want the high speed interceptor missile operational within thirty days. No excuses. Make it happen. We're going to war against Russia!"

He sent an encrypted text to Secretary of Defense Farnsworth, Senator Whitcolm, and Speaker Metzner, telling them what he needed them to do.

This is the problem with politicians and the political process—they're too undependable, he thought. I hate negotiations. I hate deals. The only people I can depend on are the ones who know I'll kill them if they don't do what I tell them to do. Fear of death is the only true basis for loyalty. No promises, no giving your word, only true loyalty matters.

* * *

Rosaq connected telepathically with the massive Zeta Grey computer system and became part of the real-time collective experience his pilots had during the recent encounter with the rogue fighter craft. The images of the enemy craft jumped and flitted rapidly. The weapon lock failure warning flashed on the main view screen. His pilots switched to manual aiming and firing control of their particle beam weapons. The amount of shots that missed their target was phenomenally high.

He initiated the interactive simulator mode with the computer and used his superior mind to aim and fire the weapons. He was able to significantly improve the number of hits against the rogue fighters, but the overall kill rate was still dismal. He reran the simulation trying several different tactics, but each time his saucer was hit and disabled within three seconds of engagement.

Rosaq focused his mind on the six-foot tall, green, praying mantis type Insectoid who had placed him in charge of the Earth Acquisition Force and connected telepathically. He shared the images of the jumping rogue fighter craft and the associated weapon lock failure. He sent his thoughts regarding possible off world sources of the technology and the known theater of operation of these craft. He waited as the Insectoid considered what course of action to take. The answer came back after a few seconds.

Locating and attacking these rogue craft on the ground became priority one. Locating the rogue base would be handled from the mother ship. Until the ground location was determined, single rogue fighters would be attacked by a minimum of three scout saucers, and multiple rogues would be engaged only when the odds were at least five saucers against one rogue. As Rosaq expected, the Insectoid made it clear that the capture or recovery of a rogue fighter, with its crew, was imperative.

Chapter 38

President Andrews sat in the Oval Office with Franks, Secretary of Defense Farnsworth, and the Joint Chiefs of Staff. Anger, defiance, and indignation were written on the faces of the defense department officers in front of him. He just needed a little more time.

"Russian armored divisions are mobilizing," Farnsworth said. "You can expect thousands of Russian tanks to flood across the borders of Ukraine and Belarus within twenty-four hours. From there they will press into Poland and then Germany. Sir, you're creating the greatest military debacle in the history of this country. Poland and Germany don't have the military resources to defend themselves without us there. You have to reverse your order to withdraw from Europe. Hundreds of thousands of people are going to die at the hands of the Russians. This is just plain lunacy, sir. You have to stop this."

Andrews remained determined to continue with his plan. The timing and sequence of events was critical to the outcome. The problem was he didn't have control over when Pasternov would make his move, assuming he was going to join the plan at all. That remained to be seen.

"Sir," the Chairman of the Joint Chiefs of Staff said. "I have to support Secretary Farnsworth. I have complete faith in the Navy and their cruise missiles, sir, but I must stand in favor of being proactive in our defense of Europe rather than falling back to a strictly defensive posture. Playing defense with the Russians is never a good strategy, sir. Too many lives will be lost."

How many lives are too many, Andrews wondered. If Pasternov didn't join with him, however many people died in the conflict in Europe would be considered the lucky ones compared to what the Zeta Greys had in mind. However bad things might look, they could always get worse. A lot worse.

"You're undoing every bit of military progress we have made against the Russians since the Cold War," Farnsworth said. "Politically and militarily, this is a disaster of epic proportions. Stop the withdrawal, now, sir, before it's too late."

Andrews shook his head. "I have a higher purpose in withdrawing our forces from Europe. We are going to need every soldier we have, right here in our own country, to fight a very vicious enemy within our borders."

Farnsworth looked suspiciously at him. "And who do you imagine that enemy would be?"

It doesn't take much imagination to know who your enemy is when they're abducting and killing your people, Andrews thought.

"Unfortunately, I am not in a position to explain it all to you at this time. Suffice it to say that you are going to have to trust me for a few more days. Then I can read you in on what's really going on."

Farnsworth wasn't buying it. Andrews could see it in his eyes.

"Sir," the Chairman said. "You can tell us right now. We have the highest security clearances in the country."

Farnsworth was staring at him: suspicious, disbelieving.

"Actually, you don't," Andrews said. "I didn't either, so just bear with me for a few more days. That's all I ask."

Andrews watched them leave, frustration and resentment clearly etched on each face. I've asked them to trust me, he thought. If they can't, this whole thing could blow up in my face. The problem was Farnsworth. He knew more than he was letting on, but what did he know? And where did he get the information?

He picked up his secure phone and called Admiral Hollis.

* * *

That evening, President Andrews and his personal Secret Service detail walked through one of the tunnels that led from the White House to a remote building. From there they traveled by car to Camp David.

At 11:00, the brightly glowing craft silently glided over the treetops and settled into the clearing inside Camp David. Andrews, dressed in an Air Force flight suit, swiftly approached as the canopy opened.

"Good evening, Commander," he said.

Diane removed her helmet. "Good evening, sir, where are we off to tonight?"

He smiled at her. "Ten miles north of the Great Wall of China, northwest of Beijing."

She nodded in acknowledgement. "We're going to have

to stay at lower altitudes, if you don't mind, sir. We have a lot of saucers looking for us."

Andrews climbed onto the wing. "Understood. Any problem in getting us there in half an hour?" he asked as he settled into the back seat.

"Not unless we get spotted by a saucer, sir. All bets would be off at that point."

She handed him a helmet.

"Then let's get to it."

She checked Andrews's harness and helmet, then took her seat.

The fighter craft rose silently into the night and shot due north at forty percent thrust. Within ninety seconds they had crossed over into Canadian airspace.

"The Canadians don't know we're coming through. Neither do the Russians. The Chinese president is the only one who knows we're on our way," he said.

She chuckled to herself. "No worries, sir. By the time they can get a pilot pointed in the right direction, we'll be long gone."

Diane angled the craft slightly east, crossing the western edge of Greenland on their way north. The moonlight reflected off the ice and snow as they crossed the top of the world, creating a surreal scene of shifting shades of gray and silver beneath them. At the fifteen-minute mark, the sky lightened in front of them. The sun appeared to rise in the south as she took him over Russia and into China. The craft settled down into the wide courtyard of an old gray stone Buddhist temple high up on a mountain. The Chinese president and his armed guards were the only people visible. The canopy lifted and Andrews stepped out into the bitter cold air. He heard it close as he walked into the temple behind President Hua Chung Hei.

"Just out of curiosity," Hua said, "how long did it take

you to fly here from Washington? Or is that classified information?"

Andrews checked his watch. "Twenty-two minutes. We took the scenic route."

Hua chuckled. He had spent two years at Yale University when he was young and had learned a number of American sayings.

The two presidents sat on folding chairs next to a small, ornate, round wood stove in the center of the room.

"I have watched with great curiosity as you moved your army and air force out of Europe," Hua said. "I must admit I am amused that you do nothing as Pasternov moves his tanks toward your NATO partners. Do you actually trust him?"

Andrews smiled and nodded. "As much as I am going to trust you,"

Hua smiled. "Meaning what, exactly?"

Andrews leaned forward. "I need your help. I am willing to trade the technology you see in the courtyard outside for your assistance in fighting the Zeta Greys."

Hua's expression turned serious. "You have no idea what you are up against. You can't win against them."

Andrews moved further forward and said confidently, "I can and I am."

Hua shook his head. "I sent our best troops against the Greys in an underground base deep in Mongolia. I don't even know if we killed any of those small creatures. What I do know is only four of our people survived. From the limited reports I have, some kind of ray gun was used by the aliens. It vaporized my soldiers. There is nothing I can do to help you."

Hua sat back and folded his arms across his chest.

"We, too, have had our encounters with the alien flash guns. We are currently building a prototype portable particle beam weapon, but that is a ways off yet. What I am offering you is the means to shoot them down and stop the incursion of their saucers into our atmosphere. If we can cooperate on that, we can stop the flow of material and creatures both on and off the planet. We can break their supply chain."

Hua scoffed. "Starve them out? Is that what you are suggesting?"

"Partially. They make their own nutritional liquid in the underground bases, and since they need to be fed only once in every six weeks, they can survive for years. What I am saying is that we need to isolate the saucers from the underground bases first. That craft outside is fully capable of accomplishing that task. Plus I know you have the atmospheric heaters and electrification technology we need as a weapon against the saucers in the ionosphere. You are going to need a certain parts per million metallic content of aluminum and barium in the upper atmosphere in order for it to work."

Hua shook his head. "What you propose is very risky."

Andrews shrugged. "And you think what the Zeta Greys are already doing and where their program is going isn't?"

Hua pushed his lips together. Andrews didn't see any fear in Hua's face and posture, just deep anger and hatred. He could tell Hua already knew what the Zeta Greys were doing.

"I have twelve training simulators already in the air on two C-130 cargo planes. Just tell me where you want them and they're yours. Underground training and launch facilities are an absolute necessity, as are particle beam cannons. The full build specifications are included with the simulators. I can deliver twelve craft and four cannons in ten days, complete with strategy, tactics, and build specifications. All I ask in return is your help fighting the Zeta Greys."

Hua drummed his fingers on his knee.

"Pasternov is joining you?"

Hua seemed very skeptical.

"Yes, I believe he is."

Hua broke eye contact, glanced around the room, and returned his gaze to Andrews.

"I will defer my decision until I see whether Pasternov actually joins with you."

Andrews nodded slightly. Hua was making the first of many steps that needed to take place. Waiting for Pasternov was both cautious and reasonable under the circumstances. "That's fine. I just need to know where you want the training simulators. Your people are going to need all the time with them they can get."

Hua watched him carefully.

"So you are giving me the simulators and the cannon design before you get my decision?"

Andrews nodded. "I don't think it's much of a decision. Either we stand and fight together, or we lose the planet to the Zeta Greys."

Hua looked skeptical, but at least he was still listening.

"When and if I decide?"

He's going to join with us, Andrews thought. If he were going to walk away, he would have done so by now.

"Seed your skies with nanoparticles of aluminum and barium. I will also need the complete input from the incoherent backscatter array in Shanghai and temporary operational control over your transmitter in Xinjiang. Once you build your own command center, we will return operational control for your part of the planet back over to you. Then you can coordinate the electrification of the upper atmosphere with us to destroy the saucers. Do that and I will deliver the fighter craft with all of the build specifications and material processes needed for you to build your own fighters. You'll have everything you need."

Hua nodded to his assistant, who wrote a location in GPS coordinates on a piece of paper and handed it to Andrews, who, in turn, handed a USB drive to Hua.

"Three files. The first contains your internal enemies—the second has the names of people you can trust. The third file is the particle beam cannon design. This should help you come to a decision."

Hua looked suspiciously at the USB drive.

"And I'm supposed to believe what's on here. How did you come by this information?"

Andrews smiled. "Through the people from the Tau Ceti star system. They have already accomplished what lies before us. You have some of them working for you. It's all in the file."

Chapter 39

"I need to get this set of coordinates to two planes I have in the air," Andrews said.

"Admiral Hollis can handle that for you, sir," Diane said. She turned on the encrypted radio. "Jink to base, do you copy?"

Her stomach tightened with the risk of using the radio.

"Base to Jink, copy?"

The Zeta Greys would certainly pick up the encrypted signal.

"Boss there?"

Got to make this quick, she thought.

"I'm right here," Hollis replied.

Andrews explained what he needed. Hollis confirmed

the two planes received the location and clearance to land from Chinese air traffic control.

"Anyone around?" Diane asked.

She waited nervously for the reply.

"Clear skies, Jink."

So far, so good, she thought.

"Roger that. I'll have him back in a few."

The sun set behind them as they continued their winter trek north into the darkness of the Arctic Circle. Diane's radio crackled to life as they entered the northern expanse of Canada.

"Base to Jink, copy?"

Her stomach tightened into a knot.

"Jink here."

She looked around quickly, scanning the skies.

"We have a saucer intrusion over the north pole. Three bogies high on your six. We are scrambling two craft to assist."

They picked up our radio transmission, Diane thought. "ETA?"

"Twelve minutes."

She cringed. "Acknowledged."

She pushed the thrust to seventy percent and turned off the radio.

"What's going on?" Andrews asked.

"We have three scout saucers coming after us from outer space. I'm going to need your help."

Of all the times, she thought.

"We'll have reinforcements in twelve minutes, right?" Andrews asked.

She scanned the navigation display. Everything in front of her was wilderness. No place to hide, she thought. The only other place to run was up and that was filled with more saucers.

"Too long, sir. Those scout saucers will catch up to us in less than two minutes. Directly in front of you is the round radar screen. The saucers will appear as red dots. Think of the screen as a clock face, twelve at the top, three on the right side, six on the bottom, and nine to the left. We are the center of the screen. When one or more of the red dots gets close to the center, I need you to call out the position of the red dot as a number on that clock. Got it?"

For the first time she wished this was a three-seater instead of a two. She desperately needed Ryan to be there.

"I think so, yes."

She closed her eyes for a moment. Ryan ran all of the electronic countermeasures and both power generating units on the fighter. If they were to crash, Andrews wouldn't be able to shut down the antigravity drive. The impact would rupture the antimatter containment tube and trigger an explosion. Well, not an explosion, exactly: an annihilation event, where matter and antimatter annihilate each other, releasing a tremendous amount of energy in the process. She doubted there would be enough left of either one of them to identify.

"When I turn, the whole screen is going to shift in response, so the clock numbers will change. I will need updates on the closest red dot. We good?" she said, trying to shake the images of death and destruction out of her mind.

"Yes, yes, I can do that."

Despite his eager and confident attitude, she was convinced this was not going to end well.

"Okay. One other thing," Diane said. "The craft is going to start shaking violently. You haven't had the opportunity to adjust to it, so just do the best you can."

She cringed at what he was about to experience.

"I can see the three dots moving up from the bottom of the screen now," Andrews said. "There's a thin red line sticking up from each dot."

Focus on what's happening right now, she reminded herself.

"Elevation indicator," she said. "When the line goes up

the saucer is above us, down is below us. No line means it's the same altitude."

Her adrenaline rush had started.

"So right now they are at six o'clock high, correct?"

Her pulse rate accelerated.

"That's correct. You can drop the o'clock, sir. Six high is fine."

Time seemed to slow down during combat. She felt her awareness expanding as well.

"Okay. I think I've got it."

She silently thanked Dr. Cowen for the meditation exercises. Maybe she could make it through this battle.

"You ready?" she asked.

She took a deep breath.

"Yes," he answered.

Diane turned the jinking control on.

"Oh my God," Andrews said. "This is awful!"

She started breathing hard.

"Just concentrate on the screen, sir."

She checked to the left and the right to see if she could see any more saucers closing in.

"The three dots are spreading out and the lines are shrinking," Andrews said, tension clear in his voice.

"They've started their attack run. Where are the dots now?" she asked.

His voice was louder now. "Seven, six, and five. Almost even with us now."

Diane broke hard left and down. As she came closer to the ground she pulled up and swung left.

"Ten o'clock high!" Andrews called out.

Diane continued up and left, selected single fire, and pulled the trigger as the scout saucer swept across in front of her. The shots missed.

"One, low."

She released the trigger, banked right and down, and squeezed the trigger again. The second scout saucer fired back at them, missing. Her third shot connected solidly with the saucer, sending it into a slow downward spiral.

"Six even and two high!"

She banked right and pulled up, firing again at the scout saucer she had missed before. Banking left and diving after the saucer she finally hit it near the left edge. The saucer banked away, dropping rapidly to the ground. There was a loud crack. The strong jolt pushed through her from her right as a light flash from the saucer behind her struck her wing.

"Six high and very close!"

She swung hard right, flipped the firing control to the two shot mode, and pushed the thruster to eighty percent. Letting her instinct guide her, she pulled the trigger. Both shots hit the saucer near the center. She glanced at her cockpit indicators. Her fighter craft was losing power, the controls were sluggish and they were losing altitude rapidly. She turned the radio back on.

"Jink to base. Mayday, mayday. We have been hit on the starboard wing. We are going down. Baffin Island, six-two point four-five-two north, seven-one point nine-eight-four west."

There wasn't enough time to repeat the location.

"Copy, Jink. Backup is eight minutes out. We have you on satellite. Are both of you okay?"

She swallowed hard. "Affirmative. Two bandits down, one saucer hit, but still functional." She glanced at her watch. "Activating locator beacon in seven minutes, forty seconds. Jink out."

She shut off the radio.

"Are we going to crash?" Andrews asked.

She glanced one last time at the navigation display.

"Where is the remaining saucer?"

She glanced from side to side.

"Eight o'clock high."

So behind and to the left.

"How far from the center of the screen?" she asked.

He hesitated. "About an inch?"

Do the unexpected, her intuition whispered.

"Okay, this is going to be close."

Diane used what power remained in her craft for a power dive straight down at the ground.

"Shouldn't we be trying to stay up?" Andrews asked.

"Not with an active saucer behind us. The sooner we get on the ground, the better."

She had to get the cockpit as far away from the annihilation event as she could.

"But . . ."

She pushed the control stick forward.

"Hang on!"

Chapter 40

Diane pulled the ejection lever. The cockpit with the canopy attached exploded out of the fighter craft and a drogue chute deployed from the back. The ground was rushing at them at a terrifying rate of speed when the main chutes deployed, violently yanking them forward in their seats. The shock wave from the fighter craft hitting the ground and exploding rocked them and drove them sideways. They crashed through the top canopy of evergreen trees and jolted to a stop as the main chutes caught on the tops of the trees.

"Don't move," Diane said.

They hung in the air, twenty feet above the ground. She squeezed a hand grip low on the left side of her seat, releasing the parachute cords from the cockpit. They fell the last twenty feet, landing on a foot-thick bed of snow over pine needles.

The cockpit bounced, jarring them down into their seats. They landed tipped to the right. The canopy unscrewed from the cockpit and rose into the air at a sideward angle. She unbuckled her harness, scrambled out, and helped Andrews out of his harness. As he climbed out, she grabbed the survival kit from the cockpit and gripped his arm.

"You okay?" she asked.

He looked totally disoriented.

"Nauseated and shook up, but, yeah, I'm okay."

Right, she thought.

"Good. We gotta go, now."

She pulled him quickly away from the cockpit and threaded her way through the tree trunks.

"Shouldn't we stay here?" Andrews asked.

Bright white light glared down from above the trees. She grabbed Andrews by the arm and tried to pull him behind a tree. A flash of light hit the cockpit. The blast from the explosion ripped Andrews from her grip and threw him into the snow eight feet away. Flaming pieces of metal and pine bark flew between the trees and sliced into the snow. A bent strip of metal from the canopy stuck out of the tree just beyond Andrews. She ran to him, checking for blood on his clothes. The force of the blast had ripped his helmet off.

"Aaah!" Andrews said, as she rolled him over.

"Sir, are you hit?" She frantically ran her hands over him looking for metal sticking out of his body. "Where does it hurt?"

"What?" He looked dazed and disoriented.

"Can you stand up?" she asked, pulling on his arms. "We have to get out of here!"

Andrews groaned as he struggled to stand. "I think . . . "

"Can you walk?" She pulled his arm over her shoulder and started moving him forward. She spotted his helmet and picked it up. A four-inch gash ran across the top of his helmet, slightly in back of center. Edges of a fine wire mesh inside the helmet were torn open. She felt her eyes widen as she realized how close Andrews had come to being dead. She had to get him away from the crash site. Gradually his legs took over and he was walking on his own.

They continued trudging on through the snow and bitter cold for three hundred yards. Diane pulled Andrews behind a large tree, opened the survival pack, and handed him a thin metallic survival blanket.

"Wrap this around you. It will keep you from freezing and help hide you from their sensors."

He unrolled the thin sheet and slipped it around his shoulders.

"Cover your head, too," she said.

Her hope was that the foil might help make up for some of the damage to the helmet. Andrews flipped the foil sheet over his head, glanced up, and said, "I never thought of myself as a foil hat kind of person."

Diane smiled and shook her head. He's going to do all right, she thought. He's certainly got enough guts.

They pushed on through the deep bed of white snow with tan pine needles being pulled to the surface by their feet. After another two hundred yards she turned to the left for thirty yards, then doubled back for fifty yards. She handed him the locator beacon and her watch.

"Stand with your back against this tree. When the watch reaches exactly 12:18, flip this switch. Then don't move." She handed him the helmet, wondering if it still worked. "Put this on over the foil blanket, it'll help keep the Greys from reading your mind or planting thoughts in your head." He put on the helmet.

She took the .45 automatic pistol out of the survival pack along with the tactical flashlight and moved over three trees. She pulled back the slide on the .45 and slowly let it close, loading a round into the chamber. The tactical flashlight was a high intensity LED model used by Special Forces. She wrapped the survival blanket around herself and faced the tree, glancing around it once every few seconds.

Three minutes later she sensed movement ahead and to the right of their position. In the dull light that filtered down through the trees from the saucer above she saw three small figures following the tracks in the snow. The beings appeared almost childlike, except for the large heads.

Diane's hand started shaking, her heart racing. In her mind she saw these creatures circled around Daniel, tormenting him, hurting him. Her breathing deepened. They took him, she thought. They took Daniel.

One Zeta was walking in the tracks she and Andrews had made, with the other two spread out twenty feet on each side. They walked slowly, swiveling their heads from side to side, searching for any sign of their quarry.

She was shaking now. How could she ever hold the pistol steady enough to actually hit one of them? She focused on Daniel again. You took my brother, she thought. Anger rose within her chest and flooded into her head. She clenched her teeth and glanced at Andrews. You're not taking anyone else, she thought. The trembling in her hand slowly stopped.

So far, they weren't picking up her or Andrews's thoughts or location. That was good. The creature closest to them stopped and turned in their direction. Crap, she thought, Andrews's helmet isn't working like it should.

Andrews turned on the locator beacon. The closest Zeta began walking in their direction. It picked up the radio transmission, she thought, in addition to his location. The other two continued following the tracks in the snow. Twenty seconds, Diane thought, and our fighter craft are going to be here.

The Zeta kept walking straight at them. It was now less

than eighty feet away. She glanced around the tree again. The other two Zetas were now headed toward them, too, but still farther away. She felt totally wired from the adrenaline rush. Because of the helmet she couldn't hear the slight crunching of the snow as the creature came within fifty feet of them. The closest Zeta stopped and swiveled its head from side to side.

What does it see? Diane wondered. She glanced over at Andrews. He was breathing rapidly, his breath pushed out from under his helmet, and drifted slowly to the side in the frozen air. She couldn't say anything to him—the creature was too close. She held her breath, counted to ten, and glanced around the tree again.

The Zeta was walking straight for Andrews's tree carrying something in its left hand. She glanced again. It was fifteen feet away now. She had a clear field of fire, no trees in the way. The horrifying thought that she was using the president as bait crossed her mind; not that she could do anything about it now. She raised the flashlight on the left side of the tree and the .45 on the right. She slid slightly to the right to get a better view.

She switched on the flashlight, aiming it at the Zeta. It tried to shield its eyes from the bright light. She quickly aimed and fired the .45 as the little creature raised its left hand toward her. The bullet hit the Zeta in the head, throwing it backward into the snow. The other two Zetas started to run at her, then stopped. They quickly turned back for the saucer and ran in that direction.

Our fighters are here, she thought. Two seconds later she heard several sharp metallic cracks followed by the sound of limbs breaking as the last scout saucer fell into the forest and crashed to the ground.

She motioned for Andrews to stay where he was. He nodded and she headed off in the snow toward the crashed saucer, moving quickly from tree to tree. Between the trees she got a brief look at one of the Zetas as it reached the saucer. A shot from one of the particle beam cannons on a fighter craft sliced through the creature as it came into the open, dropping it to the ground. The other Zeta hid behind a tree. The fighters kept moving, sliding from side to side over the trees. The fighter craft fired their cannons, blasting holes through tree trunks, trying to hit the remaining creature. She knew the Zeta didn't show up very well on the night sensors of the fighter craft. If it weren't for the snow and freezing temperatures, it wouldn't show up at all. She, on the other hand, would show up more of a bright red color on their screens, so she wasn't worried about friendly fire hitting her.

She closed in on the Zeta from the back as it jumped from tree to tree trying to avoid the cannon blasts. It raised the thing in its hand and fired it at the fighter craft, vaporizing three-foot diameter tunnels through the limbs of the tall trees. It moved to the right. Anticipating that it wanted to get back to the saucer she moved forward and left, staying behind tree after tree. After several cannon blasts from the fighter craft above, the creature bolted to the left. The Zeta paused behind a tree. Diane aimed and fired, striking it in the back of the head.

She signaled three short blinks upward with her tactical flashlight to let the fighters know everything was clear, then she slowly approached the saucer. It was tipped on its side. The sharp edge was buried two feet into the snow, pine needles, and frozen ground. She looked for a door in the saucer, but didn't find one.

She checked the body of the Zeta Grey she had shot. It was lying still in the snow. A thin green fluid seeped out of the head, turning the surrounding snow bright green. She turned away as bile flooded up her throat pushing to be expelled. She stepped away, opened her face shield, and retched beside a tree. Breathing deeply, she spit the remaining bile out of her mouth. Diane picked up a handful of clean snow and put it in her mouth. It melted quickly. She rinsed her mouth and spit out the remaining fluid.

Diane put her arm out and steadied herself on a large tree, breathing deeply until the dizziness subsided. As she became calmer, she closed her face shield, turned, and focused her attention on the dead Grey. There was an oblong hole in the snow beside the creature. She reached into the snow and extracted a flashlight shaped object with smooth, rounded edges and a row of three buttons running lengthwise in the middle of the device. This must be the thing that was vaporizing tunnels through the tree limbs, she thought. Could be useful.

Diane jumped as she caught movement in her peripheral vision. She spun in that direction and aimed the .45. The Zeta hit by the particle beam cannon from one of the fighter craft was still moving. She approached cautiously, keeping the gun aimed at its head.

God, these things are ugly, she thought. She got a whiff of the creature's odor. They stink, too. Daniel must have been terrified by them when he was abducted.

Diane glanced at the flashlight shaped object in her hand. All three of the Greys had one. Where was this one's? She walked slowly up to the squirming creature, and checked its hands. Empty. She found the hole where it had been dropped and dug it out of the icy snow. The creature's odor was definitely offensive. The closer she got, the stronger her revulsion. She shined her tactical flashlight on the creature's head. Cat-like slit pupils in the large black eyes closed quickly in the bright light. She jumped back. Her heart was pounding, her breath rapid and ragged. Her hands trembled as she aimed her gun at its head again. The thought of running away was tempting her. She looked at the two objects in her hand, and carefully slid them into pockets on her flight suit.

It's unarmed, she thought. At least I *think* it's unarmed.

How would I actually know?

She crept closer to the thing and watched it wiggle from time to time. It could be just a nervous response—or seizures. Either way it was still dangerous. She looked at its flattened face, tiny nose, and small slit of a mouth. The eyes drew her attention. She couldn't help but look into its eyes. I'm safe from telepathic influence as long as I have my helmet on, she reminded herself. Then she thought about Daniel again, trying to imagine what they had done to him. Anger and resentment mounted as she stared into the creature's eyes. She pointed the .45 between its eyes. You may not remember or care about Daniel, she thought, but I do.

She pulled the trigger.

She retrieved the third weapon from the dead Grey fifteen feet from where Andrews was still leaning against the tree.

She took off her helmet. He did the same. "It's over," she said. "We're safe."

He breathed out heavily and bent forward, hands on his knees. "Thank you."

She saw the flickering light from tactical flashlights moving through the trees in the distance.

"Over here!" She waved her flashlight back and forth to signal them.

Chapter 41

"We've lost four out of six fighter craft in the last two days," Diane said. "If we go out again, I'm afraid we'll lose not only our last two craft, but the crews as well."

Hollis nodded. "I understand your concern, Zadanski." Sitting across the table from her in the debriefing room, Hollis glanced at his watch. 0200 hours. "We have ten more fighter craft arriving in approximately two hours. That'll give us half a squadron. New pilots and RIOs will be here sometime tomorrow."

Diane was relieved that new fighter craft were arriving, but her encounter on Baffin Island weighed heavily on her mind.

"The other thing that concerns me is confronting the Zetas on the ground. We need more protection."

Hollis tipped back in his chair, his brow furrowed.

"We hadn't thought much about that," Hollis admitted. "We were thinking only of combat in flight."

Diane glanced down and shook her head.

"Well, what happened on Baffin Island changes that. We came close to losing the president. Wearing the helmets helped a lot. I think the heat reflecting emergency blankets helped too, but they're too small; we need them larger, or we need the reflective coating built into the flight suits."

Hollis put his hand to his mouth, deep in thought. Then he spoke, "You're thinking they react to infrared?"

Diane nodded. "The first Zeta I shot was following the president's breath. I don't know whether it could see the water vapor in the air, or the heat from his breath. Either way, the Zetas seem to have excellent vision in darkened areas."

Hollis grabbed a pen and made some notes. He glanced up at her, then back down as he wrote some more.

"Considering the size of their eyes, I can't say I'm surprised. What else did you notice?"

Hollis wiggled the pen in his fingers.

"They don't have any outer ears to gather sound, so their hearing isn't that good. I was able to come up from behind two of them. I think the cold snow helped to dampen the sound, but still . . ."

Hollis nodded and wrote more notes. "Okay, that's interesting, but I don't see how that helps us much at this point."

Well, I do, Diane thought. I've got to make this clear. "My concern is that we're going to have more encounters with the Zetas on the ground. We know we're going to lose fighter craft, but in a majority of those cases the crew is going to survive."

The furrow in Hollis's brow was back. He paused, then said, "I'm rethinking what you said about their vision. We have sightings of saucers during the day, but the vast majority of contact with the Zetas themselves takes place at night. You may be on to something."

Okay, she thought. I'm getting through. That's a relief. "In addition, I used our tactical flashlight as a distraction by shining it at the Zeta. It was startled and tried to shield its eyes from the bright light. That gave me the time I needed to aim and shoot it."

Hollis still appeared to be deep in thought. "What about the second Zeta you shot?"

The image of the ugly dead Zeta and the green fluid leaking into the snow flashed into her mind. The nausea returned as well, just not as strong. She took a breath, trying to calm herself.

"What my intuition is showing me is that the Zetas depend heavily on their strongest senses, which are telepathy and sight in low light levels. Our helmets seem to eliminate their telepathic control of our minds, but I think it works the other way around, too. The helmet limits their ability to sense our presence and location, probably by shielding our thoughts from them."

Hollis nodded and jotted another note. "Interesting. I will have the reflective coating built into the flight suits. What else?"

Diane paused to think.

"I feel like we need a way to communicate when we're not in our fighter craft, but it's not really formed in my mind yet. I'll let you know when I figure it out."

Hollis shook his head again. "You don't have to figure these things out on your own," he said. "You can bounce ideas off Theo anytime you want. We have a direct underground line with Ceti Research. Here's his extension number." He handed her one of Theo's cards. "Anything else?"

Diane paused and glanced around the room.

"I need to know more about the Zeta Greys. How can I get that information?"

Hollis shook his head. "As you are aware, this whole business is very compartmentalized. I'm not going to be able to get authorization."

She lowered her head, breathed out, and looked back up at him. Compartmentalization was good for security, but it was leaving too many people in the dark about the enemy they were fighting.

"Please see what you can do. What we don't know right now has the potential to kill all of us."

Hollis looked at her, worry deepening in his expression. "I'll see what I can do. Good job out there. Get some rest."

She nodded and stood. "Yes, sir."

As she walked back down to her quarters the three alien weapons weighed heavily on her mind. I should have mentioned them. I should have turned them in for reverse engineering, but my gut tells me to hang on to them. I just hope I'm doing the right thing.

* * *

Diane unlocked the door to her quarters.

"Hey," Ryan said softly from down the hall.

She turned to him.

"How did your mission go?"

She looked down at the floor. "I almost got the president killed."

Ryan appeared shocked. "You were with the president?"

She nodded. "I used the radio when we were too far from home. It attracted three scout saucers. I should have waited."

Ryan shook his head. "Look, this is my area of

expertise. If you were flying in a remote area, the radio was the least of your concerns—especially at night. Our fighter craft glows bright white at night. It's visible from thousands of miles in space. Whether you used the radio or not, they would have spotted you."

Diane hung her head. "It was a critical mistake. I lost our fighter. I shouldn't be flying."

Ryan motioned for them to go into her room. "I understand your concern. Under ideal circumstances, or as a training exercise, the loss of our craft would be a serious consideration. But we're at war. We're going to lose fighter craft and people. I'm just thankful that you and the president are still alive."

She sat on the bed, tears forming in her eyes.

He sat next to her and paused before speaking. "You feel like you can't be trusted as a pilot?"

She nodded.

He began chuckling, quietly, but she was irritated.

"This isn't funny," she said. "I almost got the president killed!"

He was trying to stifle his laughter. But he couldn't. "You don't get it, do you?"

She looked at him. "What do you mean?"

He smiled. "I fly with you all of the time. I have no control over what you do or how you fly, and frankly, I wouldn't want to be anywhere else. You're the best pilot I've ever seen."

Her heart was pounding and she felt short of breath.

He shook his head. "You still don't get it. Hollis picked you because if he'd sent anyone else, both the pilot and the president would be dead. You're that good."

She looked over at him.

"I put my life in your hands every time we strap into that fighter craft. I trust you. I believe in you. I care about you." He reached over and took her hand in his. "All I want is for you to go back to trusting yourself—believing in yourself—and being as confident in that pilot seat as you have ever been."

She squeezed his hand.

"My personal feelings aside," he said. "You have to get your head and your heart back into being the best pilot there ever was. You were born to fly one of these things. No doubt in my mind about it. There's no room for doubt in your mind, either. Forget about almost getting the president killed. Almost doesn't matter. The president is alive because of your skill and dedication. Please, let that sink in."

He stood, kissed her on the forehead, and left.

She sat there in a state of shock, mouth open, staring at the closed door. God, she thought, I had no idea he felt this way.

Chapter 42

President Andrews walked unsteadily into the residence in Camp David.

"Sir, are you all right?" James, his head Secret Service agent asked.

Andrews was feeling dizzy and having trouble with his balance.

"It was a rough night, James. I think I'll stay here for a few days. Please bring my wife first thing in the morning."

Andrews stumbled and grabbed onto a chair for support.

"Yes, sir. I'm calling the doctor. You don't look good."

James rushed over to help him.

"Yeah, I've got a really bad headache and I'm feeling nauseated again."

James encouraged him to take a chair.

"Again, sir?" Then James said into his wrist microphone, "I need the on-duty doctor and six additional agents in the residence now, and wake FLOTUS. I don't like the way this feels. Get her in the beast and on the road, now."

Andrews stood, stumbled into the bathroom, and retched into the toilet.

"And get the chief of staff and Harriet, his secretary here, too."

Dr. Wilkins, the on-duty doctor, rushed in through the front door. "Where is he? What happened?"

James pointed to the bathroom.

"What happened?" Dr. Wilkins asked again. He shined a small flashlight in Andrews's eyes, checked his heart and lungs, and took his blood pressure and temperature.

"I have a helicopter warming up," James said. "Does he need to go to Walter Reed?"

"I don't know yet," Dr. Wilkins said. "His vitals are good." The doctor took the president's head in his hands. "Sir, can you tell me what happened?"

"Partly," Andrews said. "Let's say I was in a plane that shook very violently, and bounced around a lot. I don't think anything is broken, but I'm nauseated. I have a severe headache, and my joints hurt. Other than that, I think I'm all right."

Dr. Wilkins looked horrified. "I want to take him to Walter Reed, full physical and neurological workup. I don't want to take any chances."

Andrews pulled his wallet out of his pocket and removed a card. "Call this number first. Ask for Dr. Cowen. Then you can make your recommendation."

Andrews slumped onto the floor of the bathroom.

The doctor called the number and conversed for five minutes. Then he said, "Okay. Have the chopper stand down.

Take him to the clinic. I want a CT scan of his head and chest just to be on the safe side. I have a sedative for him. After the scan, get him into bed."

Thankfully, Andrews could lie down for the CT scan. By the time it was done, he was feeling much more comfortable and drowsy. He quickly fell asleep when he got into bed.

* * *

Sean Wells sipped his morning coffee in his room at the Washington Hilton in northwest D.C. He had a local news station on the TV with the sound muted. On the screen, red and blue flashing lights with two plumes of smoke rising in the background caught his attention. Breaking News was boldly displayed across the bottom of the screen. He turned on the sound.

"Initial reports indicate that a plane or a helicopter has crashed in the countryside behind me," the young woman said. "We think there are two crash sites, judging from the smoke, and that a small plane may have collided with a helicopter. At this time we do not know what kind of helicopter or other aircraft was involved or how many people might have been on board. The local police have the area closed off. We were able to get this before the police escorted us from the area."

A shifting telephoto view of a helicopter crumpled on the ground filled the screen. Black smoke billowed from the wreckage with occasional orange flames piercing the roiling dark cloud. Sean stood and moved closer to the screen. A police officer appeared, holding his hand in front of the camera. The video restarted and played again.

"Oh no." Sean grabbed his cell phone and called his editor.

"Ed, are you watching this on the news?"

Sean looked carefully at the helicopter wreckage shown on the screen.

"Watching what?"

He checked the bottom of the screen. "It's a local station near D.C. The reporter is Virginia Cummings. She's at the scene of a helicopter crash. From what I can see, it looks like the kind and color of the president's chopper. Is there anything on the major news feeds?"

He walked closer to the screen.

"Let me check . . . So far nothing. What do you think is going on?"

He looked at the wreckage more closely. "I don't know. Every time they move the president by chopper they always use three of them. Keeps everyone guessing, you know?"

It was a live feed with no DVR. He couldn't pause or back it up for a second look.

"So it can't be that," Ed said. "There's only one crash site, right?"

Sean's heart was beating faster.

"No. I saw two smoke plumes. We have at least two crash sites."

Did they bring down two of the three choppers? Did the president get away?

"What is the local reporter saying?" Ed asked.

Sean put his left hand to his chest.

"She thinks a small plane and a helicopter collided in the air."

"Well then it can't be the president. They close the airspace every time he flies."

The screen view switched back to the local reporter. "As you can see, off to the right side, a third plume of smoke has appeared. It looks like three aircraft may have been involved."

The camera view shifted to the right. Two Maryland

state troopers were rushing over.

"This area is closed," the first officer said. "You have to leave, now."

The camera switched to Virginia Cummings.

"Officer, we have a first amendment right to be here. This is public property. You can't just order us to leave."

The officer shook his head. "This is a matter of national security," he said as he grabbed the camera.

The view on the screen blurred as the camera moved rapidly, and then the screen went black.

"What the hell? Ed, are you getting any of this?"

Sean glanced at his watch: 7:18. Hell of a way to start the day.

"No. Nothing is on the major news feeds. Wait a minute . . . One of our younger interns has something. It's a new Twitter feed: hashtag president dead. I can't verify it. Someone thinks the president has died."

Chapter 43

"Mr. President?"

Andrews opened his eyes.

"Sir," Franks said. "I hate to wake you up, but we have a situation."

Andrews sat up and tried to clear his mind. "What happened?"

"Sir, I'm afraid this is my fault. I'm so sorry."

Andrews dressed quickly. "Just tell me what happened."

"When you left the White House last night the plan was that you would be back before morning."

"Yeah?"

Franks was uncharacteristically nervous.

"But then you stayed here and the First Lady was

whisked away in the middle of the night. They came and got me and Harriet. When I found out we were all going to be here for a few days I started cancelling your appointments. Harriet and I were calling people and then it occurred to me. People would be suspicious about the president disappearing in the middle of the night and showing up at Camp David unannounced. You know?"

Franks was rubbing his hands together and shifting his weight from one foot to the other.

"Go on."

Franks glanced at the door. "So I thought the optics would be better if the public saw you leave for Camp David this morning. I had Agent Dodd made up to look like you. He walked out of the White House, waved to people, and got on the chopper."

Andrews finished tying his shoes. "Okay."

He stood, walked out of the bedroom, and into a madhouse. Secret Service agents were running in and out of the residence, phones were ringing, and three TV screens showed video of the crashed helicopters.

"What the hell happened?"

Franks rushed up next to him. "That's what I was trying to explain, sir. All three helicopters were shot down on their way here to Camp David. Last communication with Marine One said multiple missiles had been fired from the ground, sir. No chatter, no warning, nothing. The attack was a total surprise, sir."

Andrews checked all three screens. "Casualties?"

Franks shook his head. "No survivors, sir. At least eight are dead. Maybe more."

Andrews turned and looked Franks straight in the eyes. "My wife?"

Franks shook his head again. "She's here, sir. She's safe."

Andrews's head was swimming. "I need some coffee."

"Right away, sir."

Andrews walked over to Secret Service Agent James. "I thought those helicopters had countermeasure and jamming systems on them."

James turned to face him. "They do, sir. Initial examination of the crash sites indicate that Russian SA-24 Grinch shoulder-launched missiles were used. Those are reasonably countermeasure resistant. Our people on the scene are reporting that they believe at least ten missiles were fired at each helicopter, sir. It was a turkey shoot. No chance of surviving it."

Andrews's shoulders drooped. "Any idea who's behind the attack?"

James glanced at the screens. "No, sir. Too early to tell."

Andrews closed his eyes momentarily and exhaled— hard. "So this wasn't a lone nut with a missile."

"No, sir, it wasn't. At least thirty to thirty-five people had to be involved for a coordinated attack like this to succeed."

The expression on James's face was grim, but determined.

"Could someone have leaked the flight plan?"

James shook his head. "Not the way it works, sir. The route to or from Camp David is changed every time. Out of twenty-five different routes, six are chosen at random. The final flight plan is selected by a roll of a die, once the choppers are in the air. No one on the ground knows the flight path."

Andrews stepped closer to the main screen. "So someone either got incredibly lucky, or . . ." He turned to face James.

"This was a major military-level operation with coordinated supply, deployment, and intelligence support,"

James replied.

Andrews closed his eyes, breathed out, and tilted his head back.

"Your coffee, sir," Franks said.

Andrews opened his eyes, breathed in and out, looked at Franks, and took the coffee. He turned back to James. "What would be the first outward sign that I was moving by helicopter?"

"The three helicopters would be moved out of the hanger at Andrews Air Force Base. Second step would be to close the airspace for all routes from Andrews to the White House, and third, from the White House to Camp David."

Andrews took a cautious sip of coffee. It was too hot, as usual.

"So if someone were watching the hangar, how much advance notice would that provide them?"

James rubbed his lips as he thought. "Twenty, twenty-five minutes before the chopper lands at the White House. Another ten to fifteen minutes before they take off again."

Andrews blew across the top of his coffee, trying to cool it down. "And how soon does the airspace get closed?"

James pressed the ear-piece to his ear with his finger. "Within seconds. Excuse me for a second, sir."

James spoke into his wrist microphone, then returned his attention to Andrews.

"So someone could either know, or strongly suspect, Marine One would be on its way to Camp David thirty to forty minutes before it would be shot down?" Andrews asked.

James paused for a moment. "Yes, sir. I'd have to agree with that assessment."

Andrews frowned. "Meaning someone would have that long to put thirty to thirty-five people in place. That could be done, couldn't it?"

James shrugged. "Maybe. But that doesn't take into

account the different flight paths, sir. To cover all of the routes would take almost eight hundred and fifty people. The logistics are huge and unlikely."

Andrews took another cautious sip of his coffee and walked over to the window.

"How long into the flight would someone be able to determine the general flight path, and how long before the helicopter would reach the attack site?"

James followed him over to the window. "The final route could be determined within three minutes with maybe another twelve minutes travel time to the kill zone. I see what you're thinking, sir. Prepositioned groups could be centrally placed so they could move up to seven or eight miles in either direction to get to the kill zone. That would reduce the manpower requirement to around a hundred people. Operationally, that's doable."

Andrews again tested his coffee. It was just about the right temperature now.

"That means there would have to be some noticeable ground traffic between when Marine One left the White House and when the choppers were shot down."

James nodded. "Yes, sir, it does."

Andrews took several swallows of his coffee. "And someone on the inside feeding them intel."

James glanced at the floor. "Yes. That, too."

Andrews nodded slightly and finished his coffee. He motioned for Franks to come closer.

"Get a hold of Michaels over at the NSA and Butler at the NRO. See if there were vehicles in motion around the attack zones prior to the ambush. I also want Clemens from the FBI in here ASAP. Things are going to move quickly now and we need to be faster."

Franks moved off quickly while Andrews turned back to James.

"You were a Special Forces commander for a while before you came over to the Service," Andrews said. "Who would be able to do something like this and how long would it take to get everything operational?"

James paused for a moment. "Strategically, it would have to be someone like Russia or China—a player with deep resources and wide connections. The missiles used were Russian, but those are available on the black market anywhere in the world. Tactically, mercenaries would make the most sense, but it would take a long time to move them into the country without alerting us."

Andrews nodded and pursed his lips. "What if the mercenaries lived here?"

James looked at Andrews, shock registering on his face. "That would be extremely troubling, sir. That would mean someone inside our own system tried to kill you."

Andrews turned away from the window and took a chair.

"How long to put the arms and the people together and preposition them?"

James walked slowly over to a chair and sat down. "Twelve hours, maybe less. What are you thinking?"

Andrews set his coffee cup down on the short table. "With hundreds of billions of dollars flowing from the military to our defense contractors each year, I'm thinking I may have underestimated their desire for money and overestimated their dedication to our country, and that miscalculation has just turned deadly."

James's cell phone buzzed. He answered and listened. "Our agents on the scene have confirmed that the body in Marine One is Agent Dodd. I'll inform the White House that you are alive. Stephanie Peterson can hold a press conference and let the public know before this spins out of control."

Andrews held up his index finger. "What if we don't?"

James frowned. "Don't what?"

Andrews turned to face agent James. "We don't know who is behind this attack. We need to think things through before we do anything else. I've already got eight dead and three Marine helicopters destroyed because I didn't think things through clearly. We can't afford another mistake. Right now, whoever did this believes they have succeeded. What would be the next logical step?"

James tipped his head slightly to the right. "The Twenty-fifth Amendment to the Constitution provides for the vice president to become president."

Andrews nodded slowly. "But can Harper be sworn in as president before my death is confirmed?"

James shook his head. "We have confirmation. Agent Dodd is dead, and you're sitting right here."

A plan was forming in the back of Andrews's mind.

"Yes. But what if we hang on to that information until the medical examiner makes the identification official?"

James seemed confused. "I suppose we could, but that would merely delay the inevitable for a few hours. What would we gain?"

Andrews nodded as the plan became clearer by the second.

"Time and evidence. We need to get back into the White House, quickly and quietly."

He stood up.

"You think once they find out you're still alive they'll mount another attack?" James asked, following Andrews.

"I'm sure of it."

James's brow wrinkled. "But the White House is a hard target, sir."

Andrews looked at him. "Then we need to make it harder."

* * *

President Andrews walked into the back of the residence where his wife would probably be asleep. She was up, but still in her bathrobe.

"We have to return to the White House."

She looked at him with an exasperated expression on her face. "So what's going on? How did it go with President Hua?" She was clearly puzzled by the sudden change in plans.

"The meeting with Hua went well, but we had some trouble on the way back."

She frowned. "Anything serious?"

He glanced at the floor. "Yes. We were attacked by three saucers. I've got to say, that Navy lieutenant commander is one of the best pilots I've ever seen. She saved my life."

Martha plopped down into a padded chair in the bedroom, shock filling her face. "The aliens went after you?"

He shrugged. "They may or may not have known I was in the fighter craft, but either way it was a very close call."

Martha shook her head. "That's very frightening."

He nodded. "It gets worse. This morning Franks had Dodd made up to look like me and put him on Marine One to come out here. All three choppers were shot down en route."

She recoiled in shock. "Sidney Dodd?" Tears flowed down her cheeks. She looked horrified.

So it's true, he thought. She and . . .

He had trouble looking at her. His heart ached with betrayal, rejection. He had to keep himself together. The country was in a crisis. It wasn't supposed to matter that he and his marriage were also in a crisis. He had to focus on the country to the exclusion of everything else. But she was also in so much emotional pain that it was tearing him apart, right along with her.

"I'm sorry," he said softly. "It was an assassination

291

attempt. They killed Dodd thinking it was me."

She looked up at him, the horror in her face deepening.

"Oh, God." She slumped back in her chair and stared at the floor. "Then we need to stay here, where the military can protect us."

How am I ever going to be able to fix this? he wondered.

"It's too isolated here. Yes, the military could protect us, but a target out of the public view might be too tempting. We need to be back at the White House. We can move into the residence section of the underground bunker."

She looked up at him in surprise.

"You think we need to be in the bunker?"

"Yes. The assassination attempt didn't come from another country, or from the aliens; it came from inside our own system! At this point, I don't know who I can trust, and who I can't."

Her mouth dropped open.

"What about Vice President Harper? Is he in danger?"

Andrews broke eye contact with her.

"I'm sure he's being protected. Right now whoever did this doesn't know I'm still alive. My guess is that Harper is being prepped to become president as we speak. I've never trusted him. He threatened to split the party and force us to lose the election if he wasn't made vice president. He wasn't even on my list as a running mate. The party picked him against my objections. As far as I know, he could be deeply involved in this coup against me. That's why I never included him in the information about the Zeta Greys. I just can't trust him."

She nodded, a bewildered look on her face. "How much time do we have?"

Andrews checked his watch. "Not much. I think the safest thing we can do is sneak back into the White House through the underground tunnels before anyone realizes I'm not dead."

Martha looked down at her robe. "Then I need to get dressed. What about Franks and Harriet?"

Andrews looked at her. He felt like a chasm had opened up between them. She was drifting away and he didn't know how to stop it.

"They'll have to come with us and stay out of sight until we have a better handle on what's going on and who's involved."

Chapter 44

Sean Wells watched in stunned silence as the announcement scrolled across the bottom of his hotel TV screen: "Marine One shot down. No survivors." He waited as an impromptu press conference was being put together. An empty podium with a dozen microphones dominated the center of the screen. Several minutes later Vice President Harper walked briskly to the podium with Secretary of Defense Farnsworth behind him.

"It is with great sorrow that I announce that Marine One has been shot down with President Andrews aboard. There are no survivors. I want to assure all Americans that a full and complete investigation is taking place. What we do know at this time is that Russian shoulder-fired missiles were used to bring down Marine One. We will find the people behind this tragedy and they will be brought to justice. I, as vice president, stand ready to take President Andrews's place in leading this great nation in these troubled times. Rest assured that order will be restored in the world through American leadership. Secretary of Defense Farnsworth has a few words he would like to add."

Farnsworth stepped to the podium. "President Andrews's recent withdrawal of our military forces from Europe has destabilized the entire continent. As I speak, Russian tanks are racing across Ukraine and Belarus to attack our NATO allies. This unprovoked aggression cannot, and will not, go unanswered. As soon as Vice President Harper is sworn in, the order to withdraw our troops from Europe will be rescinded. We cannot, and will not, stand idly by while hundreds of thousands of innocent lives are lost to Russian aggression. I assure all of our NATO allies that we will be there, in their hour of need, to defend them with the full might and force of the United States military. Order will be restored, I promise you that."

Sean Wells muted the TV and thought, Is this the start of World War Three? If so, I sure picked the wrong time to be in Washington, D.C. He wandered over and looked out the window of his hotel room. On the other hand, this could be the right time for a really big story. He called his editor.

"Ed, where is Harper's swearing in going to take place?"

He heard the rustling of some papers. "The Oval Office, why?"

The idea was just starting to form in his mind. "Are they allowing the media in?" They should for something like this; it's politics at its best.

"They are, but for only a very select few."

Uhh-huh, Sean thought. "Are we on the list?"

His gut was telling him there was a rat in the middle of

all of this, and the only way to find out was to be there.

"One slot. No cameras, no sound support. One person as a witness, that's it."

Sean nodded. "I need to be there. I want that slot."

Ed paused before asking, "Why?"

"Too many things aren't adding up. Something fishy is going on."

That tingling sense of excitement ran up Sean's spine. "Like what?"

There's a bigger story here; he could feel it in his bones.

"Marine One was brought down by Russian shoulder-fired missiles, right?"

He could sense Ed's confusion over the phone. "Yeah, what about it?"

Sean nodded and smiled. He could see it clearly now.

"Andrews ordered our military out of Europe. Why would Russia go after Andrews? That would only guarantee a military response. Why not sit back and let the Americans walk away? I mean, it doesn't make any sense."

Ed was back to his usual devil's advocate personality. "It does if Russia is going to war. What about all of the Russian tanks heading into Europe?"

Sean grinned. "I know, I know. That's what's fishy. We aren't seeing what's really happening. All we see is what somebody wants us to see. Something big is happening behind the scenes. That's why I have to be there."

Ed paused for a moment. "Okay, you're in."

Chapter 45

"Theo, you got a minute?" Charlie asked.

Theo was rushing around Ceti Research doing physical things, trying to keep his mind from panicking. From the thoughts Charlie was picking up, that wasn't going to work.

"Can't it wait? This thing with the president is critical." Theo picked up some papers on his desk, quickly read them over and set them back down.

"It concerns that, at least by inference." Charlie waited for Theo to refocus his attention on him. "We need some additional leverage to bring about full disclosure."

"The president may be dead for all I know and you want to talk about disclosure?"

Charlie waited, reading Theo's thoughts and emotions. He just needed a short break in Theo's attention. Finally it came. "He's alive and well."

Theo looked Charlie in the eyes, sighed and said, "I should have thought to ask. You, of all people would know. Sorry."

"I think we need to recruit someone into Ceti Research to help guarantee full disclosure of the Zeta Grey presence and the corruption involved," Charlie said. "I ran a security clearance. Here's the result." He handed the sheets to Theo.

"A reporter?"

Theo's shock registered in his expression, thoughts, and feelings.

"Your CIA recruits reporters all the time. They have access and believable cover. He's honest and ethical. I think he's a good choice."

Charlie calmly listened to Theo, weighing the pros and cons in his mind.

"You sure we need this?"

Theo was still wavering, but leaning in favor of the plan. "Yes, we do," Charlie said.

He sensed the uncertainty in Theo's mind. "How and when?" Theo asked.

Charlie smiled. "I'll handle that. All I need is your approval."

Theo looked at the security clearance sheets one more time. "Go ahead," he said, as he left the room.

Charlie typed the information into the computer and created a new Ceti Research ID card and security clearance file.

* * *

President Andrews paced back and forth in his private room just off the Oval Office. Deputy Director Michaels from the NSA and Director Clemens of the FBI entered quietly.

"Farnsworth received an encrypted text message right after our troops began to withdraw from Europe. The Speaker of the House and a senator on the Armed Services Committee received similar texts. It took a while, but the NSA decrypted the text messages. Now we know who is involved and at what level."

Andrews read the pages in silence then said, "I guess it makes more sense now. I'm just shocked at who has betrayed me. The mercenaries who shot down Marine One were employed by Conrad Kaplan. I want him arrested and brought to justice."

Director Clemens nodded. "Yes, sir, the Seattle field office is already on that. They should be able to handle it quickly and quietly."

Andrews drifted back over to the door leading to the Oval Office, and waited for his cue.

* * *

Sean stood against the back wall in the Oval Office waiting for the ceremony to begin. The official White House photographer would record the ceremony. Vice President Harper waited next to the chief justice of the Supreme Court in front of the presidential desk. Farnsworth was present along with the top officers from the different branches of the military. James, the head of the Secret Service Presidential Protection Detail stood in front of the president's private door on the side of the Oval Office.

Sean's curiosity piqued as a man with an FBI ID card on a lanyard around his neck entered from the hall entrance, walked quickly over to Vice President Harper and whispered something in his ear. Harper appeared shocked. When the FBI agent whispered the news to the Secretary of Defense, Farnsworth looked *horrified*. Vice President Harper turned to face the crowd in the Oval Office.

"I have just been informed that the body on Marine One was not President Andrews."

Sean grinned. "Then where is the president?"

"He's right here," James said as he opened the door and President Andrews stepped through.

"M-Mr. President," Farnsworth said. "I—I'm so glad you're okay."

Farnsworth was clearly caught off guard.

"Of course you are," Andrews replied. "The Secret Service and the FBI have some questions for you, so if you will follow the agents behind you . . ."

Farnsworth glanced around. Four Secret Service agents surrounded him.

Sean smiled and thought, This is an even bigger story than I expected.

"Ladies and gentlemen of the press, I must ask you for an indulgence," Andrews said. "You are here as witnesses to a major event in American history. There are more people involved in the attack on Marine One. We need time to identify and locate all of them. I must therefore ask you not to publish or leak anything to the public until we have those people in custody. Each of you will have the inside scoop on the people and events related to the attack on Marine One."

Murmurs ran through the small group of reporters.

"For how long?" a reporter asked.

For almost being killed, Sean thought Andrews looked surprisingly confident and in control.

"Twenty-four hours," Andrews said.

Not very long, Sean thought. "Are you asking us, or is this a demand?"

Andrews looked directly at Sean. "Officially, I'm asking for your cooperation."

Sean grinned. "And if we don't cooperate?"

Andrews looked totally serious. "Unofficially, I will hold you liable as accomplices after the fact for treason and the murder of eight people. I think you can find it in your heart to help us out for twenty-four hours. Don't you?"

You're going to owe me big time, Sean thought as he nodded. And I won't hesitate to call in the favor.

* * *

FBI director Matt Clemens entered the Oval Office. Andrews motioned him over to the couch.

"Is Farnsworth talking?" Andrews asked.

Clemens smiled. "He is. He couldn't wait to cut a deal."

Andrews nodded. "Is he naming who else was involved in the attack?"

"To the extent that he knows, yes. With the death penalty hanging in the balance, his lawyer is encouraging him to cooperate fully."

He should die for what he's done, Andrews thought. But if we can get the rest of the people involved in this assassination plot, it just might be worth watching Farnsworth rot behind bars.

"What about satellite coverage of vehicles in the area of the attack? Any progress on that?"

Director Clemens pulled a packet of files and photos from his briefcase and set them on the low table in front of the couch.

"Yes, sir. We currently have eighty-seven people identified and under surveillance. Mercenaries, as you suspected."

Andrews leafed through the files. "Any defense contractors involved?"

Clemens nodded. "Two, so far. Still checking on a third. We should have an answer on that within the next six to eight hours."

Andrews reached into his pocket and withdrew a USB drive.

"I have a list of people I want investigated. This list is for your eyes only. Keep these people and any of their associates out of the loop. You'll find supporting documents and some additional comments in the file on this drive. Time is of the essence."

Clemens took the flash drive and headed out the door.

* * *

"We need to talk," Andrews said.

Martha turned to face him. "I was just changing clothes for dinner, what's going on?"

He looked around the bedroom, glanced at the original landscape painting hung on the wall. His heart felt heavy, and his breath was shallow, nerves tightened his stomach.

"About Sidney Dodd," he began softly.

A pained expression filled her face. She looked away, tears forming in her eyes.

"I know you two were close." He glanced at the floor, searching for the right words.

"Close?" She stood with her mouth slightly open, a look of dismay on her face. "What do you mean by close?"

"I . . ."

She put her hands on her hips. "What are you saying? You think Sidney and I were close? You think we were what? Having an affair? Is that what you think?"

He shrugged. "You just seemed so attentive to him. So . . ."

"Attentive?" She stepped forward, the flush of anger coloring her face. "When was I attentive to Sidney Dodd?"

He swallowed hard. "The limo. In Finland."

She scoffed. "And after all these years together you think I'm that kind of woman? You actually think I would do something like that? What's wrong with you?"

Breathing rapidly, he stepped forward. "You just looked so happy to be next to him, fussing over his makeup, his appearance."

She glanced away from him and then back, focusing her incredulous expression on him. "I was helping you! You were the one who had to meet with Pasternov in secret. That whole thing was for you! Sidney had nothing to do with anything else but keeping your precious secret. How could you?"

He held out his arms. "Look—"

"No. You look!" She shook her head. "I've been here for you, supporting you and the horrible demands of this job. I don't deserve to be treated like this." She grabbed her clothes from the bed. "Tell the staff I'm having my dinner alone."

"Martha . . ." He reached out for her.

"No! I've had enough." She stormed out of the room. "I'm staying by myself."

* * *

Agent James entered the Oval Office and closed the door. Andrews motioned to a chair.

"I have a very personal question and I need a completely honest answer from you."

James sat slowly, concern wrinkling his brow. "What do you need to know?"

Andrews hesitated. "Sidney Dodd and Martha."

James frowned, apparently considering exactly what Andrews was asking. Then he relaxed and his shoulders slumped. "You're thinking they were . . ."

Andrews stared back, waiting to hear what James would reveal.

James shook his head. "I know where each of my agents are at all times, just as I know where you and Martha are every minute of the day and night. They were never alone together, if that's what you're getting at. Sidney Dodd was a good and faithful agent. He never did or said anything questionable. His death is a great loss to us and should be to you, as well."

Andrews nodded. "It is. I just needed to make sure."

"The time they spent together was when she was coaching Dodd on your mannerisms and expressions. There was never anything beyond that."

Andrews smiled and stood. "Thank you. I appreciate your honesty."

Chapter 46

"At dawn the situation with the Russian tanks on the border of Poland reached a critical point," General Lansdale said. "As you can see from the satellite image on the main screen, Russian tanks have reached the border. They're marshalling their forces for a massive invasion."

It was 1:00 a.m. President Andrews once again sat in the Situation Room with the Joint Chiefs of Staff. If Pasternov was doing what he suspected, now would be the time. "Have any Russian tanks actually crossed the border?"

"They are all in position to do just that."

Andrews looked General Lansdale directly in the eyes.

"I know I'm a civilian, and I don't have the military experience you do, but I do have a question. Hypothetically, if you were in command of the invasion of Poland, from Russia's perspective, would you proceed without full air support?"

General Lansdale stood watching Andrews, but said nothing.

"General Tessier. How long would it take the Russians to move their air force assets into position to support an invasion force the size of the one on the border of Poland?"

General Tessier squirmed in his chair. "Two to three days. Thirty to thirty-six hours in an extreme emergency. They would need jet fuel, replacement bombs and missiles, repair parts . . . All of that would be brought in by trucks or trains."

Andrews nodded in acknowledgement. "How many Russian air force assets are in motion?"

General Tessier looked away from Andrews and just sat quietly, staring at the table.

Director of National Intelligence Grunwitz's phone buzzed. He read the text. "Sir, we're getting preliminary reports that some Russian generals on the front lines have . . . died."

"Meaning?" Andrews asked.

"One moment, sir." Grunwitz typed quickly, paused, and typed some more. He read the text on his phone and looked up at Andrews. "How did you know, sir?"

Andrews relaxed back in his chair. "Know what?"

Grunwitz glanced at his phone again.

"Top Russian generals are being purged, sir. A major shake-up is taking place in the Russian military. You knew this was going to happen, didn't you?"

Andrews leaned forward and placed his hands on the table. "I told you Russia is not our enemy." Pasternov was in, Andrews thought. Only Hua remained uncommitted.

"You knew the movement of thousands of Russian tanks was a ploy to get the generals out of Moscow. Pasternov moved his forces to the border of Poland in order to protect himself from a military coup."

Air Force General Tessier's phone also buzzed. He read the text on the screen. "Sir, Russian planes are in the air, but they are not headed for the eastern border. They seem to be involved in some sort of aerial spraying. I don't understand, sir. What's going on?"

Andrews nodded at Franks, who opened the door to the Situation Room. Six military police officers stepped into the room.

"Be grateful that we do things differently than the Russians," Andrews said. "General Lansdale and General Tessier, you are both under arrest for treason and murder. General Parsinian and Admiral Dosinski, while you were not directly involved in the plot against me, you had some knowledge of what was happening and you did nothing to warn me, or to stop the attack on Marine One. You are hereby relieved of command. I expect your letters of resignation on my desk within the hour. You will find that a number of your colleagues also have been arrested and even more are joining you with letters of resignation. After you resign, the FBI will have extensive questions for you to answer, so don't be in a hurry to go anywhere. Attempt to leave and you will be arrested."

Chapter 47

Sean Wells strolled along a sidewalk not far from the White House at 2:00 a.m. He had been tipped off by one of his informants that something big was happening. This better be worth it, he thought. Middle of the winter, middle of the night? What could be this important? Nothing much seemed to be happening. He stomped his feet on the sidewalk, trying to keep the circulation going. The lights were all on in the West Wing, but that must happen from time to time anyway. This wasn't his usual haunt, so he wasn't sure.

He had a camera with a good telephoto lens hanging around his neck. He raised it and took a look as several people emerged from the West Wing door. He took his first photo. Two men in suits with an army general wedged between them got into a large black car. He watched through the camera lens as the vehicle swung around and headed north. The license plate started with the letter J. He took his second shot of the plate. Department of Justice, he thought. FBI, maybe? Then an Air Force general emerged from the door accompanied by two more men in suits just as another black sedan pulled up. What in the world? The general had his hands behind his back. Handcuffs? Sean took several more photos. Could the first general have also been in handcuffs? It was hard to tell.

A third car pulled up to the door. A Navy admiral walked out the door and ducked into the black sedan. No handcuffs, but he was still escorted by men in suits. Sean continued to take photos. As the vehicle swung around he captured the J on the license plate. He pulled his phone and called his editor. After four rings an angry voice answered, "What?"

"Ed, it's Sean Wells. Have the presses started printing the paper for the morning edition?"

"Yeah, we put that to bed two hours ago. Why are you calling me at this hour?"

It figures, Sean thought. "Because you may want to set up for a special edition. Something is happening at the West Wing. It looks like some of our top military leaders are being hauled off by the FBI."

He gave Ed a moment to wake up.

"The what? How many?"

More people came out of the door.

"Here comes the fourth one in the last five minutes. Hang on." He shot more photos. "You know how we're waiting on that story about the shoot-down of Marine One? The twenty-four-hour hold will be up at ten in the morning."

He shot two more photos.

"Yeah, what about it?"

Sean grinned. "I think this is the other shoe dropping. From what I can see, some of our top military brass could be involved."

There was a long pause from Ed's end of the conversation.

"Are you serious? An attempted military coup? Here?"

Sean took another photo. "I'm serious. There are only twelve of us in the media with an inside track. This is huge. Here comes number five. At least he's not in handcuffs."

Sean held the phone against his shoulder as he refocused and took three more photos.

"Handcuffs? Some of the top brass is in handcuffs?" Ed said, apparently trying to contain his excitement.

"One that I know of for sure, probably two," Sean replied.

Over the phone, he heard sounds of movement from Ed.

"You getting pictures of this?"

Sean snapped another photo. "Oh yeah."

More background sounds coming from Ed's phone.

"I've got you on speaker. I'm getting dressed. I'll be in the office in twenty minutes. Email me those photos. Don't wait. I don't want you arrested and your camera confiscated."

Ed was right. He needed to get these photos into the *New York Times* system before anything happened to them. "Okay, sending now."

Sean ended the call, pulled the connecting cord from his coat pocket and plugged the phone into the camera. He set up the email, slipped the phone into his side pocket, and continued shooting the parade of black sedans escorting military leaders from the White House. By two-thirty the cars stopped arriving and no more men came out of the doors.

Sean checked his phone. All of the photos had been sent. He called for a cab and started walking toward Pennsylvania Avenue. The same thing had to be happening at the Pentagon, but with the location and layout, he wasn't going to be able to get anywhere near the place.

* * *

Sean went through the photos from the White House and cross-referenced them with known profiles of America's military leaders and Charlie's files. Everyone in question was a member of the Partnership. He held his hand over his mouth as the inevitable conclusion swirled to the front of his mind.

He's taking down the Partnership, Sean thought. Or at least he's trying to . . .

The Partnership had the protection of the attorney general, but who was protecting the president? Politically, Andrews would soon be under siege. This was a hornet's nest of epic proportions. In Sean's experience, you didn't survive without powerful friends, and right now, Andrews didn't seem to have any.

Chapter 48

Diane knocked on the door to the security office of Peregrine Base.

"Zadanski," Collier said. "What's on your mind?"

He sat back and cocked his head.

"I've been thinking a lot about my encounter with the Zeta Greys on the ground."

She fidgeted with her hands.

"On Baffin Island?"

"Yeah." She stuffed her hands into her pockets. "I was lucky there were only three of them. If they got into the base, we wouldn't have any weapons that would be effective against them. With their telepathic ability and night vision, we'd be in real trouble."

Collier seemed amused by her nervousness. "You think

they could get into the base?"

She glanced around the room. "Yes, I do."

He sat up, his expression turning serious. "You apparently have an idea. What is it?"

She scrunched up her face. "Do we have any flashbangs?"

He looked puzzled. "No. Those would be used by only special forces, SWAT teams, or the FBI."

She nodded and paused to think. "They're very bright and loud, aren't they?"

"Very much so, yes, and they have a substantial physical shock wave."

She smiled. "On Baffin Island, my tactical flashlight momentarily blinded one of the Zetas. How many flashbangs can you get for us?"

He typed on his computer. "Here it is: the M84 stun grenade. How many are you thinking?"

She drummed her fingers on the door jamb. "A couple hundred?"

He looked at the screen and shrugged. "Okay, I'll see what I can do."

* * *

That afternoon Diane lowered the landing pods and brought her craft to rest in the flight bay of Ceti Research. Theo stood, grinning, as she opened the canopy and stepped out onto the stone floor.

"You're here," Theo said.

She laughed. This was only their second meeting together and already they had a thing going. It was silly, but she liked it. "I'm here."

Theo reached out and took her by the hand.

"I have several things planned for you. Would you like

the grand tour of Ceti Research first?"

"Sure. How did you come up with the name, Ceti Research?"

He glanced around to make sure no one was within hearing range.

"I named it Ceti Research in recognition of the profound help and support we're getting from the people of the Tau Ceti star system."

Diane stopped and faced him. "I thought we were being helped by Etnar, from the Andromeda Council."

"We are," Theo said. He lowered his voice. "You should have seen the device President Andrews got from Etnar. It was about the size and shape of a quarter. All I had to do was set it down next to one of our network computers and it loaded all of the designs and specifications for your fighter craft and the particle beam cannons onto our database. It was amazing."

She raised her eyebrows. "And the Tau Ceti connection?"

He nodded and grinned. "We still needed help in understanding and implementing the advanced designs. That's where the people from Tau Ceti came in. They helped us with everything."

Diane looked around. "Are they here now? Could I meet one of them?"

Theo's grin spread across his face. "Actually, you already have."

I have? she thought. Not you, I hope. That would be really awkward.

"He works here. He's my second in charge."

"He's here?" Diane asked. "Could he tell me more about the Zeta Greys? I'm feeling really frustrated by all the compartmentalization and security at Peregrine Base. I need to know more. It's important to me, maybe vital to our fight against them."

Theo extended his arm, pointing down the hall. "Sure. His office is right over here."

He escorted her through several halls and into a large room.

"You were here with Etnar," Diane said. "Charlie, right?"

Charlie was sitting at his desk. He motioned to the chair across from him.

"I have a few things I need to check on," Theo said. "I'll be back in a bit."

Charlie smiled. "You're wondering about the Zeta Grey hearing ability."

Diane was surprised that he knew.

"Admiral Hollis forwarded your concerns to us. We're putting together a sound-based communications system. Infrared suppression will also be built into the new flight suits."

Diane's mouth dropped open slightly. They were taking her suggestions seriously.

"Yes, we are," Charlie said. "I can read your thoughts, quite clearly, actually. Close your eyes for me. Breathe in and out. Slow your mind down. Can you do that?"

Diane wondered what he was up to. His request seemed harmless enough, so she did what he asked.

His thought came into her mind: *Let's try an experiment.*

She opened her eyes and looked at him. He simply sat there gazing at her. She hesitated briefly, then closed her eyes again.

His thought came to her again: *Clear your mind and relax.*

She breathed in and out slowly, relaxing more with each breath. This was just like the meditation exercise Dr. Cowen taught her.

Very similar, his thought replied in her mind. *Good. Slow your mind down even more. Relax.*

But how? she thought.

Unclutter your mind. Let go of your doubts. Are you willing to trust me?

She hesitated, but then thought, *Yes.*

Ask.

Who are you? she thought.

First you need to understand what I am.

Okay, what are you?

I am a bridge between your civilization and mine.

A bridge?

My mother was what you refer to as a contactee. My father is from the Tau Ceti star system. They met when she was a young human, what you call a teenager. A relationship developed over many years. They came to love each other very much, even though their time together was limited. My mother made the decision to have a child with him. He didn't ask, she did.

She must have really loved him, Diane thought.

She still does.

So you're . . .

Half Tau Cetian human and half Earth human.

Your mother?

Raised me here. I spent most of my time learning the ways of Earth humans. I also spent some time with my father on his ship.

Did you . . .

Go to school? No. There was no need. Through my father I gained the equivalent of several advanced college degrees in a matter of weeks.

Telepathically?

Yes, through question cascades, just as you are doing now.

Who is your father?

He is an emissary to your world. If you are successful in defeating the Zeta Greys, he will become an official ambassador from Tau Ceti.

She was stunned. Charlie was the son of a future ambassador from another star system.

In a telepathic society we don't have names; we know each other intimately through our thoughts. A name serves a purpose only in an anonymous society, such as yours.

Anonymous?

Because you don't communicate mind-to-mind, you don't really know each other. You remain anonymous to each other except for the name chosen for you at birth.

You have a name—Charlie.

A compromise. In my father's world there are no names, but my mother insisted that I have one if I was to live here, on planet Earth. So, Charlie, a single name.

The compromise between your mother and your father, she thought.

Yes.

The history of the relationship between Charlie's mother and father flooded into her mind. It was as if she had grown up with them as well as her own mother and brother. Two lifetimes, shared instantly and intimately.

The Zeta Greys? she asked.

Are an artificial telepathic society. The small Greys do not think for themselves. They are the worker class. They follow orders. The taller Greys can think, gather information, analyze and pass questions up the chain of command. You can consider the taller Greys as middle management.

To?

Usually an Insectoid.

A what?

The image of a seven-foot tall, green creature, like a

giant praying mantis with folding forearms, a rounded triangular head, and large multi-celled eyes appeared in her mind.

Very dangerous, very powerful telepathically and physically.

Here?

Sometimes. Not often.

But the small Greys?

Workers. When they encounter a new situation, they pass questions and observations up the chain of command telepathically and wait for new orders.

Time delay?

Depends on the situation. For conditions similar to past experiences, a few seconds. For something entirely new, ten to fifteen seconds.

Interesting. Is telepathy affected by distance?

Yes and no. For weaker minds, such as the small Zeta Greys, effective telepathic communications are limited to several miles. For the tall Greys, a thousand miles or more. For the Insectoids, there is no effective limit.

You and your father?

If he's within your solar system, I can communicate with him.

Is he here now?

Yes.

She took a deep breath and slowly breathed out.

Life in your father's world?

In a natural telepathic society, with every thought known by everyone around you, conformity becomes imperative. Any thought, or the beginning of any desire, outside of the accepted norm becomes known and is rejected by those around you. Self-discipline and focus are instilled in you from the very beginning. That never changes.

Your society has rules?

Yes, an extensive set of rules everyone learns and follows.

The Zeta Greys have rules?

Much more so than a natural telepathic society. They are very regimented.

And here on Earth?

Earth human thoughts and desires are not normally registered in the conscious mind of other Earth humans. You remain anonymous, not connected, not part of the whole of society.

Alone?

Yes. Earth humans remain separate, unconnected, billions of tiny islands, isolated by a vast ocean of doubt, unknowing.

But you and I are communicating mind-to-mind.

You are strongly intuitive, that opens a path that I can use.

And love? she thought.

One of many attempts to connect with others.

Many?

Fear, anger, guilt, resentment, bitterness, hatred, culture, religion, class, race, educational status, social status, language . . . All are attempts to connect with others in one form or another.

But most of those things tend to divide us.

Yes, they do. This is why you, as Earth humans, are still at war with each other. This is why the Zeta Greys control your world. They have unity of purpose, unity of mind. You do not.

But aren't your people at war with the Zeta Greys?

As a matter of survival, yes. They make our response necessary.

Are there other human races?

Yes, many. The Andromedans are a very advanced human race.

Etnar has a name, Diane thought.

Contrived, for your convenience.

Are they at war?

No. Their advanced technology protects them.

But with their advanced technology, they could easily win against the Zeta Greys, Diane thought. *They could wipe the Greys out.*

To kill serves no purpose to them. Life is sacred. Violence serves no purpose, has no value. They seek only an end to war and violence. Nothing more, nothing less.

But the Zeta Greys?

Part of the answer you seek is a matter of biology. In the Corporate Alliance, the Insectoids, the Reptilians, and the Greys each have a single brain. As such their only purpose is to prey on others. Being telepathic doesn't change that.

We, as humans, Charlie went on, *have a double brain; the result of billions of your years of evolution. We have the simple brain of the reptiles and the insects, what you call the limbic brain. We also have a mammalian brain, which creates the tribal or herd mentality. Through the mammalian brain Earth humans organize and band together based on race, religion, culture, and ideology.*

A three dimensional image of the human brain appeared in Diane's mind. The limbic brain was red in color. Behind that was the Cerebellum in pink. Above and surrounding them were the eight lobes of the mammalian brain, colored from blue to gold, back to front respectively.

But, most importantly, Charlie's thoughts continued, *we also have what you call the frontal lobes. This gives us the ability to transcend our lower instincts for violence, killing, and conquest resident in the limbic brain, and to overcome the separation and distrust of the mammalian brain. Through the frontal lobes, Earth humans can transform themselves and their lives into a state of cosmic communion with their interstellar human neighbors.*

Like you?

Yes. Like the Tau Cetians, Andromedans, Sirians, Vegans, Pleadians, and hundreds of other human races.

How do we become like you?

Through knowledge, tolerance, understanding, patience, kindness, to help, support, guide, and especially a willingness to be of service to others . . .

And to love?

Yes. To love unconditionally is the last barrier. When you Earth humans can connect through your heart, your mind will open, you will hear the thoughts of others, you will feel their emotions, you will connect with each other's inner lives. When your people can accomplish that, war among yourselves will become impossible. Then it will be time for you to join us, the rest of the human family, out among the stars.

She opened her eyes and said aloud, "Thank you."

"You're welcome," Charlie said.

Diane got up and left.

She was dazed. Her mind was spinning. She tried her best to not let it show.

Chapter 49

This changes everything, she thought. It wasn't just the words he shared with me; it was the images, the history, and the relationships. My God. I had no idea I could get whole sections of information all at once like that.

It's basic biology taken to extremes. Insects, reptiles, and computers: Single function brains evolved into incredibly advanced technology and telepathy, yet they retained their basic predatory instincts. That's why the Zetas are here; they're natural predators. They see us as prey, cast into the artificial structure of a corporation based on profit and loss, assets and liabilities. They see us as assets to be seized, used, and turned into profit.

Then there's the cloned body angle: Our bodies provide the basic building blocks for their bodies, and for their food.

They didn't come to share technology with us. The technology and power they offered was bait, and we swallowed it hook, line, and sinker.

Humans—advanced humans—like Charlie and his father, are much more evolved, brain-wise. We have dual layered brains: We have a choice, but too many of us function from the simple reptilian section of our brain: fighting, stealing, and taking from one another, focused on the selfish, greedy little reptilian layer of our brains. No wonder we can't get along.

The mammalian layer of the brain is better. At least groups of people get along and band together, but none of the groups get along well enough with each other. We're still at war; one group against another. Insects, reptiles, then mammals, and finally the emerging awareness within the frontal lobes. But do we actually use the higher section of our brain? Apparently not, at least rarely. No wonder this world is in such a mess.

So how do I change the situation? I have to start with me. Charlie said my intuitive ability was a path he could use. Maybe I can, too. Maybe that will open my real human brain.

* * *

"You look really wired," Theo said as Diane walked through his office doorway.

"Yeah, I—that was really intense."

Theo nodded. "You get used to it after a while. Any other questions?"

She shook her head.

"Good. I've arranged dinner, if you have the time."

She smiled. She had never felt both this nervous and excited at the same time. It felt nice. "This sounds like a date."

"It does, doesn't it?"

He smiled and opened a door at the back of his office.

"With all of the security, this is about as private as it's going to get."

The doorway led into his apartment, which was moderate in size and spartanly furnished. A small table had been set up, complete with tablecloth, two tall white burning candles, two chairs, two place settings, two small vases, each holding a single flower, and a heated stainless steel covered dish in the center.

"It's not fancy," he said. "But under the circumstances, I hope it will do."

She smiled. "It's wonderful."

They talked as they ate, getting to know each other better. He reached across the table, resting his hand on the tablecloth. She smiled and placed her hand in his. After a pause in the conversation, he got up and extracted two small plates of red velvet cake from the little refrigerator. They held hands as they finished desert.

Finally he stood, lifting her hand. She followed and stepped closer to him. She kissed him without hesitation. It was a long, wonderful kiss that tingled from the top of her head to the ends of her toes. She hugged him, held him close to her. Desire built within her. She wanted more, but didn't know if this was the right time. Too much was happening.

"Can you stay?" Theo asked.

Diane lowered her head. "As much as I would love to . . ."

Theo held her tight. "It's okay," he whispered in her ear. "I don't want to understand, but I do."

She kissed him again and slowly pulled away. "I have a war to get back to. The Zetas are more active at night. I have to be there."

He held her hands in his. "Of course you do. Be safe, be careful. Now that I've found you, I don't want to lose you."

She nodded. "Me, either. I just don't know when . . ."

He kissed her gently. "Until then."

* * *

Diane gathered her squadron in the corner of the cafeteria the next morning.

"We've been looking at this all wrong," she said.

All she got were puzzled looks in return.

"What do you mean?" Clay asked.

Diane grinned. "What do you do when you discover your home is overrun with insects and reptiles?"

Clay shrugged.

"You call the exterminator," Helen said.

Clay glanced at Helen.

"Exactly. We're not underdogs fighting a hopeless battle. We're not the orphan squad—we're the *exterminator* squad. We're here partially because we don't have families. That doesn't mean we're expendable; it means we have to focus a hundred percent on our job with no divided loyalties."

Diane looked at the faces of her teammates. She had their full attention.

"Our world is being overrun by simple-minded pests in flying saucers. Technologically advanced, yes, but the end result and the methodology is the same. This world is ours. We are the top predators on this planet and the Zeta Greys are the prey—they just don't know it yet. We're exterminators. We kill saucers and Zeta Greys. Period. That's our job."

She put her hand out into the center of the group.

"Are you with me?"

The other pilots and RIOs placed their hands on hers.

"Huaah!" they yelled together.

* * *

Sean Wells spent most of the day reviewing his articles and investigation documents over the phone with his editor. Now that the White House had officially notified the twelve news outlets that they could run with the attempted assassination story, it was time to include the story on Conrad Kaplan and what he was doing.

"These are very dangerous people," Ed said. "I don't want any of them coming after you."

Sean shrugged. "I've received death threats before. It's just a part of dealing with greedy, crooked people. This won't be any different."

Ed replied urgently, "This guy has trained killers on his payroll."

Sean nodded in agreement. "In Africa, not here."

Ed's devil's advocate personality was pushing through again. "You don't know that. Kaplan could be one of the people behind shooting down Marine One."

He had a good point, Sean thought.

"Okay, you're right. We don't know for sure. If he had been, Andrews would have him in handcuffs by now, which means they have the people responsible in custody. We can publish the article about Kaplan."

Ed wasn't buying it yet. He needed more reasons to publish the article.

"Look, all of the electronic media are releasing the assassination story today, right now. People will already know most of the details before our paper sees any ink. What the others don't have are the photos of generals in handcuffs being taken out of the West Wing—*and* the Kaplan story. What do you want to do, run the Kaplan story some other time? This is the perfect timing. It makes us stand out above the other news outlets."

There was the usual pause from Ed. "We're creating

guilt by association, you know that, right?"

Sean smiled. "It's two different stories. People will see that. It'll be fine."

Another pause. "I don't know why I let you talk me into these crazy ideas of yours."

Sean chuckled. "Because my crazy ideas and articles sell a lot of papers, that's why."

Chapter 50

The violent pounding on his hotel door jarred Sean Wells from a deep sleep. He staggered over to the door and peered through the peephole.

"Charlie," he said under his breath. He opened the door and let the strange kid in.

"You have to leave, right now."

Sean glanced at the clock on the desk. "It's a quarter to five. What do you mean I have to leave?"

Charlie pushed past him. "The paper with your article about Kaplan is hitting the street."

The kid sure seems wound up, Sean thought.

Charlie turned to face him. "The story has been online for just over three hours. Kaplan has two men on their way over here to kill you."

Sean's mouth fell open and his eyebrows raised. "What? How do you know that?"

Charlie shook his head. "No time to explain. Throw on some clothes and grab your computer. We've got to go, now!"

Sean dressed quickly and started to pack his suitcase.

"Leave it!" Charlie said. "Let's go!"

Sean grabbed his computer, cell phone, and camera as they ran for the door. Halfway down the hall Charlie grabbed his arm. "They're in the elevator."

Sean stopped and stared at Charlie. "Stairs?"

"No time," Charlie said. They stood in a long hallway. The entrance to each room was set back about six inches from the main wall with the recess extending a foot on both sides of the door. Charlie guided him into a recess with his back to the wall.

"Stand here," Charlie said. "Close your eyes and don't move. Stay perfectly still."

The bell dinged from the elevator and the door opened. Sean swallowed hard and tried not to think about what was about to happen. The sound of footsteps approached. He held his breath. He felt relieved as the footfalls continued past him down the hall. He breathed out slowly and opened his eyes. Two men in dark suits walked down the hall away from him. He glanced at Charlie then back at the two men as they stopped at Sean's room. They each drew a weapon with a suppressor attached. One swiped a card in the door lock, opened the door, and both men entered the room.

"Let's go," Charlie whispered as he grabbed Sean's arm.

"What the hell just happened?"

Later. It was something he heard in his mind, but not with his ears. He looked at Charlie as the strange kid guided him to the elevator. Charlie pushed the button for the main lobby and then the button to close the door.

"Why did they walk right past us? They had to see us standing there."

Charlie shook his head. "It's easier to let people see what they expect to see."

What they expect to see? Sean thought.

Charlie looked at him and nodded.

"So you're saying . . ."

Charlie held up his hand, glanced from left to right, and pushed the button for the second floor. The elevator slowed, stopped, and the door opened.

"This way," Charlie said. He guided Sean out onto the second floor, down the long hall and into a stairwell. "There's a man waiting in the lobby."

Sean pulled back and stopped. "And you know that because?"

Charlie turned to face him. "I can hear their thoughts. It's a four-man team: two shooters, a back-up man in the lobby, and a driver outside."

This was just getting too strange. "You can hear their . . . What do you mean you can hear their thoughts?"

The kid looked frustrated. "I have to get you out of here first, and then I can explain."

Charlie led him out the east door, across the grass, and over to a silver compact car parked on Nineteenth Street.

"Is my boss at the paper in danger?"

Charlie pulled out onto the empty street and headed northwest. "Call him. Tell him he needs police protection, now!"

Sean grabbed his cell phone and called Ed. Full-fledged panic was starting to set in. "Come on, come on, I know it's early . . . just answer the damn phone."

"Wells? What is it now? Do you know what time it is?"

Sean breathed a sigh of relief. "Yeah, I know exactly what time it is. Call 911. Get the police over to your house right away. I just missed two guys with guns who were sent to kill me. You could be next on the list."

There was that irritating pause again. "The article?"

Sean glanced behind them to see if they were being followed.

"Yeah, I should have listened to you. Get the cops around you and your family. I'll call you when I can."

He disconnected and turned to Charlie.

"Now do you want to tell me what the hell is going on?"

* * *

Admiral Hollis greeted Captain Jakovic as he entered the newly finished master control room for Operation Planetary Shield, deep inside Peregrine Base. The OPS center was round, fifty feet across, with a domed ceiling. Around the perimeter large display screens showed space debris and functioning satellites in orbit around the planet. With the network of incoherent back scatter radar arrays and receivers, they could track objects as small as an inch in low earth orbit. The OPS center had operational control over the global network of ionospheric heaters, also known as over the horizon radar (OTH-R), or high frequency active auroral research projects (HAARP). The OPS center gave him command authority over the particle beam cannons put in place to protect the transmitters from a Zeta Grey attack.

A twelve-foot diameter, two-foot thick laminated blast door stood open. In the event of an attack, the blast door would close automatically and seal off the OPS center. The walls, floor, and ceiling had the same protection as the door: laminated layers of armored steel, depleted uranium, and high strength ceramic. The OPS center had its own air and water supply, originally developed for nuclear submarines. Below the floor of the OPS center was another floor for the main computer system, accessible by a spiral stairway.

"Captain Jakovic, how many facilities do we have online?"

Jakovic pointed to a large display.

"The incoherent back scatter radar facility in Shanghai has just joined us, bringing us up to fifteen receiving stations. That allows us to monitor the entire globe for saucer intrusions."

Hollis scanned the displays. "And transmitters?"

Jakovic pointed to additional displays around the room. "Fourteen. Xinjiang, China has not joined the planetary shield network yet. Russia now has four facilities online. Novgorod and Nakhodka have been online and ready for the last two days. Irkutsk joined us late yesterday along with the Antarctic facility. Particle beam cannons are in place in Russia and currently under construction in China."

"So we still have a hole in the shield."

Jakovic nodded. "Yes, sir, over the Pacific Ocean, east of China."

Hollis shook his head. "Let's hope we can bring that station online before the Zetas figure out we don't have complete coverage."

"Understood, sir," Jakovic said, checking the displays one more time.

God, I hate rushing this, Hollis thought. But we're out of time. "We're seeing a significant surge in saucers entering the atmosphere. We have to put a stop to this before we get overwhelmed. This is where we draw the line. Activate the shield."

"Aye, aye, sir." Jakovic turned to the control center. "Initiate Operation Planetary Shield. No one in, no one out."

Chapter 51

"I have notified key members of Congress that I am taking these extreme measures and defensive posture in the hope of discouraging a direct attack on the White House," Andrews said.

He had moved his family and close staff members into the residential section of the underground bunker beneath the White House, along with his personal military unit and Secret Service detail. "We have a lot of very upset people out there and I want to minimize any bloodshed that might take place."

Doug Franks frowned. "This seems extreme to me. You think someone would actually launch a direct attack on the White House?"

Andrews carried an armful of his most important files into the elevator. "If they thought it would succeed? Yes, I do."

Franks stepped into the elevator. "The optics on this make you look paranoid. Shouldn't we at least *appear* as though things are normal?"

The elevator door closed. "Residential bunker," Andrews said. It felt as though the bottom fell out from under them.

Franks grabbed the handrail. "I'll never get used to this thing dropping like that."

"Get used to it. We're going to be down here for a while."

Franks held tight to the handrail. "You make it sound as if we are at war."

Andrews looked over at him. "We are at war."

* * *

"Where is Andrews?" Conrad Kaplan demanded.

"He's moved his wife and close staff into the underground bunker," Senator Whitcolm said.

Kaplan poured some bourbon into a glass from the minibar in the stretch limo. "Protection?"

Whitcolm handed him several sheets stapled together and took the glass.

"His Secret Service detail plus his personal military unit, all heavily armed."

Kaplan scanned the pages. "So a direct assault isn't likely to be successful. Andrews is a cagy adversary, I have to grant him that. I have a number of people currently in sensitive positions inside the military on retainer. One of them has some intel you may find useful. I'll make him available to you. Does Andrews know about our association with the Zeta Greys?"

Whitcolm took a sip of the bourbon. "I think so. He hasn't been officially read in, but he seems to know what's going on."

Kaplan scowled. "What proof or evidence does he have?"

Whitcolm shook his head. "Nothing. All of that material is very closely contained. We'd know if anything was missing."

Kaplan looked out the side window of the limo momentarily, then turned to Whitcolm. "Okay, you can use the 'UFO nut' label to discredit whatever he has to say."

Whitcolm grinned. "I know exactly how to handle that. He'll look like a complete mental case by the time I'm done with him."

Kaplan finished his own glass of bourbon. "Good. I want you to move quickly on this. I need Andrews removed as soon as possible, you understand me?"

Whitcolm raised his glass to Kaplan and smiled. "Consider it done."

* * *

"Okay," Charlie said. "About what happened in the hotel hallway: They didn't expect to see anyone in the hallway, so I reinforced that expectation by projecting the image of an empty hall into their minds. That projection temporarily took the place of what their eyes were seeing, so our presence didn't rise to the level of conscious recognition."

Sean folded his arms over his chest and slid slightly away from Charlie.

"I know, you don't believe me, which is fine. I don't have to prove anything to you one way or the other. What I have to do is try to keep you alive."

Sean's heart was already racing with adrenaline. Now it was pounding.

"Why would you care?"

Charlie glanced at him and then back to the road ahead.

"Bottom line? I need to use you as leverage against the political system. I need to expose certain things and you are in a unique position to make that revelation believable."

So he's keeping me alive so he can use me, Sean thought. How refreshing.

Charlie looked at him and laughed out loud.

"So you . . ."

Charlie nodded. "Of course."

Sean had never encountered anyone like Charlie before. He found it nerve-wracking and intimidating.

"Relax," Charlie said. "What I need is actually right up your ally."

Sean's curiosity took over. "So you want me to do what, exactly?"

Charlie glanced at him then looked back at the road. "I want you to write about the crooked and corrupt dealings between corporations and politicians."

Sean nodded slowly. "Like Conrad Kaplan and the Africa thing?"

"Yes, you did well with that. You were willing to risk your life to tell the truth to the public. By doing that, you earned my trust. Those code name operations you wanted to see? The files are in the trunk. When I get you settled in for the night, they're yours."

* * *

Conrad Kaplan's special phone buzzed. It was an encrypted message from USAP317. The FBI had an arrest warrant for him. They were also tracking his private jet. They would be waiting for him when he landed. The message ended with a single word: EVADE. He stood, walked forward, and leaned into the cockpit.

"We need to make a change in airports. Use Paine Field

instead."

Nick Chambers nodded. "I'll notify ATC of the change."

Kaplan reached out and grabbed Chambers's shoulder. "No. Don't do that. Just change course and land at Paine Field."

Chambers shook his head. "I can't do that. We won't have clearance to land. We could collide with another aircraft."

Kaplan dug his thumb into Chambers's shoulder. "It's not a request; it's an order. Take the risk."

Chambers winced in pain, then nodded. "As soon as we divert from the flight path, they're going to send pursuit aircraft after us."

Kaplan released Chambers's shoulder. "So what else is new?"

Chambers didn't say anything else. During the approach he banked to the north and lined up on Paine Field.

Kaplan texted his helicopter pilot with instructions, returned to his seat, and buckled in. Alarms started going off in the cockpit as the jet nosed down for a landing.

"They're not going to like this," Chambers said.

They already don't like it, Kaplan thought. And they're going to like it even less before I'm done with them.

Kaplan's private executive jet landed at Paine Field in Snohomish County north of Seattle just missing a Cessna taxiing onto the runway. The Cessna had quickly turned onto the grass in order to avoid a collision with the jet. Kaplan exited the jet and ran for his helicopter as it swooped in from the south. He climbed in and put on the earphones as his pilot lifted off and headed east for home.

"Stay low and turn off all tracking devices."

His pilot looked over at him. "Copy that, boss. Going dark."

Kaplan looked down through the clear bubble of the

helicopter as six black SUVs rushed into Paine Field and surrounded his jet. They'll be at my home and business, too.

"Follow the terrain, head north, then swing across the water north of Friday Harbor, got it?"

His pilot scanned the air around them, dropped to just above tree level, then said, "Got it, boss."

Kaplan took the battery out of his phone and settled in for the rough flight as the helo swooped and lifted just over the treetops. Forty-five minutes later his helicopter skimmed above the water and landed momentarily on Point Caution, in the San Juan Islands Marine Preserve. He hopped out onto the gray rocks as the helo lifted off, banked back over the water, and disappeared back toward the mainland.

He walked to the edge of the stone point, removed the SIM card from his phone and tossed the card into the waves. He watched it disappear into the churning gray-green water before he turned south and walked into the dense forest of the preserve.

* * *

Sean and Charlie took turns driving. By early evening they were in Nashville, Tennessee. Charlie drove to the airport and parked in the short term lot.

"Wait here."

He got out, pulled a carry-on case from the trunk of his car, and walked through the arrivals door. Thirty minutes later he pulled up in a rental car.

"Let's find you a hotel room."

Sean followed him to a big chain hotel near the airport. Charlie went in, registered, and led him to the room.

"Isn't a hotel next to an airport a little obvious?" Sean asked.

"Not really. They will know you didn't travel by air, so

hotels by an airport will have a very low priority in their search for you. You'll need to use cash for food, gas, and lodging—no cards, no checks—so pick places carefully. You can use the same fake ID you have for undercover investigations. How much cash do you have?"

Sean felt uncertain about everything that was happening, but Charlie did prevent him from being shot. That counted for something. "Roughly? Around four hundred."

Charlie dug into his pocket. "I've got about three hundred. This should get you through the next three to four days."

Sean pocketed the cash. "And how do you know what ID I use for investigations?"

Charlie looked at him. "How do you think I know?"

Sean closed his eyes. "You hear my thoughts." He looked at Charlie again.

"And everything else. There are no secrets, not anymore."

Sean breathed out heavily. "Swell. Where am I supposed to go?"

Charlie opened the hotel room door. "Datil, New Mexico."

Sean's skepticism was rising. "To see?"

"Most of it's in the files." Charlie walked out toward the car. "For the rest, you'll know it when you see it. In case you get stopped, it's safer if you don't have all of the details until you actually get there." Charlie carried the box of files into the hotel room, set it and the keys to the rental car on the table. He took a plastic ID card on a lanyard out of his pocket and handed it to Sean. "Don't use this until you have to."

"What's Ceti Research?" Sean asked, reading the card.

The image of a tall, thin, man jumped into Sean's mind along with his name, position, and background.

"Oh, wow," Sean said.

"That should get you through." Charlie walked out of the room, got into his car and drove off.

Sean dug into the code-named operation files as soon as the door closed. At two in the morning he had to force himself to get some sleep. He had no idea about what had actually been happening. Now, he wished he didn't know anything at all.

* * *

Conrad Kaplan walked out of the trees at twilight and headed south into Friday Harbor. He bought a cheap phone and made a single call.

"Get the crew together, we're leaving tonight."

There was a short pause. "How long?" the man asked.

Kaplan glanced around. "A week, maybe more."

He hung up, found a restaurant for dinner, and reconsidered his plans as he ate.

I'll need to give Harper a chance to settle in as president and Mohr time to perfect the interceptor missile, he thought. Once that's done and the ridiculous warrant for my arrest is set aside, I can return in time to see Russia incinerated by nuclear tipped cruise missiles. What a sight that's going to be!

At eight that evening he strolled down to the marina and boarded *Dominator II*, his escape yacht. He had been careful to register the eighty-four-foot yacht under a series of shell corporations spanning six countries and three continents. He pulled the burner phone from his pocket and dropped it into the sea. He had this plan in place for the last four years in case he had to disappear for a while, and now certainly seemed to be the right time.

"Supplies are loaded," Captain Walters said. "Where do you want to go?"

"Hawaii."

Walters nodded and turned to his crew as Kaplan headed down the steps to his state room. It would take several hours to get through the Strait of Juan de Fuca and out into international waters. He was still deeply chilled from his time in the forest. Maybe a glass of Bourbon would help. Maybe two or three glasses would be better.

Chapter 52

Senator Whitcolm called the Senate Armed Services Committee together early in the morning. The closed-door session took place in a medium-sized, maple-paneled chamber away from the main hall. The meeting began before the regular crowd of legislators arrived. The senator stood before the twenty-six members looking as grim and serious as he could manage.

"I have just received some very disturbing news. According to the limited statements I have available from my sources inside the military, President Andrews has delivered some highly advanced military hardware to Russia. I don't have exact details on the hardware, but I have been assured that the nature of the equipment will profoundly alter the military balance of power in the world toward Russia, and ultimately, against the United States."

Shocked murmurs raced through the committee.

"Do you have documentary evidence to support the statements?" Senator Stevens asked.

Whitcolm carefully choreographed his response.

"No. Andrews has been very careful not to leave a document trail. But I do have the sworn testimony of an Air Force officer who witnessed the transfer. This is giving direct aid and support to the enemy. The president has committed treason and must be held accountable before any more damage is done."

There was visible skepticism from members of the president's party. One of them asked, "Has there been any response from the president?"

Whitcolm stepped forward cautiously.

"My chief of staff has just returned from the White House. Not only has Andrews refused to comment, he has barricaded himself in the underground bunker and is refusing to see anyone personally. All we got was a twenty-second video conference. That was it."

He watched the indignation ripple through the committee.

"I can understand his being concerned after the shoot down of Marine One, but this seems excessive to me," Senator Stevens said.

"It is," Whitcolm affirmed. He looked at the floor for a moment, then at the members of the committee. "I now have very serious doubts about Andrews's sanity. Given the shake-up in the military he has created—arresting and firing our country's heroes, questioning the loyalty of our defense contractors, and now his bunker mentality—I believe Andrews is no longer fit to be our commander in chief."

Serious concern was building in the committee, just as he planned.

"You think the president is mentally ill?" another senator asked.

Whitcolm shook his head. "Worse. I believe the president has had a psychotic break. We cannot leave him in control of this nation's nuclear capability, let alone our country's entire military force. Andrews has come unhinged. We have to remove him from office today."

Senator Stevens shook his head. "That's not going to happen without concurring medical opinions and supporting documentation."

Whitcolm held his hands out in front of him, palms up.

"That's why I propose an emergency joint meeting of the House and Senate where we demand that Andrews publically appear before us and answer our questions. I believe what he has to say will remove all doubt regarding his sanity."

* * *

Sean Wells checked the rental car agreement in the glove compartment, just in case he got pulled over. It was registered in the name of his undercover identity. The strange kid certainly knew what he was doing.

Slowly, Sean was connecting the dots. The information in the code word files was difficult to believe, but it certainly explained some of the mysterious things that had been going on. The disturbing photos and reports of bloodless animal mutilations swirled in his mind as he drove through Memphis and across the Mississippi River into Arkansas. No known medical procedure could result in the type of organ removal these revealed. The majority of mutilations involved mostly large farm animals, and had not been performed where the remains were found. The carcasses had been dropped from a height of twenty-to-thirty feet, based on the indentations in the ground. Some had been found impaled on tree branches or hung up in electrical lines.

Speculation was rampant and varied, running the gamut from secret military operations and sacrificial cults to UFOs and blood-thirsty aliens. The two consistent factors were the lack of any blood or bleeding of the tissue, and the ground impressions. The high-level military investigation and analysis uncovered almost identical reports going back into the early 1800s, precluding man-made flying vehicles as the means of dropping the carcasses. Even older reports, going back centuries, had been referenced with the caveat that the sources were either unknown, or of questionable heritage. Sean had read enough scientific papers to know that "unknown sources" and "questionable heritage" meant the information was considered valid, but nobody wanted to stake his reputation on it.

One of the other files, under the code word M-12, not only connected the mutilations to specific types of UFOs, but to a particular alien species of small Greys. The indication was that these creatures had been visiting our planet for several thousand years. Records provided by Charlie included photos of dead alien bodies, as well as live ones in captivity. The analysis of the advanced technology used by the Greys was both tedious and intriguing in its detail. According to the stamps and markings on the reports, the subject of alien life and UFO technology had been afforded a classification all its own, well above top secret, by the Eisenhower administration. Apparently, most of the more recent Presidents had been deliberately kept out of the loop.

Sean considered pushing on to his destination in New Mexico, but he was inexorably drawn back to the code word files. His desire to know the truth forced him to stop and spend the night just east of Oklahoma City.

* * *

"Sir, you need to respond to this right away," Franks said. He handed the single sheet of paper to Andrews.

"Whitcolm," Andrews said. "It figures." He read the statement carefully.

"He's accusing you of high treason and of being mentally unfit for office. He claims that you have become delusional. This is a Joint Resolution of Congress, demanding that you appear today in open session and answer the charges against you. This is a political trap, sir."

Andrews sighed. "Of course it is. I would expect nothing less from Whitcolm."

Franks's agitated state was intensifying. "If you don't appear by noon today, they will vote to impeach and remove you from office. You have to do something."

Andrews balled up the notice and threw it in the waste basket. "Here's what I want you to do first."

* * *

Whitcolm read the president's answer to the Joint Resolution of Congress and smiled.

As I expected, he thought. Andrews is using National Security to exclude the public from the hearings. A closed hearing isn't going to change the outcome, though. We can still hold the impeachment vote in public.

At ten o'clock in the morning, Whitcolm sat in the Judiciary Committee room of the House of Representatives, where the committee met in closed session, Congressman Russell, from the State of Washington, presiding. Whitcolm watched as Air Force Major Steven Cline was sworn in.

"Major Cline," Congressman Russell began, "according to your sworn statement, you flew a C-130 cargo plane into Russia and delivered classified technology to the Russian military by direct order of President Andrews. Is that correct?"

Major Cline was in full dress uniform and appeared calm. "Yes. We landed at the Bada Air Force Base near the Yablondovoi Mountains in southwestern Russia."

Congressman Russell turned to face the Judiciary Committee. "You said 'we'?"

He watched the faces of the committee members as Cline answered.

"Yes. There were two C-130 transports involved. Ours carried six large crates, as did the other plane."

Congressman Russell turned quickly toward Cline. "And inside these crates?"

Cline shrugged. "I don't really know, sir. The crates were accompanied by armed people dressed in civilian attire. We were informed that the crates themselves were classified top secret. We were not allowed anywhere near the crates."

Russell nodded slowly and paced to the other side of where Major Cline sat. "And the armed civilians, did they return with you or did they go with the crates?"

Cline shook his head. "They went with the crates, sir."

Russell paced back in front of Cline again.

"And you are certain the crates were classified top secret?"

Russell turned quickly to face Cline.

"Yes, sir. Absolutely certain."

He stepped closer to Cline. "You are also certain the orders came directly from President Andrews?"

Cline nodded. "Yes, sir. Directly from the president."

Russell turned to face attorney Sylvester Burton. "Mr. Burton, you represent the president. Do you have any questions for this witness?"

Burton didn't bother to stand. "No questions."

Whitcolm smiled. Everything was going according to plan.

"What evidence do you have in defense of the president?" Russell asked.

Again, Burton didn't stand. "I have been informed by President Andrews that he has no statement to make at this time, Congressman."

Whitcolm's grin widened. It was obvious Andrews had nothing with which he could defend himself.

"This is the appointed time for us to hear any and all evidence, counselor," Russell said emphatically. "There is no later."

Burton calmly replied, "The president is not making a statement at this time."

Whitcolm stood and headed for the door as Russell made his final statement.

"Then we vote based on the evidence before us. Pursuant to Article Two, Section Four of the United States Constitution, President Andrews stands accused of treason, an impeachable offense. All in favor of approving the Articles of Impeachment raise your hands."

Whitcolm turned as he reached the door. All but one member of the Judicial Committee raised his hand.

"The Articles of Impeachment are approved and forwarded to the full House for a hearing and a vote."

* * *

"There isn't enough time." Andrews paced around the residential section of the bunker under the White House. "Whitcolm is pushing the impeachment process as fast as he can. He knows physical evidence is extremely hard to get due to the secret nature of UFOs and alien technology. I can't go in there empty-handed. He plans on humiliating me in front of Congress and the public. I need more time."

"Then take more," Martha said. Her anger at him still

showed, but it seemed to be fading. "You're the president. You don't serve at the pleasure of Congress. Can't you just appeal whatever they decide to the Supreme Court? That should give you all the time you need."

Andrews shook his head. "I can't. There's no precedent. In fact, the Supreme Court has specifically stayed out of any impeachment proceeding. If the House votes for impeachment and the Senate convicts me, it's over. I have no recourse."

Andrews nervously rubbed his hands together.

"So what evidence can you put together in your defense?" Martha asked.

He closed his eyes and rubbed his temples. "On such short notice, I don't know."

Martha stared at him. "You could call that cute Navy lieutenant commander who flew the fighter craft the night you were attacked. I'm sure she'd be happy to corroborate your side of things."

Andrews turned and looked at her, surprised at her comment. She was still angry, but she had a very good suggestion. "The night of the attack. You may be on to something . . ."

Chapter 53

Senator Whitcolm spent the rest of the hour talking to members of the Senate while Congressman Russell passed out copies of Major Clines's sworn testimony to other House members. At eleven o'clock the full House of Representatives met with the Senate also in attendance.

"Due to the immediate nature of the charge of treason against President Andrews and the national security implications involved," Speaker of the House Metzner began, "we are meeting as a joint session, in order not to delay the impeachment and removal process. Serious concerns have been voiced regarding President Andrews's state of mind and his ability to continue serving as commander in chief. If the House votes to impeach, the Senate will then commence the trial of President Andrews. If Andrews is convicted of treason, or if he is found to be incapable of continuing as president, he will be arrested and Vice President Harper will be sworn in as president.

"You have in your hands the sworn testimony of Air Force Major Cline. Transfer of top secret information or technology in any form to an enemy is, by definition, treason. Russia is a confirmed enemy of the United States. President Andrews has until noon to defend himself against this charge. Is counsel for the president present?"

Attorney Sylvester Burton stood. "I am. President Andrews has assured me he will appear and address all of your questions."

People milled around as the hands of the clock slowly crept by. Thirty minutes passed, then forty-five. Twelve noon arrived without any sign of Andrews.

"The time for President Andrews to appear and testify has passed," Speaker Metzner said. "Impeachment is a public proceeding. Open the doors and let the public in."

Reporters and other interested people rushed into the room and balcony, shuffling and pushing for a place as history was about to be made. After ten minutes, Speaker Metzner called for order.

"Because of the serious nature of this proceeding, the vote will be taken by roll call. Congressman Smithers of Alabama, how do you vote?"

Congressman Smithers stood. "Yes for impeachment."

The roll call vote continued with about ninety percent of the members voting for impeachment. Whitcolm paced in nervous anticipation as the votes for impeachment accumulated. Two hundred and sixty-eight votes would be needed to impeach. As the votes in favor climbed over two hundred and forty, President Andrews and his entourage entered the room, unannounced.

"Mr. Speaker, may I have the floor?" Andrews called

out.

Speaker Metzner appeared thoroughly annoyed. "The time to present your case has passed, Mr. President. We are voting now."

Andrews smiled. "Has the time passed for the truth?"

Metzner glanced around without saying a word.

"What I have to say concerns national security. Have the public removed from the room."

Speaker Metzner reluctantly nodded to the sergeant-at-arms, who started clearing the room of the public. Shouts and howls came from some of the people as they slowly left. Once peace and quiet was restored, Andrews stepped to the podium at the center of the room.

* * *

"What I am about to reveal to you is classified top secret," Andrews said. "All leaks and violations of security will be prosecuted to the full extent of the law."

Senator Whitcolm smiled and stepped forward. "Mr. President, do you deny that classified technology was delivered to Russia?"

Andrews placed both hands on the podium. "No."

Whitcolm nodded. "What was the nature of the technology?"

Andrews glanced around at the people in the chamber. "Twelve flight simulators were delivered to Russian President Yuri Pasternov as part of an agreement for our two countries to join forces against a very dangerous common enemy."

Whitcolm grinned. "You are indicating that Russia is no longer our enemy?" He turned to face the members of Congress.

"I am." Andrews stated.

Whitcolm turned back to Andrews. "Then who is?

China?"

Andrews shook his head. "No. I have also shared the same technology with China. Both Russia and China are our allies. We are in this fight together."

Whitcolm feigned surprise. "Fight? A fight against whom?"

Andrews glanced at the members of Congress again. They were all paying close attention to his answer.

"Not a whom, a what. The night before Marine One was shot down I met with Chinese President Hua in China. On the way back, I was almost killed by this new enemy. Were it not for the skill and courage of a very dedicated pilot, I wouldn't be here now."

Whitcolm moved closer to the podium. "And what is this so called new enemy?"

This was the moment Andrews was waiting for: "It's easier to show you."

Andrews turned to a side door and nodded. Franks opened the door while three soldiers carried in black body bags. The expression on Whitcolm's face dropped, and he turned pale. The soldiers walked straight to the center of the room, unzipped the body bags, and dumped the dark gray bodies of three dead Zeta Grey aliens out onto the expensive carpet of the House floor. Whitcolm appeared horrified, as did Metzner. Several members of Congress turned and covered their mouths as they ran for the restrooms. A distinctly offensive odor permeated the room.

"This race of extraterrestrial is known as the Zeta Grey. They have been visiting our solar system for all of our recorded history. They have taken a keen interest in us only since we developed nuclear weapons. They have conned us, manipulated our minds, invaded our planet, and our military system. There are approximately eighteen thousand of them currently on our planet, mostly in underground military facilities. They are a violent, ruthless, despicable race of alien clones. They use our people for genetic material and as a food supply. Most major governments of the world have contracts with these creatures, including us."

He watched the look of horror spread through the members of Congress.

"We mistakenly believed we would receive very advanced technology in exchange for the lives of some of our people. In the past, our political leaders believed the sacrifice of some innocent souls was worth what we expected to receive in return."

Andrews leaned closer to the microphone and lowered his voice slightly.

"I am here today to tell you that not only was that wrong, but we have been had. The Zeta Greys have no intention of delivering on their promise, ever. We have received nothing useful in return. Certainly nothing that justifies the lost lives of thousands of our citizens."

He paused for effect. "Yes, thousands."

As he let that sink in, he made eye contact with as many members as he could.

"In the last year, the Zeta Greys have abducted over forty thousand people worldwide. In excess of ten thousand people per year are never seen again. Those who are returned have been physically abused, psychologically damaged, chipped, tracked, and controlled for the rest of their ruined lives."

He looked at Whitcolm, who was backing slowly away.

"Make no mistake about it. We are at war. We have Russia and China at our side—humans fighting against the Zeta Greys. We have the technology to defeat them, but we have been able to build only a small percentage of the very advanced fighter craft and exotic weapons we need to do the job. Several of our major defense contractors have been corrupted by the influence of the Zeta Greys and the money that flows into their coffers."

He looked directly at Speaker Metzner. "That stops now. I have a list of over four thousand people who have or still are cooperating directly with the Zeta Greys. I also have a list of twelve thousand other people who have been corrupted by the Greys and are working indirectly with them. All of those people are now being arrested or at least detained."

Whitcolm slowly moved for the door. Andrews turned to face him. "Senator Whitcolm, congratulations. You made the short list. You are under arrest for treason against the United States and complicity in the deaths of more than four thousand of your fellow Americans."

The Secret Service quietly took Whitcolm into custody.

"Speaker Metzner, you also made the list."

Secret Service agents put Metzner in handcuffs and led him out the door.

"What I need from the rest of you, today, is an off-the-books authorization for one trillion dollars to expand the new United States Space Command so we can kick these stinking creatures off our planet. Similar measures are being introduced in Russia and China as we speak. I expect your authorization on my desk by the end of the day. And in case you're wondering, I have more alien bodies where these three came from. It's time for us to take our planet back."

Andrews turned and walked out the side door leaving the three dead Zeta Greys lying on the floor, thin green blood seeping into the carpet.

* * *

Representative George Elias of Missouri delivered the approved authorization bill to President Andrews at the White House later that afternoon. He was scanned for proper ID, weapons, and then brought down to the underground bunker.

"So what happened after I left?" Andrews asked.

Elias still looked somewhat shaken up by the experience.

"The impeachment vote stopped—the whole thing was dropped. The biggest concern was what to do with the dead bodies. Several people came over to get a closer look, but mostly no one could stand the stench. They finally decided to move the bodies over to the Smithsonian."

Andrews nodded. "The discussion on the appropriation?"

Elias shook his head. "There wasn't much. Mostly everyone agreed that the expense was both necessary and reasonable. It passed both the House and the Senate by voice vote. I don't remember hearing a single nay."

Andrews signed the appropriations bill, finalizing the process to make it official.

"I've got to say," Elias said. "I'd heard rumors about UFOs and aliens from a few friends, but I never even considered that they could be real. It just seemed too weird, you know?"

Andrews sat back in his chair. "And now?"

Elias shrugged. "You don't have to show me more than once. You said they tried to kill you?"

Andrews nodded. "Yes, they did."

Elias paused, apparently thinking things over. "They're that dangerous?"

Andrews stood. "More so than you can imagine."

Chapter 54

Diane studied the new rules of engagement against the Zeta Greys. Now that they had a full squadron of twenty-four fighter craft, they could begin to project overwhelming force against a small group of saucers. With the significant losses the Zeta Greys were experiencing against Diane's squadron, the saucers were fleeing rather than attacking them. She liked the new rules: They were winning.

Rules, she thought. Her mind drifted back to the question cascade she had experienced with Charlie. In a telepathic society, everyone follows the rules. That was especially true for the Zetas. That's why the jinking worked: It was random—it didn't follow the rules. The Greys couldn't adapt to something spontaneous. That was an Earth human quality—spontaneity. The telepathic civilizations considered

Earth humans to be inferior because we couldn't communicate mind-to-mind. But that also left us free to be spontaneous. That's one thing we do that's not a weakness; it's a strength.

She had received the information from Charlie in a few seconds, but it was taking her days to absorb what the information meant. She was still connecting the dots, realizing the implications, and understanding the relationships between everything he shared with her.

This whole thing isn't as simple as I had imagined, she thought. Just like most of our human relationships: It's complicated.

* * *

Diane had been watching a new pilot, Eric Thorensen, go through his first flights. He was good, she thought. We could use more like him. It didn't take long for the squadron to nickname him Thor. With twenty-four craft in the squadron, Diane broke them up into four flight groups of six fighters each. She placed Thor in her flight group so she could see how he performed in combat.

The scramble alarm sounded. "Saucer intrusion! Saucer intrusion!"

She ran for the elevators and joined Ryan on their way up to the staging deck.

"I thought the planetary shield was operating," Ryan said. "How are they getting through?"

Diane shrugged. "Maybe they're not. We'll have to hear what Hollis has to say when we get into our fighter craft."

They quickly changed into their flight suits and ran to their craft. As Ryan powered up the fighter and went through the preflight checklist, Diane listened for Hollis's directions.

"Four saucers have been located operating close to the ground. Coordinates are being sent to your displays. Flights alpha through delta are assigned to targets one through four respectively. Go get 'em people. Stay aware, and stay alive."

The targeting assignment appeared on Ryan's screen "Okay. Our target is in Costa Rica, heading south. If we stay low and come up from behind it, our ETA is three minutes, thirty seconds."

She nudged the thruster control forward. "Roger that."

She guided her fighter craft up the access shaft and took her place on the front left of the flight deck. The red lights were flashing and the blast door was already rising as she arrived. The entire squadron was in place as the lights turned to solid green.

Diane and the other five fighter craft in her flight group swung north, circled tight around the mountain with Peregrine Base carved inside, and headed south at fifty percent thrust. They quickly slipped through one mountain valley after another, using the landscape as natural cover, swinging southeast over Mexico and Central America. When they reached Costa Rica, she guided her flight out over the Pacific Ocean, staying close to the water. The saucer was now off the coast of Peru and gaining altitude.

"Increase thrust to seventy percent and start firing at five miles from the target," Diane ordered.

"Effective range of our cannon is only three miles," Ryan reminded her.

Diane checked the other craft in her formation. Everyone was holding in tight.

"We're not trying to hit them—we're just giving them a reason to run."

She smiled. Chasing was a lot safer than them shooting back.

"Copy that," Ryan answered.

The six fighter craft moved in perfect synchronicity as they pulled up at the lone saucer above them.

"Eighty percent thrust," Diane ordered.

The saucer bolted vertically before any cannon shots had been fired, racing into the upper atmosphere.

"Jink to base, let me know when you have the target in range."

She checked the formation one more time.

"Copy, Jink," Peregrine Base replied. "Three seconds, two, one."

"Flight Alpha, break, break," she ordered.

The six fighter craft banked down toward the ground and decreased speed. Diane looked back at the saucer. A bright blue glowing light appeared in the sky around it followed by half a dozen lightning bolts striking the target. The saucer, carried by its momentum, arced up, and over, slowly beginning its long tumbling fall to the ocean below.

"Jink to base. Target one is down. I confirm target one has been hit and killed. The shield is working."

She could hear the cheers from Peregrine Base over the radio.

"Roger that Jink. Return to base."

She was about to issue the return command when Ryan interrupted, "Hold on. I show at least twenty bandits coming out of the Andes Mountains at high speed. ETA is twelve seconds."

It's never clean or simple, is it, Diane thought.

"Flight Alpha, engage!"

The six fighter craft turned east and flew straight into the saucers.

"More bandits coming in behind them. This is going to get messy!" Ryan shouted.

She saw Thor make his first kill as she swung and dipped, shooting another saucer in the process. She smiled. He was going to do just fine. She focused on shooting two more saucers.

"Thor is hit," Ryan said. "He's dropping."

Diane glanced at the falling fighter craft. Movement in her peripheral vision drew her attention. A large saucer, approximately a hundred feet in diameter, swooped in below them from the east. It slowed dramatically in front of Thor and projected an intense blue light onto his craft. Thor was no longer falling to the ocean below. He was being sucked up into the large saucer!

The battle was chaotic and changing rapidly. Diane weaved and shot, hopping over one saucer and shooting another. When she managed to glance back at Thor, his craft was disappearing inside the large saucer backwards, with his cannons pointing away from the saucer. Nothing he could do, she realized. Just like her brother, Daniel.

The fighting continued until the large saucer disappeared at high speed back into the mountains. As soon as it was gone, the remaining scout saucers broke off the attack, scattered and vanished into the distant mountains.

"Let's go get 'em!" Buddha shouted.

"Negative," Diane said. "This was a trap. It still is. If we follow them into the mountains, we all die."

* * *

Sean Wells pulled into the small parking area in front of the guest ranch on U.S. 60 in Datil, New Mexico. He was surprised they were still open, being the off season for tourists. He ordered the meatloaf special for dinner along with some peach pie for dessert. They obviously had rooms available and he was in the area where he was supposed to be, so he registered to stay for several nights. He just didn't know how or why it was so important for him to be in this place in the middle of nowhere.

* * *

Rosaq watched from the deck in the side of a remote mountain near the border between Peru and Bolivia. The bright blue tractor beam moved the captured rogue fighter craft into the wide cave and placed it on the flat stone surface. The two occupants were unconscious. Workers cut the clear canopy from the craft and extracted the crew. Their flight suits and uniforms were removed and they were placed naked on examination tables. Tissue samples were taken and a physical exam completed.

Earth humans, Rosaq thought. That answered the first question. This was not an off-world group of rogues stirring up trouble. This was the first phase of a rebellion.

The human who had been in the front seat of the craft woke slowly. Rosaq leaned over the human and stared into his eyes, initiating neural engagement. He followed the optic nerve into the recesses of the brain and extracted all of the information about Peregrine Base, the planetary shield being put into place, and the technical specifications for the fighter craft.

* * *

When Diane and her squadron returned, Hollis and Theo were waiting for her.

"What happened?" Hollis asked.

She looked at the floor. "It was a trap, sir." She looked up at him. "They sacrificed four saucers to draw us out."

Hollis looked surprised. "Do you think they knew about the planetary shield?"

Diane shook her head. "I don't think so, sir. The whole thing seems to have been set up for the sole purpose of capturing one of our craft with its crew."

Theo sighed. "How much did the crew know?"

Hollis breathed out and closed his eyes momentarily. "Pretty much everything about Peregrine Base, its defenses, layout, and the fighter craft."

Theo nodded. "Then that's what the Zetas know now. What about the location of Ceti Research?"

Hollis shook his head. "The three of us are the only people here who know."

Theo relaxed a little.

"So what's going to happen to Thorensen and his RIO?" Diane asked.

Theo glanced at the floor. "It's not like there's ever going to be a prisoner exchange. They're probably already dead."

The pain from the loss of Daniel swelled in her chest with the addition of Eric Thorensen and his RIO. She tried to remember the name of his RIO, but it just wouldn't come to her mind. She closed her eyes and tried to stifle the sobs pushing their way up. She turned away from Hollis and Theo as the tears flooded down her cheeks. Her breath came in jerks as she wept.

Theo stepped up behind her and wrapped his arms gently around her, giving her a soft hug.

"I'm so sorry," he said.

* * *

Hollis called the flight crew together and announced that their new flight suits had arrived and were ready for them in the conference room. As they entered, Dr. Theo Shugart stood at the front of the room.

She looked at him, unable to smile from the loss of Thorensen. He gave her a concerned look.

"Please take a seat. These are your new flight suits." He

held a suit in his right hand and a helmet in his left for them to see. The suit was a highly reflective chrome color, as was the helmet. "You'll notice that each suit has a backpack built into it. On the side are the connections for the cooling system, oxygen, carbon dioxide removal, and communications—all combined into this master connector. Your fighter craft are being modified for the new suits as we speak and should be complete by tomorrow morning."

"That suit looks like something from a bad 1950s science fiction movie," Ryan said.

Theo chuckled. "We thought so, too, but it turned out to be the most efficient design. Infrared emissions are almost zero. The backpack has a dry ice core that will maintain temperature inside the suit for twenty minutes outside of the fighter craft. The cooling pack is primed by plugging into the fighter craft and putting your helmet on. Cooling is activated by unplugging with your helmet on. Remove the helmet and the backpack systems shut down."

"The out-of-craft communications?" Diane asked. She still couldn't shake the loss of such a promising pilot. It was too much like losing Daniel all over again.

Theo tried to smile, then nodded. "The sound based system works remarkably well. The little bar on the collar of your flight suit is a combination microphone and speaker. It works through the radio system as long as you're plugged into the fighter craft. Once you unplug, it goes into sound mode as long as you have your helmet on."

Helen Catalano raised her hand. "Range?"

Theo turned to face her. "It depends on your surroundings. It has an echo inside hallways—can't help that— but outside you can talk easily up to two hundred feet away."

Helen and several other pilots nodded in approval.

"How often does the dry ice have to be replaced?" Simmons asked.

Good question, Diane thought.

"You will need a new dry ice canister snapped into place in the backpack for every mission. This is something your new flight techs will do as soon as the scramble alarm sounds. By the time you get to your ready room, everything will be ready to go."

Diane smiled. This whole operation was coming together. She liked it—a lot.

"We sometimes fly outside the atmosphere. If our canopy springs a leak, will the new flight suit protect us?" Ryan asked.

Theo shook his head slightly.

"Only to a degree. The suit is not a true pressure suit, but it will provide you with basic protection for twenty minutes or so."

Helen raised her hand. "You have a lot of boxes there, how many suits do we get?"

Theo glanced at the stacks of boxes.

"Two suits each. We don't want anybody unable to fly because of a damaged suit. The remaining boxes are filled with backup suits and replacement parts. The flight techs will inspect your suit after each flight and replace anything that's worn, damaged, or questionable. Any more questions?"

There weren't. The new suits were picked up as the team disbursed.

Diane arranged to have dinner with Theo. It would be in the cafeteria, without any privacy, but it would have to do.

* * *

President Andrews watched on the security monitors, as crowds gathered in front of the White House. In excess of ten thousand veterans had gathered to protest. Some were across the street in Lafayette Square, others stood in front of the

Capitol Building, with the rest spreading out into the National Mall. Another twenty thousand were traveling by bus and would arrive over the next two or three days.

"The rumor has spread," Doug Franks said, "that withdrawing our troops from Europe means a massive reduction in military personnel and defense contracts. Active members of the Armed Forces are scrambling to find a way of not being phased out and losing their careers."

"If they only knew," Andrews said. The current U.S. military had just over two million members, including reserve units. The new space-based military would need more than seventeen and a half million members from the U.S. alone. "Instead of downsizing, we need a massive upgrade, not only in people, but in equipment, and technology. Tanks, bombs, bullets, ships, missiles, and planes are going to become as obsolete as horses, spears, and arrows. We need to reorganize everything, from the top on down."

Franks sat in a chair opposite Andrews. "You have any people specifically in mind for that?"

Andrews sighed as his shoulders slumped. "Unfortunately not. My hope is that with younger military officers being promoted to fill vacancies, we can identify those who are naturally inclined toward our new vision, and place them in key positions of influence."

Franks scooted forward. "And what, exactly, is our new vision?"

Andrews glanced at a display screen showing the crowds gathering outside.

"The old vision was of a world divided with U.S. military might intimidating other countries into either cooperation or submission through regime change. By keeping the world divided and squabbling, we could maintain control. But that is just managing an ongoing crisis; it's not an actual solution."

Andrews paused to gather his thoughts.

"My new vision is of a world joining forces for survival, with our new space technology leading the way to security and eventual prosperity. This new understanding of energy and technology has the potential of opening a whole new future for mankind. Unfortunately, it will also mean the demise of many cherished institutions and vested interests."

Franks shook his head. "Those walls will not come down quietly."

Andrews nodded in agreement. "No, they won't. But those businesses and structures will come down at some point, one way or another. We're just going to make it happen sooner rather than later."

* * *

Rosaq connected with the Insectoid telepathically. The ground base for the rogue fighter craft was located. He reviewed the computer-generated, three-dimensional layout of that rogue base. The arrangement of interconnected tunnels and rooms indicated the base was heavily defended. Rosaq provided details on the placement and capabilities of the large particle beam cannons obtained from the crew of the captured rogue fighter craft.

Now he knew the rogue base and fighter craft were all manned by Earth humans. There were rumors the captured crew had heard that the off world technology assistance had come from an Andromedan, but Rosaq was skeptical. What someone from the Andromeda Council would be doing here was a mystery. There were no known contracts or protection agreements between the Andromeda Council and Earth, which made the technology transfer illogical. No ships had shown up on their sensor arrays, but Andromedan technology could cloak any number of ships from them, or make millions of ships appear where none actually existed. It certainly added an unanticipated element of risk.

The information from the captured crew and the analysis of electromagnetic transmissions and field strengths, indicated the Earth humans had a planetary shield almost in place, and Peregrine Base was the command center. There was one glaring defect in the planetary shield coverage, which Rosaq needed to exploit to bring in more saucers and workers.

Excellent, he thought. A decapitation strike was the obvious solution. There were two other locations with possible rogue fighter craft activity on the other side of the planet, but it wasn't significant. Twenty scout saucers and a transport would be more than sufficient to eliminate each of those.

Rosaq finalized his battle plan. Experience with the rogue fighters indicated that they were formidable, but subject to overwhelming force. Therefore a massive assault against the base was in order. He calculated his losses and the resources the rogue base was now known to have, took the worst-case scenario, and doubled it. He was going to need hundreds more scout saucers, at least five transport saucers full of workers, all armed with flash guns, and three portable particle beam cannons. He had a new strategy to deal with the fighters, too.

With the new saucers, the rogue fighters would be overwhelmed, the base defenses overcome, and his ground force would eliminate every living thing in or around the rogue base. That would put an early end to this foolish rebellion.

Chapter 55

The scramble alarm sounded at 4:06 in the morning. Diane jumped from her bed and raced for the ready room. This would be the first flight in their new suits. The flight techs were just finishing up prepping the suits as she and Ryan ran into the room. The process of getting into their flight suits went faster with help from the tech support people. Within twenty seconds she and Ryan were sprinting for their fighter craft.

Ryan completed the preflight checklist. Diane nudged the controls and headed for the flight deck. Hollis was there, as usual, giving them the details of the mission.

"Multiple saucer intrusions over the Pacific Ocean, northeast of Guam. You will have the support of six fighter craft from the Russian Space Command. China is still spraying the upper atmosphere and their Xinjiang facility is not yet under our control. We need to stop these saucers, people. Get out there and take them down. Stay alert and stay alive. Go get 'em!"

The launch lights turned from red to green. Diane and her squadron sprang from the flight deck, swung around Peregrine Base, and streaked west over the mountains. As the twenty-four fighter craft cleared the coast of Southern California, she led them low over the water at sixty percent thrust.

In eighteen minutes they contacted the lead pilot from the Russian Space Command.

"ETA?" Diane asked.

The Russian Space Command leader's English wasn't bad.

"Less than sixty seconds, Lieutenant Commander Zadanski. I am Senior Lieutenant Nikolaev, at your service. What is your plan?"

She smiled as she adapted to his Russian accent.

"We come in low and underneath the saucers, then up. Shoot everything that isn't made on planet Earth."

She had heard rumors about the skills of Russian pilots from her time on the *Ronald Reagan*. She was curious to see how they performed.

"Roger that. Commencing attack run in thirty seconds."

Well, she thought, I'm about to find out.

"Copy, Nikolaev, see you in the wild blue yonder. Good hunting."

The tactical display in the fighter craft gave Ryan the direction and distance to the enemy saucers, but no information regarding the size of the target. Diane was the first to get a visual on the saucers.

"Ry, look at the size of those things."

Two large saucers, roughly a hundred yards across, were being escorted into the atmosphere by several hundred of the scout saucers they had encountered before.

"This isn't an incursion; it's an invasion," Ryan said.

Diane had a sinking feeling in the pit of her stomach. This wasn't going to be easy.

"Jink to all fighters: Do everything you can to get through the scout saucers and take down the transports. They're priority one."

She turned on the jinking control.

"Roger that," Nikolaev said. "Initiate jinking." He repeated the instructions in Russian for his squadron.

The scout saucers quickly divided into two groups. The first came directly at them firing as soon as they were in range. The second group clustered close around the transport saucers, forming a protective barrier against attack.

Diane engaged the first two saucers in front of her, bobbing and weaving as her shots zeroed in.

"Ry, watch our six, I'm going in a little deeper."

She slipped past three other saucers in an attempt to get a shot at a transport.

"Two on our six. Not going to work."

She flipped around, shooting another saucer in the process. The two saucers behind her closed in, firing in a rapid coordinated sequence. Instead of firing back, she dived and swung to the left, then hard right, coming up behind them. Within three seconds she had hit both saucers, sending them into a twisting fall to the ocean below.

That was new, she thought. In her peripheral vision she caught four saucers coordinating fire on one of her teammates. The fighter craft was hit on its right wing and started falling to the ocean.

They should be able to get out, Diane hoped.

She swung to the left and fired at the group of four saucers, hitting one before the formation broke and the saucers scattered. Then six saucers formed a quick hexagonal formation and focused their fire on a single fighter craft from Nikolaev's squadron. The fighter was hit and started dropping.

They're focusing their fire around a single craft, she realized, trying to overcome the effect of jinking, and it's working!

"Jink to all fighters: If you see four or more saucers forming up and facing you, do not engage—repeat, do not engage. Break and evade! Break and evade!"

She banked along the side of six other saucers forming another hex pattern and opened fire. Two saucers were hit before they realized she was there. The other four broke away before they could hit another member of her squadron.

"Jink to all fighters: If you are to the side or the back of saucers forming up together, attack as soon as you see them."

The response of both her squadron and Nikolaev's brought joy to her heart. Conversation between pilots coordinated a bait and attack strategy. One fighter would drift off on its own. As soon as the saucers closed formation to go after it, several fighter craft would zoom in from the side and back, taking down the saucers in the formation.

Nice try, Zetas, Diane thought. Coordinated firing works for you, but your formation makes a target rich environment for us.

The number of saucers versus fighter craft was shifting dramatically in favor of the fighters as the two large saucers disappeared over the ocean to the east.

"Nikolaev, our two squadrons can handle what's left of these scouts, how about we take on the transports?"

There was a pause before Nikolaev answered. "What is the saying, 'go big or go home?' "

Diane smiled. "That's the one."

"See?" Nikolaev said. "Now you're thinking like a Russian."

Diane and Buddha broke from the dogfight with

Nikolaev and his wingman on their left. The four fighter craft accelerated with thrust at eighty percent. The saucers were staying well below the ionosphere where the Planetary Shield weapons could get them, but still high enough for high speed. Within three minutes Diane, Nikolaev, and their wing craft were closing in on a transport saucer. Half of the scout saucer protection squad broke off and engaged them. The four fighter craft seemed heavily outnumbered.

"Spread out. Let's start with Buddha playing bait."

She heard Buddha chuckling over the radio. "Roger that, Jink."

Buddha pulled away from the other three fighters and started shooting at several saucers. Six saucers formed a hex pattern focused on Buddha.

"Here we go. Break and evade!"

Buddha dived and twisted as Diane and the two Russian fighters closed in and shot down the saucer formation.

"I'll go next," Diane said. She pulled away, going after two isolated saucers as six more came together in formation right behind her.

"Break now," Ryan said.

She pulled up, twisted, and spun over the saucer formation as her three teammates took out the six saucers still in formation. Two more times the bait and attack worked, at which point the remaining saucers returned to protect the transport saucer.

"Ideas?" Diane asked.

It felt strange to see the Zetas on defense.

"Two teams from opposite directions?" Nikolaev said.

She could see that working.

"Or each from four different directions?" Buddha said.

Four directions makes more sense, she thought.

"It leaves us without any backup," Diane said.

Following a brief pause, Ryan said, "Actually, the rest

of our fighters are on their way. Twenty seconds out."

"Ours, too," Nikolaev said.

She looked at the scout saucers packed around the transport. "The Zetas are willing to sacrifice their scouts to protect the transport," she said. "I think we should take them up on it. Spread out, no closer than two miles, and see how many we can pick off before the rest of our fighters get here."

They broke in four different directions and began firing into the pack of scouts. The Zetas were firing back, but between the jinking and the distance, they weren't hitting anything. Then the scout saucers swarmed at them.

They must have realized that when the rest of our fighters got here, we were just going to sit back and pick them off one at a time, Diane realized.

"Attack!" Diane ordered.

All four began their attack run on the transport. The scout saucers moved to block their shots from hitting the transport, but with the speed and spontaneous changes in direction of the fighters, simple blocking wasn't working. Diane swung up and as the scout saucers moved to block her shot, she dived, spun, and swept under the transport saucer. She fired several shots, hitting the underside before breaking off. Nikolaev was doing the same thing from the top. Buddha followed her lead and hit the underside two more times before peeling away.

The transport saucer slowed and began to tip to the front. The last of the scouts abandoned the falling transport and flew directly at them. Diane took out three more saucers before being shot several times by the saucer swarm. A beam shot through the canopy and blasted fragments throughout the cockpit. Ryan yelled out in pain.

"Ry, you hit?"

She shot and hit another scout saucer as the rest of her squadron arrived.

"Aaah, jeez, my left shoulder. I don't think the beam hit me. Just shrapnel."

Her fighter craft was losing power rapidly.

"Hang on Ry, I'll get you out of here."

Diane aimed at one more scout and pulled the trigger. The cannons did not fire. She pushed the control stick forward and dived for the ocean below.

Chapter 56

"Mayday! Mayday! Jink going down!"

She reported her position as she saw Nikolaev falling from the other side of the battle. Two saucers came after her, but Buddha swept in from the side and shot them before they could get to her. Two more saucers came at Buddha, managing only one hit on the left wing. He was losing altitude and had limited maneuverability, but he circled her falling craft, following her down, protecting her so she wouldn't get hit again.

After falling for several minutes Diane pulled the ejection levers, separating the cockpit from the craft. The chutes deployed, slowing their descent into the rolling ocean. She took a quick survey of her surroundings. Nikolaev and Buddha had both ejected and were drifting down into the water below. Nikolaev's wingman was still flying, following them down, circling to provide both protection and a location for their rescue.

Diane's cockpit hit the water with the front edge down. The impact drove the capsule as deep as forty feet under the water. Thirty seconds later they bobbed to the surface.

"Ry, you okay?"

"Maybe. We have sea water pouring into the cockpit. We're going to sink!"

He sounded panicky.

"You think it was worth it to take down one of the transports?" she asked, trying to get his mind off the flooding cockpit.

"Yep. I just wish we knew how many more got in before we got there."

Ryan seemed to be refocusing his attention away from panic.

"Yeah," Diane replied softly. "If this was the Zeta Grey invasion force, we're going to find out soon enough."

Diane was knee deep in sea water as the capsule dipped to the front. Ryan released his harness and moved around in the back of the cockpit capsule moaning and grunting with every breath.

"What are you doing?"

She turned her head to look at him. He was facing the back of the cockpit. "According to the tech manual, we have a small inflatable raft down in here, somewhere."

Her eyebrows rose. "We do?"

He grunted again. "That's what it said. Didn't you read the manual?"

She scoffed. "I read the flight parts, not the rest of it."

He groaned after he hit his head on the canopy. "Well it was in there."

He grunted as he reached behind his seat.

"You remember exactly where it's stowed?"

He strained as he reached deeper behind the seat.

"Not exactly, but it's either under or behind my seat." He pulled his arm free. "Well, it's not behind the seat."

"You sure it's still there after the last round of improvements?"

He reached under his seat. "You know, they could have improved the fighter to the point where the inflatable raft is no longer there."

She grimaced. "That would figure. The most advanced fighter craft on the planet and we can't find the life raft."

She and Ryan were both breathing heavily.

"We're sinking. You find the raft yet?" Diane asked.

He shook his head. "No. It's not here."

Diane unbuckled her harness and looked back at Ryan. His disappointment over the missing raft was clear in his pained facial expression.

"Let me guess—you can't swim," she said.

He didn't answer.

"In the Navy, they made sure everyone could swim. They had classes."

"Yeah, well, they had classes in the Marines, too. I was just never that good at it, and that was a while ago, you know?"

She reached back and gripped his right arm. "Ryan, I've got you. I'm not going to let you drown, okay?"

He looked back at her and nodded. He just didn't look convinced.

Ryan activated the release mechanism. The canopy unscrewed and opened as more sea water poured in from the front. They pushed free as the capsule sank beneath the waves and disappeared into the depths below. For a few minutes the flight suits easily kept them afloat, but slowly the sea water seeped into the collar and began filling the suit, which got heavier as they started to float lower in the water.

"We're going to drown! We have to get out of our suits!" Ryan shouted.

Diane thought back to her training at Annapolis.

"Yeah . . . no. We take the suit off, but we use it as a floatation device."

Ryan shook his head. "It's too heavy, it'll drag us down."

She spoke as calmly as she could. "It'll be fine, Ry. Trust me."

They took their flight suits off and resealed them where the zipper was located. They scooped air into the legs of the suit to use them as a V-shaped floatation system. It felt good to Diane to get out of the hot suit. The sea water was warm and refreshing by comparison, but she knew that seventy-eight degree water was still twenty degrees below body temperature. At some point hypothermia would set in.

"We need to stay close to conserve body heat," she said.

He was looking away from her. "I don't think that's going to matter."

She frowned. She thought he would want to be close to her. "Why?"

He pointed across the rolling moonlit waves to a fin breaking the surface of the water fifty yards away.

"At least it's only one shark. It could be worse," she said.

Ryan used his right arm and paddled away from her.

"Ry, what are you doing?"

The shark slowly circled, closing in. "It's curious," Diane said. "Don't move. Maybe it'll go away."

Ryan turned and yelled, "I'm bleeding, Jink, I want you as far away from what's going to happen as you can get."

Now she felt panic rising in her chest. "Ry . . . No!"

Ryan continued to paddle farther away. "Stay away! I

mean it. Stay away!"

She stayed still as the shark came within three feet of her. The shark drifted by, moved away, and came back. It brushed against her. It was all she could do to not scream in panic. The shark drifted away from her, but still circled Ryan at about twenty feet away.

* * *

I've got to keep it away from her, Ryan thought. He paddled harder to draw the shark farther away from Jink.

The shark fin cut through the top of the water as it followed the blood trail straight to him. Panic filled his chest. He held his helmet firmly in his right hand as the shark charged at him. His left shoulder was bleeding, making it the shark's primary target. He pushed the helmet against the shark's mouth, turning in the water, forcing the vicious thing off to the side. It circled and took another run at him.

The shark pushed straight into him. Ryan punched it in the nose with the helmet. The shark whipped its head from side to side, trying to get past the helmet. It was all Ryan could do to keep the helmet between him and the shark. The force of the attack propelled Ryan back in the water. He reached out with his left hand and dug his thumb into the shark's eye. The shark whipped to the side, slashing into Ryan's left arm with its razor-sharp teeth. He yelled out in pain.

* * *

Diane was so focused on the shark attack that she almost didn't hear the dull thump of distant helicopter blades. The Navy chopper slowly approached, its searchlight sweeping the rolling sea from side to side. As Ryan continued to struggle with the shark, the deafening pulse of the blades flared the water into a swirling maelstrom and the brilliant searchlight lit up the water around her. She pointed to Ryan.

* * *

It was difficult enough for Ryan to see the shark in the moonlight. Now, with the swirling water around him, he lost track of where the shark was. He spun around, looking, but no fin was in sight. The searchlight lit up the ocean around him. He looked down into the water. There, coming up from twenty feet below him, was the shark. Ryan pulled his legs up into a ball as the shark lunged at him. He held the helmet in both hands and thrust it into the gaping rows of triangular teeth. The force of the impact threw him up, nearly out of the water, and spun him around. His helmet was yanked away as it became wedged in the shark's mouth. Ryan fell out of the V-shaped legs of the inflated flight suit, and plunged down into the water.

The searchlight turned the water a pale light green. A shadow moved above him in the glow. He moved deeper in the water as he tried to get away. Something grabbed his arm and turned him around. The mouthpiece of a scuba set was thrust into his mouth and a blast of air filled his lungs. He turned to face a Navy rescue diver in the water with him.

As they broke the surface, Ryan shouted, "There's a shark! Jink, where is she? Is she okay?"

"She's fine," the rescue diver said. "I put D2 shark repellant in the water. The shark is gone."

Ryan desperately looked around him, trying to locate Jink. He couldn't see her.

"Where is she?" he shouted.

The rescue diver hooked a harness around him and snapped the lift cable in place.

As he was hauled up into the air, the chopper swung over until the searchlight was centered on Jink. She was alive.

That's all that mattered to him. She was alive.

* * *

Once Diane was lifted aboard the chopper they moved over to pick up Nikolaev and his RIO. A Navy corpsman cut Ryan's blood-soaked uniform off of his chest and examined the wounds. He sprinkled a powder into the gashes on Ryan's arm and his shoulder to stop the bleeding and wrapped the wounds with gauze. The corpsman went on to check the rest of them for injuries. He looked at the uniforms and the strange patch on the shoulder, but he didn't say anything. When he saw Nikolaev's name in Russian Cyrillic above the right pocket, he turned and stared at Diane.

"It's okay," she said, "he's with us."

The corpsman looked at the Lieutenant Commander insignia on her uniform and nodded.

"If you say so, ma'am."

She held her eyes firmly on the corpsman. "I do. He's with us."

The corpsman wrapped each person pulled from the sea in a blanket as they headed back. The chopper landed on the rear deck of a destroyer. A Navy commander came out to greet them as they climbed out of the helicopter.

"I'm Commander Snyder," he said as he shook hands with Diane. "Come on inside and get some food and hot coffee. I have orders from the president to get you back to land on the first available high-speed transport. I've got a doc on board who can stitch up your injured man. We'll fly you back to the carrier as soon as we're in range, ma'am. Until then all of you are invited to enjoy our hospitality."

"Which carrier?" Diane asked.

"Ma'am?" he asked as he turned to face her.

"Which aircraft carrier are we going to?"

He grinned. "That would be the *Ronald Reagan*, ma'am, out of San Diego."

Chapter 57

What are the chances of not meeting someone I know? Diane wondered as the transport helicopter made its final approach to the *Ronald Reagan.* She watched carefully out the window as the chopper hovered briefly and then settled down on the flight deck. She breathed out quickly and momentarily closed her eyes as she recognized Commander Chase standing there, fists on his hips, waiting for them.

God, this is awkward.

When the door slid open, she hopped out, and walked straight over to Chase.

"Zadanski," he said as he looked her uniform over.

"Sir, I . . ."

Commander Chase's expression hardened as Nikolaev came to a stop next to her.

"Consorting with Russians? What the hell is going on, Zadanski?"

She shook her head. "Sir, it's need to know. I can't really explain beyond that."

Anger flared in his face. "Follow me."

Commander Chase turned, walked briskly to the door in the superstructure at the edge of the flight deck, and up two flights of stairs to his office. As they entered, Chase pointed to the two chairs opposite his desk.

"Sit."

Diane and Nikolaev sat as instructed.

"Sir, I can't really explain this to you. It's highly classified and compartmentalized."

He shook his head and breathed out hard. "You're going to have to give me more than that, Zadanski, otherwise I don't know when we are going to have a high-speed transport available to get you back to the States. You understand what I'm saying?"

She looked down at the floor. "Yes, sir." Her mind scrambled for a way to explain why they were there. "We work directly for the president. Again, it's strictly need-to-know, sir."

Commander Chase tipped back in his chair. "I'm aware of President Andrews's orders. I need to know something about what's going on before I allocate my resources. I see that it's lieutenant commander now."

Is that what he's upset about? My promotion?

"Yes, sir, it's critically important that we get back as soon as possible. Our national security is at stake."

He just sat there and stared at her for what seemed like an eternity.

"That's a convenient excuse, Zadanski. I've used it several times myself. I might be able to get the resources you need in a matter of a few minutes, or it could take several hours. I need to be convinced, so spill it."

She glanced at Nikolaev and then back to Commander Chase.

"It can't go any further than you, sir," Diane said. "I need your word."

He nodded. "Done."

She took a deep breath, then said, "Sir, in all of your experience as a pilot and a Commanding Officer have you ever seen or encountered a UFO?"

His expression darkened.

"We don't report those, for obvious reasons."

She nodded. "Have you ever seen how they can turn at right angles and accelerate to tremendous speeds?"

He didn't seem to like where the conversation was headed. "Your point being?"

He crossed his arms over his chest.

"They're actually very dangerous, sir. Just because you can't get close to them in an F/A-18 Super Hornet doesn't mean they're not hostile. They don't shoot at you because they don't have to, sir. It's just easier for them to fly away."

Commander Chase leaned forward and put his hands flat on his desk. "And you know this because . . . ?"

She leaned back, uncomfortable with the situation.

"I've shot down around twenty of them. I've also had two of our fighter craft shot out from under me, sir."

Commander Chase appeared clearly shaken by the news. "We're at war? You have a fighter craft that can shoot down UFOs?"

Finally, I'm getting through, she thought.

"Yes, sir. Our new fighter craft makes an F/A-18 Super Hornet look like a bicycle with cardboard wings on it. I'm Commanding Officer of an advanced squadron out of the United States. Senior Lieutenant Nikolaev, here, commands another squadron out of Russia, and a third squadron is forming up in China. It's a fight to the death, sir, and we really need to get back—right now."

Commander Chase picked up the phone on his desk, pushed a button, and said into it, "I need a V-22 Osprey, fully fueled and on the flight deck, right away." He hung up the phone. "Thank you, Zadanski. I always wondered if your talent would ever be fully utilized. I'm satisfied now that it is."

He stood and extended his hand to Nikolaev.

"It's an honor to meet you, Senior Lieutenant. I've been informed that two Russian fighters will be here within the next two hours to take you and your RIO back home. Don't let her down. She's very special."

Nikolaev stood at full attention. "I know that, sir. She has our full respect."

Chase finished shaking Nikolaev's hand and then turned to Diane.

"Zadanski . . . I hardly know what to say. You make me so proud. I . . ."

"Thank you, sir. It means a lot to me." She shook his hand and smiled. "We really have to go, sir."

He nodded sadly. "Of course."

She led Nikolaev through the maze of corridors to the flight deck.

"Do you think he will keep our secret?" he asked.

"Yep. It's ingrained in military plots to never talk about UFOs. It'll be fine."

Nikolaev smiled. "Until we meet again, as you say, in the wild blue yonder."

They shook hands and she walked over to the waiting Osprey.

Yeah, she thought, if we manage to stay alive that long.

Chapter 58

Sean's head was feeling stuffed with new information to the point where he needed some air. He strolled out the back of the guest ranch to the corral and barn that housed the horses. He put his right foot on the lower railing and rested his arms on the top of the corral fence, staring into the distance.

"Can I help you?"

The difference between the man's western drawl and Sean's own New York accent made him smile.

"No, just thinking."

He turned to face the man.

"Well there's enough room for plenty of that out here. If I can do somethin' for ya, just say so."

Sean nodded.

The ranch hand turned away.

"You know," Sean said. "I've got kind of a crazy question, if you don't mind."

The ranch hand turned around.

"You ever heard of animal mutilations?"

The man stared at him.

"Ever seen a UFO?"

The man walked over to Sean. "You with the government?"

"No. The *New York Times*, actually."

The ranch hand looked around.

" 'Cause I reported some of that stuff years ago. Got a visit from some men in black suits: Made it clear I didn't see anythin'. I've kept my mouth shut. I don't want them comin' back."

Sean nodded. "I understand. I wouldn't want them coming back either. So . . . off the record, totally anonymous, what do you know?"

The man stepped closer.

"Seen both. Lost three horses over the last five years. Dangdest thing I ever saw. Clean round cut, no blood."

Sean tipped his head slightly to the side. "Genitals?"

The man nodded. "Yep. Seen some eyes and other organs taken, too."

This was consistent with what Sean had read. "Dent in the ground, like they were dropped from the air?"

The man stopped and stared at Sean. "You know an awful lot for a stranger. Who are you, really?"

Sean showed him his *New York Times* press ID and said, "I'm investigating a story. A friend told me to come out here so I could see for myself."

The man looked around at the sky. "Well, if you're looking for UFOs, you've come to the right place. We see 'em every night, dartin' around in the sky. Come on out tonight about an hour after dark. You'll see 'em."

Was this why Charlie wanted him out here in Datil, New Mexico?

"Thanks," Sean said.

The man nodded and walked off.

So, Sean thought, I'm in the right place.

* * *

Diane arrived at Peregrine Base late that afternoon and reported in to Hollis.

"Do we have a count on how many saucers got in through the hole?" she asked.

"Several hundred, I'm afraid. The Xinjiang transmitter is online now and the aluminum and barium are up to usable levels in the upper atmosphere, so however many saucers we have to deal with is fixed. The planetary shield is complete. The Zetas can't get any more saucers in."

"At least one large saucer is here. I don't know how many more slipped in before we got there, but my impression is that it was an invasion level force."

Hollis nodded and glanced at the floor. "That agrees with my assessment. We recorded seven large saucers entering. Your squadron shot one down, as did you. That leaves five out there, somewhere."

Diane looked up at the ceiling for a moment as she collected her thoughts.

"We lost seven fighter craft in the battle. The Russians lost two. We need replacement craft, and we need them now."

Hollis blew air out through his lips. "Four new craft are here now. We will be back up to twenty-four craft before tomorrow morning. President Andrews has the funding and the production facility has set up in a new place. They will have six times the manufacturing capability."

"Will have" wasn't helping her feel secure at the

moment. "Any news from Russia and China?"

Hollis nodded again. "Both the Russian and Chinese Space commands will be up to twenty-four fighters each within the next day to day and a half. We're going to be as ready as we can be, given the timing."

She sighed. "I just hope it's enough."

Chapter 59

Diane sat on the bed in her room and held the Zeta Grey flash gun in her hand. It's not like it came with an instruction manual, she thought. Three buttons . . . three levels of power?

She examined what she assumed was the front—the flat end. It looked like some sort of a lens inside a rotating collar. Focus control? Like our tactical flashlights? It was time to find out.

She slipped the flash gun into the inside pocket of her coat and headed for the main entrance to the underground base. When she reached the main security checkpoint they stopped her and asked her to wait for Captain Collier.

He arrived three minutes later and asked, "What's this all about?"

"I need some air," she said.

Collier stood there and looked at her. "You're going to have to do better than that. What do you really want?"

She glanced around the room. "Okay, I need to try something out."

He tipped his head. "Like what?"

She hesitated. "Can't you trust me on this?"

He shifted his weight to his other foot. "Maybe. It depends on what it is."

How was she going to explain this? "Look, I really don't want to make a big deal out of this, but I think it could lead to something important."

Collier took a step closer to her. "And you can't tell me?"

She shook her head. "No. Consider it something personal."

Collier studied her for a long minute. "How long do you need?"

She glanced around the room again. "Twenty, maybe thirty minutes."

He turned his head and stared at the exit for a few seconds then settled his gaze back on her. He walked over to the desk, picked up the phone, and called Hollis.

"Yes, sir, Zadanski is asking to go outside for twenty to thirty minutes." He looked back at her. "She has the same look in her eyes as the night she went to the simulator room." He continued to stare at her. "Yes, sir, the night she figured out the jinking." He glanced at the exit again. "Yes, sir, I agree." He hung up the phone. "You want an escort?"

She closed her eyes for a moment. "No."

He rubbed his chin, apparently deep in thought. "Personal, right?"

She nodded. "Right. Personal."

He glanced at the blast door again. "Okay if I wait at the mine entrance for you?"

She hesitated. "I guess."

Collier took a coat from the rack and an H&K MP5 with two extra magazines from one of the guards.

"Open the blast door, then close it again when we're clear."

He led her out through the mine entrance into the dark of the winter night. The moon was up and the light snow on the ground allowed her to see where she was going.

"Thirty minutes, I come looking for you," he said.

She smiled. "I'll be fine, thank you."

Diane wandered south through the canyon for about five-hundred yards and stopped. She stood silent and watched the scrub surrounding her. She saw what appeared to be a coyote investigating a hole in the ground. She raised the flash gun in her right hand and put her thumb on the rear button.

Sorry if I get this wrong, she thought. She pressed the button.

There was a quick strobe of bright light from the weapon, similar to the electronic flash from a camera. The coyote dropped to the ground and four birds fell out of several trees. She slowly approached the coyote and cautiously put her hand on its chest. It was still breathing.

Stun function, she thought. Handy. She studied the trees. The birds had fallen off of limbs spread out over forty feet apart. She had been maybe sixty feet away from the coyote.

So, wide angle. She rotated the front collar to the right, aimed off to the side into the scrub and pressed the front button. The flash was definitely more intense. A three-foot diameter tunnel appeared in the scrub brush. She walked to the tunnel and examined the ends of the branches. They were cut clean. She worked her way for fifty feet next to the hole cut in the scrub brush. The diameter seemed smaller. She pressed on. At a hundred feet the ends of the branches were smoking and no longer cleanly cut. Beyond that, the void in the brush shrank in size. A little farther and she found the end of the hole created by the flash gun.

Interesting. Almost a hundred and fifty feet effective range. Not bad.

She worked her way back through the scrub to where she'd started. She looked for the coyote and the birds that had fallen to the ground. All of them were gone. She looked at the flash gun again and thought, Okay. Back button is for stun, front is for vaporize. The middle button must be for kill. This can work.

The wind picked up from the southeast. At first it felt like it was getting warmer; then the snowflakes drifted down at an angle. Diane stopped and looked at the night sky. Clouds were moving in quickly from the west, obscuring the sparkling stars.

She put the weapon back into her coat pocket and headed back to the mine entrance.

"I was about to come looking for you," Collier said.

Diane shrugged. "No need, I didn't get lost."

Collier nodded. "Didn't think you would. Figure out what you needed to?"

She smiled as she passed him. "I think so."

He looked around at the blowing snow and shivered. "Then let's go back inside. It's really cold out here."

* * *

Diane knocked on Helen Catalano's door and Clay Obers's door.

"My room, ten minutes," she whispered. "Come alone."

Helen arrived first, two minutes early. Clay was one minute late.

"What's going on?" Helen asked.

Helen and Clay glanced at each other, worry filling their faces.

"Back on Baffin Island I picked up some things from the dead Zeta Greys. I've been trying to figure out what to do with them."

Helen and Clay looked relieved.

"Do with what?" Clay asked.

Diane picked up her coat revealing the flash gun on the bed.

"Is that what I think it is?" Clay asked.

Diane nodded. "It's a Zeta Grey weapon. On Baffin Island it was blasting holes through the trees. I collected three of them. Finally got a chance to try it out."

Clay grinned.

"And?" Helen asked. She couldn't take her eyes off the flash gun.

"Back button is for stun, middle button kills, front button vaporizes. Rotate the collar to the right for narrow beam, left for wide angle."

Clay stepped forward to get a closer look. "Range?"

"Narrow beam vaporize, fifty yards max. Wide angle, I don't know. I didn't want to draw too much attention."

Clay nodded. "Hollis is going to want those to go into research. He'll want you to turn these in."

Diane paused and looked at Helen. "I know. My intuition tells me to hang on to them, at least for a while."

Helen nodded slowly, indicating she suspected what Diane had in mind. "You said you had three of them?"

Diane opened a dresser drawer and handed one to each of them.

"Our secret?"

Helen took one gently in her hands, grinning.

"For now," Clay said.

Helen nodded in agreement.

"Be careful, there doesn't seem to be any safety on them. Accidental discharge could be very bad," Diane said.

Clay took the remaining flash gun. "Got it."

Helen hesitated, then asked, "You know about . . . ?" She nodded her head toward Clay.

Diane smiled and nodded. "That's why I asked both of you."

Helen smiled. The expression of appreciation on her face was all Diane needed.

"Thanks," Helen said.

Clay smiled and nodded in agreement.

"I'm guessing that they will wear down and need to be recharged at some point, and I have no idea how we would do that, so . . ."

A new loud alarm sounded.

"Battle Stations! Battle stations! All hands on deck!" came over the PA system. Helen and Clay ran to their rooms. "Saucer intrusion! Saucer intrusion! Multiple incoming saucers! Battle stations! Battle stations!"

Diane joined the rush of people in the hall as she headed for the elevators. She, Clay, and Helen were all carrying their flash guns. Ryan was the last person to jump into the elevator as the doors closed. His left arm was in a sling.

"You're injured. You need to stand down," Diane said.

Ryan shook his head. "And leave you out there alone? Not on your life."

He took the sling off and tossed it into the corner of the elevator. "Never wanted the stupid thing anyway."

He glanced down at the device in her hand and looked back up at her.

"Later," she whispered.

The door opened and they ran to their ready rooms. With their flight suits on they ran to their fighter craft, climbed in, cinched the harness, and plugged into the master connector for the cooling and communications system. Ryan powered up the craft and went through the preflight checklist.

"We're good to go," he said.

Diane nudged the thruster, retracted the landing pods, swung into the vertical shaft, and up to her place on the flight deck. Hollis stood by the blast door. When the flight deck was full he hit the button and the massive blast door raised, red lights flashing.

"Multiple saucers, all converging on this base," Hollis said. "This is it, people. The big guns will be more effective against saucers at a distance. Once they get through that, it's going to be up to you to take them out. Stay sharp, stay aware, and stay alive."

The first big particle beam cannon fired with a horrendously loud *crack*. It was uncomfortably loud even from inside the fighter cockpit with a helmet on. The sound drew Diane's mind back to the night her brother was abducted when she was less than a hundred feet from a lightning strike. That event had shocked her down to the bone and left a bitter taste in her mouth. She stayed as far away from lightning as she could ever since then.

Lightning, she thought. Why did it have to be like lightning? She shuddered involuntarily. It's not really lightning, she rationalized, it just sounds like it.

Her breathing became more rapid. For the first time it seemed to take forever for the blast door to open. She couldn't wait to get away from the deafening sound of the cannons.

Chapter 60

Sean Wells wandered out the front door of the guest ranch and looked around. The sound of distant thunder reached his ears. He searched the sky. The western two-thirds of the sky was covered with clouds. That's when he noticed the flashes of light in the sky to the southeast. Dots of light moved swiftly across the sky from the east. The light flashes weren't lightning. They were coming from the ground, hitting the dots of light, and making them disappear.

This is it, he realized. Something huge was going on and he needed to see what it was. He ran to his room, grabbed his camera, jumped into his rental car and headed east on U.S. 60. Snow was starting to drift in from the south. He kept looking up at the sky, enthralled by the display of lights and brilliant white flashes on the horizon.

$$* * *$$

More of the big particle beam cannons were firing—three, four shots per second. The launch lights turned green. Diane and the other first eleven pilots bolted from the flight deck as the rest of the fighters flew up the access shaft and took to the air. The falling snow became a blizzard pressing on the front of the clear canopy. They had to rely on just their instruments to fly.

"Stay low," Diane said. "Let's come up from their bottom side. Initiate jinking."

The big particle beam cannons were firing rapidly now, with almost constant shockingly loud cracks, making it difficult to hear commands over the radio.

"All RIOs, boost the volume on your comm sets to overcome the sound of the cannons."

We could fly above the clouds and the snow, Diane thought, but I think the element of surprise is more important—provided we don't fly into a mountain.

"Affirmative," came back over the system.

The fighter craft spread out, trying to cover the base. In the distance a hundred or more saucers dropped out of the sky after being hit by the big cannons. Even more raced across the horizon in the attack.

Scout saucers were getting through the cannon defense system here and there. Individual fighter craft were moving quickly to intercept. So far the losses are all on the Zeta Grey side, Diane thought. But that will change as more saucers get past the big cannons.

"All of the saucers are well above the clouds," Ryan said.

Oh crap, she thought. "Spread out fast!" she ordered. "We have saucers coming in close to the ground, hidden by the snow. Move out low and engage!"

She and Buddha swung to the south down the valley and then east through the first mountain pass. A dozen saucers hovered just above the ground on the other side of the low pass, opening fire on them as they crested the edge of the pass.

"I need back up!" she shouted as she opened fire.

She banked hard left as Buddha peeled off to the right. They both swung around and came at the group of saucers from opposite sides, firing into the group. On the navigation display she could see the movement of four saucers that broke off from the group, two on her side, two on Buddha's.

"Only two against one?" she said. "I like those odds."

She banked and dipped as she used her targeting radar to lock onto the targets. She fired at the two saucers in front of her, hitting one, and then the other.

"Four on your six!" Ryan shouted.

She swung up and over in a sharp curl, firing upside down at the saucers closing in on her, hitting two more enemy craft. She spiraled down into a small break in the trees and came up at the far side behind the two remaining saucers, shooting as she rotated upright. One saucer broke left while the other turned sharp right. She banked left and closed in, shots first hitting the outer edge of the saucer and then the center. As soon as the saucer tipped, she banked back toward the pack hovering near the mountain pass.

"Bandit four high!" Ryan shouted.

Diane banked up and to the right. The saucer was accelerating up and away rapidly.

Why isn't the main pack moving? she wondered. They're trying to draw us away. Why?

She whipped around and aimed back at the pack of eight saucers still hovering near the mountain pass. Two more fighter craft slipped over the pass and engaged the hovering saucer pack. The saucers broke from their position and bolted away from the base, staying close to the ground. She, Buddha, and the other two fighter craft chased after them, engaging and hitting them one after the other. From what she was hearing over the radio, the other fighter craft teams were having similar encounters, all chasing fleeing saucers away from the base.

The realization struck. Yes! Away from the base!

* * *

Sean drove as fast as he dared while keeping track of the moving white lights and the flashes from the ground. The whole scene was now to his right, south of where he was on U.S. 60. The snow was getting heavier, obscuring his view of the lights in the sky. In his peripheral vision he thought he saw a dirt road zoom by. He braked to a stop and backed up. He hadn't gone more than a hundred yards before he saw it. He swung onto the dirt road and headed south into the darkness, his surroundings punctuated by faint flashes of light as if a massive lightning storm were happening in the clouds above him.

* * *

"Jink to base. Do we have infrared satellite coverage around the base?"

"Yes," Hollis said. "Saucers are bright yellow, moving away from the base at high speed. Fighter craft are in pursuit."

Diane shook her head. "What about something only slightly warm? Something on the ground maybe?" There had to be something not so obvious going on.

"Checking . . . Oh no. I have two, maybe three hundred objects on the ground surrounding the base at a distance of ten to twenty miles. They're only slightly warmer than the ground. They must have snuck in during the early evening and set down on the ground, waiting."

"They landed, shut down, and cooled off so we wouldn't see them on our sensors," Diane said. "Except now the falling snow is colder. We can see them again.

"Jink to Squadron One: All units return to protect the base. Break off and return to protect the base!"

She whipped around and pushed the thruster control higher.

"Most of the squadron is at least two to three hundred miles from the base," Ryan said. "We can be back in thirty seconds."

Her heart was pounding. "Yeah," she said. "And in that short time, disaster can strike."

* * *

"Transmitter facilities are all under attack," Captain Jakovic said. "Particle-beam-equipped ships are engaging the saucers. Holding their own so far."

This was the first time Hollis had been in the middle of a real battle. Everything before had been simulations or training exercises.

"Any activity in Russia or China?" Hollis asked.

"Affirmative, sir. Reports of multiple saucers attacking both bases are confirmed. Fighter craft responding."

Hollis blinked hard. This is too soon, he thought. I don't know if they're ready for a major assault. I don't know if we are, either.

* * *

Something smashed into the ground in front of Sean, sending dirt flying at him through the snow. He slammed on the brakes, sliding to a stop only three feet from the object. He slowly got out of his car to see what it was. His mind flashed back to the code name files that Charlie had given him to read.

I'd say this looks like a flying saucer, he thought.

He set his camera for wide angle and took several photos. The booming sound was almost continuous now, but still off in the distance. He held his hand up close to the saucer-shaped thing. He touched the smooth surface. It felt warm to the touch. He wandered around the thing, examining it in detail.

If it's some kind of flying saucer, he thought, there has to be a door somewhere.

He returned to the rental car and opened the glove compartment, retrieved a small LED flashlight, and then returned to the thing stuck sidewise in the ground. As he was examining the object something heavy landed in the brush about sixty feet off the road. He headed over to find out what it was.

* * *

Diane keyed the radio. "Jink to base. What's happening?"

"We have approximately two hundred fifty saucers lifting off the ground and inbound at low altitude," Hollis said. "The cannons aren't able to shoot at the ground. We need help, now!"

Diane swore under her breath. "On our way!"

She tried to imagine what the base would look like under such a heavy attack. She skipped over the mountain pass and banked north, up the valley toward the base, Buddha right behind her. Whatever she imagined didn't prepare her for what she encountered.

Dull flashes of light penetrated the snow storm in front of her. She cringed at the loud cracks from the Zeta Grey saucers. They're firing at the cannon emplacements in the mountain, she thought. We could already be too late. Motion on her navigation display indicated multiple targets charging directly at her. The targeting radar located and locked onto six new bandits.

"This is it, Ry, we're goin' in."

She started firing and hitting saucers as fast as she could.

"Give 'em hell!" Ryan yelled.

She banked and dipped to exaggerate the jinking effect as the saucers opened fire at her. She fired back, hitting one after another. With so many targets in front of her, it was hard not to hit one. Fighter craft from her squadron flooded over the mountains, in from the north end of the valley and filled in behind her. The front layer of saucers accelerated to engage the inbound fighters. One saucer seemed to fly directly at her. Even after it was hit, it tried to collide with her. Diane jerked the control stick at the last moment to avoid the collision. The belly of her craft scrapped against the saucer as she passed by it.

This is intentional! Diane realized. She struggled to regain control over the rising panic in her chest. Her hands were trembling as she tried to stabilize her craft.

"Jink to Squadron One. Saucers are trying to ram us. Heads up. Don't let them get too close!"

She went into a roll to avoid another collision, firing and hitting three more saucers. She heard a sharp metallic *crack* and felt the strong jolt on the left as her craft went into a tight spin.

"Jink is hit. Going down!"

Another light flash from a saucer hit them on the right side. They were already low and the spin made ejection risky. She grabbed the ejection levers and paused, letting her intuition guide her.

She pulled the levers and the cockpit exploded from the fighter craft. The drogue chute deployed pulling the main chute out and open. They slammed into the ground shortly after they felt the jerk from the main chute. Stars floated in her vision from the impact and everything around her was spinning.

* * *

Sean found an orange and white parachute draped over the bushes. He heard motorized screws running and then the sound stopped. He was breathing hard, trying to contain the panic spreading through his body. He cautiously approached with his small flashlight illuminating the limited area in front of him. He stopped when he saw two figures in chrome suits and bowling ball type chrome helmets climb out of an oblong container with a clear lid. He froze.

Aliens, he thought. What the hell do I do now?

One of the beings removed the helmet and said, "We need your car."

"What?" Sean said.

The being without the helmet looked human.

"We need to borrow your car."

Sean's mind froze for a moment.

"You speak English." He glanced back at the crashed saucer. "How do you . . . ?"

The other one also took off the helmet.

"Sir, I'm Lieutenant Dunlap. We need to borrow your car. National security. We have to get back. Now."

Sean's mind was scrambling, trying to sort everything out. "I can drive you."

Dunlap shook his head. "No. You can't go with us. They'll take control of your mind."

Sean was about to ask, Who are "they?" and then thought better of it.

"It's all of us or none of us," Sean said. ". . . unless you're going to kill me to get the car keys."

The two people in chrome suits glanced at each other. "Sir, it's a secure area. Authorized personnel only."

The Ceti Research ID card from Charlie, Sean thought. "I have authorization," he said. He pulled the ID card out of his suit pocket and handed it to them.

Both of them examined the card. "You know the director?"

"Yes," Sean said, as he recalled the image from Charlie. "Theo, tall thin guy, Dr. Shugart."

They whispered with each other for a moment. "Okay, but I drive. They'll make you crash the car."

Dunlap handed the ID card back to Sean. "Wear this around your neck. It might stop somebody from shooting you by mistake."

How reassuring, Sean thought. He looped the lanyard over his head.

"The keys?" Dunlap demanded.

Sean handed the keys over and led them back to the car.

* * *

"Ry . . . Ryan, you okay?"

Diane's speech sounded a little slurred to her.

"Ahhh . . ." came from behind her. "Is this what it's like to die?"

"No. Pain is the one true indicator that you're still alive. Pop the canopy. We need to get out fast!"

The screws unwound and the canopy rose. She unbuckled, disconnected the master connector and climbed out to the right side. Diane reached back in and grabbed the flash gun. She took the .45 automatic from the survival kit and handed it to Ryan.

"What are you going to use?" he asked.

She held up the flash gun. "I'll get you one as soon as I can. Then you can ditch that antique."

Ryan released the master connector and harness and climbed out of the cockpit. They scrambled under some scrub brush and crawled away from the cockpit shortly before it was hit by a blast from a saucer. They were still a mile from the base, trying to stay under cover.

The snow was letting up. She looked at the sky. Fighter craft and saucers darted up, down, and to each side in a violent fight to the death, flashes of light filling the night sky like too many fireworks. Diane stood and watched for a moment. This was the first time she had been able to watch the jinking of the fighter craft from the ground. Even though both the saucers and her squadron glowed bright white in the night sky, the jinking made her teammates both obvious, and difficult to follow. They moved in fast random patterns that made it look as if they weren't really there, but some kind of a rapidly shifting mirage. No wonder the saucers were having so much trouble hitting them.

Ryan touched her on the arm and motioned toward the base. The moonlight filtering through the snow gave them enough illumination to see. Saucers and fighter craft were falling out of the sky at an alarming rate, with the downed saucers outnumbering the fighter craft by about five to one. Her squadron had now penetrated the outer defense layer of the scout saucers and was engaging the ones shooting at the cannon batteries.

But the hope rising in her chest was dashed as she saw more saucers pouring over the mountains to the east.

Chapter 61

Diane and Ryan moved quickly on foot toward the stricken base as more and more saucers and fighter craft fell from the sky. By the time they had covered the first half mile, the battle above them was over. Not a single fighter craft remained in the air. The saucers took up protective positions around the base as three transport saucers glided over the mountains and landed in the valley near the mine entrance.

She and Ryan located several empty ejected cockpits with main chutes tangled in the scrub brush.

"Where are they?" Ryan wondered.

She pointed toward the base.

Someone in a chrome flight suit stepped out from the scrub brush and waved.

Three more team members emerged from the brush.

Helen was one of them.

"What now?" Helen asked.

"Now we try to save the base," Diane said. "You still have your weapon?"

Helen showed her flash gun.

"Good. Time to go hunting."

The group of six worked their way through the brush and an accumulating array of crashed saucers and fighter craft littering the valley floor. Some fighters had crashed with the cockpit intact, holes blasted through the clear cover. Others lay with the canopies open and the flight crew not far away. By the time they were a quarter mile from the base entrance, the group had grown to around twenty people, half armed with .45 automatics, the rest with nothing.

"Stay here," Diane said. She and Helen crouched and moved quietly through the brush. Within fifty yards they spotted a Zeta Grey walking, apparently on perimeter patrol.

"What do you think?" Helen whispered. "Is this weapon going to work silently?"

Diane nodded. "Silently, yes. But the Greys will see the flash, especially in the nearby area." Huh, she thought. They don't know we have any flash guns. They'll think it's another Zeta and come to assist. This can work!

Helen looked at the flash gun. "So we'll have company?"

Diane sighed. "In short order."

Helen looked at Diane. "So what do we do? Hit it with a rock?"

A rock? Diane thought. "Actually a rock isn't a bad idea. How's your throwing arm?"

Helen shook her head. "Not worth beans, yours?"

She looked around at the ground. There were rocks, but they were under an inch and a half of snow.

"I can manage. Sneak in closer. I'll find a rock and

move to the left, see if I can lob it over its head. When it turns, use the narrow beam kill function."

Helen rotated the collar to the right on the flash gun. "Got it."

Diane moved slowly through the brush, picking the widest path to avoid making any sound from her flight suit rubbing on the sagebrush. She picked up a stone the size of a baseball. This should work, she thought. She moved as close as she dared in the light snow, watching the Zeta. It turned in her direction. Diane froze, her heart thumped in her temples. The creature seemed to look at her for a moment and then looked away.

The suit's working, she thought. There's enough light. It must be the reflective coating on the outside of the suit. It's reflecting the snow and bushes around me. Without infrared, it can't see me very well.

When it turned away from her she threw the stone. It landed on the other side of the Zeta. The creature spun quickly and fired its flash gun into the brush. A flash from Helen's weapon dropped the creature to the ground. Diane ran from the brush, snatched the flash gun from the little creature and pointed to Helen's right.

Helen darted to the right as Diane ducked back into the brush and moved left. Fifteen seconds later another Zeta came running between the bushes. She pressed the kill button and the flash dropped the Zeta in its tracks. A second later she caught Helen's flash in her peripheral vision. She grabbed the weapon from the Zeta and headed back to meet Helen.

"Okay, now we have five weapons. Let's get back to the others."

They handed out the three new weapons and showed their teammates how to use them.

"Let's spread out," Diane said. "There's a Zeta patrol line about fifty yards ahead. You'll have only about fifteen seconds before another Zeta shows up, so be prepared for company. Each Zeta will be carrying one of these. Make sure you get the weapon and then go for cover—the next one will be coming in fast. Try throwing a stone over their heads to get them to turn away. Keep in mind that they have very good vision at night, so throw the stone only when they're looking away. They shoot as soon as they see or hear anything. You don't want to be in front of them."

Diane thought of something else. "And one more thing. If one looks at you, stand perfectly still. Don't move when they can see you."

The group spread out and slipped between the bushes. At fifty yards in, Diane and Ryan encountered another Zeta, standing still, facing them. It raised its arm and pointed the flash gun in their direction. She and Ryan froze. A flash from the left drew the Zeta's attention. It turned and pointed the flash gun to her left. Diane pressed the kill button and the Zeta fell to the ground. She rushed forward and picked up the Zeta's weapon, but instead of heading back, she went forward with Ryan right behind her.

"Now you've got a real weapon," she said as she handed the flash gun to Ryan, and showed him how to use it.

They moved silently through the brush until they came in view of the first of the three transport saucers. It was a hundred yards across and fifty feet tall with dozens of Zetas walking around the open ramp. Light filtering from inside the transport silhouetted the Zetas against the shadow of the saucer.

"Any ideas?" Ryan asked.

Diane took a quick count of the Zetas. "Nope. Too many of 'em to take on directly."

Ryan sounded like he was breathing hard. "So, let's wait."

It'll give him a chance to rest, she thought. "We need to

give our team time to get into position."

After a few minutes the saucers high in the night sky started moving north.

"Look at that!" Ryan said.

Diane smiled. "I think the cavalry is arriving."

Ryan stared at the saucers disappearing to the north. "But we lost all of our fighter craft."

Not all of them, she thought. "My guess is that's Nikolaev's squadron from Russia."

Ryan turned to face her. "They came all the way over here to help us?"

Ryan sounded surprised. "Yep," she said, "and the squadron from China should be right behind them."

She watched overhead as fighter craft engaged the saucers high in the night sky. More saucers than fighters were falling to the ground.

"Not bad," Ryan said. "Someone put their time into training."

A new group of fighter craft flew down the valley from the north.

"Chinese Space Command," Diane said as the fighters opened fire on the three large saucers on the ground.

Zetas ran in every direction, firing their flash guns up at the fighters, which were still well out of range.

"Attack now," Diane ordered as she bolted from the cover of the scrub brush.

She and Ryan ran for the transport saucer through the short scrub and sagebrush along with a dozen of their teammates, all firing flash guns into the panicked group of Zeta Greys. The Zetas fired back, killing several small groups of her teammates before the last of the Zetas fell to the ground. As they closed in on the transport saucer, more Zetas poured down the ramp. Diane and her teammates opened fire, dropping one Zeta after another in the rapid strobes of flash gun discharges.

Diane and Ryan rushed up the ramp and into the saucer, shooting Zeta after Zeta on their way inside.

As they peeked above the floor of the saucer from the ramp, two tall Greys were running at them with flash guns.

She pressed the kill button and dropped the two tall Greys to the floor.

The inside of the transport saucer consisted of multiple rows of bed-like small imprints for Zeta Grey bodies in them. Ryan checked around the inside of the saucer, excitedly waving her over.

"Look, storage bins," he said.

Ryan held up more of the Zeta Grey flash guns.

"Hand 'em out. We can use 'em."

She looked around. "No more Zetas inside."

Ryan stepped close to her. "Look at all of the recesses. There must be room for two or three hundred of the small Grays."

Diane's heart sank. "Yeah," she said. "And right now they're all inside our base, killing our people."

* * *

Sean rode in the back seat with the two people in chrome suits and helmets in the front. With the helmets on, Sean couldn't talk with them. Questions flooded his mind as the car raced on into the night. The car came to a skidding halt as two more people in chrome suits stepped from the brush to the road.

They crowded in next to Sean in the back seat. Both of them looked him over as they got in, but he couldn't see anything through the chrome coating on the front of the helmets. The booming sound had stopped and the bright flashes in the night sky had also come to an end. He began to wonder exactly what he had gotten himself into when the car slowed and drove carefully around another saucer-shaped thing stuck sidewise in the ground.

Once back on the dirt road they sped up.

Chapter 62

"We need to secure the other two large saucers before we go into the base," Ryan said. "Can't have them coming up behind us."

Diane glanced to the north where the two remaining transport saucers landed. "No, we can't have that. Let's go."

People still in need of Zeta Grey flash guns picked them up from where the small bodies had fallen. Others raced into the large saucer, emerging armed with the weapons.

Diane led the group north to find the next saucer. They moved noiselessly through the low brush. The size of the saucer made it visible from two hundred yards away, even in the relative darkness. They approached in a crouch, looking for patrols or sentries. So far, there weren't any.

The Chinese fighter craft flying above had disbursed

most of the Zetas. As they got within fifty yards of the saucer Diane saw flashes of light. Flash guns, she thought.

She worked her way closer to the saucer. The Zetas were involved in a deadly flash gun fight on the other side of the transport saucer. Diane led the charge out of the brush firing at the back of the Zetas.

Caught by surprise in a crossfire, some of the Zetas fell before they realized they were in the middle of two firing lines. Diane's mind was jumping faster than she could move, her heart raced, and her breath was rapid as if she had run a mile at top speed. She aimed and fired the flash gun in rapid sequence. In her peripheral vision, some of her teammates fell to the ground.

Is this it? she wondered. Dr. Cowen's question about being willing to die in combat drifted through the back of her mind. She had been so sure she would prevail flying in combat that actually dying didn't have a real feeling to it. Now she wasn't so sure.

Finally the last Zeta dropped to the ground. Eight of her teammates were on the ground, killed by the Zetas. Diane cautiously walked under the saucer, scanning the edge of the brush for any more Zetas.

Clay stepped out of the brush.

"Appreciate the assist," he said. "Saucer to the north is secured."

Helen came running up to Clay.

"The one to the south is, too," Diane said.

Clay and Helen hugged, awkwardly, it turned out, because of the size of the helmets.

"Then let's finish this quickly," he said. "Most of them are already inside the base."

Diane smiled at seeing the two of them together. "I know."

Clay went up the ramp and into the saucer with Helen

and Diane right behind him. The two tall Grey pilots were aiming flash guns as Clay pressed the kill button on his weapon.

"He who hesitates . . . " he said. "Time to go inside the base and find out how bad it is."

Diane's group formed up with Clay's group and they all headed for the mine entrance. Two small Greys stood guard, one on each side of the mine.

"This is the tricky part," Clay said. "Getting close enough without being killed."

"Not really," Diane said. She looked around and found a stone the right size. She picked it up and handed it to Clay.

"That's an old trick."

Diane chuckled. "Not to them it isn't."

Clay took the stone, waited for the Greys to look to the side, and threw it off to the right of the mine entrance. When it hit, the two Greys turned and fired into the brush. Diane and Clay fired, killing the two creatures.

"It's a good thing you hung on to these things," Clay said. "Without them we wouldn't stand much of a chance. I thought we should turn them in so they could be reverse engineered."

Diane turned to look at him. "And now?"

He grinned. "We have enough for everyone in the squadron with plenty left over for research. Good call."

Diane led the group into the mine entrance. Where cameras had been mounted, large divots of rock were now blasted out. They found eight dead Zetas lying next to the wall, obviously hit by the particle beam cannons. The cannons themselves were gone, having suffered the same fate as the cameras. The Zetas had used the vaporize button on the flash guns.

Farther into the mine was the blast door. A huge hole had been cut through the door by a particle beam weapon.

"The vaporize button on the flash gun?" Helen guessed.

"I don't think so," Diane said. "Too precise. Besides, I don't think these things have enough power to cut through high density materials like the blast door."

Diane stepped through the hole in the door and checked the security station. Only fragments of the table, chairs, and other equipment remained. So far no human bodies had been found. Either the security team withdrew, or the Zetas had simply used the vaporize function. It was hard to tell.

They moved on through the second damaged blast door, down the smooth hall, and into the elevator lobby.

"Which floor?" Helen asked.

The echo from the smooth walls was interfering with the sound-based communication system, but it was tolerable.

"Yeah," Clay said. "The Zetas will be waiting for the door to open. Then they'll blast us with the flash guns. No way."

Diane paused and thought for a moment. "Actually, I like the elevator idea," she said. "We go down the stairs. When we're ready, someone sends the elevator down to the floor. When the Zetas are all looking at the empty elevator, we fire. Simple."

Ryan stepped forward. "I can send the elevator."

He looked like he was in a lot of pain from the capsule impact, added to the shark bites.

"Good idea," Diane said. "You stay here. We've got this."

Diane led the group down the stairwell. She took a quick glance through the safety glass in the door. Four Zetas were walking toward the elevator in the main residential hallway. She nodded to Clay, who waved his arm out into the open center of the stairwell. Ryan waved back from above. Clay came over and gripped the door handle, ready to pull it open. Diane kept glancing through the glass.

"Almost there," she said. "Now!"

Clay yanked on the door. As it flew open Diane and two others fired into the hallway. The four Zetas fell, but eight more ran in from the other hallway. Flashes back and forth left all the Zetas and three of Diane's teammates dead. Mad Dog was screaming in pain, missing most of his arm.

"My arm! It's on fire! I'm burning!" he shouted.

Diane checked the stump sticking out from his shoulder. It was cut clean and cauterized. Her heart was aching at the personal losses taking place.

"I've got him," Helen said. "Go get those bastards!"

Diane led the group down the hall. "We have to get to the armory," she said.

Clay was right behind her. "Why?" he asked. "These are better."

Diane shook her head. "Flashbangs."

Clay smiled. "I get it."

They worked their way down the hall, around the corner, and into the security office. Four more security officers lay dead on the floor. Clay opened the door to the armory.

"Everything's still here."

Diane looked around. "Of course—they know guns are useless. Get the flashbangs."

They handed out boxes filled with a dozen flashbangs per box. Each teammate took and carried a box under arm. Once the twenty-four boxes were divvied up, they moved on.

The team methodically cleared the residential level, room by room. The residence rooms were empty, no people and no Zetas. Diane motioned them over to the stairs leading up to the operations level.

As they climbed the stairs, the sharp *crack* of a particle beam weapon echoed down the stairwell. The closer they got to the operations level, the louder the sound grew.

"The Zetas are cutting through the blast door into the

OPS center," Diane told her team. "We have to hurry!"

She glanced through the safety glass in the door. No Zetas in the alcove. Ryan had finally caught up with her. She and five teammates slipped into the alcove with their backs against the stone wall. Diane took a quick peek around the corner. No Zetas there either. The whole group rapidly made their way down the hall to the main corridor. Sneaking up to the corner, she took another quick peek.

The main corridor was packed with Zeta Greys. She could hear gunfire from the main control room, probably shooting through the expanding hole in the blast door. Not going to work, she thought.

Clay held up a flashbang. They were ready.

Diane held up three fingers, two, one, and then pointed to the hall. Ten people rushed into the main corridor, pulled pins, threw flashbangs and ran back into the adjoining hall. Diane knelt down and peered around the corner to see what would happen. Flashbangs clattered down the main corridor, drawing the attention of the Zetas. The closest Zetas used their flash guns in vaporize mode to shoot the skittering canisters before they could go off.

Oh crap! Diane thought.

The Zetas started running at them, flash guns in hand.

"Run!" Diane shouted.

The hallway was too long and the group was too slow reacting. The Zetas were going to round the corner with their weapons in vaporize mode. None of them was going to make it. Clay pulled the pin on a flashbang and dropped it on the floor near the wall as he started to run. Diane followed his lead, pulling pins and dropping flashbangs as she ran.

Her mind raced. We're doing what the Zetas expect us to do: We're running. What won't they expect?

"Stop!" she ordered. "Turn to face them, but lie down on the floor. Fire as soon as you see them."

The first flashbang went off just as the leading edge of Zetas rounded the corner. The first dozen or so Zetas were stunned and disoriented, dropping their weapons and covering their eyes. They staggered in every direction, hindering the rest of the Zetas from moving quickly into the narrow hallway. As the next batch of Zetas pushed through the crowd, the second, then the third flashbang went off.

Diane's group opened fire into the mass of staggering Zetas. They were bumping into each other, tripping over fallen creatures, and stumbling into the walls. It was working—the Zetas didn't expect to see them lying on the floor.

And the flashbangs were working, too. Throwing them from a distance gave the Zetas too much time to react. She repeatedly fired her flash gun into the stunned crowd of Zeta Greys. Clay and Ryan started lobbing more flashbangs over the group of Zetas falling to the floor. The canisters fell into the pressing mass of Zetas pushing around the corner from the main corridor, exploding in the crowd and disorienting all of the creatures.

"Now! Get up and attack!"

Diane and her teammates stood and attacked, some firing their flash guns while others pulled pins and threw flashbangs over the heads of the Zeta Greys. The flood of Zetas pressed relentlessly toward the hall. Flashbang canisters ricocheted off the far stone wall of the main corridor and fell into the fumbling crush of creatures. Carefully, Diane and her group stepped over the accumulating bodies of Zetas, fired into the mass of stunned creatures, and threw flashbangs over the heads of the crowd.

The Zetas that were still functioning were at the far side of the stunned aliens, unable to see what was happening. She saw three Zeta Grey heads sticking up above the others.

Tall Greys, she thought. They can think, analyze, and give orders.

"Aim for the tall Greys," she ordered. "Those are the ones in charge."

Because the small Zetas were all the same height and their heads were so large, none of them could get a clear view of the situation, and the flashbang canisters fell to the floor almost unnoticed. The three tall Greys turned and ran.

Chapter 63

Sean looked at the huge saucer that sat across the road in front of them. As they got out of the car, he could smell a strange odor in the air. He took several more photos and then walked forward, following the four people in the chrome suits. He stopped when he saw the first dead alien and took another set of photos. It looked just like some of the depictions of short Grey aliens in the code word documents.

They're real, he thought. That's when it dawned on him: The electromagnetic shield. It wasn't for incoming warheads; it was to stop flying saucers. But they were already here. How much worse was this situation going to get?

* * *

The loud crack of the particle beam cannon stopped as the remaining Zetas rushed toward the center of the battle. Diane, Clay, and Ryan pressed themselves against the stone wall, allowing their teammates to move forward and throw the canisters they carried. The main corridor was filled with rapid flashes as Diane and her team crawled over piles of dead Zetas, pushing the battle to the heavily damaged blast door of the OPS center. Finally the last small Zeta fell to the floor, dead.

"The three leaders ran this way," Diane said.

Clay and four others followed her down the wide hall to the intersection where two smaller passageways split off—one to the right, the other to the left. The passageways were empty. Diane felt a flush of warmth inside her suit and thought, The dry ice is gone. Three to five minutes before we pass out from heatstroke.

Which way? she wondered. Diane looked right, and then left. The passageways lead to the particle beam cannon rooms, but the cannons had all been destroyed by fire from the saucers, coming from the outside.

"Outside," she said to herself. But at this level it was a shear drop outside the cannon ports to the valley below. There was nowhere to go. She looked at the door to the stairs. Up or down? The lower level cannon ports had the same problem—shear outside drops—so up. The top of the mountain was rounded, allowing the Greys to walk out of the cannon ports onto the rocks outside, where they could be rescued.

Diane raced to the stairwell door, glanced through the safety glass, and pushed the door open.

"Which way?" Clay asked.

She looked up the stairs. "They're going up. It's the only way they can get out of the base."

Clay looked confused. "There aren't any doors up there."

She shook her head. "The cannon ports must have all

been blasted open. They can crawl out through them."

They climbed the stairs to the next level, watching for any sign of the tall Greys. Sweat poured down Diane's face, into her eyes, and down into the legs of her flight suit.

"We can't take our helmets off without revealing our position and subjecting ourselves to Zeta Grey mind control," she said.

Clay breathed out hard. "We're going to have to split up."

Diane shook her head. "No, it's too easy for them to pick us off. Let's stay together."

Clay shrugged. "Then which way?"

Diane looked around. "Give me a chance to think." She closed her eyes, calmed her mind. In the far reaches of her awareness she could sense the three tall Greys, communicating mind-to-mind. She took a deep breath and let it out slowly, willing her mind to ignore the heat inside her flight suit, the sweat in her eyes, and the fluid building up around her legs.

"Up," she said. "Top level."

The six of them raced up the stairs. At the top landing Clay took a quick look through the safety glass and yanked the door open. They sprang into the passageway, aiming the flash guns to each side. Nothing.

Diane closed her eyes again and tried to sense where the tall Greys were. She turned slowly to the right, then to the left. She was aware that they were close, but the right seemed to be just like the left. There wasn't any difference. So what do I do? she asked herself. Flip a coin?

Then it dawned on her: There was a third passageway, just around the corner from the stairwell.

"This way."

They ran down the narrow hall to the set of steps at the end. Diane held her flash gun steady as she slowly climbed the eight steps to the upper landing. The blast door was partially open.

"They figured out how to get the blast door open," Clay said.

She nodded. "You got any flashbangs left?"

Clay shook his head.

"I've got two," one of the others said.

Another member of the flight crew stepped forward. "I've got one."

"And I've got another," a third member said.

Diane stared at the flashbangs they held in their hands. "That's it? Four?"

Clay nodded. "All at once?"

Diane glanced at the open blast door. "They could be gone already. Try one."

Clay took a flashbang, pulled the pin and tossed it around the door and into the room. There was a very bright flash, and then nothing.

"The flashbang got vaporized, so they're still in there."

Diane jumped across the opening, forcing her back to the wall next to the door. She rotated the collar on the front of her flash gun for wide angle.

"Okay. All three flashbangs at once: three, two, one!"

Her team pulled the pins and threw the flashbangs around the blast door. As soon as Diane saw the first of the flashes vaporizing the flashbangs she swung her arm into the doorway and pressed the vaporize button. The second and third flashes from the tall Greys rapidly followed the first and happened just before the flash from her own gun discharged. Diane sprang into the doorway pressing the vaporize button again.

Parts of two of the tall Greys that hadn't been vaporized fell down the pile of rubble, while the third one struggled, missing an arm and part of its torso. Diane rotated the collar to narrow beam, aimed, and pressed the middle button. The last tall Grey tumbled down the rubble and rolled out onto the floor among the debris from the battle.

Diane looked around at the carnage and quickly removed her helmet, breathing in cool fresh air at last. They rushed back to the main hall and the blast door to the OPS center.

* * *

Sean Wells followed the four people in chrome suits in through what appeared to be an old mine entrance.

Where the hell are they going? he wondered. He entered into a room with concrete walls, floor, and ceiling through the remains of some kind of heavily reinforced round door on massive hinges. So, not a real mine, he realized. He took a picture of the damaged blast door and a piece of desk that had been shoved against the right wall.

"Hey!" someone shouted at him. "What are you doing? This is a secure area!"

Sean held up the Ceti Research ID card. "You know Theo?"

The man examined the ID, looked at Sean sternly, turned and walked deeper into the hallway off to the left.

Sean checked the room over quickly. Probably a security station, he thought. He continued following the pilots in chrome suits down the hall and into the stairwell. They walked down flight after flight of steps until they emerged into a hall. Sean walked past about a dozen dead aliens and took more photos. The hall had rooms set off to the side.

They look like dorm rooms, he thought. Could be residences for a military base.

He followed them over to another stairwell, and climbed up what seemed like endless sets of steps. At the top landing they opened a door and entered a small alcove. The obnoxious odor he encountered outside was overwhelming in the hallway.

* * *

"It's over!" Diane shouted. "How are the people in the control room?"

Jed Collier stuck his head through the large hole in the blast door. "Zadanski?"

"Yes, we're here."

He sighed in relief. "We thought you were all dead, and we were next. When we lost communications we . . ."

Diane nodded. "I know. We thought you guys were dead, too."

Jed Collier stepped back and Hollis stuck his head into the gaping hole.

"What's it like outside? Losses?"

Diane glanced at the pile of dead Zeta Greys. "The Russians and Chinese have a few fighter craft left. We don't. Outside looks like the world's largest advanced tech junk yard. Crashed saucers are scattered over a two or three hundred mile radius. I don't know how you're ever going to keep this quiet."

Hollis shook his head. "We're going to have to try. I have to call the president. See if you can get the blast door open. We need to assess the damage and figure out how long it's going to take to rebuild the base."

"And how long it's going to take to get new fighter craft," Diane added.

* * *

Sean walked through the alcove and turned into the hall. He stopped at the sight of more dead aliens and took more photos. The stench from the aliens was nauseating. He walked cautiously forward, stepping over the dead bodies. He also saw people in chrome suits lying on the floor, dead, he assumed. It was clear some horrific battle had taken place here. The end of the hall was knee-deep in dead aliens.

He stepped carefully over the bodies and into the main hall, taking more photographs as he went. Several dozen people in chrome suits stood thigh-deep in dead aliens near the other end. He made his way closer to the group of people.

* * *

Diane looked at what remained of her teammates, proud of the victory they had made over the Zeta Greys. Among the people in flight suits was a man in a wrinkled polyester business suit.

"Who the hell are you?" Diane demanded.

"Sean Wells." He held up the Ceti Research ID card. "You know Theo?"

"I do," she said. "I've been to Ceti Research, and I don't remember seeing you there."

The look of lost confidence on Sean's face made her approach him.

"Any other ID?" she asked. "Empty your pockets."

She went through his wallet: New York driver's license and a *New York Times* press pass.

Diane tipped her head back and looked at the ceiling. Oh crap, she thought. This is the last thing we need. She looked back at him and asked, "How did you get in here?"

He looked around like he was a little unsure of himself. "I came in with some of your pilots. They needed my car to get back here."

Diane shook her head. "What I mean is why did you come here, to this specific spot?"

Sean shrugged. "Honestly? I was invited."

Diane put her fists on her hips. "By whom?"

"A strange kid named Charlie."

She handed Sean's ID card to Jed Collier, who ran it through the security system.

"He's legit, including his security clearance."

* * *

"Peregrine Base is going to need major repairs, but it'll be functional again in the near future," Admiral Hollis carefully explained to President Andrews. "The manufacturing center for the fighter craft hasn't been discovered by the Zeta Greys, so it's still in full production."

He heard Andrews sigh.

"I'm ordering the National Guard and all military in the area to close off that entire section of the state," Andrews said. "I think releasing news that a nuclear spill has taken place will help keep people out of the area. No one wants to be around radioactive contamination."

Hollis made a note in his briefing pad. "I think that's wise," Hollis said. "I've requested that several Russian and Chinese fighter craft remain in the area, at least until we can have a few fighters of our own flown in to protect what's left of the base."

Hollis paused, considering just how to word his next bit of news. "We have an unexpected guest in the base."

"Who?"

Hollis cringed. "Sean Wells, from the *New York Times*."

There was an uncomfortable pause. "How the hell did he get in there?" Andrews sounded furious.

"Apparently, he was invited." Hollis closed his eyes as he waited for Andrews to respond.

"Let me guess—by Charlie?"

Hollis nodded to himself. "None other."

Chapter 64

Conrad Kaplan listened carefully to the reports coming in over the radio. The impeachment of President Andrews had been dropped without explanation. He found the arrest of Whitcolm and Metzner equally troubling. The Partnership had taken an unexpected blow, but they would recover. He sat back, thinking, as his yacht, *Dominator II* sailed for Hawaii.

I need time to rethink my plans. I need a place out of the reach of the U.S. government, a country without an extradition treaty.

He checked his reference books and climbed the stairs to the pilot section of his sail boat.

"Captain, we need to change course."

Walters turned to face him. "Where to?"

Kaplan looked out over the endless sea. "Vanuatu. Do

we have enough supplies?"

Walters smiled. "I know a quiet little place where we can stop along the way. It's not going to be a problem."

Kaplan nodded. "Do it." He turned and went below to his state room.

* * *

Sean Wells walked slowly with the group from Peregrine Base to where the memorial service would be held.

What a strange and twisted path this has been, he thought. From climate change deniers to corporate corruption, an attempted coup, and on through chemtrails to a planetary shield against hostile extraterrestrials.

What he needed now were the words to explain to the rest of the world what it all meant. The *New York Times* may, or may not, be willing to tell the whole story. That remained to be seen.

President Andrews seemed at least partially open to eventually disclosing the whole truth: that alien visitors are a reality and we are secretly fighting to save our planet from a desolate future—that a heartless and despicable extraterrestrial race stalks the people of our world, silently and secretly plotting our demise.

Climate change remained an open question as to whether it was real, or simply a cover to fund the secret planetary shield technology. As far as Sean could determine, only time would sort that one out. Either way, it was all Pulitzer-Prize-winning material, and he had the only inside track. For an investigative journalist, it just didn't get any better than this.

* * *

Diane Zadanski, Admiral Hollis, and the remaining

members of Squadron One gathered to pay homage to their fallen warriors. Of the forty-eight pilots and RIOs at Peregrine Base, thirty-seven had perished in the last battle, plus another eighty-six of the base personnel. A private cemetery had been constructed in a remote valley a mile south of the entrance.

Admiral Hollis stepped in front of the small group.

"I'm not very good at this. I view each of you the way I would my own children, if I had any. The fact is you are my family. I take the loss of each person as a great loss to me, personally, and a tragedy for humanity. I am extremely proud to have every one of you as a vital part of my family, and I grieve the passing of each brother and sister in this military version of my household. I . . ."

He breathed heavily and glanced around. Tears welled in his eyes.

He needs help with this, Diane thought. She stepped forward.

"I can do this, sir," she said quietly.

He slowly stepped off to the side as she turned to face the group.

"We have come together, here, in the quiet and privacy of the wilderness, to pay our last respects to our friends and comrades-in-arms. While the public may never know of their bravery and ultimate sacrifice, we will hold their heroism in our hearts and minds from this day on."

She held her arm out toward the rows of white stone crosses.

"Each cross bears the name and rank of our country's newest heroes. A place for the branch of service has been left blank, so that we may more openly declare their courage and defining place in history at some point in the future. I personally pray *that* time is not too far away. This level of commitment and sacrifice needs to be acknowledged and revered, if not for them, then for those who will follow in their footsteps.

"To our friends, I say, in parting, that we will see you all when we meet again in the wild blue yonder."

Diane turned to face the graves.

"Atten-*hut!*" Clay said.

They all raised their right hands in slow salute as taps played in the distance. As the sound of the bugle drifted off, Diane said, "Rest in peace, knowing that we will not rest until our enemy is vanquished and security is restored to our world."

* * *

President Andrews stood in the small semiformal dining room in the bunker under the White House. Martha came through the open doorway from the kitchen carrying two glasses of red wine. She handed one to him.

"Peace offering?" she said.

He took the glass of wine and nodded.

"You seem deep in thought," she said.

Andrews took a long sip of wine before answering, "I was just thinking how much things have changed since I took office. Back then I thought we were leading the world in technology, and that Russia was our biggest concern. After meeting Charlie and Etnar, my whole perception of humanity has changed. My hope was to limit war in our world. Instead, I've started a new war with creatures from another star system. With the size of the battle in New Mexico, I don't know how long I can keep this secret."

She took a small step closer to him. "So what do you think would happen if people found out we're not alone in the universe?"

He took another swallow of wine. "All of our major social systems are based on beliefs that are now hopelessly out of date. Religion, political parties, military power, our financial and educational systems—all of them would have to be profoundly revised. The chaos in the world would be devastating. Everything would fall apart."

She glanced down and smiled to herself. "You think people would panic?"

He nodded. "I really do. I think they would lose confidence in everything. I can't tell the American people we're in the middle of a war with aliens. It's too great a shock. I have to find a way to do this gradually."

She nodded slowly. "You're not the first to wrestle with this decision, you know." She sipped at her wine and set the glass down on the table. "Spain and Brazil admitted that UFOs are real. They declassified all of the documents pertaining to flying saucers and aliens and made them available to the public. Nobody panicked. There was a collective sigh of relief that their government was finally being honest with them. I think the same thing would happen here."

He shook his head. "But this isn't Spain, or Brazil. Disclosure could be devastating."

She looked up into his eyes. "I think you're over-estimating the fragility of most people. I've checked on the polls. Eighty percent of people think the government is hiding information on UFOs. Only fifteen percent think UFOs are not real, half of the people think they are, and thirty-five percent either don't know, or don't care."

She watched his face carefully.

"But what about people's faith in religion, government, finance, and academic institutions?"

She shook her head slowly. "I don't think it's going to matter. People will go on believing what they believe. People who go to church will continue going to church. People who go to college will still go. People are creatures of habit. You said your perception of humanity has changed. How, exactly?"

He took a deep swallow of wine.

"I suppose I have lost some of my arrogance." He

looked at the expression on her face. "Okay, more than some."

She chuckled and looked up at him again.

"Meeting people who know all of my thoughts and motivations is a very humbling experience. In learning about other, more advanced human races, spread throughout the galaxy, I now see our civilization differently."

She stepped a little closer to him. "It sounds like you've benefitted from the experience. I think others would, too. How do you see us now?"

He swallowed the rest of his wine and placed the empty glass on the table.

"I see us advanced over where we were, but not as advanced as others. I see us on the threshold of a huge leap in awareness, knowledge, and technology. We're close to a fundamental transformation in not only our society, but in our civilization. In the foreseeable future we will conquer the Zeta Greys, visit all of the planets in our solar system, and make our first trip to another star. We are coming of age as part of the human community in the galaxy."

She smiled and nodded. "You sound more hopeful that doubtful."

He stepped closer and put his arm around her. "I am, actually," he said.

She looked up into his eyes again. "That's what you need to share with the people of this country—your hope, your confidence, and your vision for the future."

He furrowed his brow slightly. "That we're coming of age as a human civilization?"

She smiled. "Yes. What you believe in your heart, others will also believe. That is the defining mark of a true leader."

She put her arms around him. He looked back into her admiring eyes.

"Then that is what I'll do."

38317395R00244

Made in the USA
San Bernardino, CA
08 June 2019